HORROR FOR GOOD

HORROR FOR GOOD

MARK C. SCIONEAUX

R.J. CAVENDER

ROBERT S. WILSON

Horror For Good
A Charitable Anthology

Cutting Block Press, LLC.
6911 Riverton Drive
Austin, Texas 78729
www.cuttingblock.net

This is a charitable anthology. All revenues, less direct costs for production, marketing and distribution (net profits of each purchase, estimated to be at least 10% to 15%) will be donated to amfAR, The Foundation for AIDS Research. For more information on amfAR, please visit: www.amfar.org.

Jeff Strand's Story "The Apocalypse Ain't so Bad" was originally published by Cutting Block Press in *Horror Library, Volume 3* (2009)

Joe McKinney's story "Sky of Brass, Land of Steel" was originally published as "Coyote Season" in *The Harrow Vol 9, No 10* (2006)

G.N. Braun's story "Autumn as Metaphor" was first published by Bendigo T.A.F.E in *Painted Words* (2011)

Ray Garton's story "Reception" was originally published by Subterranean Press in *The Girl in the Basement and Other Stories* (2004)

Gary McMahon's story "Road Flowers" was originally published by Ash Tree Press in *Pieces of Midnight* (2010)

Tracie McBride's story "Baptism" was originally published by *Hecate Magazine* (2009)

Ramsey Campbell's story "Dead Letters" copyright © 1978 by Ramsey Campbell, later reprinted by PS Publishing in *Told by the Dead* (2003)

F. Paul Wilson's story "Please Don't Hurt Me" was originally published by Maclay and Associates in *MASQUES IV* (1991)

Jack Ketchum's story "Returns" was originally published by Gauntlet Publications in *Right To Life* (2002)

Laird Barron's story "Shiva, Open Your Eye" Originally published in *The Magazine of Fantasy & Science Fiction* (2001)

Joe R. Lansdale's story "On a Dark October" was originally published in *The Horror Show.* (1984)

— CREDITS —

Editors in Chief:	Mark C. Scioneaux
	R.J. Cavender
	Robert S. Wilson
Reading/Selection Team:	Mark C. Scioneaux
	R.J. Cavender
	Robert S. Wilson
	Jennifer Wilson
	Selene M'Only
	Ann Magee
Formatting:	Boyd E. Harris
Layout and Design:	Bailey Hunter
Cover Art:	William Cook
	www.bloodrelated.wordpress.com

— TABLE OF CONTENTS —

A Message from the HWA President - *Rocky Wood* 7

The Journey of Horror For Good - *Mark C. Scioneaux* 9

Autumn as Metaphor - *G.N. Braun* 15

On a Dark October - *Joe R. Lansdale* 19

Mouth - *Nate Southard* 25

Blood for the American People - *Lisa Morton* 39

Reception - *Ray Garton* 53

The Long Hunt - *Ian Harding* 61

The Apocalypse Ain't so Bad - *Jeff Strand* 79

The Gift - *Monica O'Rourke* 91

The Silent Ones - *Taylor Grant* 99

Sky of Brass, Land of Iron - *Joe McKinney* 113

Consanguinity - *Lorne Dixon* 137

Dead Letters - *Ramsey Campbell* 151

The Monster in the Drawer - *Wrath James White* 159

Baptism - *Tracie McBride* 169

Atlantis Purging - *Boyd E. Harris* 181

Returns - *Jack Ketchum* 197

The Other Patrick - *Brad C. Hodson* 205

A Question of Morality - *Shaun Hutson* 223

The Meat Man - *Jonathan Templar* 227

A Man in Shape Alone - *Lee Thomas* 239

Solution - *Benjamin Kane Ethridge* 253

To and Fro - *Richard Salter* 261

Please Don't Hurt Me - *F. Paul Wilson* 275

The Depravity of Inanimate Things - *John F.D. Taff* 283

The Lift - *G.R. Yeates* 297

The Eyes Have It - *Rena Mason* 307

Road Flowers - *Gary McMahon* 319

The Widows Laveau - *Steven W. Booth & Norman L. Rubenstein* 333

This Thing That Clawed Itself Inside Me - *John Mantooth* 349

Somewhere on Sebastian Street - *Stephen Bacon* 357

June Decay - *Danica Green* 369

Shiva, Open Your Eye - *Laird Barron* 387

—A Message from the HWA President

I am very pleased to congratulate the editors— Mark C. Scioneaux, R.J. Cavender, and Robert S. Wilson on *Horror For Good*. And to commend you for buying this anthology, the proceeds of which benefit amfAR, the Foundation for AIDS Research, which is one of the world's leading nonprofit organizations dedicated to the support of AIDS research, HIV prevention, treatment, education, and the advocacy of sound AIDS-related public policy.

Horror For Good is not just a title—it is an expression of the heart and soul of the horror literary community. Like all literary genres, horror can be insular, but of course our readership spreads out across the wider community worldwide. Horror is the original form of storytelling, going back to the caveman's fire and the savannahs of Africa, when hunters told of the fearful creatures and natural phenomena they had encountered. And the genre is alive and very well in the 21st century.

One of the things that mark our genre and we who write in it, is the tremendous generosity of spirit that is inherent in our colleagues. In recent times, I have been involved in fundraising and increasing awareness around ALS/MND (or Motor Neurone Disease) and I never cease to be humbled by the generosity of so many writers, and so many fans and readers from the horror community. I am sure this has been exactly the experience of the editors in compiling this anthology and I congratulate the authors who have donated reprinted, rare, and original stories. Many of them are members of the Horror Writers Association, the leading professional writers' group in our genre, and they do themselves and the entire membership proud by choosing to participate.

HIV/AIDS is a disease that has struck the wider public

consciousness on a number of occasions since it first appeared on our radar in the 1980s. As medical breakthroughs, funded by Government and private foundations such as amfAR, have reduced the fear of the disease in the wider community, it seems to have disappeared from the mass media. But I am sure we all know someone, or know of someone, who has been touched by the disease, and while awareness and prevention has been largely successful in "First World" countries, the same cannot be said of many countries in Africa and Asia in particular. Everything that amfAR and similar organizations can do to raise awareness (and defeat popular myth in these "Third World" cultures) and aid in prevention in those countries is critical not only to the individuals involved but to the entire economic and cultural future of nations.

In reminding us of HIV/AIDS and the continuing fight to improve the medical response, awareness and prevention, the editors have delivered an anthology that is entirely readable in its own right, and reminds us once again that horror can heal, as well as terrify.

Rocky Wood
President, Horror Writers Association

—THE JOURNEY OF HORROR FOR GOOD

by Mark C. Scioneaux

My uncle, Louis "Setchie" Scioneaux Jr., lost his courageous and hard fought battle with AIDS and Hepatitis on February 1, 2002. On that day, the world lost a man who embodied what was good about humanity: love, passion, selflessness, and a sense of humor. His ability to make those around him laugh was so contagious that he could turn a complete stranger into a friend within minutes of knowing him. Currently in the United States, approximately 49 others will lose their battle every day, and for 154 the battle will have just begun.

My Uncle Setchie was diagnosed in a time where the life expectancy for someone with AIDS was only two years. He lived for 10 years past the average. My family was blessed to get that extra time, though it didn't make saying goodbye any easier. I was 18 at the time, and still didn't understand the complexities of how the world worked. Death was something that was fortunately foreign to my family, but I lost my uncle and my godfather; my family lost a son, a brother, and a friend. The world lost an artist and something beautiful never to be recaptured again.

Ten years went by, and though life moved on, his memory never faded. In fact, his paintings adorn the wall of my home; a constant reminder of his presence in my life. I was always interested in writing and for reasons unknown, horror appealed to me. In the years that followed, I went on to publish a novel as well as several short stories. I pursued my writing more seriously and started networking with fellow authors like myself. I was introduced to the Kindle Horror Books group on Facebook.

KHB is an ongoing network for horror writers and readers to interact with one another in an honest fashion. An idea popped into my head one day. Here in this group were so many talented authors; why not get together and put an anthology out? But for what purpose? For our own reasons of hopeful fame and glory, or maybe for another cause? The idea of charity was the clear answer.

The first person who should be commended is my friend and business partner, Robert S. Wilson. A brilliant author and editor, he immediately teamed up with me and allowed this idea of mine to take off. He is a genuine, honest person who looks to help others before himself. A devoted father of two and husband; I am lucky to know him. I envision him and I having a partnership in the horror writing world that will last for years.

Author Christine Sutton worked hard to develop our Facebook page when we first started. She researched various charities for our cause to support and selected three. Though I had a vested interest in an AIDS charity, I had to follow the rules of the group vote. To my delight, amfAR won out. Since 1985, amfAR, The Foundation for AIDS Research, is one of the world's leading nonprofit organizations dedicated to the support of AIDS research, HIV prevention, treatment education, and the advocacy of sound AIDS-related public policy. This charity gave the best chance to not only help those living with AIDS in the USA, but also worldwide.

Robert and I began to solicit some of the biggest names in horror since we both felt it could never hurt to try. We didn't expect to receive such a big response from these titans of the writing world, but we did. To our surprise, many great authors pledged their help. It seemed everyone wanted to send a story in, and did just that. Submissions went from five a week, to ten. Then twenty. And then more. Our little project had picked up steam, almost too much steam for two indie writers to handle. We needed help. Professional help to prevent this train from derailing before it had even left the station.

Enter R.J. Cavender. A Stoker-nominated, industry-respected editor in the horror writing community, R.J.'s eye for detail and commitment to quality is unmatched. He took the challenge of *Horror for Good* head on, rounding up friends and numerous contacts to donate their time and services to ensure that this act of charity did indeed remain so. People like Steve Booth and Bailey Hunter donated their professional services and time to ensure *Horror for Good* would have the quality look that the collection of stories deserved. I'm not sure what R.J. saw in us that made him take the risk he did, but it speaks volumes to his class and character that he took a chance with us. I am lucky to call R.J. Cavender my friend.

With R.J. came Boyd E. Harris and Cutting Block Press, offering their services to us for publishing and marketing. I will always be thankful to Cutting Block for believing in our cause, and stepping up to take on the responsibility of publishing this anthology. We had the credibility now, and the horror world opened up to us like a surging floodgate. Submissions came in by the hundreds. Questions from interested parties followed, as did offers for radio interviews, blog tours, and other promotional ventures. Support on Facebook soared, and it seemed even more people wanted to help.

We couldn't have handled all the submissions we received if it weren't for three wonderful women who volunteered their time to read hundreds of submissions from the slush pile. Jennifer Wilson, Selene M'Only, and Ann Magee, from the bottom of my heart, I thank you. Because of these three, I can say every story submitted was read by a member of the *Horror for Good* team and received a fair chance. We all discovered many new authors that we will continue to follow. Everyone who submitted brought their best work to the table, and we were the lucky ones for it.

The cover art was graciously donated by William Cook, a New Zealand native, who is a talented poet, author, and illustrator. He gave us access to every piece of work he had created and left it to us to choose any we would want. We chose the two hands reaching for one another. Though I am not sure of the original meaning behind the work, to me it represented a helping hand reaching out to another in need. Robert and I thought it was perfect, and William happily donated it to us.

We needed a cover that would live up to the contents of this book, and I feel we achieved that.

The authors contained within these pages are a mix of some of the brightest stars and some of the most promising new talent in horror. They have donated their stories, consisting of rare reprints, personal favorites, and brand new, never-before-published tales. I cannot thank them enough, just as I cannot thank everyone enough who submitted a story to our anthology. It is my hope that you, the reader, will enjoy these tales crafted by some world-class storytellers.

Along the way I came to know an author that many may not know, Joel Marc Andre. Although he's not an author within these pages, Joel, to me, embodies what this project is all about. In speaking with him, I learned a few things that spoke volumes to the kind of man he is. In 2008, he did a series of charity items for the ASPCA, as well as several charity auctions that year. In 2009, he ran an event to bring in proceeds for a local homeless shelter. In 2010, he did a "Haunted Tour" in Phoenix, AZ for the Children with AIDS project. Just recently, he donated all royalties for the month of February from one of his e-books to the American Heart Association. Joel is a man who knows how to help others, and then goes home and writes horror, taking great care and skill to keep the two worlds separate. People like Joel are the reason why *Horror for Good* has been so well received. Just because we write about ghouls, gore, and death, it doesn't mean we do not care about the needs of others.

The heart of the horror community is on full display, and it stretches from the very top with Horror Writers Association President Rocky Wood, all the way to an author whose first ever published work will appear in these pages. The Horror Community *has* heart! A large, caring, blood-drenched heart.

In closing, the biggest "thank you" goes to you, the person who has purchased and is holding this book right now. I want you to know that you have just made a donation to amfAR, The Foundation for AIDS Research, and all the profits generated from your purchase went directly to them and no one else. You helped make a difference today, and on behalf of all the editors and authors, I thank you. So sit back, dim the lights, and prepare to be immersed into a dark world of terror. And remember that this is horror for *you*. Horror for me. Horror for Setchie. Horror for the 49, the 154, and the many others affected by this terrible disease. Horror for amfAR. Horror for a cure.

This is *Horror for Good*.

—G.N. BRAUN

G.N. Braun was raised in Melbourne's gritty Western Suburbs. He is a trained nurse and holds a Cert. IV in Professional Writing and Editing. He is currently studying Dip. Arts (Professional Writing and Editing). He is the author of *Boneyard Smack*, *Bubba wants YOU*, and *Insurrection* (all available as free downloads from Legumeman Books), as well as "Santa Akbar!" (*Festive Fear: Global Edition*, out through Tasmaniac Publications in Australia). He has had numerous articles published in newspapers. He is the current president of the Australian Horror Writers Association, as well as the director of the Australian Shadows Awards. His memoir, *Hammered*, was released in February 2012 by Legumeman Books.

—Autumn as Metaphor

By G.N. Braun

I feel nothing.

My daughter is gone; forever lost to me. Her life reduced to mere memories. The autumn leaves fall outside her window. She always loved autumn, and I think I may have loved her most of all this time of year.

She used to kick through the piles of fallen leaves, laughing like a loon. I loved her laugh; loved the way her cheeks would flush with delight; loved her youthful exuberance.

She would lie on the ground and pile leaves over herself—hidden—a shivering pile. I'd pretend I couldn't see her; I'd call her over and over while she'd lie giggling, trying hard not to shift the leaves but failing. The remembered sound of shuffling leaves brings tears to my eyes.

I don't know if I can live without her.

I don't know if I even want to.

She lies there now, under a pile of leaves. Browns and oranges speckled with red, the colours of life and death; the brown of soil, the orange of sunsets, the red of blood.

I sit and wait in darkness. The house is cold. Sooner or later someone will find her, but it won't be me. There's no sound from under the leaves. No giggling or movement. This time the red is more blatant. This will be the last time she lies under a pile of leaves. After this, she'll be under the brown earth.

Far under. Far away.

I sit and wait for someone to arrive. They'll come calling sooner or later. Night stretches; the house is silent. The clock in the hallway ticks, measuring my guilt and remorse in chronological slices.

Finally, I hear a distant shuffle, the sound of leaves rustling at the front door. I'm sure I locked it, but the hinges creak as it eases open. Slight, hesitant footsteps, the crunch of dead leaves; these sounds break the silence as I wait for someone or something to relieve my loneliness and assuage my guilt. The study door rattles, opens. Nothing but shadow beyond. A tiny shape gradually enters, brown and yellow leaves swirling at her feet as though in a breeze, yet no breeze stirs the room. I can't raise my eyes to meet hers. It would be too much, too hard. I wait for her to reach my side, to whisper in my ear that she loves me.

I try not to giggle. I fail.

She is here now, with me. I am there now, with her. We're together again.

Far under, far away.

—JOE R. LANSDALE

Joe R. Lansdale is the author of over thirty novels. He has written somewhere in the vicinity of four hundred shorter works, fiction and non-fiction, essays and opinion, introductions. He has written for film, television, and comics. His novella *Bubba Ho-Tep* was the source for the cult film favorite of the same name. He has won numerous awards, including The Edgar, eight Bram Stokers, The British Fantasy Award, The Inkpot Award, The Herodotus Award, The Grinzani Cavour Prize for Literature, and many others. He produces films and avoids wearing stretch pants. He lives in Nacogdoches, Texas with his wife and superhero dog, Buffy.

—ON A DARK OCTOBER

By Joe R. Lansdale

For Dave Silva

    The October night was dark and cool. The rain was thick. The moon was hidden behind dark clouds that occasionally flashed with lightning, and the sky rumbled as if it were a big belly that was hungry and needed filling.

    A white Chrysler New Yorker came down the street and pulled up next to the curb. The driver killed the engine and the lights, turned to look at the building that sat on the block, an ugly tin thing with a weak light bulb shielded by a tin-hat shade over a fading sign that read BOB'S GARAGE. For a moment the driver sat unmoving, then he reached over, picked up the newspaper-wrapped package on the seat and put it in his lap. He opened it slowly. Inside was a shiny, oily, black-handled, ball peen hammer.

    He lifted the hammer, touched the head of it to his free palm. It left a small smudge of grease there. He closed his hand, opened it, rubbed his fingers together. It felt just like...but he didn't want to think of that. It would all happen soon enough.

    He put the hammer back in the papers, rewrapped it, wiped his fingers on the outside of the package. He pulled a raincoat from the back seat and put it across his lap. Then, with hands resting idly on the wheel, he sat silently.

    A late model blue Ford pulled in front of him, left a space at the garage's drive, and parked. No one got out. The man in the

Chrysler did not move.

Five minutes passed and another car, a late model Chevy, parked directly behind the Chrysler. Shortly thereafter three more cars arrived, all of them were late models. None of them blocked the drive. No one got out.

Another five minutes skulked by before a white van with MERTZ'S MEATS AND BUTCHER SHOP written on the side pulled around the Chrysler, then backed up the drive, almost to the garage door. A man wearing a hooded raincoat and carrying a package got out of the van, walked to the back and opened it.

The blue Ford's door opened, and a man dressed similarly, carrying a package under his arm, got out and went up the driveway. The two men nodded at one another. The man who had gotten out of the Ford unlocked the garage and slid the door back.

Car doors opened. Men dressed in raincoats, carrying packages, got out and walked to the back of the van. A couple of them had flashlights and they flashed them in the back of the vehicle, gave the others a good view of what was there—a burlap wrapped, rope-bound bundle that wiggled and groaned.

The man who had been driving the van said, "Get it out."

Two of the men handed their packages to their comrades and climbed inside, picked up the squirming bundle, carried it into the garage. The others followed. The man from the Ford closed the door.

Except for the beams of the two flashlights, they stood close together in the darkness, like strands of flesh that had suddenly been pulled into a knot. The two with the bundle broke away from the others, and with their comrades directing their path with the beams of their flashlights, they carried the bundle to the grease rack and placed it between two wheel ramps. When that was finished, the two who had carried the bundle returned to join the others, to reform that tight knot of flesh.

Outside the rain was pounding the roof like tossed lug bolts. Lightning danced through the half-dozen small, barred windows. Wind shook the tin garage with a sound like a rattlesnake tail quivering for the strike, then passed on.

No one spoke for awhile. They just looked at the bundle. The bundle thrashed about and the moaning from it was louder than ever.

"All right," the man from the van said.

They removed their clothes, hung them on pegs on the wall, pulled their raincoats on.

The man who had been driving the blue Ford—after looking carefully into the darkness—went to the grease rack. There was a paper bag on one of the ramps. Earlier in the day he had placed it there himself. He opened it and took out a handful of candles and a book of matches. Using a match to guide him, he placed the candles down the length of the ramps, lighting them as he went. When he was finished, the garage glowed with a soft amber light. Except for the rear of the building. It was dark there.

The man with the candles stopped suddenly, a match flame wavering between his fingertips. The hackles on the back of his neck stood up. He could hear movement from the dark part of the garage. He shook the match out quickly and joined the others. Together, the group unwrapped their packages and gripped the contents firmly in their hands—hammers, brake-over handles, crowbars, heavy wrenches. Then all of them stood looking toward the back of the garage, where something heavy and sluggish moved.

The sound of the garage clock—a huge thing with DRINK COCA-COLA emblazoned on its face—was like the ticking of a time bomb. It was one minute to midnight.

Beneath the clock, visible from time to time when the glow of the candles was whipped that way by the draft, was a calendar. It read OCTOBER and had a picture of a smiling boy wearing overalls, standing amidst a field of pumpkins. The 31st was circled in red.

Eyes drifted to the bundle between the ramps now. It had stopped squirming. The sound it was making was not quite a moan. The man from the van nodded at one of the men, the one who had driven the Chrysler. The Chrysler man went to the bundle and worked the ropes loose, folded back the burlap.

A frightened black youth, bound by leather straps and gagged with a sock and a bandana, looked up at him wide-eyed. The man from the Chrysler avoided looking back. The youth started squirming, grunting, and thrashing. Blood beaded around his wrists where the leather was tied, boiled out from around the loop fastened to his neck; when he kicked, it boiled faster because the strand had been drawn around his neck, behind his back and tied off at his ankles.

There came a sound from the rear of the garage again, louder than before. It was followed by a sudden sigh that might have been the wind working its way between the rafters.

The van driver stepped forward, spoke loudly to the back of the garage. "We got something for you, hear me? Just like always we're doing our part. You do yours. I guess that's all I got to say. Things will be the same come next October. In your name, I reckon."

For a moment—just a moment—there was a glimmer of a shape when the candles caught a draft and wafted their bright heads in that direction. The man from the van stepped back quickly. "In your name," he repeated. He turned to the men. "Like always, now. Don't get the head until the very end. Make it last."

The faces of the men took on an expression of grimness, as if they were all playing a part in a theatric production and had been told to look that way. They hoisted their tools and moved toward the youth.

What they did took a long time.

When they finished, the thing that had been the young black man looked like a gigantic hunk of raw liver that had been chewed up and spat out. The raincoats of the men were covered in a spray of blood and brains. They were panting.

"Okay," said the man from the van.

They took off their raincoats, tossed them in a metal bin near the grease rack, wiped the blood from their hands, faces, ankles and feet with shop rags, tossed those in the bin and put on their clothes.

The van driver yelled to the back of the garage. "All yours. Keep the years good, huh?"

They went out of there and the man from the Ford locked the garage door. Tomorrow he would come to work as always. There would be no corpse to worry about, and a quick dose of gasoline and a match would take care of the contents in the bin. Rain ran down his back and made him shiver.

Each of the men went out to their cars without speaking. Tonight they would all go home to their young, attractive wives and tomorrow they would all go to their prosperous businesses and they would not think of this night again. Until next October.

They drove away. Lightning flashed. The wind howled. The rain beat the garage like a cat-o'-nine-tails. And inside there were loud sucking sounds punctuated by grunts of joy.

— NATE SOUTHARD

Nate Southard's books include *Lights Out*, *Scavengers*, *Red Sky*, *Just Like Hell*, *Broken Skin*, *This Little Light of Mine*, and *He Stepped Through*. His short fiction has appeared in such venues as *Cemetery Dance*, *Black Static*, *Thuglit*, and *Supernatural Noir*. A graduate of The University of Texas with a degree in Radio, Television, and Film, Nate lives in Austin, Texas with his cat. You can learn more at www.natesouthard.com

— MOUTH

By Nate Southard

More.

The word was still a whisper, barely more than a breath, but Gary knew it would get louder. It always did. Once it got so loud he couldn't ignore it, he'd have to obey. He hoped to find a way to shut it out, but so far all his attempts had failed.

Gary sipped his coffee, wishing he had enough energy to run, and watched half a dozen residents of the Juniper Ridge apartment complex chase a squirrel. Each time they came close to grabbing the little bastard, he felt his entire body tense, the anxiety and excitement creating a terrible friction inside him. When the animal switched direction and scurried free of their grasp, the friction disappeared beneath crashing waters of disappointment. He wanted to join them, but his legs were too tired. Just climbing from his bed, making the coffee, and then plopping down in the camping chair that decorated his balcony had stolen what remained of his strength. In a few hours, maybe he could join the hunt, but he hoped the group would catch the squirrel by then.

He could go to a pet store, buy a rabbit. That would work well. One of the more astute portions of his brain told him that might be a bad idea, though. Already, a lot of the complex residents had hit the local pet shops, and while the shopkeepers might enjoy the sudden rise in profits, sooner or later they'd grow suspicious. Already, the local Humane Society had stopped adopting animals to the folks living in Juniper Ridge. Gary knew because he'd tried, swearing up and down that he wanted to give an abandoned boxer a good home. They'd fed him a spiel about the breed and weight restrictions at apartment complexes, but he knew the truth. They suspected something, and that something was The Mouth.

More.

After streaking in circles for a moment, the squirrel bolted up a nearby tree. Two members of the crowd giving chase were children: a girl of less than ten whose hair was matted with weeks of grease and grime, and a boy of about the same age wearing nothing but white briefs. The kids started up the tree at once, climbing like monkeys. Below them, the adults pointed and shouted, telling them where they saw, or thought they saw, the squirrel. Their clothes were soiled and tattered, their faces streaked with dirt. In the weeks since they'd discovered The Mouth, the entire Juniper Ridge complex had fallen into a state of almost perpetual filth. Hair became tangles that were almost dreadlocks. Clothes smelled bad enough to be sniffed out from around corners and behind doors. Just looking at the crowd huddled beneath the tree inspired Gary to lift his own T-shirt to his nose and give it a whiff. Pretty bad, but not horrible. If he felt like it, he'd change in a few days.

He wouldn't feel like it, though. It was only due to The Mouth's understanding and mercy that he'd been allowed to sleep, that he had a cup of coffee in his hand instead of a squirming, terrified cat or other animal. Maybe that meant The Mouth could be quenched. He suspected the truth was something more ominous, though. Could be The Mouth was simply toying with them, all of them nothing more than rats in a cage or ants in a plastic farm. Or maybe The Mouth knew they needed rest, that they'd break if it worked them too hard.

That final possibility bothered Gary the most. It meant The Mouth was smart and knew their limits. And that meant there was no end in sight.

These thoughts tumbling through his brain like jagged rocks, Gary sipped his coffee and watched.

More.

* * *

The squirrel bit Cali's hands four times before she finally grabbed hold of it and smashed its skull against the tree. For a hot instant, when her hands were burning and the blood was starting to seep from the bites there, she'd thought about throwing the stupid thing against the parking lot. If she'd done that, however, one of the grown-ups would have grabbed it. Then, they'd give it to The Mouth, and she didn't want that happening. She liked feeding The Mouth more than anything else in the whole world, and she wasn't about to let no grown-up do it just because they were bigger and a stupid squirrel had hurt her hands.

"Idiot," she whispered to the limp mass of fur and broken bones in her fist. Then, she smiled.

"Gimme it."

A tiny gasp filled her throat when she heard the boy's voice. She couldn't remember his name, wasn't even sure she'd ever learned it, but she didn't like what he'd said or the way he'd said it. Carefully, she leaned to one side so she could look down at him. He crouched on a branch just below her.

"Gimme," he said again. His face was blank, his eyes black and hard.

"No. I caught it."

"So?"

"So, I'm gonna take it."

For a second, the boy did nothing but look at her with those eyes. Then, his face scrunched up in a collection of angry creases, and one of his hands curled into a white-knuckled fist.

"I'm taking it. It's my turn."

"We don't take turns. It doesn't work that way."

"It does now. You can go next."

A trick! She knew it as soon as the boy said it. If she gave him the squirrel, there wouldn't be any next. He'd lie and change the rules, find some reason for it to still be his turn.

More.

"I know," she answered, starting to feel anxious.

"So gimme," the boy said.

"I wasn't talking to you. Go away!"

"Gimme it, and I will."

She stuck out her tongue. Yeah, it was a kid thing to do. She didn't care. "Find your own. This one's mine."

"It belongs to The Mouth."

"I know that." It came out as a shout, almost a scream. Something pushed at the back of her eyes, forcing water down her cheeks. Why wouldn't the boy leave her alone? She knew the squirrel belonged to The Mouth, but it was hers until she dropped it down the hole. "I know, I know, I know. But I get to give it, so go away!"

Somehow, the boy's face scrunched up even more, so that he barely looked like a boy at all. Instead, he looked like an old man or a troll, something ugly and gross. She was about to tell him so just to hurt his feelings, but then his face changed into a boy's again, a smiling boy. The smile creeped her out, but she wasn't sure why until he stood on top of the branch, reached up with one hand, and grabbed hold of her ankle with strong fingers.

"I'll pull," he said. "I'll pull you right out of the tree."

"No, you won't." Cali didn't like the way her voice had gone all soft and whispery. She sounded scared, and she guessed there was a good reason for that.

The boy nodded slowly. "I will. You could break your leg. Or your neck. If you break your neck, you die, and then one of the grown-ups will give you to The Mouth."

Her breath disappeared, and her entire body felt like she'd just been tossed into a cold swimming pool. Would they do that? No one had fed a person to The Mouth, and she figured no one ever would. There had to be some kind of rule against it. The Mouth liked birds and squirrels and mice and kittens and turtles and puppies and even grown up cats and dogs, but it had never wanted a person. But The Mouth had never asked for anything specific, just *More*.

The boy tugged on her ankle, and a short screech burst out of her. She started sobbing, diving forward to wrap her arms around the tree limb. In her tiny, iron fist, she felt the squirrel grow cooler and cooler. She thought of the sounds that would come when she gave it to The Mouth: the crunching and tearing and the wet noises that she couldn't quite define. Then, she thought of the sounds *she* would make in The Mouth. No way. She couldn't risk it. Sniffling and crying, something clucking hard in her throat, she reached down and handed the boy the squirrel.

Cali heard a giggle, followed by the heavy sound of the boy landing in the grass. The giggling became laughter that trailed away, and she knew the boy had gone, running toward apartment 414 and The Mouth.

Slowly, her sobs died down into quiet sniffles. Now, she'd have to start all over.

More.

"I know," she said through tears.

* * *

Tara tried to concentrate. She thought if she put her mind to it, really focused and got her thinking straight, she could figure out how long it had been. When she didn't try to focus, the answer bounced all over the place. Sometimes, she thought she'd been watching The Mouth for hours. Other times, she knew it had been months, maybe close to a year. Each time, she remembered Marco with the pickaxe he'd bought at the hardware store, the way he'd dragged the washer from its cubby hole and started swinging at the linoleum beneath, how the flooring had peeled back like great scabs until the pickaxe began ringing off concrete. She recalled how she'd asked what he was doing, how she'd screamed the question at him, and how he'd answered with a voice so calm it had terrified her.

"There's something underneath."

For a long time, she'd tried to ignore him, had cranked the volume on her stories and pretended there was nothing strange happening. When the apartment management started knocking on the door about noise complaints, the panic inside her had boiled, and she'd begged Marco to stop, to listen to reason before they found themselves homeless.

"Almost done."

He'd broken through the concrete just as management unlocked the front door and pushed their way inside, and she'd heard the voice for the first time, the same voice she heard all day, every day, that never died and that always demanded *More*.

And now she heard the voice again. It kept her awake almost constantly, her mind balanced on a point between exhaustion and what had to be insanity. The world moved in shapes and colors around her, and she constantly fought to keep everything in focus.

Focus. Focus was the key, and she knew it. Enough of it, and she avoided slipping into the strange state almost everybody else in Juniper Ridge exhibited. Even now, more than a dozen filthy, stinking residents littered what had once been her living room. They slept on the floor and the couch. Another filled the space that served as her lone hallway, blocking both the bathroom and bedroom with her naked bulk. All of them lay where they had collapsed, too exhausted after finding food for The Mouth. Marco moved between them, shoving aside those who took up too much space.

The front door opened, knocking against the top of a sleeping man's head, and two adults in tattered clothes entered. Tara knew from the way they kept their hands cupped in front of them that their offerings were small, but she still had to see. It was the role she'd either assigned herself or been forced into by The Mouth. She couldn't remember anymore, wasn't sure she'd ever known. Just like how much time had passed, the answer swam in and out of her head, changing all the time. Maybe it was the exhaustion, or maybe she'd simply forgotten what was real.

More.

The first person, a woman whose T-shirt smelled like rotten meat and had stretched and torn at the shoulders, stepped up and presented her gift. It was a dead bird, a cardinal. It lay in the cup of her hands like a strange sculpture, all odd angles and pain. Tara examined it for a second and then nodded, stepping aside so the woman could drop her dead bird in the hole that had now been widened to almost four feet, nothing but darkness inside. She didn't bother watching. When the chewing sounds came, she knew the woman had dropped her offering.

She looked at the old man who stood in front of her, at the exhaustion that filled his eyes like fog and the terrible way his entire body sagged. He held up his hands, and she saw hope in his features before she looked down to see the dead crickets he held.

Please accept it, she thought. She didn't know if The Mouth could hear her. Most of the time, she hoped it couldn't, but now she wanted her plea to break through.

The answer came the way it always did, appearing in her mind without words or commands, just a feeling she couldn't ignore, couldn't resist. Without warning, she slapped the old man's face. The hope crumbled, and depression rushed in to fill the cracks. She hated herself as the man turned and left the apartment. He'd spend the rest of the day searching for something to feed The Mouth, and if he didn't make it back home before fatigue claimed him, he'd sleep on the ground, his pillow either dead grass or oil-soaked concrete.

It had to change. Tara knew it, and sometimes when she looked in Marco's eyes—she couldn't recall the last time they'd spoken—she could tell he knew it, too. The Mouth held too much control. From the moment it first spoke directly into their minds, it had taken over their lives. What would it do when they ran out of things to feed it? Would they be next? Sometimes the questions kept her awake even when the fatigue was a lead weight on her shoulders, dragging her down, down, down.

Shaking her head, she made the questions disappear. She feared The Mouth would catch on, would sense her betrayal and punish her for it. Worse, she feared it would punish Marco, the man she still loved with some piece of her heart The Mouth had forbidden.

And the rest of the world wasn't helping them. She wondered about that sometimes, why the police never bothered them and no one cared that the rent or utilities hadn't been paid in months. Or years. Or hours. She made sure to never consider it too long, because the possibilities frightened her.

Marco entered the kitchen and leaned against the counter. He watched her with tired, pleading eyes, and she saw tracks in the grime on his face. Tears of frustration and fear had cut those tracks, she knew, just as she knew a matching set adorned her own face. Silently, she prayed as she stepped toward her husband. She wanted to speak, but she didn't really remember how to form words. Instead, she placed her hand on the counter and slid it toward Marco's. She reached with her little finger, hoping for the slightest contact. Her eyes never left his, and for the first time in months she felt her heart accelerate.

They touched, the skin of their fingers sticky with dirt, and Tara watched her husband shudder. The beginnings of a smile appeared on her face. She still had him, and he still had her. That counted for something. It kept the nightmare at bay.

More.

She jumped, gasping, and jerked her hand back to her side. Marco's face crumbled, and he turned from her, shuffling back to the living room, where he stepped over comatose bodies and rubbed his face with his hands.

Tara watched him, and her heart felt like ashes. Something had to be done. Searching her mind, she hoped she'd find the answer.

* * *

A year had passed. At least, Gary thought it had been a year. He remembered the leaves turning colors and falling to the ground, remembered them growing back. Most of the dead leaves remained in the Juniper Ridge parking lot, a carpet of decay in orange, red, and brown. The entire community smelled like rot now. In addition to the leaves and the unwashed state of every resident, most of the older tenants had failed to last through the winter. For some reason, no one had fed them to The Mouth. He didn't understand why they'd been left to decompose in their apartments, but he suspected it was a mercy. If The Mouth developed a taste for humans...

He shut out the thought before it could percolate.

Everything required concentration now, and he'd grown better at it over the preceding months. When he kept his thoughts sharp and controlled, he could resist The Mouth just enough to function like a normal person. More than once, he'd considered letting his concentration slip or disappear altogether. He'd moved beyond Juniper Ridge enough times to know the world had changed. There must be mouths everywhere. It was the only way to explain how people had transformed so drastically, how ugly and vicious and desperate they'd become.

When he saw the deer, he'd decided to do something. It was dead, a recent kill found on the side of the road. Why no one had dragged it to The Mouth was anyone's guess. Maybe the vehicle that struck it had already been loaded with morsels, or maybe it had been hit by somebody who'd pulled their will together long enough to decide escape was a good idea. Either way, he'd known the relatively fresh carcass presented a way to fight back.

Now, the dead deer filled his living room floor. He'd feared someone would see him drag the remains up the stairs by a chain, but some stroke of luck had left him unnoticed. Since that time, he'd made quick runs to abandoned hardware and grocery stores, grabbing anything he thought might hurt The Mouth. Already, he'd soaked the deer's carcass with bleach and rat poison and a dozen different insecticides. He kept the windows open and wore a painter's mask, and still the stink was overpowering. The smell scared him, because surely someone would realize what he was doing. Hopefully, The Mouth had kept everybody too tired, too close to insanity to be a threat. Preparing for bed, knowing he'd show all his cards the next day, he prayed long and hard, and hoped somebody could hear him.

When Gary woke, he slapped himself across the face before The Mouth's voice could enter his thoughts. The daily ritual worked once again, and he crawled out of bed, his stomach a flutter of excitement and fear. His mask had shifted in the night, and the smell of bleach and other poisons made him dizzy as he sat on the edge of the bed. Pulling the mask back into place, he smiled. It was good to feel things again. For too long, he'd been just shy of an automaton.

He changed into one of the dirt-caked outfits he kept in a pile in his closet. So far, no one had seen through his disguise. With enough luck, no one would until he'd dumped the poisoned deer down the hole and fed it to The Mouth. After that, they could do anything they wanted. As long as he did some damage, he didn't care much. Still, he grabbed his car keys and stuffed them into his pocket. His car held just over half a tank, and if he could reach it, he'd drive as far as that tank would allow.

Wrestling the deer down the stairs proved just as hard as dragging it up, but he did it without getting crushed. Without his mask, the smell stung his nostrils. His back ached, and his arms burned, but he refused to rest until he reached apartment 414.

As he approached The Mouth's home, the fear that roiled in his belly crept up his spine and threatened to set his mind on fire. What if somebody tried to take the deer? He'd seen similar things happen, The Mouth inspiring violence like he'd never seen, and he wondered if he could kill someone if they threatened him. If it needed to be done, he'd try his best. All of this served a greater purpose, even if that purpose amounted to no more than thumbing his nose at death in the moment before it took him.

More.

The closer he came to building four and the dreaded apartment, the louder the voice grew. He hoped that meant The Mouth sensed his offering and wanted it, but the frightened parts of his brain said his concentration was crumbling, that soon he'd be the same as he'd been for months, just another mindless body kept around to bring food. Once he made sure no one was looking, he squeezed his eyes shut and lined up his thoughts. Everything became neat and orderly, and the voice quieted some, now little more than the tapping of a fingernail against a windowpane.

Please, God, he thought. *Please. If you're still there, help me.*

He dragged his prize through the door of apartment 414.

* * *

Tara knew the next offering was a large one before she saw the man wrestle the deer's corpse through her door. The Mouth's wanting was a hook in her brain, and she felt its greed tugging harder and harder. All through her living room, the others gasped and grumbled, both jealous and dismissive of the man's offering. Her eyes met Marco's and she saw worry in them. She knew why. If violence broke out among the people gathered in their apartment, they'd never be able to stop it. The crowd would tear apart both of them in their frenzy to please The Mouth.

Jesus, she wished she had the courage to do something.

Panting, the man dragged the dead animal around the corner and into the kitchen. He had a chain around its limp neck, and she saw the links dig into the corpse's flesh as well as that of his hands.

A thought wedged in her brain, but she couldn't understand it. Something about the man's hands. Was there something wrong with them? She found herself staring as the man grunted and struggled to maneuver the dead animal into the narrow space. Could they even fit the deer down the hole? Maybe they'd need to cut it into pieces. Without thinking, she opened a drawer and retrieved a butcher knife, one of the many kitchen utensils they never bothered to use anymore. Surely, it could slice through the meat.

Behind her, The Mouth demanded the man move faster. Tara felt this more than heard it, The Mouth's hunger like a charge traveling the length of her spine. She moved to help the man, to start cutting pieces off the deer, and he pushed her away, his hand strong against her shoulder. For a moment, their eyes locked, and what she saw stunned her. Clarity. This man wasn't like the rest. He knew what he was doing, and he was in charge of his actions.

In the next instant, the smell struck her. Bleach and other chemicals raced up her nostrils, not the rotting scent of dead meat. Terror filled her. This man meant to hurt The Mouth, maybe kill it. He could free all of them, but what if he didn't succeed? What would The Mouth do to them if he angered it? The questions whipped through her head like leaves on an October wind, and the man was standing at the hole, peering into it with a smirk on his face, and she knew she had to do something, but she didn't know which action was right until she made up her mind and plunged the knife deep into his back.

He didn't scream or shout or make any noise but a small gasp. Slowly, he turned to face her, but she couldn't see his expression through the tears that filled her eyes. Already, she thought she'd made the wrong choice, that she should have helped him instead.

With one groping hand, the man tried to grab hold of the knife she'd buried in him. His knees buckled, and he fell. Tara dove, trying to catch him, but she was too slow, too tired. The man's body hit the ground and then tumbled into the hole. A scream erupted from Tara's mouth, but it disappeared beneath the crunching and tearing noises. It had tasted a person now. She felt The Mouth's pleasure through every piece of her, a riptide of enjoyment that made her want to die.

More!

Somewhere in the distance, she heard shouts, violence. Marco called to her, but she couldn't answer, could do nothing but curl into a ball beside the deer carcass and sob. Too late. They'd lost.

* * *

Cali watched the boy. He lay in the grass, naked and filthy. His thumb filled his mouth. A grin stretched Cali's lips because the boy didn't know yet. In his exhausted dreams, he probably thought The Mouth still wanted animals. Cats and dogs and mice. Squirrels. Her grin widened to a smile.

A heavy rock occupied her hands. Cali lifted it and giggled.

—LISA MORTON

Lisa Morton is a screenwriter, author of dozens of short stories, and one of the world's leading Halloween experts. Her first novel, *The Castle Of Los Angeles*, won the Bram Stoker Award for First Novel, and her first collection, *Monsters Of L.A.*, was released in 2011 by Bad Moon Books. Coming in 2012 are *Witch Hunts: A Graphic History Of The Burning Times* (McFarland), co-written with Rocky Wood and illustrated by Greg Chapman, and *Trick Or Treat?: A Cultural History Of Halloween* (Reaktion). She lives in North Hollywood, California, and can be found online at www.lisamorton.com

—Blood for the American People

By Lisa Morton

Tom leaned back against the closed front door and stared at all the blood. He sighed once, and began mentally cleaning the apartment.

The couch had taken the worst of it. Fortunately it was cheap and typical, and he could replace it in hours.

Likewise, the carpeting—standard issue low pile, light beige. Unfortunately, he'd have to redo the entire living room. He hoped it hadn't completely soaked through to the padding.

The walls.

Now Tom groaned, used a gloved hand to lock the front door behind him, and carefully crossed the room. As he stepped around the coffee table (which, to a cursory glance, looked untouched), he noticed a crimson-splotched hand just behind the sofa. He walked another yard, and saw that the hand had been severed from the rest of the body, which was apparently also behind the couch; he saw a leg flung into a far corner of the room, having just missed the window treatments.

Jesus fucking Christ.

In his career as a highly discrete "cleaner," Tom had dealt with a number of messy disposals—a man who'd been stabbed roughly 50 times, a woman beaten by a team of three professionals—but he'd never seen blood splattered at this magnitude before. He leaned over the couch and saw entrails three feet away from the main trunk of the body; and there, on the tasteful wallpaper—were those claw marks?

What the fuck did the killer use? A goddamn tiger?

Tom glanced at the pale, dead face, and saw the features frozen in a grand-finale expression of terror and agony. Just after he'd accepted the job and had been given the address, Tom ran a check and found out the apartment was rented to a Morgan Dempsey, a minor-league employee of the State Department. Mr. Dempsey was so far down the food chain he didn't even have a memorable title, but apparently he'd pissed somebody off.

Bad.

Tom tore his gaze away from Dempsey's wide eyes and focused again on the task at hand. He realized this job would require more than just new furniture and fresh paint; the crime scene was severe enough that he couldn't possibly remove all evidence in a day. He'd dispose of the body, get the furniture and carpeting and wallpaper in place, then—since he'd been assured by the client that he had an unlimited expense account—he'd grease a few palms.

And, most importantly—he wouldn't ask any questions.

* * *

The man on the other side of the desk gave Tom an envelope of cash and a smile. "Your fee and your expenses." As Tom pocketed the envelope, the flabby, middle-aged man with the ugly comb-over chuckled once. "I don't know how you do it. I hear the D.C. forensics team hit the apartment this morning, and came away with nothing."

Tom let his relief course silently; outwardly, he nodded, apparently confident, sure of his own skills.

The client, Mr. Dickson, squinted. "My contacts said you were good. I trust it would be acceptable to hire you again in the future...if necessary, I mean?"

"Of course."

"Do you have any idea what we do here, Mr. Lightenour?"

Tom glanced around the walls. The Founding Fathers Foundation was housed in a converted residence, one of those old, thin two-story houses squeezed into parts of Washington like celery sticks in rancid dip. Dickson's office had once been a den, probably; it was spacious, with expensive pastel wallpaper and genuine antiques for furnishings.

Tom hoped he'd never have to clean it. Just the chair he was sitting on was probably irreplaceable.

He shrugged in answer to Dickson's question. "All I know is that you're one of those high-powered think tanks."

Of course he knew a bit more than that.

He always investigated a client before he accepted a new job. The Founding Fathers Foundation was a conservative think tank, with a mission statement that read like a Cliffs Notes version of the Pledge of Allegiance. Funded by private and corporate sponsors, it boasted an annual budget of nearly $50 million, and its dozen officers and trustees had their fingers in nearly every slice of the policy pie. The Foundation supported supply-side economics, the Monroe Doctrine, a strong national defense, and traditional American values...which *it* defined, regardless of how traditional they really were. Tom figured the fine folks who made up FFF had probably been involved with everything from the invasion of Iraq to the death of the public health care option. Tom's own politics—on the rare occasions when he thought about them—leaned considerably to the left of the FFF's, but he had to respect their strength. And, of course, their money.

Suddenly a low female voice sounded behind Tom. "Oh, sorry, Dix, didn't know you had company..."

Dickson waved a hand. "Quite all right, Anita—we're almost done here."

Tom rose, turned—and stopped just short of gaping.

The woman who stood in the office doorway wasn't Hollywood beautiful, but her shoulder-length, thick, light brown hair, half-lidded smile, and hip-cocked pose all smacked Tom like a bolt of erotic lightning straight to the crotch. He froze as he felt himself harden, hoping she hadn't noticed.

No woman had ever had such an effect on him.

She shifted slightly, the filmy material of her bright red dress hissing slightly as it slid over her thighs, and Tom felt another arc of pure sex. "Oh...you must be Mr. Lightenour," she said, letting his name slip from her tongue like drops of hard liquor.

Tom swallowed, unsure of how to answer—or that he even could answer—when Dickson rose from behind the desk. "Mr. Lightenour was just leaving—"

"I was hoping we might discuss some other business," she said.

Dickson and the woman stared at each other for a moment, eyes narrowed, nostrils flared. Then Dickson twitched and backed down, rustling papers as he looked away. "Fine."

The woman gestured out of the office, and Tom followed as she led him down a short hallway to another room at the rear of the house.

He worked to recall her from the FFF website, and remembered her on the page listing the Foundation's Board: She was Anita Curran, a Rhodes Scholar and CEO of at least one major corporation before joining FFF. In the accompanying photo she'd looked attractive, but more like a well-groomed middle-aged executive, not the most desirable woman Tom had ever met.

She paused before an office door that had her name on it. Tom entered, then she stepped around him, silently closing blinds, turning locks, and flipping off light switches before launching herself at him.

The miniscule part of Tom's mind not currently connected directly to his cock told him to resist, to take his money and run, to never accept another job from the Founding Fathers Foundation...but that part was quickly silenced by tongue and taste and hair and nails and the musky hot scent of her.

It was over in minutes, leaving them both sweaty and panting. As Tom re-buttoned his shirt, he glanced at her and saw her eyes flash in the dim light, and for a moment he had the unsettling sensation that he'd just fucked an animal in heat.

But when she told him she'd call him later, he didn't say no.

* * *

She did call, two nights later. This time they met at an

expensive hotel where the desk clerks welcomed her by name and had a room key waiting.

It began as quickly as it had in her office, but lasted longer this time and took place in a king-sized bed. When they finally pulled apart, Tom was too drained to do more than just stare at the ceiling.

Anita rose, used the phone to order room service, then lit a cigarette and stood naked before the fifth floor window, looking down at the lights of Washington.

"You smoke," he said, watching her.

"Is that a compliment or an observation?" She didn't turn, only took another drag.

"It just surprises me."

Tom could hear amusement in her voice. "You only live once, right?"

"You don't seem like a conservative scholar."

Now she did turn to look at him, and he felt a chill ripple up from the small of his back. "What do you know about the Founding Fathers Foundation?" she asked.

"No more than what's on the website."

She nodded, then turned back to the view and the cigarette. The lights seemed to fascinate her, and he saw the hand without the cigarette spread on the cool glass as if she could reach through and take the city. She didn't say anything else.

* * *

Two weeks later, she gave him an address and told him to meet her there at 7 p.m.

They'd rendezvoused a total of six times, but each meeting had consisted entirely of sex (*really amazing fucking sex*, Tom reminded himself) in a random hotel or her office. They never left the room, didn't enjoy a night out on the town, didn't talk much before or after. She certainly had never invited him home.

But when Tom pulled up before the tasteful two-story house in Georgetown, he knew it was hers. Somehow that realization made him more anxious, not less.

He parked, walked to the front door, rang the bell. Moments

later he stood in Anita's large, elegant living room, hearing cloth tear as she raked her nails down his back and ran her tongue along his jaw.

She abruptly pulled away from him, spinning to the window. Tom ignored his throbbing crotch and tried to follow her glance, but saw only the night sky over the affluent cityscape.

"It's time," she announced, and took his hand, leading him out of the room.

They went through the kitchen, around the island with its copper pans and chrome fixtures, to a basement door. She opened it, turned on lights, and led him downstairs. The basement looked typical—boxes, old furniture, gardening tools—except for a solid metal door wedged into one wall. Anita opened it to reveal a small, sterile room within: One wall held a bank of video monitors, there were racks of canned goods and supplies, and a cot against the third wall.

"I'll be damned," Tom said, taking it all in, "a panic room. I've never seen one in person before."

Anita reached around him to close the door, then stepped away from him. "I want you to watch me, Tom."

He grinned. "Is that all?"

Her response was nearly a physical slap. "Goddamnit, *watch me.*"

Silent, chastened, he nodded.

She reached back to a shelf and brought forth a vial of pills; twisting the lid off, she poured about ten into her palm. She threw the pills into her mouth, and washed them down with a long pull from a bottle of water.

"Anita, what the hell...?"

"*Just watch.*"

Next she removed her clothing, which she carefully folded and placed on a shelf. By the time she finished, Tom could see the drugs working on her—her eyes were losing focus, her limbs moving as if she were underwater.

She lowered herself to the cot, stretched out there, and promptly lost consciousness.

Jesus...what is this, a suicide attempt? Christ, Anita...

Tom was debating whether to call 911 when she quivered.

At first he thought she must certainly be convulsing from the medication—but then he saw that somehow her bare skin seemed to be darkening. He bent closer to her, breath held, and saw that it wasn't that the flesh was changing color, but that it was growing hair.

Tom backed up so quickly that he rattled the shelving unit behind him. He stared in disbelief as she changed:

Limbs lengthened and bent. Features changed shape and color. Thick gray-brown fur covered her. The spine curved. A tail sprouted.

In less than thirty seconds, Tom stood over a large wolf that was twitching slightly in a sedative-induced sleep. She growled softly, Tom saw canines that were nearly as long and thick as his little finger, and he knew exactly who/what had killed the young man in the State Department.

He turned and stumbled out the door, slamming it behind him, double-checking it even when he heard the catch of the heavy interior latch.

But he didn't leave. He paced for a few seconds, until his heart slowed, and then he found a cracking old leather armchair and fell into it.

Jesus, I've been fucking a wolf, he thought, and allowed himself a time for hysterical laughter. Then, when that had passed, he thought about what to do.

And decided simply to wait.

* * *

He dozed off for a while, but jerked awake when he heard the door opening. Adrenaline flooded his system and brought him to his feet, but before he could run, the door was pushed back, and he saw her.

Fully human again. Partly clothed. Looking dulled, as if she was still slightly wrapped in the sedative's embrace.

"I need coffee," she announced before heading up the stairs, leaving him to follow. He saw morning light streaming in through the kitchen windows, and realized the night had passed.

He sat at the dinette silently while she went about the absurdly normal motions of making coffee. Finally, she brought two steaming mugs to the table, sat down across from him, took a sip, and eyed him contemplatively.

"You stayed."

He nodded, his throat dry, his stomach in rebellion at the thought of coffee, which he swallowed anyway.

"I was bitten four years ago..."

Tom remembered the website. "When you joined FFF."

"Yes. It's kind of...let's say, a condition of being part of the Foundation—"

"Wait—do you mean that all of you in the FFF are...?"

"Of course. I was turned by Dickson."

Tom tried to imagine the pudgy, balding bureaucrat as a sophisticated predator, and was surprised to find that he could.

"The wolf," Anita said, drawing his attention back to her, "it changes you even when the moon's not full. Makes you faster, smarter—"

"More vicious." Images of shredded limbs and flung-about organs in the young man's apartment made Tom push the coffee aside.

"Yes," she said, and Tom wondered if her teeth weren't still longer, more pointed than they should have been. "We are more aggressive. But that's good for our work."

"For planning wars and police actions, you mean."

She laughed, then stroked his hand, and Tom had to stifle an urge to pull away. "God, Tom, you sound so liberal."

"So what did he do? That kid in the State Department."

She sighed and looked away. "He had the bad luck of walking in on a cabinet head in a...well, compromising position."

"And that cabinet head is yours?"

She didn't answer, just turned that glistening smile back on him.

"So," he said, doing his best to hold her gaze, "what about me? How can you let me just walk away knowing what I know?"

Anita rose languorously from her chair, padded around the

table, and draped herself over Tom until she could whisper into his ear.

"Darling, every wolf needs its dog."

* * *

She was right, of course. She was always right.

If Tom tried to tell anyone—cops, media, iReporters, another think tank—he wouldn't be believed, but he would be dead, because the wolves of the Founding Fathers Foundation had his scent now and would hunt him down.

So he served them. He cleaned up when they tore apart an influential talk show host's assistant who was regularly blowing the blowhard. He disposed of a blood-soaked car when they attacked a street hustler who'd sold drugs to an evangelical leader.

And he had a great deal more mind-numbing sex with Anita, the kind of sex that left him chafed and sore. Normally Tom would have done anything for that kind of sex, but his bouts with her also left him scared out of his wits. Even though she had told him she would only change on full moon nights, he knew she could strip the skin from his bones any time she wished.

The street hustler had been killed during a new moon.

But they also paid Tom well. It was amazing what money and sex had done to silence his conscience. He sometimes found himself embroiled in late-night arguments with himself, reasoning that he might as well be on the winner's side; or that he could take their money until he was wealthy enough to turn on them.

Or he could beg them to turn him.

Whenever the full moon came again, and he locked himself away in his apartment, imagining Anita roaming the streets, her smooth ash-colored fur protecting her from sight and cold, her attuned senses leading her to the prey, the remorseless kill...he wished he was with her.

Nearly a year after his first job for FFF, he awoke the morning after a full moon to receive his latest assignment. He was sent to a house in a New Jersey suburb, where he found the mutilated remains of a woman—and a baby girl. She still wore the shreds of a pink jumper and booties.

For the first time in his professional life, Tom vomited upon viewing the scene, then immediately cursed himself for creating a major evidence stew; one more thing to clean up. He forced himself not to wonder what anyone could have done to deserve this, or what anyone could be to commit this. He focused solely on the practicalities, and he walked through the actions like a stone man, a robot.

A dog.

When the job was finished, he returned to FFF and found Dickson waiting with the pay. "I trust everything went well...?"

Tom didn't answer. He took the money, left Dickson, walked down the hall to Anita's office and threw the door open.

She was on her cell, and looked up in irritation. "I'll have to call you back," she said, watching Tom as he closed her door and then paced before her large, neat desk.

"Tom, what—"

"Bite me."

She blinked in surprise, and then laughed.

"I saw what you—or one of you—did last night, to that woman and the baby. And I almost couldn't handle it."

Anita leaned back in her chair, eyes narrowing. "That's unfortunate, but—"

"So turn me. Make me like you."

She gawked for a moment, her mouth actually hanging open. Then she said, with some amusement, "You can't be serious."

"Why not?"

"Because," Anita said, rising from her chair, causing Tom's stomach to constrict in dread as she walked around the desk to him, "you will never be one of us."

She started to reach for him, but Tom leapt away. "I would be if you turned me."

Her amusement vanished, replaced with a fury that made her eyes glitter; flop sweat broke out on Tom's brow as she advanced. "What do you think I was before, Tom? Some weak-kneed left-winger with a useless fucking degree in Liberal Arts and a collection of Indigo Girls albums? Some halfwit jabbering of equality and socialism? Some naive *dog* who stupidly dares to dream that it can be a wolf?!"

She backed him into a corner, and now pushed her face up to his. "If you want to know the truth, even the sex has started to get boring. I'd like your dick better if it was attached to a backbone." Anita's nose wrinkled in disgust, and Tom knew she'd smelled his fear. She turned away, didn't bother to look back as she added, "Get out. FFF is finished with you, and so am I."

He left while he could.

* * *

Tom had a month.

Somehow he knew she wouldn't risk attacking him while in human shape. He wasn't some spaced-out junkie too doped to put up a fight; no, he knew she'd wait to let the wolf take him.

If he ran, she'd find him. There was nowhere he could hide, no one he could talk to.

He only had one chance: To fight back.

FFF's offices had its own security, and he knew he wouldn't be able to get near her while she was human. That was fine; he wasn't sure he could kill her while she still looked like Anita, and while he still wanted her.

Tom searched the internet, found YouTube instructional videos on how to cast bullets, and bought the molds, ladles, and other equipment online. It took him a few tries to get it right. Tom didn't like guns—he'd never had to use one in his work— but he did own a Smith & Wesson 327 that held eight rounds, so he made eight bullets. He went into the woods and fired one as a test, to be sure it wouldn't shatter or melt. He was satisfied with the results. He had seven bullets left.

He thought it would be enough for her.

* * *

The night of the full moon arrived.

Tom had been his usual careful self as he'd arranged (under a false name) to rent the isolated cabin. He couldn't afford to have his D.C. neighbors hearing gunshots, or wolf howls. Or seeing him lug a body out to his car.

He knew she'd find him anyway.

It was past midnight as he sat in the cabin's main room, the gun cradled in his lap, a fire blazing in the old-fashioned hearth behind him. The moon had risen several hours ago, and outside he saw pines and scrub bathed in light the color of her fur.

Finally, he heard the small scratch at the door.

Tom stood, holding the gun firmly in both hands, pointing it at the room's single large window. He knew she wouldn't get in through the door, but could easily leap past the glass, enduring only a few small cuts. He hoped to take her down in mid-leap, but would fire the rest of the rounds into her, just to be sure.

The hair on Tom's arms stood on edge as he heard her howl...and then he heard the answering howls of other wolves. Of course she hadn't come alone. She'd brought the entire FFF board with her. Their kind always hunted in packs.

Tom's knees gave way and he sagged into the chair, cursing himself for his arrogance. He'd really believed he'd meant enough to her that she'd want to deal with him alone. Of course they'd tracked his online activity, knew how much silver he'd bought, and had calculated how many bullets he had. She had maneuvered one of the others to take out the window first. Maybe she even had human assistants out there, preparing to open the door, to let them in to tear apart their dog in bites that would kill him, not change him.

She'd been right all along. He could never be like them.

Tom raised the gun to his own head as the first wolf crashed through the window.

—RAY GARTON

Ray Garton is the author of over 60 novels, novellas, short story collections and media tie-ins. His 1987 novel *Live Girls* was nominated for the Bram Stoker Award and has become a classic of the genre. In 2006, he received the Grand Master of Horror Award. His latest novel, *Meds*, a thriller about prescription drugs, is available as a trade paperback, for Kindle from Amazon, for Nook from Barnes and Noble and in several ebook formats at www.fictionwise.com. He lives in northern California with his wife Dawn. To keep up with new releases, read interviews and reviews, participate in contests and interact on the message board, please visit the official Ray Garton website at www.raygartononline.com

—RECEPTION

By Ray Garton

Frank sat on the couch watching television. A commercial was on. He jotted something down in a spiral-bound notebook in his lap, writing quickly.

Seven-year-old Kami perched on the cushion beside him and said, "What are you writing, Daddy?"

"Just some stuff," he said distractedly. "Why don't you go play, sweetheart."

"Can I have cookies and milk?" she said.

Frank reluctantly put the notebook and pen on the rolled arm of the couch. He got up and hurried to the kitchen. He quickly found a package of Chips Ahoy cookies in the cupboard, put four on a paper plate, poured some milk in a glass. He put the cookies and milk on the dining room table.

"There you go," he said.

"Thank you, Daddy."

Frank went back into the living room. His mouth dropped open when he saw the silent blue screen on the television. He grabbed the remote from the end table and flipped through the channels. They were all an empty blue screen. Cable was out.

He took his iPhone from his pocket and called the cable company.

"Yes, I'm calling because my cable is out."

The woman on the line asked for his address and he gave it to her.

"We're working on it, sir," she said.

"Do you have any idea how long it'll be?"

"All I can tell you is that we're working on it."

He hung up and paced for a while. Then he went to the window and looked out at the front yard, at his Dodge Ram parked at the curb.

Frank didn't park in the driveway anymore. He hadn't since the accident. It hadn't happened in the Ram, but that didn't matter. It had happened in the driveway. Almost three years had passed, but it felt like yesterday. When he closed his eyes, he could feel the Chevy pick-up's left rear tire bump over something as he backed out of the garage. He heard Kami's scream. He'd stopped the pick-up and gotten out. He'd seen Kami standing nearby with both of her little hands over her mouth. He'd seen the lower half of Frank Jr.'s body sticking out from beneath the pick-up. Frank Jr.—they'd called him Franky—had been nowhere in sight when Frank had started the engine and backed up. When he thought back on it now, he imagined he'd heard Franky's chest being crushed beneath the tire, his ribs breaking, although he hadn't at the time. Franky had been just a few weeks shy of his eighth birthday.

Frank had sold the pick-up and gotten a good deal on the used Ram. But he never pulled into the driveway anymore. Because then he would have to back out, and he could never do that again.

He went over to the television, hands on his hips, elbows jutting at his sides. The reception had not returned.

Frank tucked his lower lip between his teeth and chewed on it. He wondered what he was missing.

He needed something to do, a distraction. He decided to do some housework. Then he would cook dinner for Grace. But he left the television on even though the screen remained blue. He wanted to know as soon as the reception was restored.

* * *

Grace came home to the smell of garlic. The table in the small dining area was set.

"Hi, Mommy," Kami said as she hugged Grace.

"Hi, sweetie. What smells good?"

"Daddy cooked dinner."

Frank came out of the kitchen. "Fireman's stew, a salad, and garlic bread," he said.

Grace smiled and said, "Well, aren't you good to me."

"Don't be silly," he said. "You're the one who works. I should do this every night."

She embraced him and they kissed. "How are you?"

"Fine," he said with a smile.

She saw the blank blue screen on the television. "What's wrong with the TV?"

"Oh. Cable's out." He went over to the end table, picked up the remote, and turned off the television. "Dinner's ready," he said.

Grace went to the bedroom and changed into jeans and a sweatshirt.

Over dinner, she was pleased to see Frank smile as they talked. He even laughed a few times. He was doing so much better. He'd gone into therapy immediately after the accident. He'd seen Dr. Stack, a family therapist, twice a week for a while before backing off to once a week. Grace had seen Dr. Stack for a time, too. She'd been so angry at Frank at first and she had to learn to let go of that, had to see things from Frank's point of view, feel his pain. The first year without Franky had been tough on both of them. Even Kami had seen Dr. Stack several times.

A couple of weeks ago, Frank had said he didn't think he needed the sessions anymore and had stopped. Grace had been uncertain about that at first, but he was so obviously doing better that she thought it was probably all right for him to at least take a break.

Frank had been a newspaper reporter at the *Redding Record-Searchlight*. He'd been in line for a promotion to associate editor when the accident happened. He'd quit work with the assurance that his job would be waiting for him when he was ready to come back, but the promotion went to someone else. Grace had gotten a job at a small advertising firm to make ends meet.

He'd been so silent and morose at first. For a year, his facial expression had not changed once. Now, he was so much more like his old self. The difference was staggering.

"Honey," she said as they ate, "you seem to be doing so well. Have you considered going back to work?"

He nodded. "Yes, I've thought about it. I think I may be ready to do that very soon. What about you? Ready to quit?"

"No. As a matter of fact, I thought maybe I'd keep working. We could have Mom take care of Kami in the afternoons when she gets home from school. It would be nice to have two incomes, don't you think?"

"You like it that much?"

"I love it. I'd forgotten how much I enjoyed working. When we lived in Vacaville it was such a hassle. You know, driving into San Francisco every day, the awful traffic. But I love the work, I love advertising. And here in Redding, the traffic's no big deal at all. I'm really enjoying my job."

He smiled. "That's great, honey. I'm glad."

After dinner, they washed dishes together, then went into the living room and watched television—the cable was working again. He had a notebook in his lap. During the commercials, he scribbled in it.

"What are you doing?" she said.

He shrugged. "A little writing."

"Really?" She smiled. "You miss it, don't you?"

"Yeah, I guess I do."

"Can I see?"

"Oh, no. It's nothing. Just...messing around."

That night in bed, they made love. It was better than it had been in a long time. Since before the accident. Grace fell asleep, content in the crook of his arm.

* * *

Grace woke to find herself alone in bed and looked at the digital clock on her nightstand: 3:11. She heard something, sat up and listened. The television was on in the living room with the volume low. She got up and put on her robe.

Frank was on the sofa writing frantically in the notebook.

He wore a T-shirt and boxer shorts. The lamp on the end table provided the only light besides the glow from the television. She walked into the living room, but he did not notice her.

"Honey," she said.

He was so startled, his entire body jolted and the notebook dropped to the floor. He bent down and picked it up, kept writing. When he was finished, he looked up and smiled at her. It was a big smile. Too big. A sheen of perspiration gleamed on his forehead and upper lip.

"What are you doing up?" she said as she approached him and rubbed one eye with a knuckle.

"Oh. Um. I-yuh, I couldn't sleep."

"What're you—"

He looked at the television. "Shh!" He leaned forward and watched a commercial. He started writing again.

She sat down beside him.

Frank stiffened, scooted away from her a bit. "Um, why don't you go back to bed, hon. I'll be in later."

"What are you writing?"

"It's nothing. I'm just—"

She reached over to take the notebook, but he jerked it away from her.

Grace frowned. "What's wrong?"

"Nothing's wrong."

"Why won't you let me see what you're writing?"

Another commercial came on and Frank focused his attention on it. He put the notebook in his lap and started writing again.

"What are you writing?" she said.

"Look, I'm kind of busy here. Why don't you go back to bed?"

"You're sweating, Frank. What's wrong?"

"Go to *bed*," he snapped.

She flinched. "I'm not going to bed until you tell me what's wrong with you. Frank, you've been doing so well. I don't understand, what are you doing up at this hour, sweating like you've been on a run?"

"You wouldn't understand."

"Try me."

He focused his attention on another commercial, wrote in the notebook again.

Grace stood and folded her arms tightly across her breasts. "Are you going to talk to me?"

An old black-and-white movie came on and Frank sat back on the sofa wearily, sighed. He wiped his forehead with the back of his hand.

Grace went to the television, bent down, and punched the power button. The picture blinked out.

Frank sat forward again and said, "No! Turn it back on!" He looked around until he found the remote on the end table, pointed it and turned the television back on.

As he was doing that, Grace went to him and took the notebook from his lap. On the page were written lines in quotes, and within each line, certain words had been circled.

"What is this?" she said.

He stood and snatched the notebook away from her. "I *said* you wouldn't understand." He sat down on the couch again and watched the old movie.

Grace took a deep breath, sat down beside him, and put a hand on his shoulder. "Frank, you...you're scaring me."

"There's nothing to be scared of. Everything's fine."

"Something's wrong."

"Nothing's wrong, everything's fine now. He's *telling* me everything's fine."

"What? Who's telling you everything's fine?"

The gray light from the television sparkled in the unspilled tears in his eyes. He turned to her and smiled as one of the tears fell.

"Franky."

A cold feeling spread in Grace's chest. "What?"

"He's been telling me that everything's okay. That he doesn't hate me for what I did. That he knows it was an accident."

"When...how has he told you this?"

"I noticed a pattern. In the commercials. About six weeks

ago. At first, it was only in the mornings. Then it started in the afternoons, too. Now it's all the time. Certain words in certain phrases. I was watching TV one day, and it just...it just became *obvious* to me. It clicked. I started writing them down, and I've been getting all his messages."

The cold feeling spread to her stomach.

"He's telling me it's okay, that he doesn't hate me for what I did. That he knows it was an accident. It's in the commercials. It's all in the commercials."

She squeezed his shoulder and said, "Honey, did you...did you tell Dr. Stack about this?"

"No. That's why I stopped seeing Dr. Stack. Now that Franky is talking to me, I don't need Dr. Stack anymore. Franky's talking to me, and everything's okay. Everything's fine."

The cold spread through Grace's entire body and she shivered.

Frank smiled and placed a hand to her cheek. "Our boy is talking to me now, and everything's just fine."

—IAN HARDING

Ian Harding is a U.K.-based fantasy and horror writer. His short fiction has appeared in *Fear Magazine*, in the Maynard and Simms anthology *Darkness Rising*, and in *All Hallows*, edited by Barbara Roden. Next year sees the publication of the first installment in a brand new trilogy for young adults about a virus outbreak epic entitled *DOGZ*.

—THE LONG HUNT

By Ian Harding

McNichols caught up with the boy outside the bus depot in Los Alamos, New Mexico. It had been three hard months since their last encounter.

For a fortnight the August sun had flung hellish heat from white skies, and McNichols was sheltering under the awning of LaundroCity on Dowd Street, sipping a Coke and keeping an eye on the depot steps opposite.

The boy had gone in and hadn't come out.

Earlier he'd glimpsed the scarlet sneakers, the lime-green backpack...and his heart had lurched into a hard thump as recognition lit his brain. He hadn't moved—had hardly breathed—as he watched the small figure slalom through the thin crowds, quick and sharp as a rat, then bound up the depot's granite steps and disappear inside.

That had been 20 minutes ago.

McNichols finished his soda, binned the can, and stepped out. The heat poured over his scalp like pan-warmed syrup. Across the street, the yellow depot sign hung over the concrete pillars of the shady entranceway, and he felt his nerves knot.

He crossed the street thinking about the butchery of three months ago. That had been in Hook, Kansas...or had it been Sheeton? No, Hook. Sheeton had been the pedigree dog breeding farm, kennel after kennel of drained trophy-winners. The boy drank dog blood when he couldn't get anything more refined.

Hook had been the Richards family, up from the wheat and dust of Luxton County for a fortnight of boating on the Winsor

Lakes. McNichols had tracked the boy to the shore of Great Winsor just as the family's hired yacht was drifting back to the jetty, blown by the freshening wind.

He'd stood on the boards over the water, braced for a fight. Maybe even the final fight. But the boy wasn't there. McNichols had frowned into the lake, trying to see past the waves lapping up, the sun-glare. Maybe the boy was still down there, sharking through the shadows and weed-fronds, the Richards' blood skimming off his small hands in pink clouds. But he saw nothing.

The yacht knocked against the wooden pilings by his feet.

The family was arranged in the bottom of the boat with their backs against the gunwales, legs stretched out, ankles together. Mum and Dad and the two kids. The bottom of the boat was dark with blood. Their heads had been taken and swapped around. Mr. and Mrs. Richards stared from the shoulders of their children. But the sight McNichols couldn't endure was the faces of the twins—girls—on the adult bodies. No pain in those blue eyes. No fear. Just puzzled sadness.

He'd turned and gone back to his stolen Cherokee. He wasn't weeping. He didn't weep...hadn't since the day his son was taken from him. Instead, he raged. Like a furnace beneath his breastbone as he drove away.

Now he stood at the foot of the depot steps and the entrance gaped like a lair. He felt old. The years weighed in him. His teeth were bad and needed work. His back ached and rankled after only a few hours of walking now. His hips gritted and needled, especially in damp weather. He was prone to migraines last thing at night that sometimes got so cripplingly bad that he ground his teeth and wished it would all end. He felt slow and badly prepared. He couldn't stalk at speed the way he used to, and hurrying was out of the question. The long hunt had turned him into a relic of himself.

He was a joke. An *old* joke.

* * *

The boy wasn't coming out. So what was he *doing* in there? McNichols went in. The depot was a twilight cave, the air diesel-choked and humming with engines. He walked the passenger concourse past a Starbucks, a magazine stall, tourist information, rest rooms. Buses were pulling into or backing out of a fishbone pattern of parking bays, reversing alarms beeping.

He could *feel* the boy was close—somewhere just beyond the press of the immediate crowd. An electric, lurking feeling like an approaching thunderhead. He watched the passengers come and go. Their ignorance filled him with low dread—familiar as the feel of his crumbly teeth to his tongue.

He went forward through fumes and caught sight of a man turning away from a burger stall, a quarter-pounder in one fist, a coffee in the other. Good trainers. Good haircut. McNichols shouldered into him automatically.

The man staggered back a step. The coffee didn't spill. The burger didn't fall. McNichols gave the man a look of abject apology.

"God, man, I'm sorry. *Real* sorry—"

There was a moment in which the man considered him. McNichols knew it could go either way—run smooth or turn raucous.

It ran smooth. Due, in McNichols's opinion, to his age. Some folk simply could not be shitty to the old, like they were born with an inhibitor.

"S'okay, fella," the man said. "No harm done."

McNichols gave a civil nod and peeled away towards a restroom with the man's wallet up his coat sleeve. He felt fossilised by the years, but his pick-pocketing skills hadn't rusted.

He locked himself in a stall, broke open the wallet, and pocketed 80 dollars in cash. Everything else went down the pan...but only after he'd lingered over the photo of the boy in backyard sunshine that Mr. Haircut kept in there.

Outside again, that thundery feeling was heavier. The boy was close. McNichols scanned for him, but saw nothing. Just folk coming and going, a bus backing out, pigeons squabbling high up in the iron roof rafters.

He looked back at the bus. It was nosing forward now,

swinging towards the white glare of the exit.

Was the boy on it? No. The bus was leaving but the feeling remained.

He scanned again, turning a slow circle. And something happened then that was the boy's doing...and he knew he'd been seen.

"*Daddy?*" someone called out—someone sounding so much like Ricky that McNichols had to close his eyes. It wasn't Ricky, of course. Ricky was dead these fifteen years. And how was his dead son supposed to call to him from somewhere up by the roof anyway, among the ironwork and the pigeons?

Not Ricky.

McNichols was about to look up—could feel the stiff wires and ratchets in his old neck getting ready to move his head—when he caught sight of the boy through the plate glass of the ticket office.

Ventriloquism. An old trick. To unsettle and confuse. It had happened before—voices from the TV, voices from the full moon, from the mouths of the dead. But the boy had never used Ricky's voice before. A vile new twist.

The boy was standing second from the desk in a queue of ten or so. The two desk clerks were working hard in their heavy-looking TransAm uniforms. They were trying for happy helpfulness but only managing sweaty doggedness. A desk fan turned its head.

The boy looked straight at him through the glass, and smiled. It was a beautiful smile, open and warm. Like the boy was overjoyed to see him. And because the smile was his son's, because it was Ricky's, the sight of that smile made him feel damned.

The moment passed. The flabby couple at the head of the queue turned away from the desk and the boy broke eye contact with him and stepped up. The top of his sandy-blond head barely cleared the desktop. The ticket seller had to boost herself off her stool to look down at him.

McNichols watched the boy buy a bus ticket with cash, the bills dug from his jeans pocket in a crumpled ball. He watched how the boy melted the desk clerk's heart. He had a ticket in seconds, no problem. The clerk just handed it over. McNichols suspected something was at work here—some trick of suggestion. The clerk hadn't stood a chance.

It occurred to him that he could attempt the assassination now. To hell with Academy laws stipulating deep isolation and zero witnesses...laws to which he had, long ago, put his signature and made his pledge.

It couldn't be here. Too public.

The boy turned away from the desk and made for the door with his newly-purchased ticket in his small fist and McNichols felt it. The fear about which all hunters were warned. Desert fear. Because it was a likelihood that the last struggle would have a desert setting. Ancient place of temptation and bone.

He stepped forward and met the boy square-on coming out of the office. Both stopped on their own side of the door threshold, the boy looking up, McNichols looking down.

The boy's face was tender and beautiful. And McNichols felt his heart clench with vast love and unendurable shame despite the years since Ricky had lived and laughed.

The boy's face lit up. He gulped with delight.

"Look, Daddy!" he cried suddenly. "I got me a ticket! Can we go on vacation, Daddy? Can we? Pleeeease?" The boy waved the ticket between them like a small flag.

McNichols shut his eyes. In the cave of his head he did what he could against the heartbreak. But he was still pierced.

"Sure we can," he said, opening his eyes again, playing along. "Where we going? What does it say on that ticket there?"

The grin became a frown. The boy held the ticket up so that McNichols could read what was printed on it. A sham, of course. The boy could read.

"It says Tonloose," McNichols said, his mouth suddenly dry as ashes. So. Here it was. The desert.

"Tonloooose?" the boy echoed, pulling the word into something charmingly puzzled. And McNichols was pierced all over again.

"Say, Daddy!" the boy sing-songed, his grin back. "I know

Tonloose! Sure I do! That's in Arizoner! Am I right, Daddy?"

"Don't call me that," McNichols said.

The boy went on like he hadn't heard.

"Arizoner's hot, ain't it, Daddy? Real hot! There's desert there, Daddy! Cactuses and rattlers and rock!"

"I'm not your daddy," McNichols said into the boy's face. "So don't fucking call me that. You understand me?"

Now there was a perfect little frown on the boy's face.

"Daddy, what's wrong? Don't be mad at me."

McNichols bore down on his rage. The boy was goading him and he hated himself for his lack of grit. If only the boy didn't look the way he looked. God, he felt old. Hollow with heartbreak.

He stepped aside and the boy trotted merrily past him, off to catch his ride. But before he disappeared in the throng, he turned back.

"Go get a ticket, Daddy! Hurry up! I'll see you on the bus!"

Then he was gone.

McNichols stood by the office door as people filed past him. This was it. After 30 years. This was it. All he'd trained for. All he'd sacrificed. A desert showdown.

He went to buy his ticket.

* * *

The bus rumbled up the exit ramp and into the burning day.

McNichols selected his seat—left side, towards the rear—for the solitude it gave him. The Tonloose-bound TransAm with its broken AC, greasy headrests, and 60-passenger capacity was maybe half-filled.

There was a young woman with a toddler opposite. The child was damp-haired and mewling in the heat. The woman was pretty in a worn way, wearing a simple dress and clodhopper work boots. She showed McNichols a wan smile as she stowed her daughter next to the window, planted a bottle of water in the child's hands, and settled down beside her.

She turned to McNichols as the bus rolled down Hetten Avenue, saying, "Gonna be a hot drive, I'm thinking."

He agreed with a nod. His attention went to the front of the bus. The boy had placed himself beside a right-side window, two seats back from the driver. A mountain of a woman had wedged herself in beside him, making opportune use of the bonus seat space the boy provided.

With a pinch of alarm, he saw they were already talking, their heads bent together in a chatty fashion. He wanted to do something about that, and quickly, for the woman's sake, but he couldn't think of a ruse to separate them. Yet.

"You going far?"

It took him a moment to catch up with the question. The young mother was leaning towards him across the aisle, smiling tiredly.

Her daughter looked tired too, peering at him around her mother's freckled shoulder.

"I don't rightly know, ma'am," he told her. "Depends how things work out with my youngest, Charlie."

A lie came automatically and without guilt. If she pushed for more, he could give it.

He tilted sideways in his seat and stole another glance forward. They were chatting now like regular buddies. Suddenly, chillingly, the boy laughed—a peal of bright, childish giggles that carried down the length of the bus.

"I'm leaving my husband," the young woman told him. This came with flat simplicity and no hint of emotion, as neutral as a weather comment.

"I'm sorry to hear that, ma'am," McNichols said. "Always pains me to hear families are busting up."

"Don't be sorry," she said immediately. "Wayne's a trash piece of shit. I just never woke up to it before." She laughed, but the laugh was empty. "Going to my sister's place in Tempe. Gonna be hot down there—but better for my girl and me."

"I hope it will, ma'am."

"Alice."

"I hope it will, Alice."

"Like that kiddie book," she said. "*Alice in Wonderland*. That's gonna be me."

She went quiet. McNichols's attention went back to the front of the bus.

* * *

The slow unrolling of the road eventually settled the big woman and the boy into silence. The boy turned to the window to watch the dusty suburbs slide by. Spears of sunlight lit up his hair as the bus swung through its turns. Then the town was behind them and the long miles opened up.

McNichols turned to his own window and let the slow slide of the dry view smooth out his coils. Unlikely the boy would try anything on the bus with McNichols keeping a beady watch on him. The long engine drone was good. His guard was slipping, but that was okay. Nothing would happen yet.

One last time he leaned sideways and glanced forward. The boy's golden head was still turned to the view. The big woman looked asleep, her head back, lips parted. Through his own window he saw road signs for Mt. Taylor and Santa Fe and Albuquerque. The bus fed south through dry valleys.

He closed his eyes. He'd been hunting for so long he felt born in harness. Idly he wondered if this really was the endgame. He'd been here before, thinking this was it, the showdown, only for it to be just another leg of the journey.

He slept.

* * *

And woke suddenly.

Not with alarm. Just a bleary surfacing. His surroundings slotting into place around him.

There was a small circle of tender scalp above his left ear that had taken the full weight of his head against the window. Now the window was still. So was the stuffy air. The seat. The whole bus. The engine, too. What was this? A rest-stop? How long had he slept?

Long enough to turn noon into late-afternoon, judging by the low slant of the sunlight.

He sat up straight and felt the warmth steal out of his blood. There was no rest-stop outside. No roadside diner. No gas station. Nothing but a twisted root of tan mountain trailing away into desert. Rock and furious heat shimmer. It looked like they'd even left the road behind.

The truth crashed into him. He'd been duped. Proved slow and old. It had happened before, but never so neatly. So calamitously.

The interior of the bus was an abattoir. It looked like an attempt had been made to paint every window with blood. As McNichols cursed the dumb fact of his age, he tottered from his seat and stood giddily in the aisle.

Was *everyone* dead? He should have done a head-count as soon as the bus rolled. He flogged himself with this thought as he wavered there in the silence of carnage. Because he had no way now of making sure all the passengers were accounted for. The bus was stacked with corpses. Maybe the boy had dragged a few off—for sport, for meat. But maybe some had escaped. No way of knowing.

The bus windows were so liberally daubed it seemed like the desert was obscured from view behind tattered red curtains. The interior of the bus had a pinkish tinge. The air was both meat-sweet and sour with cesspit gas.

He went down the aisle counting bodies...knowing it was a redundant exercise, but doing it anyway, high-stepping over pools of blood, strings of gore hanging from the ceiling like wet bunting. The big woman to whom the boy had spoken was unrecognisable as human from the waist up, a gaping sack of meat and bone. The reek of leakages, the drips and sighs of settling corpses—it was all familiar to him, but the proximity of savage death never got easier to endure. Like the sight of Alice there, and her daughter: faceless, handless, bloodless. The bus door was open and the sand flies had found the bodies. There were flies basking on the dry islands of Alice's teeth. Mother and daughter were holding hands. McNichols knew the boy had arranged them that way after death—gently pressing the palms together and knitting the fingers. Ironic tenderness after the fury of slaughter.

He ignored the horror of the driver behind the wheel until he was outside and the heat was hammering his scalp and face, and then he glanced back.

It looked like the man had been dynamited. Hardly anything left but his hands. One of them lay fingers-up in the centre of the steering wheel, caught on the spokes. The other lay on the dashboard like a bled crab. There was a wedding band on the third finger and the nails were chewed.

The bus had come to a stop on a shallow bank. A slow river of blood was crawling down the steps and pattering into the dust, thick as soup. McNichols stepped back before it reached his shoes.

He was right: the bus was no longer on the road. There wasn't even a road in sight. Just desert nowhere. Table-rocks and dust lagoons and ravines. Mountains to the west at vast remove.

He squinted into the heat. The idea of hiking through this shimmering kiln made him feel broken before he'd begun. He wouldn't get five miles.

The boy was out there somewhere. The stage was set. He wished he could wait in the shade of the bus for the boy to come to him. But that wasn't the way it worked. The long hunt had old rules.

McNichols walked into the desert.

* * *

He saw lightning ahead and knew he was getting close. The sky was cloudless. Yet there it was again—definite lightning, stabbing up from the ground in silver zig-zag branches. A flickering tree of light.

He staggered towards it like he was drunk on heat.

The first thing the boy said was: "For the love of Christ, John, why not take that coat off? This heat'll kill you, you know."

It was tempting, of course. But his coat was his protection. There were weapons in its lining.

"I'll keep it on, I think."

The boy shrugged. "Suit yourself."

He was sitting crossed-legged on a slab of rock and smiling up at John with his sweet angel's face. His lime-green backpack was off to one side. A nick of curiosity appeared in that perfect forehead.

"John? Do I upset you, looking like your poor dead Ricky?"

McNichols said nothing. He glanced off into the furious haze to settle himself.

"30 years I've been on the road after you—"

"31 last month. Answer the question, John. Do I upset you like this?"

"The man who set out to hunt you down isn't the man standing here now. So no, to answer your question. How you look doesn't upset me anymore."

The boy's hands delved into the small pit formed by his crossed legs. Up they came again...and now there was a rattlesnake looped from fist to fist. The boy was smiling at him and shaking his head.

"How right you are, John. You've changed. Not half the man you were. A shadow of your former self. How're those gritty old hips?"

"Sometimes okay, sometimes not. Okay today."

"And the migraines?"

"They come and go."

"At least they go, John, yes?"

McNichols nodded and unfastened his coat—two buttons, three. The boy reached over and placed the snake in a flexing coil by his leg. Then he fished in his lap again and pulled up a second one. This snake he placed across his thighs and stroked like it was a cat.

"What's under that coat, John?" the boy said, then giggled suddenly, like he'd been tickled.

McNichols said nothing. He unfastened the last two buttons and the wings of his coat settled open.

The boy went on. "I took everything from you, didn't I, John? Piece by piece. Did the Academy prepare you for that?"

"As well as it could."

"Bet it kept a few things to itself, though, didn't it? Bet it kept some secrets, that old place. The loneliness. The loss. Am I right, John? Loss of faith. Of family. Of time. Am I right?"

"I never did have much faith."

"But family, John. You had a family, didn't you?"

"A long time ago."

"I ate Vanessa, John. Most of her, anyway. Remind me— how long were you married?"

"Ten years."

"And little Ricky...what was he? Seven? Eight?"

"He was eight."

"Doesn't it upset you at all, John, seeing me like this? Doesn't it touch you—seeing me made in your dead son's image?"

McNichols looked at the boy and took his time. "Once. Not now."

"Ah, yes. Once. You lost it for a while, didn't you? After I took little Ricky. Wandered in the wilderness. I had to hang around until you were well enough in your head to come after me again. Remember that winter in Vancouver? How long did it take you to kick the junk?"

"Two years."

"Are you sure it doesn't bother you—seeing little Ricky in front of you now, playing with snakes?"

"You're not Ricky."

"True. But not a pang? A twinge?"

"Not anymore. It's all gone."

"You've forgotten your son, John."

"No. He's just untouchable now." McNichols showed the boy his palms. "Beyond all this. Beyond you."

"What's under your coat, John?"

"You'll see."

"Gonna kill me, John? You got a gun under there? Gonna shoot me down?"

"I'm going to kill you, yes. That's the task I swore to undertake. But not with a gun."

"With what, then? What you got under there?" The boy's

face was all sweet curiosity. His smile was gently guarded, like he suspected he was being teased. "You got a gun under your coat?"

"I told you. No gun."

"The Academy must have armed you with *something*."

McNichols shrugged and waited. Maybe fear would peep through a crack in all this giggly good humour. The boy lifted the snake off his lap and twirled it down next to the first. With a new twist of life, another snake appeared.

"What have you brought, John?" the boy said. "Hammer and silver nails? Sulphuric acid? Plastic explosive?"

"Nothing like that."

"Then what? I'm curious. I want to know what I'm facing. Don't tell me they loaned you Carmichael's needles! Surely the Holy Provost wouldn't trust you with *those*."

"The needles aren't used against things like you."

"Like me, John? And what am I, exactly?"

"A demon," he said, and the rest came by rote: "Lower denomination. Maybe a krillion. Non-hellborn. Probably mewk."

"Mewk?"

"Academy slang. One of twins."

The boy regarded him blankly. For the first time the smile was gone. "Someone's been doing their homework."

"So you are?"

"What?"

"One of twins?"

"Very sly of you, John. Next you'll be using my kin against me and asking what my real name is..."

"So there is a brother. Or a sister. You just said as much." McNichols sighed. "Anyway, I already know your name."

"Bullshit, John."

McNichols studied the boy. "You don't believe me? The Academy told us to go to primary sources. I opened a book and found your name. Easy as that."

"Again, John—bullshit."

"All right. It wasn't easy. The book was written in Syriac. I had to go to Istanbul to get it translated. Turned out it was a book of poetry."

The boy was watching him closely, no longer blinking. "I don't recall anyone setting me down in verse."

"Then your memory's failing."

Brightening, the boy said, "Was it *love* poetry?"

"Sonnets."

"The nurse! I bet it was my little nightingale! Am I right, John?"

McNichols nodded and listened to the boy's long sigh of happy remembering.

"How could I have forgotten? I found her in a hospital tent in the Crimea, mopping up after amputations. So pretty among the screams. And so passionate. It was like death had girded her loins for love. We used to sneak into the field marshal's tent while he was out on operations and make love on his ermine cushions. I say love, but really I mean fucking. Good meaty fucking. She demanded nothing less." The boy's eyes had turned wistful. He blinked back into the present. "She wrote sonnets about me?"

"Yes."

"And used my name in them?"

"Yes."

"That was careless, giving her my name," he said. "But I was in love, John. They were reckless times. All that blood and fucking." He fell silent. His attention went to the rattlesnake in his lap. He stroked the brown arrowhead with his small forefinger.

McNichols reached into his coat pocket and produced a crumpled Polaroid. The movement got the boy's attention.

"What's that?"

"Photograph," McNichols said. "You might want to see it."

Interest lit the boy's face. He held out a hand. "Let me look."

"Put the snake down first."

He obliged, just like that. The snake went down on the rock with the others. The hand reached again.

"Let's see."

McNichols handed the photo across and the boy bent over it.

"What is it?" he said, after a long peer. "Is that a wall? What's the mess on the bricks?"

He looked up and McNichols nodded. "The wall's down an alleyway in Seattle. In Longyard, past the bridge. Nothing much to look at, is it? Sort of forgettable. One of those places folk pass every day without noticing."

The boy was frowning over the photo again.

"Is that a body there, John? Somebody die and you took their picture?"

"That's right," McNichols said.

"Not very sporting of you, John."

McNichols waited until he had the boy's attention again.

"It was your brother," he said, his voice carefully bland, his gaze steady. "Your twin brother. Turns out you're mewk after all."

The boy blinked, just once. Then he calmly set the photo aside among the snakes.

McNichols said, "I'm 62 years old. I've been following your scat and murders for 31 years. But you never once asked me what I did *before* you. Weren't you ever curious?"

The boy's eyes had hardened. "I'm thinking about it now, John. I guess I am now."

"I had another assignment. My first."

"Bullshit. Hunters get one job. I know that. Then you retire. One backbreaking job of killing. What makes you so special, John?"

The composure was splitting.

"The Academy saw my skills," he said. "You've seen the evidence. It's there in the photo. You're mewk. Killing your twin was like doing half a job. It meant you were still out there. The Academy sent me out again...for you, this time."

"I murdered your family, John."

"I've lived with that half a lifetime."

"We're both alone in the world."

"Except you've just found that out," McNichols said. "Tell me, how's it sinking in for you?"

The boy's eyes darkened. "Was hunting me worth all that

grief, John?"

McNichols shrugged. "That grey taste in your mouth right now? That's grief. Maybe you can tell me."

The boy bowed his head and closed his eyes. It took McNichols a long time to realise he was crying. The tears dripped from his trembling chin and fell among the snakes. McNichols reached into his coat again and produced a box of matches and a can of lighter fluid. He placed the matches and the can on the rock by the boy's knee. One of the snakes shook a rattle at him. Coils tightened. But he wasn't bitten.

He watched the boy lift a snake and hold its coils against his neck, nuzzling it the way a real child might nuzzle a soft blanket or a stuffed toy.

"You didn't answer my question," the boy murmured. "I asked you if it was worth it."

McNichols looked at the place where the far mountains danced behind the heat.

"There's not an hour goes by I don't wish my family back again," he said. "Nothing's worth that. Not in this life. Not under this sun. The question is—can *you* stand it?"

With that McNichols turned around and walked away towards the mountains, leaving the boy to his grief. He knew he wouldn't get far before the heat brought him down. The idea didn't bother him unduly.

Later he heard the mellow boom and seethe of bursting flame. And, tangled up in that sound, the spit and hiss of burning snakes.

He didn't look back.

—JEFF STRAND

Jeff Strand is the author of a bunch of books, including *Pressure*, *Dweller*, and *Wolf Hunt*. If the apocalypse ever happens, he probably won't go on a rampage of destruction, but he makes no promises. Visit his Gleefully Macabre website at http://www.jeffstrand.com

—The Apocalypse Ain't So Bad

By Jeff Strand

If you ask me, people are unnecessarily gloomy about the end of the world. And that starts with calling it "the end of the world." It's not like the planet exploded or cracked in half or melted or anything like that. The world itself is perfectly fine— it's just that almost everybody is dead.

Here's the thing: We all *know* that it was a devastating tragedy. Why keep bringing that up? Anybody you talk to, you literally can't have more than fifteen seconds of conversation before they've gotta switch the topic to the apocalypse. I'm not suggesting that it isn't a major news story; I'm just saying that it doesn't have to be the *only* news story. Know what I'm saying? It's been almost four months.

Believe me, I've got plenty to whine about. I'm pretty much on my own at this point. For a short while after humanity's 99.7% demise, I was traveling with a woman named Cyndi. Unfortunately, I sort of botched the timing on bringing up the whole "Hey, we've gotta repopulate the earth!" topic, and I found myself surviving on my own.

Sure, the mutants are a problem. (And, yes, they're mutants—it seems like some people want to call any non-verbal human with a messed-up face a "zombie.") But they go down pretty quick with a shot to the head, and c'mon, who among us thought we'd get the chance to open fire on real people without it being a felony?

Now, some survivors did have to defend themselves against mutated friends and/or family, and there's no question that it must've sucked. If you're one of them, you have the right to be mopey. That's not who I'm complaining about. It's the folks who had to shoot three or four mutant strangers, yet act like they had to drown their own mother in a bathtub. Three words: Get. Over. It.

Would I rather the plague not have claimed billions of lives? Of course. You'd have to be a fool or a psychotic to feel otherwise. But are those billions of people going to get right back up and return to their normal routines? No. (Especially because they're *not zombies!*) It happened, the streets are littered with corpses, so let's make the best of it.

Take Disney World, for example. The rides aren't working because there's no electricity. But admit it, haven't you always wanted to get out of the car in the Haunted Mansion and just take a look around on your own? I did that a couple of days ago, and it was an absolute blast. I even tore off a piece of the wallpaper as a souvenir. Could I have done that pre-apocalypse? No way! I would've been thrown out of the park. Hell, I even got to climb on the track of Space Mountain, and there were no lines anywhere. You don't need some guy walking around in a Mickey Mouse costume to have a good time.

Food is a trade-off. I won't lie to you—I miss steak. On the other hand, last week I brought home an entire shopping cart filled with candy. That sucker was overflowing, and I left plenty on the shelves.

I guess I just don't understand people who always have a negative attitude. Life in a post-apocalyptic world isn't anywhere near as bad as movies want you to believe. It's actually kind of fun. Now I'm going to head over to Barnes & Noble and pick out any book I want.

* * *

I got bit by a mutant this morning. It was my fault; I should've been paying closer attention to my surroundings. Got me right on the arm. It hurt—oh, Christ, did it hurt. Still, my gun was within reach, and I've always been ambidextrous, so I took care of him before he was able to actually start chewing.

Infection is a concern, I'll admit, but it's not worth getting all bent out of shape over.

Trust me, I'm not taking a lackadaisical attitude toward the bite. I cleaned the wound (which did, unfortunately, break the skin) thoroughly with antiseptic, and then I covered it with a bandage. I cleaned it again every half hour after that. Yeah, it stung like crazy, but that means it's working, right? When life hands you lemons, you make lemonade, and even though the antiseptic burned worse than pouring lemon juice into the wound, I wasn't going to let it bum me out.

I knew a guy who got bit. You wouldn't believe how much he carried on, and how much of a "Pity me!" attitude he had about the whole thing. Know what he did? He said "I don't wanna become one of those things," shoved his revolver in his mouth, and pulled the trigger. Can you believe that? I mean, who kills himself over a mutant bite?

Me, I don't care if I become a shambling, oozing, moaning super-mutant, I'm not swallowing a bullet. That's the coward's way out. Screw that.

* * *

Well, it's been five days, and the bite is almost completely healed. That's how it works. When you have an upbeat attitude, your body chemistry and immune system respond accordingly. Mind over mutant.

A lot of people would've just holed themselves up in their home or apartment after being bitten like that. Not me. Know what I was doing when the pain was at its worst? I was smashing up an abandoned Volkswagen with an aluminum baseball bat. That's not something I could do before the plague, and don't try to act all high and mighty and pretend that the idea isn't appealing. In this new world, boys can be boys, and I love it!

* * *

I miss my family. There, I said it.

This feeling started while I was in a pottery store, breaking pottery. Though I was being cautious and staying out of the narrow aisles, I suddenly felt a hand grab my wrist and yank me away from the shelf. It was the nastiest-looking mutant I'd encountered thus far, and I mean both nasty as in "disgusting" and nasty as in "mean."

There were four other mutants with it. The fact that they were less nasty-looking than their counterpart wasn't much of a consolation.

I immediately opened fire, pumping a bullet into the first mutant's nose. As expected, its grip loosened and I yanked my wrist free. Another shot and the mutant was missing a goodly portion of its skull, including essential brain components. It fell to the floor.

The other four mutants lumbered toward me. They aren't exactly speedy creatures, but they aren't *that* slow. I mean, it's not like you'd feel like a schmuck and be embarrassed to tell people if one of them got you. So I quickly scooted back through the aisle until I was well out of arm's reach, and then started pumping bullets into those reeking brutes. (Have you smelled one of those things up close? Oh, man, imagine the worst case of festering halitosis you've ever inhaled and multiply it by eighteen or nineteen. Foul. Foul, foul, foul.)

I got the first one in the chest, which didn't do any good. I fired again and got it in the chest again, which continued to not do any good. But the third shot was the requisite head shot, and the mutant dropped.

Something grabbed me from behind.

I screamed and spun around, getting a damn good view of another mutant's jaws coming right at my face. I jerked my head back just in time to avoid the no-doubt unpleasant sensation of its teeth digging into my eye, then pushed the barrel of my gun against its chin and squeezed the trigger. Much splatter resulted.

I spun back around and fired at the other three mutants. I finished off the first one in line, pulled the trigger again, and heard the ever-disappointing click. Fortunately, I always carried two guns, plus a hunting knife and a grenade. I wasn't sure if it was a "blow things up" grenade or a smoke grenade (I'm not exactly a weapons specialist) but I kept it with me anyway, just in case.

I pulled the second gun out of its holster and fired, blowing a hole in the mutant's right hand and giving him an impromptu stigmata. Couldn't repeat that shot if I tried. I didn't try, because it was more important to kill them than impress myself. My next shot got rid of the mutant's ear. It howled in pain.

I took a few steps back, almost tripping over the dead mutant behind me but thankfully sparing myself that indignity. The two remaining mutants walked side-by-side down the aisle. They were both women, which sucked. There was a definite macho thrill to be found in blowing away ugly guy mutants, but shooting women—even grotesque mutated ones—made me feel like a jerk.

My next bullet shattered a pot. But my next two bullets after that got both of the female mutants in the head. Down they went. At least they weren't hot.

Then *another* mutant popped up behind me. How did I miss that they were having a frickin' mutant convention in the pottery shop?

Its teeth sank into my shoulder.

I immediately pulled away, which was a bad idea. A generous strip of flesh ripped off in the process. I fired four or five bullets into the mutant's skull before it hit the ground, and two more after.

I frantically peeked around the corner of the aisle, expecting to see a dozen more mutants coming at me with outstretched arms, but the store seemed to be empty now. My shoulder wound was bleeding profusely, and I plucked one of the mutant's teeth out of my flesh and flicked it onto the ground.

That's when I started to miss my family.

Sure, we had our little spats, but they never bit chunks out of me, and our quarrels never involved gunplay.

I pressed my hand against the injury, then quickly made my way out of the store and back home.

* * *

I'm a bit more cynical about the apocalypse these days. The bite really, *really* hurts when I use the antiseptic, and I'm seeing definite signs of infection.

I still think people complain too much about the whole situation, but the lack of qualified medical personnel is a pretty big downside. That said, I don't think that I'm going to become one of those creatures and I don't think I'm going to die. I do think that I'll be doing a lot of screaming for the next few days.

* * *

My shoulder looks like crap.

It never stops hurting. I've got aspirin but it's not doing any good. I've gone on several supply runs trying desperately to find something stronger, but those goddamn scavengers have cleared out all of the painkillers.

Not gonna die.

Might have to cut my arm off.

I don't think it's possible to saw off your own arm. I think you'd pass out from the pain, and then wake up with a hacksaw imbedded in your arm. If the infection gets worse, I'll need somebody else to do it.

Is there a tactful way to ask somebody to perform an amputation? How do you even bring up the subject? I guess you could always leave the bite uncovered, and keep the hacksaw in plain sight, and hope that they put two and two together and make an unsolicited offer.

Of course, the whole arm-removal thing is a last resort. Don't want to chop my arm off and then have some guy find me lying in a huge pool of my own blood and say "Oh, gosh, I've got a pill right here that would've cleared that up."

Think I'm gonna scream some more.

Yeah, that sounds like a good way to spend the afternoon. Afterwards I'll open a can of spaghetti.

* * *

Wow, my social skills have taken a beating since the world ended. I went out looking for survivors with medicine (y'know, for the whole arm thing). Found a family of four. Started shouting like a crazy person. I don't even know what I was saying. I know what I was *trying* to say: "Hi there, folks, I've had a spot of trouble and was wondering if you could spare some antibiotics?" But as soon as I saw them I got so excited that I lost my ability to form a coherent sentence, and the father calmly suggested, with the aid of his shotgun, that I move along.

I tried to give him the whole "I mean you no harm" speech, but he fired into the air and looked really damn stern. So I left. Couldn't find anybody else all day.

I try to continually think happy thoughts about my shoulder, but it keeps looking worse and worse. It's hard to move my fingers and elbow.

But hey, it doesn't hurt as bad anymore! It's more numb than anything. That's a blessing, I guess.

* * *

I really think this arm has to go. Better than losing a leg. Can't walk very well with only one leg. You try to run away from those mutants with one leg, and you're almost guaranteed to fall on your face unless you've had a lot of practice hopping. Me, I'd rather lose an arm than a leg, any day.

I'll be an inspiration. How many people can survive in a post-apocalyptic world with only one arm? Not too many. Amputees have accomplished many great things throughout history, and I will proudly join their ranks.

After I do some more screaming.

* * *

Know what? I think it's looking a little better. Not a lot better, but a little. Can't expect it to heal right up overnight. That would be wacky talk.

Starting to get tired of all this candy. Wish I had some pork chops. Think a nice meal of pork chops, baked potato with sour cream and bacon bits, and steamed broccoli would make my shoulder feel better. I've got the broccoli, anyway, but not the steamer.

Wish my family didn't live on the other side of the country. Sure, they're probably all dead or mutants, but it would still be nice to see them, if only for a brief visit.

Time for more antiseptic. Joy.

Almost out of it.

* * *

I've got to admit, I didn't expect to end up in a cage. Dead, maybe. Mutated, sure. Caged? Nope.

Thing is, there's something much worse out there than the mutants. Namely, a band of paranoid survivors, led by this insane gentleman named Sunshine, who are trying to rule this new world. I saw three of them walking down the sidewalk and I thought, hey, potential source of shoulder medicine! Having learned from my previous mistake, I took a deep breath, composed myself, and politely stepped into their path and introduced myself.

I remember a big wooden club swinging at my head, but the other details of the encounter are blurry.

Woke up with my hands and feet duct-taped together in a school gymnasium. About twenty other people were there playing cards and smoking cigarettes and just hanging out. The walls were lined with cots. I seemed to be the only prisoner.

Sunshine stood over me, his wild hair and facial scars a weird contrast to his serene expression. He ran his finger over my lips and asked "Are you one of them?"

"Do I *look* like one of them?"

Helpful hint: Sunshine and his band of followers are not admirers of sarcasm. When I woke up again, I was in a wooden cage in a classroom, and the rest of my body hurt even more than my shoulder. The posters on the walls indicated that it was a history teacher's classroom, which added an extra dimension of terror to my nightmare.

A little kid, maybe twelve, was crouched outside of my cage. "Got any aspirin?" I asked him.

He shook his head.

"Any chance you'll let me out?"

He shook his head again.

"Could you go get a grown-up so I can talk to them?"

He grinned. "I'm a grown-up now. I even get first pick."

"Of what?"

"Of what I eat."

I had the very unnerving sensation that this conversation was going to move in a cannibalism-themed direction, but I tried to play stupid to give myself a couple more moments of mental health. "What do you mean?"

"You're food. We're going to eat you for dinner tonight."

"I see." My mental health status dropped a few notches.

"Gotta cut off the bad parts first, though," he said, pointing to my arm.

* * *

My natural optimism faltered a bit after they duct taped me to the desk. I tried to let a smile be my umbrella, but it wasn't working. Though I explained to them all the ways in which their actions were poor ethical decisions, I wasn't being particularly coherent and my message didn't really get across.

Sunshine held a lighter flame underneath a knife that didn't look anywhere near sharp enough to do an efficient job.

I wept.

He began the unpleasant process. It took me a long time to pass out. With a better knife, I probably could've done the job myself. Live and learn.

* * *

The tile floor under my cage is spotted with blood. Though they cauterized the stump, it's still leaking a little.

I wonder what they did with my arm?

Apparently I get one more day to live before I become brunch. They're still finishing off their last batch of meat. The little kid—Toby—loves to sit outside my cage, licking his lips and rubbing his belly in an exaggerated manner.

I'm almost delirious from lack of sleep. Toby threw stuff at me all night. He'd get real close to the cage, and I kept trying to thrust my good arm through the wooden bars and grab him, but he always kept himself just out of reach.

Well, not always. I did get his collar once. He shrieked for help, and a couple of Sunshine's nutcase crew came in, pulled him free, and then beat the crap out of me.

Tenderizing me.

So this is how it ends. Tormented by a little brat, missing an arm, and about to become dinner.

I had a pretty good life before the plague.

The apocalypse sucks.

No...I'm not going to let these bastards take away my happy disposition. Screw 'em. I'll get out of this, somehow. Optimism. Optimism is the key. Nobody ever got anywhere with a can't-do attitude.

They can take away my freedom. They can take away my arm. They can take away my life. But they won't take away my smile until they eat my lips.

I try to smile. My lips are swollen from the beating and it hurts too much, so I abandon the idea.

* * *

I hear footsteps in the darkness.

They're coming for me.

* * *

Sunshine is a charismatic leader, with devoted followers who will obey his every command, even if it means marching to their death. However, the guy isn't very good at keeping everybody in the loop regarding crucial pieces of information.

Such as, my severed arm was for disposal. Not for adding

to the soup.

A lot of people got really foamy-mouthed that night, and they started to prey on each other. They grabbed Toby and pulled him in half, right in front of me. I wanted to applaud, but...well, you know...

A couple of them tried to get into the cage. It took a while, but they finally broke the lock. I scooted past them and fled out of the classroom and down the hallway, where there was carnage galore.

It was disgusting, but it was a *good* kind of disgusting, y'know?

I saw what I think was Sunshine in a few chunks on the gymnasium floor. Not completely certain—he wasn't easy to recognize. The chin looked familiar, though.

I found a gun next to a body that was missing a few feet of intestine. Fully loaded. It was empty by the time I got out of the school, but I made it to the exit unscathed.

I ran home, went to sleep, and woke up feeling refreshed. Though I'm not suggesting that my stump wasn't sore, it was definitely a more pleasant feeling than being devoured. One arm was still one more arm than I would've had if that rotten little brat had gotten his way.

After a few days of relaxation, the swelling went down, and I could smile again.

* * *

I'm wiser now. When you think about it, this whole thing was a learning experience. I'm no longer that innocent guy breaking pots. I'm not saying I wouldn't rather have my arm back, but all things considered, I think this was good for me.

Again, people need to quit their bellyaching. The apocalypse ain't so bad.

—MONICA J. O'ROURKE

Monica J. O'Rourke has published more than one hundred short stories in magazines such as *Postscripts*, *Nasty Piece of Work*, *Fangoria*, *Nemonymous*, and *Brutarian*, and anthologies including *The Mammoth Book of the Kama Sutra*, *These Guns for Hire*, and *Darkness Rising*. She is the co-author of *Poisoning Eros I and II* with Wrath James White, *Suffer the Flesh*, and the collection *Experiments in Human Nature*. She works as a freelance editor, proofreader, and book coach. Her website is an ongoing and seemingly endless work in progress, so find her on www.facebook.com/MonicaJORourke in the meantime.

—THE GIFT

By Monica J. O'Rourke

The sky was lonely somehow, and beneath its bondi blueness the old man sat, absorbing the vitamin D and loneliness and believing himself one with nature. The sky held a promise of hope, a commune with God through the vast greatness and splendor that was the universe, the clouds and winged creatures and wind, the very sky itself. Somehow he was in touch, he knew. Somehow he could visualize God's greatness through the crest of impossibly tall trees.

But the visit was fleeting, the understanding of what was being proffered equally elusive. Nothing lasted these days: not the retention of understanding, not the thought itself. But he enjoyed each moment as they happened and wondered how long they would last, and later would wonder where they had gone. But in the moment, he greedily soaked them up and reveled in them.

"Let's go, Dad." Kelly's son cleaned the fast food containers off the picnic table and dropped them in the trash.

"Already?"

But his son's attention was elsewhere, gathering his children as quickly and carelessly as he had the burger wrappers. He screamed the kids' names and would have had better luck herding cats.

"Jesus, Dad," he called over his shoulder. "Why're you just sitting there? Let's go."

* * *

Kelly shared a room with another old man named Bob, and Bob's family never came to visit, never took *him* for car rides out to the country or bought him vanilla ice cream cones with sprinkles or took him to ballgames at Yankee Stadium. *Jennie used to do these things all the time,* he thought. Maybe. He seemed to recall doing these things, seemed to recall movies and ballgames and a wife who was once alive, and he was sure he'd loved her very much. Maybe. Bob didn't have anything like that in his life. Bob spent his days rocking in a chair that wasn't a rocking chair, drooling into a bib that was usually just the front of his polo shirt. The old man would spend a stupid amount of time watching Bob do much of nothing, but it helped pass the time. And Bob always lost when they played gin rummy or backgammon.

"Joseph drove me out to the country yesterday," the old man told Bob. Bob, as usual, didn't respond.

"That was last month, Mr. West," the nurse sponge-bathing Bob told him.

"Yes, of course," the old man replied and wondered what the nurse was talking about.

That night the old man dreamt about the countryside, about the blades of grass tickling his toes when he ran across the field hand-in-hand with Jennie. He dreamt the sky was beckoning, billowing clouds forming fingers, like the fingers of God, pointing down from the heavens, though he later wondered whether he'd left the TV on. But during the dream he waited for a message. Later he figured the message had been in code, and he worked tirelessly trying to decipher it. While awake. While asleep.

God visited him again in his dreams and explained the message. But the following morning he couldn't remember what God had said. Something about the woods, something about...he sighed. He couldn't remember.

"God talked to me," he told Bob, who responded by blowing a spit bubble.

The old man wandered through the garden, a garden

comprised mostly of white-painted rocks and badly pulled weeds, an overgrowth of brambles amid clumps of daisies and daffodils struggling for breath. *Not enough staff* he was told when he asked why someone couldn't maintain it better. They offered him the job but laughed at him before he could accept.

God was silent during the day, the old man discovered, though he seemed awfully chatty at night. The old man hoped that wandering through what might pass as nature—in this pitiful section of stone and gravel in this sad somewhere-part of the Bronx he called home—might make him more receptive to God's message. *God seems like a nature freak,* the old man thought, imagining an ancient man in flowing white robes, ZZ Top beard, and Birkenstocks, throwing back granola by the fistful.

But the old man realized, when the voice came again, that it didn't belong to God. It belonged to the sky.

"Why are you talking to me?" the old man asked. "Where's God?"

God loves you, the sky replied, *but he doesn't have time for your crap.* The sky whispered in the old man's ear the secrets of the universe but made him promise not to tell. *The secrets are a gift,* the sky told him, *but they're your gift.*

The old man considered that a pretty lousy gift, though he had no one to share it with anyway. His son, Joseph, had been here yesterday and yesterday and yesterday and it was always yesterday and never tomorrow. And Bob still wasn't much of a conversationalist, so why bother?

Then the sky whispered to the old man again, and the old man nodded. The sky was wise. The sky was ancient and ethereal and knew things. The old man believed the sky would lead him, though he couldn't imagine where. He once knew but couldn't bring the thought up. So close to grasping it so often, but its ephemeral quality was like mist slipping through his mind. Like trying to grasp quicksilver, though he wondered why anyone would try. Quicksilver was toxic.

Hold my hand, the sky said, *and follow me into eternity,* and the old man thought the sky had lost its mind.

"You have no hand!" he cried and was shushed by a chorus

of nurses and physical therapists.

"Other clients are trying to rest, Mr. West."

"You have no hand," the old man whispered. "How can I grab your hand when you don't have one?" The old man drew his fingers down his chin and pondered his own question.

Metaphor, my friend, the sky responded.

The old man didn't understand what the sky meant. But he thought about it and tried to understand. A little while later he forgot what the sky had said, and this was upsetting for a moment until he forgot he'd forgotten.

When he asked a nurse where Jennie was, why she hadn't come to visit in a long time, he was told Jennie had died. He began to cry. "Why didn't I go to her funeral?" he asked and was told she had died five years earlier.

And the next day they had the same conversation, and the day after that until the old man could barely remember he'd been married.

Eternity, the sky said, *is eternal. And it's another gift, but not for everyone.*

"Who gets the gift then?"

Whoever wants it.

"I want it!"

Do you?

"Yes!"

Why?

"I want to live forever!"

Then you don't understand the gift.

"You," the old man said after grinding his teeth, "are very stupid."

The sky was silent after that for a long time, days or weeks or months, the old man was unsure. But the sky *remained* silent after that conversation, and the old man was upset and felt lonely again.

"Why won't you talk to me?" the old man howled, baying at the descending slip of moon while standing in the center of his weed garden.

You haven't asked me anything, the sky said.

"Oh." The old man shrugged. "When can I have my gift?"

That much you remember. The wind laughed softly. *You already have it, my friend.*

The old man huffed and shuffled out of the garden, back toward the building. There was no gift. The sky was trying to trick him, confuse him. The sky offered empty promises, and the old man was sick of it all. He wondered if he'd missed dinner and wondered if he'd missed his medication. Then he wondered if he even took medication.

Take my hand, the sky said, and the wind reached down to help, breathed against the old man in an effort to move him along. The trees danced and bowed in the wind, dipping their branches forward to help him along. The rocks wanted to help as well but they were rather useless.

"I don't understand. What do you want from me?" Tears rolled down the old man's cheeks, but he didn't wipe them away. He had forgotten how to cry and didn't know what to do with the wetness.

"I can't remember her face," he sobbed and then tried to recall her name. "Why can't I remember?"

The sky caressed the old man's cheek. *You've given me something wonderful*, the sky said. *You've shared your grief with me. Your loneliness. You have given me a gift that will last an eternity. I will be forever grateful.*

And with that the sky was gone, replaced by a starless night, and even the moon refused to return.

The old man felt dejected and climbed the steps to the building's entrance. But no matter how many times he tried the knob or rang the bell, he remained on the wrong side of the door. He wrapped his arms around his shivering body.

This way, the grass cried, tiny shrill voices like parakeets. Thisway-thisway-thisway.

The old man was reluctant to listen to the orders of blades of grass. But he had listened to the sky, so why not?

He followed their voices until they grew silent, and he found himself deep within the black woods, shrouded by mossy trees and dense underbrush. A fallen log provided the short respite he needed. His left hip cursed him and attempted to strangle his sciatic nerve.

The sky pulled him to his feet and pushed him gently into a field. The old man's protesting hip and joints grew silent. He walked steadily ahead without signs of a limp or hobble.

My gift to you, my friend.

Jennie ran to him and leapt into the old man's arms, arms strong and pain free, arms that could hold her tightly and without fear of end. They ran hand in hand and disappeared into a copse of shaded oaks. The old man felt good, felt energized and free, as if the secrets of the universe had been revealed to him.

And he could remember.

—TAYLOR GRANT

Taylor Grant is a professional screenwriter, filmmaker, author, actor and award-winning copywriter. He has written for both animated and live action TV series, as well as acclaimed music videos for some of the biggest music acts in the world.

Grant has written horror, action and sci-fi feature scripts for studios such as Imagine Entertainment, Universal Studios, and Lions Gate Entertainment. Most recently, he wrote and directed a psychological thriller entitled *The Muse*, currently on the film festival circuit. More of Grant's fiction can be found in the horror anthology *Box of Delights* from Aeon Press, featuring stories by award-winning authors such as Steve Rasnic Tem, Kristine Kathryn Rusch, and Mike Resnick, the literary anthology *Stories from a Holiday Heart*, the May 2012 issue of *Terror Tales* from Rainfall Books, and the April 2012 release of *A Feast of Frights* from *The Horror Zine*, featuring legendary horror authors such as Graham Masterson, Joe R. Lansdale, Simon Clark, and Ed Gorman.

Grant's next feature film, a thriller set in the Arizona desert, is currently in active development and he is also hard at work on his first collection of short stories, which he plans to publish in 2013.

You can find out more about Taylor Grant and contact him at www.taylorgrant.com

—The Silent Ones

By Taylor Grant

The phenomenon was like a cancerous growth: imperceptible at first, yet silently spreading with lethal intensity. The first sign of something amiss was a noticeable lack of mail being delivered over the course of several months. One day it simply occurred to me that my mailbox was empty more often than not. Even local ads and flyers had stopped. I checked with the post office several times but they always had my correct name and address on file. Although each time I spoke with them it seemed to take them a little longer to find it.

I never would've believed that I'd miss junk mail, but I discovered that there was something comforting about seeing your name on a mailing label. It let you know that someone— even an automated mailing service—acknowledged your existence.

The last piece of mail I received was the week of Christmas. I was excited, because I could always count on holiday cards from my mother and younger sister, Karen. Mom's cards were always sappy and included an awkwardly written personal note, while Karen's were always of the homogenized, humorous variety; your typical mass-produced greeting card.

It was Friday, December 24th, when I looked into my mailbox for the last time that side of the New Year. Inside, I discovered a single handwritten envelope. An honest to goodness letter! I actually flushed for a moment at the prospect of sitting down to read it. After all, in those days of emails, texts and instant messages, who wrote letters anymore?

But as I read the envelope I felt the blood drain from my face.

The letter was addressed to my neighbor. The postman had put it in my mailbox by mistake.

After that, things worsened. A few weeks later, I called my mother to wish her a happy birthday.

"Hello?" she answered, sounding distracted.

"It's me, Mom," I said.

"Can I call you back?" she replied in a way that told me she'd most likely forget.

I started to say "I love you," but she hung up on me.

I never spoke to her again.

Then my phone stopped ringing. I still got a dial tone when I picked up the receiver and could call out just fine. But no one called me. Not even those automated reminders for overdue bills.

It was quite humiliating coming home night after night to an answering machine that blinked zero at me. Sometimes I'd press the play button just to hear the automated recording, informing me that there are *no* new messages.

But at least it was a voice.

I even began to regret signing up for the government's "do not call list," which banned telemarketers. At that point, even a canned sales pitch would have been welcome.

There had to be some sort of logical explanation. I was a pretty rational person. My approach to life was methodical, particularly at my job where I analyzed insurance claims.

Initially, I approached my situation the way I did most things: systematically. First, I checked for any issues with the phone company. Next, I called every organization that I did business with or that I owed money. Oddly, I was unable to find any problems within any line of communication.

Every billing representative that I spoke with assured me that they would resend my bills—but for some reason they never did.

Every facet of my life became infected. At work I "slipped people's minds" on a regular basis. Missed appointments became the status quo, and people ignored me wherever I went.

I got so pissed off that I decided to skip work without telling anyone.

It was the first time I'd ever done that. I even planned it so I'd miss my yearly evaluation from my boss, just to make sure my absence would be noticed.

It wasn't and he didn't. In fact, no one did.

Fifteen years I'd dedicated to that company. And not a single person noticed I was gone.

* * *

Any attempts I made to reconnect with the world were met with a wall of indifference. At first, I tried being overtly nice to everyone, starting with my obnoxious, two-packs-a-day neighbor who sat on his porch most of the day, blowing secondhand smoke through my living room window. When that didn't work, I tried being friendly to the forever imposed upon barista at my local coffee house. Her stony-faced visage spoke of a childhood devoid of smiles. I also tried my snot-nosed cubicle mate at work and the Chinese food delivery guy with the terminal case of halitosis.

It made no difference.

When the niceties failed, I became overtly nasty. I shot people dirty looks, spat at others, even yelled at a few strangers for no other reason than to elicit a response.

No one blinked an eye.

Out of frustration, I threw a full-blown temper tantrum right in the middle of our Thursday afternoon staff meeting, just to get a rise out of someone...anyone.

Having failed to interject a single word into the discussion, I screamed at the top of my lungs, "Excuse me!"

Kevin, the lead financial analyst sitting next to me, winced a bit at the sound of my voice, but kept right on talking. Finally, I heaved my hot latte, cup and all, as hard as I could against the far wall.

Suddenly, I had everybody's attention.

"Did you just throw that?" my boss, Barry said.

"Umm...yes," I said, suddenly wishing to God I hadn't.

"Why would you do that?" Kevin asked, but there was no judgment in his eyes. It seemed to be an honest question.

I started to stammer out a poor excuse for an answer. But within a matter of seconds, I was forgotten again. It was as if I could only maintain their interest for mere moments with the greatest of outrage and passion—emotions that I normally bottled up and rarely exhibited.

I panicked at that point and ran down the halls like a lunatic under a full moon. My wild energy provoked a smattering of human response, but not much more than if I were a monkey performing at the zoo, caged behind a sheet of impenetrable glass. It proved impossible to maintain such impassioned feelings. They were like unused muscles that had atrophied; the result of a lifetime of my own passivity and apathy. I was quickly disregarded; left alone to sob on the orange and puke-brown carpet outside my cubicle.

A little while later, I gathered the wherewithal to drag myself home.

But sitting in my apartment was like solitary confinement. As I paced the floor, I thought I was going to lose my mind.

I had to find a way to engage with someone.

There was this gloomy 24-hour coffee shop down the street where local night owls perched every evening. I'd passed it countless times before, but had never felt compelled to go inside.

Until then.

I sat there for hours, soaking up the greasy walls of the dimly lit coffee shop, watching nothing but nameless faces with sunken, hopeless eyes. They seemed to be drawn to the place, like moths ticking at light bulbs. A grizzled waitress with a blank expression wafted across the floor like a specter, while the brooding clientele stared silently from the shadows.

Sometimes, while passing by late at night, I'd wondered what kind of people lurked inside this place at such an ungodly hour. Now—I was one of them. One of *them*: the silent ones; the nameless and forgotten; the in-between people that no one saw; the homeless that businessmen stepped over to get to their power lunches; the faceless figures that simply—filled up space and nothing more.

Somehow I'd become one of them.

I knew this because, for the first time in weeks—I'd been finally acknowledged. They seemed to recognize me. With a slight nod of the head or a weary meeting of the eyes, my status had been established. I was one of *them* now.

I watched them gather there all night, hovering quietly at their tables, comforted by the fact that they were not alone in their—our—misery. I had to get the hell out of there while I could. I may have been offered membership into the dead-end club, but that didn't mean I had to accept it.

* * *

I didn't go back to work. No one noticed my presence, so I doubted they'd notice my absence. Money wasn't a problem, of course. I could steal any store blind and no one would raise an eyebrow. I wish I could say that provided me with some comfort.

I roamed the streets all week, searching for human connection. The city seemed...different, almost unrecognizable. Then again, perhaps it was my growing appreciation for things. Oddly, I'd never noticed the snow-dusted desert ranges, or the tall cacti that stood sentinel in the shadows of the great mountains. I was also surprised to see such a diversity of architecture pervade the city. I heard countless birds for the first time, chirping their esoteric songs from faraway places.

New scents and fragrant flowers seemed to permeate the air wherever I walked, and the endless blue of the September sky awed me.

However, what struck me the most were the people on the streets that I used to take for granted. They were filled with an energy that I found almost impossible to describe. Children glowed with it, like tiny suns. The adults and the elderly, I observed, shone with varying degrees of this radiant light.

Whatever this energy was, I envied it. When I gazed at my own reflection, I saw none. The other silent ones were also devoid of this radiance. We shuffled through the city unseen, except by our own kind.

I suspected that I might be dead—a wandering spirit perhaps. But neither of those conclusions made sense. I had yet to see a single indication of my death: a cleared out desk at my office; a boxed up and emptied apartment; a cheap funeral with a handful of detached mourners. But there was nothing.

The world remained unaware of my disappearance.

One day I walked through a local cemetery, searching for some peace of mind. My family plot had been there for years, passed down for three generations—a giant cavity in the earth, waiting patiently for its next meal. Everyone dead in my family was accounted for there.

I was relieved not to see a tombstone bearing my name. But the relief was short-lived, for it dawned on me that I hadn't consumed anything, neither food nor water, in several days.

Somehow, I had been subsisting on...nothing.

I was not dead. I was not a ghost.

I feared I had become something far worse.

* * *

It had been well over a week since I had gotten out of bed at home. By that stage I had memorized every crack, fissure, and imperfection in the ceiling. I had yet to sleep, eat, or even relieve myself. But all of that seemed as meaningless as my life.

Now that the distractions of life had fallen away, the inevitable introspection appeared like an unwanted guest. The inescapable questions came up: What was my legacy? What had I contributed? Who the hell cared if I lived or died?

The weight of the answers had trapped me in this bed, sweating and stinking in a pool of regret. I found myself flipping through the pages of my past to discover a mental scrapbook filled with empty paper. I returned again and again to the same forgotten dream—eons ago—before the mundanities of life had slowly pushed it aside.

I once dreamt of being a man with something to say.

I saw a lovely face, peering at me through the veil of the past. Her name was Mrs. Wainwright—my exceptionally well-endowed grade school teacher. She often praised my flair for words. And that flattery led to my naïve, but wondrous fantasies about writing the great American novel (as well as fondling Mrs. Wainwright's breasts).

However, I was from a family of accountants, bankers, and financial analysts who not only scoffed at the idea of writing for a living, they made sure to humiliate me for even considering it.

I didn't have the fortitude to disagree.

Eventually my great dream faded into nothingness.

And now my very physicality, my very essence was joining that faded dream.

* * *

I shot myself in the face with a twelve-gauge shotgun.

I stole it from a local gun shop, came home, wedged it against the corner of my nightstand, stuffed the barrel into my mouth—and pulled the trigger. There was a vicious explosion as the world turned blindingly white—followed by impenetrable black. When I regained consciousness I was face down in a soup of blood, flesh and bone.

By all known laws of this universe, I should have been dead. I couldn't understand what was happening to me. It was as if this new existence wouldn't *allow* me to die.

With my remaining eye I could still see dried scraps of my brain coagulated on the wall across the room. The reflection staring back at me in the bathroom mirror made me vomit into the sink. My tongue dangled from my mouth like a dried-up, broken swing and pieces of my skull jutted from my face like shards of crimson glass.

If there was a hell, I prayed I'd find it soon. Even the devil himself would have been welcome company in such a lonely room.

* * *

I had become a human moth.

I swore I wouldn't return to the Godforsaken coffee shop, yet there I was again amongst those pathetic souls and that oppressive silence.

I was no longer allowed in the main eating and drinking area. When I stepped through the front door I was immediately directed toward a back room by a large and unfriendly fellow who practically shoved me inside.

This dark, smoke-filled room was smaller and even more congested than the main coffee shop. The silent ones back here were a whole other level of afflicted and forlorn.

My shocking visage didn't seem to bother anyone except me. As a matter of fact, this night's particularly vile looking crowd was riddled with what appeared to be failed suicide attempts. The blonde perched next to me at the tiny bar looked as though she may have been attractive once. But the precious reservoir of blood that pumped through her veins was long dried up. I could see crusted bones and shredded muscle through the tattered skin of her wrists: she had ripped them open with very little grace.

Worse off were two grim figures directly across from me: an obscenely bloated man who cradled his decapitated head under his arm like a mangled pet cat, and a figure to his right with skin so horribly burned I couldn't ascertain its gender. If you listened closely you could hear the seared flesh crackle and pop as it moved. Another gruesome character slithered across the floor like a human snake, his body reduced to a fleshy pulp—presumably after taking a nosedive off a very tall building. I nearly retched watching his shredded web of entrails drag after him on the dirt-encrusted floor.

But the worst by far was the festering abomination propped against the wall in the far corner. It was impossible to describe him/her/it. But the wretched thing was so dreadful that even the regulars wouldn't go near it.

I stepped past it later, as I moved toward the back door and heard what sounded like whimpers coming from what might have been a mouth once.

I wanted to scream at the sight of it, but I never got the chance. Just then a tall brunette woman stepped up to me and gave me the once over.

"Hello," she said.

For a brief moment I felt a rush of gratitude. I was so stunned that someone had spoken to me that I took an involuntary step back.

"Hel...hello," I replied. Or would have if it had been physically possible; my tongue was still hanging loosely from the cavity where my mouth used to be. And yet, somehow, I had communicated this simple greeting.

"You're new." the woman said matter-of-factly. She was probably in her mid-40s and had been attractive once. Her mouth didn't move when she spoke, nor did her awkwardly positioned head. It appeared as if she'd been in a serious car accident and broken her neck. I found it difficult to look her in the eyes, since they were practically vertical.

"I can hear you, but you're not talking..."

"That's the way it works here."

"Here?" What...what is this place?"

"No one knows," she said with no emotion. "A place for lost lives, perhaps."

She smiled at me then. The smile of a madwoman.

I took another step back, wanting to be anywhere but in this hellhole of a room. A man could go mad here. Clearly, some of the denizens already had.

When I left, I knew it would be for the last time. Loneliness may be hell, but it was better than facing those *things* night after night.

* * *

My life once again consisted of an empty apartment and my tedious reflections, countless days wishing for something—*anything*—to happen.

And finally, something did.

A young couple named James and Susan McIntyre moved into, or rather *invaded* my apartment. It had been vacant for a good while (I simply came home one day to find my personal belongings gone), so I suppose an intrusion like this was inevitable. I admit that, at first, I was thrilled. Their presence added some much needed color to what was beginning to feel like my own personal mausoleum. I followed them from room to room for days, listening to their intimate conversations like a man-sized fly on the wall. Sometimes I would lie next to them as they made love, trying to recall the fading memory of that experience myself.

During one particularly passionate session, I couldn't stop myself from reaching out to touch Susan. I was transfixed by her gorgeous auburn hair, which glistened with the sweat born of their lovemaking.

Her eyes locked with mine and she *saw* me.

She screamed, as I'd never heard anyone scream before. And it took her husband all night to calm her down and convince her that it was just her imagination.

Fortunately, she hasn't been able to see me since.

The weeks passed and I often huddled close to them as they talked into the wee hours, discussing the future and relishing their possibilities. Possibilities I once had, failed to notice and carelessly threw away.

One night, Susan discovered an old picture of me that had been wedged in a crevice on the top shelf of the bedroom closet. She didn't recognize me, of course, and tossed it into the garbage, where it sat for several days unnoticed.

But I noticed. I noticed how the image began to fade once it had been discarded. And by the second day, my image had vanished completely.

It was as if reality itself had forgotten me.

Any initial distractions the McIntyres provided soon soured. Their joy had become my pain—their love my hate. They flaunted their lives before me with a constant torment of shameless affection. Now, when I saw them caress each other, I could only wish I *were* a ghost so I could haunt this place and force them from my home. But I remained invisible and powerless, unable to do anything but leave the last part of my previous life behind.

Perhaps it was for the best. Yes, maybe it was time to do something I should've done years ago: leave this city behind. Why not? It was high time I explored the world that lay beyond it.

How pathetic that this had only occurred to me now.

* * *

I discovered that time had no meaning in this indeterminate state that is neither living nor dead. How long had it been now? Days? Weeks? Months?

It felt as if I'd walked several lifetimes, and yet, no matter how far I travelled—the past refused to be left behind.

However, there was something far more disturbing that I discovered during my trek. The world vanished around me with each step I took. The tastes and smells I once took for granted had now disappeared. The infinite sounds and countless textures of the earth were also gone—evaporated like yesterday's rain. As I walked, I would have given anything to hear my own footsteps again—anything to end the relentless drone of nothingness.

Though I clung to what was left of my sight, I noted that the once vibrant colors of the earth had fused into a dullish gray. My chance to experience all the wonders of the earth had simply... expired. There was no choice but to return to the city; there was no longer anything beyond it.

* * *

I am again in the darkened, back room of the coffee shop. The silent ones are all around me: the dispirited embodiment of countless promises unfulfilled, quiet desperations—and lost lives.

I glance from one hollow-eyed face to another and realize

how desperately I will miss these silent figures—for the significance of their fellowship has become clear.

In some perverse way, they are here simply to connect—to bond with others somehow. They reach out to each other to keep from fading yet again—into an even deeper, more forsaken plane of existence than this one: an unspeakably lonely place that awaits those who choose to isolate themselves.

This congregation of lost souls offered my last opportunity to avoid such a fate; a missed opportunity that I will regret for eternity.

I am fading fast, into a nether level that swallows me even now.

I am the festering abomination propped against the wall in the far corner—and even the silent ones don't notice me anymore...

—JOE MCKINNEY

Joe McKinney has been a patrol officer for the San Antonio Police Department, a homicide detective, a disaster mitigation specialist, a patrol commander, and a successful novelist. His books include the four part *Dead World* series, *Quarantined* and *Dodging Bullets*. His short fiction has been collected in *The Red Empire and Other Stories* and *Dating in Dead World and Other Stories*. For more information go to www.joemckinney.wordpress.com

—SKY OF BRASS, LAND OF IRON

By Joe McKinney

For Robert Garza, it started on a cool, breezy night in early May. He was driving home on Texas Farm Route 181 when he saw the first one moving across the road from left to right with a slow, loping gait. At first he didn't recognize it as a coyote. It didn't look right. It didn't *move* right. Coyotes were supposed to move like dogs. But there was something different about this one. It almost seemed to hop. More like a rat than a dog. Garza watched it move across the road and thought it was odd, but not particularly alarming.

Two more went by, disappearing into the cedar thicket off to his right.

A forth went by a moment later.

He waited to see if there were any more, but none came. The night was perfectly still and quiet, save for the burbling exhaust of his idling truck. He could smell the faint tinge of wood smoke on the night breeze.

He shook his head and chuckled, dismissing the encounter as just another strange thing you sometimes see on empty country roads in the middle of the night.

He drove on.

At the time, it didn't occur to him to worry.

* * *

Garza's best friend was a man named Frank Resendez. They'd known each other for almost ten years, going back to when Garza was a rookie detective assigned to the San Antonio Police Department's Homicide Unit and Resendez was his sergeant. It was Resendez, in fact, who'd talked Garza into moving his family out to Espada Ridge.

Garza would be the first to admit that Resendez was a genius. And he wasn't alone in that belief, either. He'd watched, like the kid brother of somebody famous, as Resendez's skill as an investigator and police administrator made him a law enforcement legend all across South Texas. Those same skills also earned Resendez the coveted lieutenant's position overseeing San Antonio's Homicide Unit, a job he still held, and did exceedingly well, despite everything else he had on his plate. For as successful as he was in police circles, he was even more successful writing about it. His textbook, *Criminal Investigations for the Texas Peace Officer*, was now in its fourth edition, and the money he made from that allowed him to reinvent himself yet again—this time as a major player in South Texas real estate.

Now, looking out over the 3400 acres that Resendez planned to turn into the Espada Ridge Estates, Garza felt a renewed awe for the scope of the man's vision. It was a beautiful, but hard country. Espada Ridge formed a fat crescent around the north corner of Worther Lake. Its gently rolling hills were densely covered with cedar and hardy Spanish oaks, and close to the water, there were occasional meadows that, in April, burst forth with wildflowers. In a few places, Resendez had added old-fashioned split rail fences to demarcate available lots. And, of course, there was the lake itself. Right now, it was dappled with late afternoon sunshine, a rich tapestry of yellows and reds, a pool of molten bronze.

Resendez was showing him an old country church and the ruins of six small cottages he'd found while clearing the bottom ten acres of his land. "Impossible to say how old they are," Resendez said. "Too overgrown. I bet the place is probably crawling with rattlesnakes."

Garza nodded, suddenly mindful of where he stepped. The cottages themselves were nothing special, just small moldering derelicts waist deep in yellow alkali grass. None of them had roofs, and only one still had all four walls. The weather and the years had not been kind to them.

But the church was in better shape. It no longer had a front door, and few of the gravestones on its north lawn were still standing, but it retained enough of its former self that you could tell at a glance it was a church.

"This is what I wanted to show you," Resendez said, watching with pleasure at the fascination on Garza's face. "Go on, look inside."

Garza got as far as the front steps and stopped. "Oh Jesus," he said. He put a hand over his mouth and gagged. "Something's dead in there."

"It's a deer," Resendez said.

Garza glanced at Resendez, his face wrinkled in disgust. Even after twenty years of handling homicides, the smell of rotting flesh still rattled him.

"Go on, you big baby," Resendez said. "Go inside."

Gagging, Garza went. It took a moment for his eyes to adjust to the sudden darkness, but once they did, he saw that the church was as simple inside as out, no frills, no ornamentation. It was just a large, high-ceilinged, rectangular room with a couple pews. The dead deer lay across what had once been the altar, and swarming around its carcass was a vast gathering of flies. Their murmuring buzz filled the deepening shadows.

Resendez led him around the carcass to a small wooden box tucked back into a corner. The ancient black iron lock had been forced open. "One of my workers found this yesterday while he was clearing brush for me," Resendez said. "Go ahead. Open it."

Inside lay a small brown leather book. The back flap was water-damaged, but the spine was still somewhat supple, and the pages felt stiff as he thumbed through them. The handwriting was a thin, scrunched-together scrawl that didn't yield to easy translation. It looked like a series of journal entries, with an occasional list of names and dates. Some of the earliest were from the 1720s.

"It's in German," Garza said.

"Yeah, I was hoping you could translate it. That's what you

did in the Army, right? A language officer?"

Flies buzzed around them. Garza waved a hand to shoo them away. "That was twenty-five years ago," he said. 'Rusty' didn't even come close to describing his comfort level with the German language. "I can try, I guess."

Resendez nodded and together they walked outside. The dusty haze of late afternoon wrapped around the trees. Resendez said something about wanting to know the history of the place.

But Garza was only half listening. He was watching a coyote about forty yards off, and it was watching him. Garza opened his mouth to say something about it, but the animal melted back into the cedar before he could get the words out.

He turned to Resendez. "Did you see that?"

* * *

Garza and his wife, Linda, both lay awake in bed, their eyes open in the dark, as their dog howled in the kitchen downstairs.

"Will you please go check on him?" Linda asked.

Garza grumbled something about strangling the damn dog with his bare hands and got dressed. On his way downstairs, he passed his daughter Sam's room. A white glow bordered the door. She was awake, of course, probably on her cell phone, or listening to music. For a moment he thought of getting her to do it. Guthrie was her dog, after all, and she was probably in there doing nothing, as usual.

"Screw it," he mumbled, and went down to shut the dog up himself.

Guthrie, a full grown chocolate lab, ordinarily gentle as a kitten, stood in the kitchen by the back door, barking himself hoarse. His coat bristled down his spine and his lips pulled back over his teeth in a fairly convincing imitation of a tough-as-nails junkyard dog.

"Guthrie, shut up!"

The dog looked at him, whined once, then started barking even louder at the door. Garza watched him for a second, morbidly fascinated. He'd never acted like this. Not when they lived in the city.

Of course, there, Guthrie hadn't had ten acres of land to lord over.

A part of Garza wanted to slap the dog and be done with it. But another part of him recognized something hideous in his bark. At times, it became a keening wail, almost feral, wolf-like. City dogs didn't make noises like that. And Guthrie, despite his new home, was decidedly a city dog.

Garza flipped on the kitchen light and Guthrie backed away from the door, his barks trailing off to a low, stuttering growl.

He turned on the floodlights for the backyard and looked through the window.

There was nothing there.

"Stupid dog," Garza said, and patted him on the head.

He looked outside again, his hand poised over the switch to turn out the lights, when he heard a low murmuring hum. He glanced at Guthrie, who was still growling, and then back at the yard.

There was nothing but grass and darkness beyond the trees. He hesitated for a moment, then opened the door and stepped outside—only to jump right back in and slam the door behind him.

A huge swarm of flies covered the outside of the door. He put his knuckles in his mouth to stifle the nausea threatening to overtake him.

"Jesus," he said. "Oh Jesus."

* * *

Though he was unbelievably tired, Garza stayed awake most of that night thinking about the church on Resendez's land, and the book he'd been given to translate.

It was curious how a building like that could have been spared the ravages of the South Texas weather for as long as it had. According to the book, the church had been there since at least 1728, for there had been a baptism in March of that year.

Later entries showed the church was in constant use until 1848, when the last entry was made.

But the most curious thing about the book was that it only mentioned one name—Kretschmer. Garza guessed that it was a family prayer book, which might explain why only that name was written there. The other alternative, that the little community had been so isolated that they only married each other, was too repugnant for him to dwell on.

He assumed it was a prayer book because the various authors whose handwriting he could decipher all made mention of religious rites and ceremonies. He'd skimmed over them at first, only because he figured they described conventional ceremonies, like baptism and marriage. But when he began to read them in more detail, he realized they described activities so hideously strange they could only be Satanic in design. There were so many references to demons that Garza wondered if the community's isolation was voluntary, or perhaps forced on them by horrified neighbors.

He was enough of a modern man to dismiss most of what he read in the prayer book as hogwash. But there were constant references to flies that stirred something inside him. He was almost surprised to discover this superstitious side of his personality was there, but there it was. He read the numerous entries about the flies, and how the book said they were the eyes and ears of a demon called De Vermis, which Garza guessed meant "the worm," and he found himself thoroughly creeped out. It wasn't a feeling he enjoyed.

But he hadn't known any of that when he went to Resendez's house earlier that evening. At that time, shortly after touring the church and cottages on Resendez's land and before making it back to his place for dinner, he hadn't even opened the book yet. It wouldn't be until he was alone in his own study, while Sam was upstairs doing her homework and Linda was in the kitchen doing the dishes, that he learned about the demon the Kretschmers called De Vermis.

"I suppose the first thing we ought to do is figure out how old those structures are," Resendez had said. "Once we know that, we can make more informed decisions."

They were sitting in Resendez's study, looking over some maps of the land around the lake.

"Decisions about what, exactly?"

"Well, think about it, Robert. If it's just some cowboy church, we might as well bulldoze it and move on. But if it's something else, something older—maybe Spanish—we could use that."

"Why would it be Spanish? That book was in German."

"You know what I mean. I just want to know if we can use it somehow."

"Use how?"

Resendez smiled at him patiently. "We could market it. Maybe change the name of the development from Espada Ridge to something having to do with the church."

Garza started to speak, but suddenly stopped himself. It dawned on him that he and Resendez had very different ideas about their obligations.

"Do you think we have the right to do that?" Garza asked.

"What do you mean? Why wouldn't we?"

"Well, if it is a church, Spanish or otherwise, wouldn't it fall under some kind of historical preservation act? The federal government's got that law protecting archeological artifacts."

Resendez waved the idea away with a dismissive flick of his hand. "This isn't like finding the Dead Sea Scrolls, Robert. It's just a little out of the way church the world forgot about. My point is we could use it to really give the development an identity. Make it something unique, you know?"

"Frank, I really think—"

Resendez said, "I'm not going to turn this thing over to a bunch of academics and let them put the development on hold indefinitely, Robert. You know that's what they'd do. Remember when they were building the Wal-Mart over off General Kirby Parkway and they found that old Indian village? The academics got a court order to put a twenty-million-dollar building project on hold so they could dig around for a bunch of fucking arrowheads and cornhusk dolls. You think I want that?"

"No."

"Well, you're right. I don't. What I do want is for you to translate that book. Try to get me some answers."

And just like that, Garza realized he'd been given an order. There'd be no further discussion. The matter was closed.

* * *

"Hey, honey."

"Yes, dear?" Linda said. She was dropping spaghetti into a large pot of boiling water.

"We probably shouldn't put our garbage out on the back porch anymore. It attracts flies."

"Flies?"

"Yeah. Probably other things too. I think that's what Guthrie was barking at last night."

Linda looked puzzled. "I didn't put any garbage out back," she said. "We always put it out on the side, remember?"

Garza nodded. "Must have been Sam. I'll talk to her about it."

* * *

The little town of Bonheim stood about three miles South of Worther Lake. It was a quiet crossroads for the surrounding ranches, with a little eight-man police department under the command of Chief Pablo Delgado.

Delgado was a heavyset man in his early sixties with a sunburnt face and bald head. He'd been an assistant chief in Horizon City, and the chief's job at Bonheim was his retirement gig. Bonheim was a peaceful little town that didn't demand a lot from its police force, and that suited Delgado just fine. He preferred to be easy going anyway, more like a benevolent grandpa than a serious lawman.

Garza knew that Delgado also happened to be the local expert on regional history, so he called Delgado, and the two agreed to meet in a little cafe in town.

"What kind of history do you want to know about?" Delgado asked as he managed to wrap his mouth around an enormous pulled pork sandwich that dripped red ropes of barbecue sauce onto his plate.

That was a good question, Garza thought. He didn't really know. Or he did, he just didn't know how to bring it up. How does one break the ice when talking about demon worshipping in-breeders?

In the end he decided to come as close to the truth as he could.

"I've heard rumors about a family named Kretschmer that was supposed to live around these parts," he said. "Folks I've talked to said they lived up by the lake. Near my house."

The smile on Delgado's face slipped away like a greasy egg yolk running off a piece of toast, and Garza guessed he'd hit a nerve. The man put his sandwich down and wiped the barbecue sauce from the corner of his mouth. "How'd you find out about the Kretschmer family?"

"Just people talking," Garza said. "You know the way people talk. I figured if they used to live on my land, I wanted to know about it."

Delgado looked annoyed, or maybe skeptical. He said, "Well, that's the kind of thing I wish people wouldn't talk about. This area's got a lot of good, honest history. It doesn't need a scandal to make it interesting."

But Delgado seemed willing enough to talk about the scandal. After all the horrible things he'd read in that book, and the flies at his door, and the coyotes that seemed to leer out of every dark pocket of cedar, Garza found himself keenly interested in the tale.

Most of it revolved around a man named Oswald Kretschmer, who fled Germany in the 1680s with his family to avoid religious persecution and ended up in Mexico. He relocated his family again to the area around Worther Lake sometime in the 1690s or early 1700s.

"They pretty much kept to themselves out there," Delgado

explained. "Of course, at the time there really wasn't anybody else around for them to associate with. Most of the area was a giant Spanish land grant to one of their local governors. Empty except for a few half-starved Indian tribes.

"After Texas got its independence from Mexico, settlers started moving into the area and founded this town. People avoided the Kretschmers, mostly. Though, I did read a diary once that mentioned them. It said you could always tell the Kretschmer family on account of their eyes."

"Their eyes?" Garza asked. He was leaning forward despite himself, like he was hearing dirty gossip about what the pretty secretary in the office looked like naked.

"Said to be the iciest blue you ever saw. Every single member of that family had those eyes, apparently."

"And so what happened to them?"

"Nobody knows," Delgado said. "The Texas government took a census of the area when they tried to enlist local boys into the Confederate militias, and there's no record of them in it. My guess is they packed up and went somewhere where they could still be by themselves."

Garza sat back and scratched his head. "I'm afraid I don't see the scandal in all that."

"Well," Delgado said, and he obviously found this detail distasteful, "there's the part about them all marrying each other. It was just the one family, you know. Over the space of a hundred years or so, you're bound to end up with what the law calls *marriages of consanguinity.*"

"In-breeding," Garza said.

Delgado nodded. "You know how that kind of thing gets people talking. There's more than a few references to them doing devil worship—and witchcraft too—but I think that's just people embellishing an already sordid story. The records I've seen mention birth defects and deformities and all the other things you'd expect from generations of in-breeding. Given the nature of the time it's only natural stories of witchcraft and such would start up."

Garza said he agreed, but his mind kept turning back to

that book.

And the flies.

* * *

"You did *what?*" Resendez said. "Robert, what in the hell's wrong with you? I told you I didn't want a bunch of historians crawling all over this place."

"He's not a real historian, Frank. He's just an amateur—"

"I know who he is, Robert. What I want to know is why you'd do something like that. Don't you realize how much is at stake here? We both stand to make a lot of money if we do this right."

"I was just trying to find out about the history of this place. Like you asked me to do. And I didn't say a word about the buildings you found. As far as he knows, I was just following up on idle gossip I'd heard around town."

"You mean about that devil worshipping crap you found in that book?"

Garza nodded.

"That's great," Resendez said, and then he turned and looked out the window of his study, his gaze wandering over the acres of cedar to the lake beyond. At last he said, "You know, this isn't what I wanted when I asked you to help me give this place an identity."

"You got the truth, Frank."

"Bullshit," Resendez said. "There's no truth in that book. And none in Delgado's amateur history either. The truth is what we make it."

Garza was appalled. In all the years he'd known Resendez, he'd never once heard the man say something to suggest slippery ethics. He felt like one of his boyhood heroes had let him down. But that wasn't all. For the first time, he realized that some small part of his orderly, rational mind actually believed the stories he'd read about devil worship. Maybe there was a kernel of truth in it, at least. People who isolated themselves for religious reasons usually did it because they had some off-the-wall beliefs, didn't they?

"So what are you going to do, Frank?" Garza's voice strained, his lips thin as razorblades.

"I don't know yet," Resendez said, and turned back to the window. "Go home, Robert. We'll talk later."

* * *

The next day was Monday, and work was uncomfortable. Resendez, never one to hold a grudge or let a problem bog him down, was unusually cold, and he and Garza went most of the day without speaking more than a few grunts to each other.

Garza left work about six and drove home, taking Farm Route 181 like always. As he passed the new Methodist Church just south of Bonheim, still a half mile or so from his usual turn off, he saw one of the coyotes with the rat-like gait go bounding across the road in front of him, then disappear into the cedar off to his left.

He put on the brakes. A feeling had festered in his mind ever since he saw that coyote watching him near Resendez's church that the coyotes and the flies and the church were somehow connected. His police training had prepared him to look for links between seemingly unrelated people and events, but this felt like a different kind of problem, like it wouldn't yield to conventional logic. He wasn't sure what the connection was, only that he believed one existed.

It was a cool night, and he'd been driving with the windows down. But watching the coyote shook him in a way he couldn't quite define, and he moved to roll up the windows.

He got the driver's side window secured, but when he reached over to roll up the passenger side, he stopped and jerked his hand back in horror. A huge humming mass of black, angry flies covered the whole door frame.

He backed against the driver's side door, fumbled blindly for the handle, and spilled out into the street, where he stood gaping at a living black carpet beating against his vehicle. They were actually rocking the truck with their attack.

After the shock wore off, he pulled out his fire extinguisher and turned it on the flies.

The chalky spray coated the insects, and they dropped to the road in powdery, white chunks. Their swollen bodies and still twitching wings disgusted him, but he mastered his nausea long enough to sweep the remaining flies onto the road with an old, greasy towel.

Something moved in the grass behind him. He turned, his right hand poised over the thumb snap on his holster, and saw a single coyote running with that familiar rat-like hop across the church lawn. It stopped about fifty feet away and watched him. Off in the distance, he could hear howling, a disconcerting chorus of yaps and long, mournful bays.

More coyotes came around the side of the building, moving fast. There was no point in pulling his gun. At the speed they moved, he'd probably empty the whole magazine without landing a single shot.

Instead of firing, he got back in his truck, dropped it into gear, and peeled out down the road as fast as the old Chevy would go.

When he looked in the rearview mirror, there was nothing but dust behind him.

* * *

When he arrived home, Linda was standing in the driveway. The look on her face said something was wrong. "She hasn't come home yet," Linda said.

"Sam?"

Linda nodded, near tears. "She was supposed to be home at four."

"Where'd she go?" But he had a sinking feeling that he already knew.

"She's out with Jenny and Margaret. They went horseback riding down by the lake."

"How long ago?"

"They left after lunch. I don't know."

Garza jumped back in his truck.

"Where are you going?"

"Call Chief Delgado," he told her. "Have him bring shotguns and a couple of his men. Tell him to meet me on Resendez's property down by the lake."

"Robert—"

"Go!" he said. "Hurry."

He dropped the truck in gear and sped away.

* * *

Garza raced down to the lake on a narrow dirt road he and Resendez had cut with a tractor the summer before. He took it as far as he could, then cut through the brush toward the church, his truck ripping through overhanging cedar branches the whole way.

He reached a large limestone outcropping and had to slow so he could work the truck around it. When he did, he heard Sam and Resendez's daughters screaming for help.

Their voices came from the trails above the church, and it sounded like they were getting closer.

Not thinking about anything except his daughter, he punched the gas and took the truck straight through the cedar and down the slope of the limestone outcropping. The old Chevy yawed in midair, making him feel weightless for a painful, prolonged moment, and then hit the ground with a tremendous impact.

The truck bottomed out and stalled. It wouldn't start again. He jumped out, gun in hand, and scanned the trails on the hillside above the church.

"Daddy, Daddy," Sam screamed at him. He saw his little girl holding on to the horse for dear life. Resendez's daughters came up behind her.

He ran a few steps that way and stopped. Coyotes bounded down the hill on either side of the girls, moving through the brush so easily they seemed more like shadows than animals. In the gaps between the cedar trees he could see them snapping at the bellies of the horses.

"Samantha," he yelled. "This way. Come on. This way!"

The poor girl was barely holding on. She wasn't half the rider Resendez's daughters were, and as the horses jumped from the slope to the grassy ledge of limestone on the far side of the church, she nearly popped out of the saddle.

The coyotes snapped at her feet and at the horse's belly, but Garza couldn't risk a shot. Hitting a running, dog-sized target at sixty yards with a pistol would be next to impossible, and he stood a better chance of hitting one of the girls by mistake.

"Make for that cottage," he yelled at her, and ran that way himself. It only had three walls, but it would have to do. At least that way the coyotes could only come at them from one side.

The girls raced for him and they met at the busted cottage wall. Garza shot at the coyote snapping at the horse's hooves. He missed the first shot and fired three more times. The last two shots sent the animal tumbling backwards over itself.

More coyotes raced across the grass, coming for them. He yanked Sam down and folded her into his arms while the other two girls jumped off their horses.

"Inside here," he said, packing them into the cottage. "Hurry."

He glanced inside the cottage as he pushed them inside and did a double take. Most of the floor was grown over with meadow grasses and wildflowers, but toward the back wall, someone had dug up fresh earth. There was a large mound of gray dirt and rock there, and a sizeable hole in the ground beyond it.

"There," he said.

"Daddy—"

"Go," he told her, and turned back just in time to see at least thirty coyotes going after the horses. The horses neighed and kicked. They punched the air with their hooves, their eyes rolling wildly, their lips pulled back, slinging long ropes of spit.

The coyotes tore the belly out of one of the horses and Garza couldn't look anymore. Its dying screams were enough. He backed into the cottage, moving toward the girls, who were already getting into the hole.

"Mr. Garza," Jenny said, "there's a tunnel down here."

"Get in," he said. "All of you."

"Daddy—"

"Go, Sam. I'm right behind you, baby."

They got down on their bellies and crawled into the darkness. He went after them, backing himself in just as one of the coyotes appeared at the rim.

In the fading evening light, all he saw was the jagged rows of its fangs. He fired with one hand, killing it. He backed further into the hole. Behind him, he could hear the girls whimpering, saying his name. Sam tried to hold on to him. A coyote silhouette appeared at the entrance to the tunnel and more gathered behind it. He fired, putting it down, the bark of the Glock sounding like a cannon inside the tunnel.

"Get out of here!" he screamed at the snarling animals. "Get the hell away!"

He fired two more times. The coyotes outside the hole snapped and grabbed at their dead brethren blocking the entrance, and rather than drag the carcasses out of the way, they seemed more intent on ripping their way through.

But suddenly the cannibalistic tearing of flesh and the snarling growls stopped, and everything was silent, save for the panicked shallow breathing of the girls behind him.

"Daddy," Sam said.

"Shhh, baby. Keep quiet."

He listened. From somewhere above him he heard voices shouting and men running. Then, like thunder, shotgun blasts. Several of them. A battle raged above them. And then, after a long time, that noise too went silent.

They huddled together in the dark, the girls crowding as close as they could to him. The moment seemed to go on forever.

Then, from the entrance, a thick Texas drawl: "Sergeant Garza, it's Officer Boller with the Bonheim Police Department. Ya'll all right down there, sir?"

* * *

It was getting dark when they came out of the tunnel. Resendez stood there, a smoking shotgun in his hands. Chief Delgado was there, too. He had three of his officers with him. Resendez threw the shotgun on the ground and hugged his daughters. He steered them away from what was left of their horses, and then made arrangements for one of Delgado's officers to take them home.

When they were gone, Garza retrieved a flashlight from one of the other officers and pointed it down the tunnel where he and the girls had taken refuge. The light didn't reach the end of the tunnel. When he'd fired his pistol down there, the sound had carried a long ways, and now he knew the actual distance was farther than he thought.

Probably much farther.

The hole was fresh, the ground just recently overturned, but the tunnel was obviously much older. The earth was packed tight and dry. He crumbled it in his fist. It occurred to him the tunnel was probably the same age as the cottages and church.

He went back to the clearing between the buildings. Resendez stood there with Delgado and the other two officers. Delgado clearly had no idea what the hell was going on, but Resendez's face was set and unreadable.

"This tunnel connects all these buildings, doesn't it?" Garza asked.

Resendez nodded.

"How long have you know about this?"

Resendez looked away for a second, then said, "Since yesterday afternoon."

"And you didn't say anything about it?"

Resendez looked away again.

Delgado said, "Them coyotes. I've never seen so many in one place before. They're not supposed to act that way. Matter of fact, I don't think I've ever heard of a coyote going after anything bigger than a rabbit."

Garza glanced at him, but didn't respond. To Resendez he

said, "What did you do?"

Resendez was silent.

"Answer me," Garza hissed. "What did you do?"

Delgado cocked his head in surprise. He glanced back and forth between the two of them.

"Watch your tone of voice with me, *Sergeant*," Resendez said, his face a mystery in the settling dark.

"Bullshit!" Garza shot back. "Don't you dare try to pull your rank on me. Not after what I just went through. Now you tell me what you fucking did."

Resendez glanced around. He drew a heavy breath and seemed to weigh the cost of telling what he knew. "There's a network of tunnels underneath here," he finally said. "They connect under the church. That seems to be the hub."

"What are they for?" Garza asked. "Do they go anywhere?"

Resendez nodded. "There's an entrance beneath the church."

"An entrance to what?"

Resendez just shook his head.

"It's that book, isn't it? It's all true."

Resendez hung his head in resigned acquiescence. The genie was out of the bottle, and they both knew it.

"What are ya'll talkin' about?" Delgado said.

Garza turned to him. "Do your men have enough flashlights and shotguns for all of us?"

Delgado still seemed uncertain. He looked to Resendez for guidance, but Resendez wouldn't look back.

Finally, Delgado said. "Yes, sir. We got plenty of fire power." He turned to one of the officers and said, "Bert, go and get the shotguns. Plenty of shells, too."

"What are you going to do?" Resendez asked.

"We're going down there. All of us."

"What good will that do?"

"I don't know," Garza said. "I really don't. But I think the book and those coyotes and these buildings are all connected, and I think whatever it is we're dealing with here is waiting for us down there beneath that church."

* * *

Resendez had done a lot of work in a short time. He'd peeled away the plank boards that made the floor of the altar and exposed a gaping pit leading down into darkness. Delgado and a young redheaded officer named Sturgis tried to light it up with flashlights, but only succeeded in casting an eerie, buttery glow on the ancient limestone steps.

"What are you fellas hoping to find down there?" Delgado asked.

Garza racked the shotgun, chambering a shell. "Let's go," he said. "Everybody stay sharp."

He climbed down the steps and made his way into the darkness, not even bothering to see if the others followed. The steps went down maybe thirty feet before leveling off into a tunnel. The flashlight beam hinted at other tunnels a short distance off, opening off the main passageway. Dried timbers were embedded into the walls like ribs, and he traced them with the light. Supports, Garza guessed, like the box frames miners use to prevent cave-ins. There was a faint, foul odor, like something lingering in the still air.

"Where do these tunnels lead?" he asked over his shoulder.

"The side tunnels on the right have collapsed," Resendez said. "I don't know how far back the main tunnel leads."

They went on silently, Garza in the lead, the others following. The tunnel opened up to a large, rectangular chamber, and there they stopped. Wooden platforms, the supports black with mold, ran along both side walls. In the middle of the chamber was a round stone wall, about knee-high, and inside boiled a dark, oily liquid. Toward the back of the chamber stood an altar, and as Garza looked around, Resendez made his way to it.

Once Resendez mounted the altar, he turned and looked out over the chamber. As he did, a shudder spread through the air. They all sensed it. Garza staggered to one side. Flies buzzed in his ears. He swatted at them, but nothing was there. He felt dizzy, suddenly nauseous, and he thought he could see the ghostlike shapes of men and women and even children standing on the platforms, their eyes pointed at Resendez. He shook his head and blinked, trying to clear his mind, but couldn't. What, at first, he had taken for flies buzzing in his ears now sounded like voices. Slowly, those voices became a chorus that filled the air, and when Garza strained to listen, he found their cadence familiar. He knew the words they were chanting from the book Resendez had found.

The shotgun fell from Resendez's fingertips and clattered to the ground. His hands spread wide, as though in benediction. The ghostlike visions around him became more solid. The room seemed to brighten. The voices grew louder. Resendez muttered along with them, and Garza too felt a familiar rush pounding in his veins. The words were ancient, powerful. Garza yelled at Resendez from across the chamber, his voice unable to punch through the hazy veil that had enveloped them.

Resendez went on chanting. The words moved through him, so powerful they shook the walls.

The oil in the pit began to boil, and flies crawled out of the muck, taking to the air and attacking Delgado and Sturgis. Garza felt himself lensing in and out between two worlds, the world of Delgado and Sturgis screaming in pain on the one side, and the ghost world of the voices and Resendez on the other. The part of him that watched from the ghost world filled with the awe and love of the zealot. Yet that other part, the part still attached to the corporeal world, sensed an overpowering stench rising from the depths of the pit, and was nearly overcome by it.

He could sense the ghost world gaining strength, and as he looked out over the strangely similar faces of the men, women, and children of the Kretschmer family, he could see their fiercely penetrating blue eyes staring back at him.

Their cadence grew stronger. The room shook, and clods of earth and stone crashed down around them. Something vast rose from the depths of the pit, something old and powerful. Garza could sense it pushing its way up through the earth.

On the altar, Resendez was shaking. The man he had been now gone, something different stared back from his mad eyes.

Garza grabbed the man's shoulders, but Resendez shook

him off. Any moment now and the thing rising up through the earth would be free. *De Vermis*, Garza thought. He had to break whatever had a hold on his friend, but there didn't seem to be any way to reach him. Flies yawned out of the pit by the thousands. Their buzzing made Garza's skin vibrate. He yelled at Resendez, and though their faces were almost touching, they were miles away.

Garza grabbed the shotgun his friend had dropped and punched Resendez with it. Resendez seemed to hardly feel the blow at first, but then, as he looked up at Garza, pain entered his expression.

Garza pulled him up to his feet and wrapped Resendez's arm around his shoulders.

"Come on, man, we have to get out of here!"

As Garza led him down from the altar, he saw blurry shapes he knew were Delgado and his men standing by the pit.

He yelled a warning they didn't hear.

The stone wall collapsed and the boiling, oily liquid in the pit spilled over the ground. Garza yelled again, but not in time. Sturgis was snatched off his feet and pulled into the pit by a huge, blackened tentacle.

Delgado fell backwards, a scream dying on his lips.

"Move!" Garza shouted, and ran down from the altar with Resendez on his arm. "Move, man! Move!"

He stopped long enough to grab Delgado's shirt and pull him to his feet. Then he pushed him to the door.

The three men ran for the surface.

From behind them, like thunder under the earth, something ancient struggled to break free.

* * *

They worked most of the night, packing the entrance beneath the church's altar with dynamite that Delgado and one of his men got from a nearby quarry. By morning, they were ready to light the fuse.

The blast shook the lake and sent birds sprinting to the air.

When it was done, and the land where the church had stood was just a smoking, crumbling crater in the ground, Garza went walking through the tall grass near the rim.

He walked until he saw a dead coyote, its legs bent under its body, the head twisted against the ground. Its eyes were open, bulging, and though no life lit them, they were still powerfully blue.

He stared into those eyes and thought of the thing he'd just faced. A great power had lurked beneath that church, something dark and ancient and evil beyond the narrow limits through which most men understood those words. Maybe it was still down there, waiting for another man like Resendez to open its way through the depths of rock and earth.

One thing eluded him, though. The eyes of the coyote seemed hauntingly familiar. Other eyes that same color blue had stared at him from the ghost world Resendez had opened up, but he wouldn't believe—indeed, couldn't believe, if he had any prayer of holding on to the tattered remnants of his sanity—that they were the eyes of the Kretschmer family.

Still, there was no way to be sure.

—LORNE DIXON

Lorne Dixon lives and writes off an exit of I-78 in residential New Jersey. He grew up on a diet of yellow-spined paperbacks, black-and-white monster movies, and the thunder-lizard backbeat of rock-n-roll. His novels *Snarl*, *The Lifeless*, and *Eternal Unrest* are available from Coscom Entertainment. His short fiction has appeared in dozens of anthologies and magazines, most notably five appearances in Cutting Block Press' *+Horror Library+* series, PS Press' *Darkness on the Edge*, and Edge Publication's upcoming *Danse Macabre: Encounters with the Grim Reaper*.

—CONSANGUINITY

By Lorne Dixon

Walking beside her twin brother Perry, Adelaide worried the tour guide might catch a sniff of their overcoats and recognize the clingy stench of a hundred-and-forty-year-old grave. The scent of their great, great grandfather's coffin—mold on rotten linen, wet clay, dusty human remains—lingered on their clothes, as if polyester and denim had an elephant's memory. They'd washed themselves in river water, but ever since they'd been evicted from their family home they hadn't enjoyed a proper shower, and their effort in the Sucarnoochee made little difference. If anything, it added the scaly odor of skipjack shad. They kept themselves a few steps behind the other tourists in hopes to keep suspicion, and inquiring noses, at bay.

The name on the tour guide's bright yellow name badge was *Linda*, with a tiny red heart drawn above the second letter instead of a tittle. She walked in her tan businesswoman skirt with the grace of a pair of brand new scissors, hour-a-day workout legs moving with machine precision. Mesmerized with envy, Adelaide had a tough time drawing her eyes off them. Frowning, she forced her gaze downward, studying each disappointment of her own body for the millionth time; feet three sizes too large to be feminine, swollen ankles, flabby legs, uneven pear-shaped hips, bulging stomach, a pair of ugly, drooping breasts, and wide, masculine shoulders. She hated every inch of herself.

She knew she needed to size up the crowd. The loose Mississippi gun permit and carry laws meant that any number of the big-eyed men and women in the museum could have a sidearm nestled under their belts.

She was less concerned by the security, though she noticed that Perry kept a constant, suspicious eye on the overweight, out-of-shape men in loose-fitting uniforms. Adelaide knew they didn't have guns. There was no way the institution's liberal patrons-of-the-arts benefactors would have allowed any such thing. No, if there was a threat here, it was from Joe or Jane Sixpack.

She had her own gun, a well-worn Colt 1917 handed down from her Pop, stashed in the inner pocket of her coat. It bumped against her ribs with every step. Nothing in the world felt more reassuring. Perry's gun was newer, an ugly little .22 with its serial numbers filed off. The pistol matched her brother well. He was short and wide, with an uneven, greasy mustache, a thinning hairline, and a long list of aliases. As a young felon, freshly released from federal prison, he'd burnt off his fingerprints with a kerosene lamp.

Linda led them through the prison, pointing out displays erected in cells where men had once spent long spans of their lives. Here, she informed the group, was where Jack Haley, the bank robber, hung himself from the top rail of his double-bunk. And here? That was Benjamin Roost's death row cell until he was given a reprieve by the Governor. He murdered his cellmate the next day. She told her stories with surprising candor, never betraying the fact that she must have spun the same script half a dozen times a day, every day.

Adelaide didn't give a good goddamn about Jack Haley, Benjamin Roost, or any of the other semi-infamous prisoners who had spent their sentences in these cages. She and Perry shuffled along at the back of the pack, listening without interest, waiting for the tour to bring them to their destination. Although she'd never set foot inside Camp Croix, she didn't need a guide for this tour. Her research had been extensive, if undisciplined. Barely better than illiterate, she'd never read any of the dozen books written about the Civil War-era prison or its infamous uprising, but she knew the story with sharper detail and more scope than anyone could ever have gained from a historian's retelling. Passed down through the generations, the history of this place was a rot that spread up from the trunk of the Spratlin family tree, infected each of its branches until suicides and death sentences reduced it to a withering, hollow pole. Adelaide and Perry were the last.

Linda led them through a maze of rusted bars, slanted floors, and uneven walkways. She called out for the tourists to watch their step as they descended a steep flight of concrete stairs. Bare bulbs ran along ceiling wires for lighting, casting strange long shadows down the counter-clockwise spiral of steps. At the bottom, she turned to face them and walked backward with the same feline grace as before. "These are the guard stations. You can still see where the munitions stores were located along that far wall. And now, just a tiny step, and we're entering the living quarters. The Confederate soldiers who served as guards lived in town and commuted to work every day. There were no horses to spare, so they hoofed it. But the general who ran Camp Croix lived here, inside the prison, with his family."

Adelaide attempted to visualize the empty, dingy living quarters in her great, great grandfather's time. It was impossible. She could not imagine life in these subterranean caverns. How had a family gathered around a dinner table surrounded by such gloom? Had they somehow found enough peace in these damp, concrete corridors to pray? To laugh? To grieve? To fuck? From her view, Woolfolk Spratlin and his family lived only marginally better than the inmates above.

Anticipation began to build inside Adelaide. She exhaled in quick, staggering breaths. Glancing at Perry, she saw her brother was untroubled. That'd always been the case, though. Their parents believed Perry to be stoic and fearless. They were wrong. It only took one look into his astigmatic eyes to tell the true story: Perry just didn't give a fuck, not about his family's destiny, his sister, himself, or *anything*.

As kids, Adelaide's favorite pastime was netting creek bullfrogs and bringing them back to the antique, metal-framed aquarium in the cramped bedroom she shared with her brother. *Perry's* favorite pastime was squashing Adelaide's pets with a wooden mallet. In time, Adelaide came to understand that her brother didn't enjoy killing the frogs in the least. What he enjoyed was the tears, anger, and fisticuffs that inevitably followed.

"General Woolfolk J. Spratlin ruled over the prison with an iron fist. The Northern soldiers held here feared him. He had a reputation for employing drastic corporal punishment in the everyday running of Camp Croix. Caning was common, but his favorite way to correct an inmate's attitude was to have him tied, kneeling, to the camp's flagpole. A hauling donkey would be brought over from the stockyards and backed up to the prisoner. Guards would stab the animal with their bayonets in its rear until it kicked. The lucky ones got away with broken noses and missing teeth. Some came away with faces that were, well, no longer faces."

There were nine tourists in all, five men and four women, not counting the siblings, all wearing bright yellow admission bracelets. Adelaide sized up each of them as they passed, single file, through a narrow doorway into the final room. None seemed like a particular threat, not even the tallest of the bunch, a three-nights-a-week gym membership standing in a pair of beaten-up sneakers. She'd dealt with the type before, turning a last-call bar pickup into a simple hit-and-run robbery, and knew that a single shot to the face would bring Mr. Cardio Infomercial down. Break his nose and the deal'd be done.

"Camp Croix is famous, of course, for the riot of July, 1863. Vicksburg had fallen two weeks earlier, and news had made its way back, by word of mouth, to the Northern troops imprisoned here. They overcame the guards in a three prong coordinated attack, simultaneously taking control of the courtyard, the eastern cellblock, and the watchtower. The guards were forced to the center of the complex and found themselves surrounded. They knew that because of the way the prisoners had been treated, surrender would not spare them from the inmates' wrath, so they fought to the last man, retreating underground into the General's living quarters. They barricaded themselves in and hoped they could hold out until reinforcements arrived."

Adelaide's eyes locked onto the iron door against the far wall. Green from oxidation and accented with patches of crimson rust, it was nothing like the stories she'd been told. Family lore described a towering, impenetrable metal barrier fit for a royal castle's gate.

"The General gathered his family together and headed through that door into a small room cut into the bedrock. Locking the door behind him, he intended to wait out the siege with his family." Linda gestured to the door with the grace of a game show hostess displaying a prize. "There was a problem with his plan. Inside this "safe" room, he kept a week's worth of canned provisions and water. The riot, however, lasted *three* weeks."

Once, when she and Perry were seven, her brother surprised her. Instead of killing the day's catch of frogs, he slid a lock into the ornate metal grill on the old aquarium's lid, leaving only pinholes for air. Unable to feed her pets, she'd begged Perry for the combination. When that failed, she'd tried hundreds of random combinations and watched the frogs grow weaker and weaker. The largest of the bunch, a squat, proud-looking tyrant, didn't wait long before he began eating the fresh corpses. And eventually, he didn't even wait for them to die.

"When Confederate forces finally arrived and quelled the uprising, the General emerged from behind that door. His wife and his two sons did not. Only his deaf and dumb daughter survived the ordeal. And she, naturally, was in no position to offer testimony about the horrors that happened in that dark room over those long weeks. The neat, clean pile of bones in one corner told the part of the story she couldn't. Another hidden detail of the ordeal was revealed nine months later when, at thirteen, she gave birth to a son."

A few of the tourists winced. Adelaide did not; although she wasn't really listening, she knew where the story led and easily enough deduced why they reacted. Her grandfather told the same story in Biblical terms, referencing Lot's daughters, who seduced their father, as directed by an angel, to continue the family bloodline. Adelaide had never been upset by the implications suggested by the story, but now, in the company of the pretty tour guide and the upper-class tourists, she felt a reflexive anger rise up inside her. Murder and cannibalism hadn't disgusted these people, but the creation of new life had. Scanning the small crowd, from face to face, she felt judged by their scowling expressions.

One of the tourists, a six-credits-a-year college twenty-something with a pair of earbud headphones dangling from his shoulders, raised his hand. Linda squinted and pointed. "You have a question?"

"Yeah," the slacker said through the braces-straightened teeth of a smug, interminable grin. "Did she call the baby her son, or her brother?"

A few of the others giggled

Perry didn't laugh. His temper didn't have a short fuse, it had none at all. Adelaide glanced at her brother, fully expecting him to erupt into violence, kick his heels off the floor, and tackle the dumbshit college brat. She was relieved to see Perry standing still, eyes still glazed over in disinterest.

"We really don't know much about what happened to the daughter, or her child." Linda handled the question as a serious one, not missing a beat. "Although a birth certificate still exists for the baby, no other records remain to tell us whatever became of the boy."

Records, no, Adelaide thought, *and very few left alive that knew, either.* The boy, her great grandfather, Alessander Spratlin, lived long enough to marry, spawn two children, contract Syphilis, and buy the gun he used to end his life.

Linda moved toward the door, prancing with her perfect legs and rolling, seductive hips. The tourists followed. A woman holding a tri-fold brochure in her hand asked in a thick Georgia mountain pine accent, "It says in here that there's some kinda treasure in there?"

Placing an open palm against the door, Linda turned to the woman with dimples etched so deeply into her smiling face that they must have reached back to her tonsils. "That's the mystery. When the Northern soldiers originally arrived here, the General had every one inspected." She opened her mouth and tapped her central incisors. "Back then, gold fillings were very common. We can't know how much gold the General harvested from his captives, but I can tell you this: 39,000 captured Federal soldiers came through this prison during the war, second only to Andersonville. A mass grave was uncovered in the fields behind the camp back in '83. One in every three bodies excavated showed signs of having teeth pulled shortly before their deaths. It stands to reason that a large fortune was made."

"So what happened to the gold?" the tourist asked.

Linda shook her head. "Never recovered. Some say that the General stored it in a hidden lock box in the safe room behind this door. We have no way of knowing."

Another from the small crowd asked, "Haven't ya searched?"

"Nope, we haven't a way to do so," she answered. "The door slammed shut after the General and his daughter came out in 1863 and it hasn't been opened since. There have been a few attempts to get in over the years, but it's a very thick door and the lock is very tricky. Some of the best locksmiths in the world have tried to pick their way in. None have succeeded."

The college kid called out, "Mind if I try?"

The other tourists laughed.

"Be my guest," Linda said, stepping away from the door.

The kid took two steps forward but then froze when Perry slid the muzzle of his .22 under his chin. Using the weapon to push the slacker away from the door, Perry said, "How's about y'let me give it a try first, huh?"

Adelaide rushed to her brother's side, pulling her own gun and waving it at the crowd. Shocked, they backpedaled away until she screamed for them to stop, drop to the floor, and put their hands on the back of their heads. They all obeyed, even the gym shower stud. Their eyes were glassy, some tearing. Glancing back through the living quarters, Adelaide saw no signs of any of the guards. "Stay down and nothing bad has'ta happen ta any'all. But don't make this any harder, 'kay?"

"I think I can—"

Perry spun toward Linda and stopped her mid-sentence

with a sharp blow across her face. She fell against the wall, lip bursting, and began to wail. Keeping his gun trained on her chest, he reached down, wiped a dollop of blood out of her quivering mouth with his thumb, and drew a cartoon heart over her right eye. "You stay down, too, honey-flower, or you're gonna make yourself an example."

Linda changed. The perfectly composed, conservative host disappeared and a much humbler face emerged, defiant and proud, no more than a generation removed from the indignation of back country hill folk. She spit a glob of blood into his face.

Reddening with fury, Perry wiped his eyes with his sleeve. For a moment he was still, and Adelaide thought his rage might dissipate, but then, in a flurry of spastic motion, he took hold of the cowering tour guide and wrestled her flat to the floor, swinging the .22 in wide arches, each blow kicking her head to one side, then the other. Turning her over, he pushed her face, mouth open, flat to the floor and jammed the gun under the base of her skull. Screaming, he pulled the trigger three times. The top half of her head, everything above the jawline, rocketed to the far wall.

The tourists stirred, releasing a chorus of hushed, frenzied murmurs and muffled cries. One of her father's favorite aphorisms—and he had many, preferring them to any meaningful thoughts of his own—was Ernie Pyle's famous phrase "There are no atheists in foxholes," however, looking out at the tourists, Adelaide saw exactly the opposite. The few who chose to steal a quick upward glance did so with wide, faithless eyes. She and Perry hadn't robbed them of their wallets and rings, as her brother had promised her they would, but they'd stolen their faith.

"Give 'em over," Perry said as he leaped to his feet and held out a hand. Adelaide flinched at the sight of his glimmering eyes and vicious, bestial expression. She knew the look too well. She reached down inside her coat to her waist and felt the brush of a long wooden handle. Digging deeper, into a tight pocket, she hooked her finger around the old key ring stored there and pulled it free. Heavy for their size, the edges of the two black, wrought iron keys had been smoothed by the decades, but they felt like a pair of razor-sharp weapons in her hand, instruments to be treated with the greatest amount of care and *never* entirely trusted. She'd felt that way ever since she'd pried them from her great, great grandfather's skeletal clutch. Avoiding her brother's intense, glowering eyes, she handed over the keys.

He leaned in close to her ear and blew a pungent blast of chewing tobacco and tooth decay across her nostrils, forcing her head to turn in protest. "We'll celebrate tonight, just the two of us."

Grunting, he turned to the door, slid the old black key into the lock and turned. The mechanism resisted. Rust and calcified grime trickled out of the keyhole as the lock's complex series of gears and tumblers turned. Finally, letting out a short, sharp shriek, the safe room door cracked open.

Perry grunted as he pushed against the heavy door. The hinges turned with a protesting scream, almost human, and the room filled with a cloud of fine dust that smelled and tasted like smoke. Gesturing out to the men and women on the floor, he said, "You stay here with them all." Louder, he added for the tourists, "Y'all get outta line with my sister, she'll make sure the police'll need a whole heap of chalk when they get here."

Adelaide moved the aim of her gun from one to the next, making sure they knew what it felt like to have the weapon trained on each of them. The uneven floor helped out her cause; a wandering rivulet of blood trickled its way from Linda's stumped head through the crowd. She could tell from the look in their eyes they wouldn't dare move unless commanded to do so.

Pulling his handkerchief from his back pocket, Perry took a deep breath, covered his mouth, and disappeared beyond the door. With him gone, the gun in her hand felt insufficient to control the crowd; a sudden charge by the men in the group would overtake her, even if she squeezed off a few shots. The stopping power of a handgun was less potent than many believed, she knew this and had seen the scenario play out in a boxcar in Atlanta. She wished she'd found a way to bring her brother's Browning Auto 5. That twelve-gauge shotgun could take down a steer.

Still, they were terrified and unlikely to try anything.

She hoped. Under pressure, people became unpredictable.

Inside the dark room, Perry coughed. From the echo, he sounded farther away than she would have guessed. Family lore never discussed the size of the room, only that it was bored out of the mountain, below the foundation, so she'd always assumed it to be a small, confined space. Not so, apparently.

The trail of Linda's blood trickled past the tourists and down the short hall beyond. Following a groove in the concrete floor, it turned and flowed right, avoiding the guard station, and entered the living quarters.

The thunder of boots descending the stairs hit Adelaide's ears. Captivated by the movement of the blood, she hadn't noticed the advance of the footfalls, and from the sound of it, four guards were moving in fast. Adjusting her grip on the handgun, she squeezed the trigger and sent a wild shot into the stairwell. The footsteps stopped with a rustle and a few shouts.

Drawing a deep breath, she yelled, "Don'tchu come down here—"

"—please," one of the tourists begged, "let us go—"

Another voice, this one female, groveled, "—please—"

The footsteps on the stairs began again, now cautious, but continuing down. The guards would be at the landing in a minute or less. She tugged the trigger again. Dust burst from the wall above the stairwell's mouth where the bullet struck. Adelaide took a quick backward step.

"—please, Miss, please let us—"

She heard a voice in her head, her own voice when she was younger, pleading for release, begging Perry to let her go, to get off her, to stop hurting her. Hands shaking, she fired two more shots. Far off target, they ricocheted off the quarry-rock walls.

"—God, don't shoot, don't—"

Tears came, reducing her eyesight to an unfocused, moving watercolor painting. She wiped her face and took another step back. Her foot slid on Linda's blood trail, but she righted herself before losing her balance, free hand clutching the safe room's door. It felt colder than any metal surface she'd ever touched, colder even than the keys she'd recovered from great, great Grandfather Spratlin's grave.

Two dark silhouettes appeared in the stairwell landing, guns raised. Never a great shot, Adelaide knew she had no chance of hitting them, not from this distance with blurry eyesight. Catching a fleeting glance of the men as they stormed into the living quarters, she frowned. They weren't guards. Cops? No, the uniforms were wrong.

Bolting into the safe room, she slammed the door closed.

Screaming for her brother, she spun in the darkness. Unsettled dust buzzed around her like an endless swarm of riverbed mosquitoes. The first breath she took inside the room brought her to her knees in a coughing fit. Face flushing, she lifted the collar of her shirt over her nose.

Perry's hands clamped down on her arms. Coming in close, he asked in a coarse, angry voice, "What th'fuck happened?"

"Cops," she lied.

He released her, something he hadn't done when she'd begged him in their adolescence, and stepped away. Pocketing the handgun, she lit her cigarette lighter. Through the haze of the swirling dust, she saw him turn away from her and move out of the light's reach.

"We'll deal with *that* in a moment," he muttered.

She followed him. The safe room wasn't a room at all; smooth, rounded walls reached up to a low, elongated dome ceiling: it was a short, terminated tunnel. Not the large room she suspected, the acoustics were misleading in the extreme, even her breathing echoed.

Fists pounded on the metal door. Spinning, Adelaide saw the impossible: the heavy, impenetrable door shook with each blow. A century and a half of attempts to break into the safe room had failed, but now the fists of a handful of men threatened to bring the door down. Perhaps, she thought, that the seal had weakened when it was opened. Maybe the rust and decay was all that held the hinges together?

At the back of the room, the dust cloud thinned. Pulling

his handkerchief away from his face, Perry dug at the wall, his hands uncovering the outline of a metal box hidden in a recess in the stone. "Help me."

Sliding alongside him, she worked to uncover more of the box. Once the dirt was removed, Adelaide was shocked by its condition. Untouched for several lifetimes, it looked new. In its center, Perry used his thumbnail to expose a keyhole. He grinned, revealing his incomplete set of uneven, black-tipped teeth.

"Hold the light still," he commanded her.

The pounding on the door intensified. Plumes of dust snaked back to the rear of the safe room.

Perry inserted the smaller key into the lock and turned.

The key snapped off at its midsection.

Disbelief spread across Perry's face like a falling shadow.

Adelaide reached down for the wooden handle tethered to her belt. She tightened her hand around the shaft, tore it free, and brought the mallet up over her head. Perry had just enough time to open his mouth in surprise before she brought the hammer down on the side of his face. Bone shattered. Perry staggered back, dropping the key ring.

"I sawed that key down last night," she told him as he held his head and scooted across the floor, away from her. One hand darted into his coat for his .22. Adelaide pulled her gun first, freezing him in place.

Stuttering, his mouth quivered as he spoke. *"We c-c-c-oulda been r-r-rrich..."*

"Can't buy happiness, brother," she said, reaching down and taking his gun. She swung the mallet again, hitting the same spot. He screamed and kicked away, leaving a trail of blood behind. "Maybe it all ain't your fault, that's something I been thinking. Maybe it's a curse, our family, y'know? Maybe we have no choice but to play the damned thing out."

As Perry curled into a fetal ball, Adelaide dropped the mallet. Perry had used it to kill so many of her pets, but now its killing days were over. She strode into the whirling surf of airborne dust, reaching down to retrieve the key ring as she moved. She didn't bother to cover her mouth or nose. Inhaling, she took a deep drag from her family's history. She tasted blood, fear, desperate tears, the salt of their skin against hungry lips.

Sliding the key into the door lock, she wondered if this offering of blood would pay her family's long debt. She pushed the heavy door open. The prison beyond the door was not a museum. And the distorted and tortured faces massed outside were not tourists and police officers. Spotted by blood, they wore the uniforms of Federal troops. They rushed inside, makeshift shanks and bludgeons swinging. They passed, oblivious to her, and descended on Perry. He screamed as they overtook him.

Stepping through the doorway, Adelaide ran a hand over her stomach, closed the door, and wondered whether she should consider the child within her to be her son, or her brother.

—Ramsey Campbell

The *Oxford Companion to English Literature* describes Ramsey Campbell as "Britain's most respected living horror writer". He has been given more awards than any other writer in the field, including the Grand Master Award of the World Horror Convention, the Lifetime Achievement Award of the Horror Writers Association and the Living Legend Award of the International Horror Guild. Among his novels are *The Face That Must Die*, *Incarnate*, *Midnight Sun*, *The Count of Eleven*, *Silent Children*, *The Darkest Part of the Woods*, *The Overnight*, *Secret Story*, *The Grin of the Dark*, *Thieving Fear*, *Creatures of the Pool*, *The Seven Days of Cain* and *Ghosts Know*. Forthcoming is *The Kind Folk*. His collections include *Waking Nightmares*, *Alone with the Horrors*, *Ghosts and Grisly Things*, *Told by the Dead* and *Just Behind You*, and his non-fiction is collected as *Ramsey Campbell, Probably*. His novels *The Nameless* and *Pact of the Fathers* have been filmed in Spain. His regular columns appear in *Prism*, *All Hallows*, *Dead Reckonings* and *Video Watchdog*. He is the President of the British Fantasy Society and of the Society of Fantastic Films.

Ramsey Campbell lives on Merseyside with his wife Jenny. His pleasures include classical music, good food and wine, and whatever's in that pipe. His web site is at www.ramseycampbell.com

—DEAD LETTERS

By Ramsey Campbell

The séance was Bob's idea, of course. We'd finished dinner and were lighting more candles to stave off the effects of the power cut when he made the suggestion. "What's the point? The apartment's only three years old," Joan said, though in fact she was disturbed by this threat of a séance in our home. But he'd brought his usual bottle of Pernod to the dinner party, inclining it toward us as if he'd forgotten that nobody else touched the stuff, and now he was drunk enough to believe he could carry us unprotesting with him. He almost did. When opposition came, it surprised me as much as it did Bob.

"I'm not joining in," his wife Louise said. "I won't."

I could feel one of his rages building, though usually they didn't need to be provoked. "Is this some more of your stupidity we have to suffer?" he said. "Don't you know what everyone in this room is thinking of you?"

"I'm not sure you do," I told him sharply. I could see Stan and Marge were embarrassed. I'd thought Bob might behave himself when meeting them for the first time.

He peered laboriously at me, his face white and sweating as if from a death battle with the Pernod. "One thing's sure," he said. "If she doesn't know what I think of her, she will for the next fortnight."

I glared at him. He and Louise were bound for France in the morning to visit her relatives; the tickets were poking out of his top pocket. We'd made this dinner date with them weeks ago—as usual, to relieve Louise's burdens of Bob and of the demands of her work as a nurse—and as if to curtail the party Bob had brought their flight date forward. I imagined her having to travel with Bob's hangover. But at least she looked in control for the moment, sitting in a chair near the apartment door, away from the round dining table. "Sit down, everybody," Bob said. "Before someone else cracks up."

From his briefcase where he kept the Pernod he produced a device that he slid into the middle of the table, his unsteady hand slipping and almost flinging his toy to the floor. I wondered what had happened in the weeks since I'd last seen him, so to lessen his ability to hold his drink; he'd been in this state when they arrived. As a rule he contrived to drink for much of the day at work, with little obvious effect except to make him more unpleasant to Louise. Perhaps alcoholism had overtaken him at last.

The device was a large glass inside which a small electric flashlight sat on top of another glass. Bob switched on the flashlight and pressed in a ring of cork that held the glasses together while Marge, no doubt hoping the party would quieten down, dealt around the table the alphabet Bob had written on cards. I imagined him harping on the séance to Louise as he prepared the apparatus.

"So you're not so cool as you'd like me to think," he said to her, and blew out all the candles.

I sat opposite him. Joan checked the light switch before taking her place next to me, and I knew she hoped the power would interrupt us. Bob had insinuated himself between Stan and Marge, smacking his lips as he drained his bottle. If I hadn't wanted to save them further unpleasantness I'd have opposed the whole thing.

A thick scroll of candle smoke drifted through the flashlight beam. Our brightening hands converged and rested on the glass. I felt as if our apartment had retreated now that the light was concentrated on the table. I could see only dim ovals of faces floating above the splash of light; I couldn't see

Louise at all. Silence settled on us like wax, and we waited.

After what seemed a considerable time I began to feel, absurdly perhaps, that it was my duty as host to start things moving. I'd been involved in a few séances and knew the general principles; since Bob was unusually quiet I would have to lead. "Is anybody there?" I said. "Anyone there? Anybody there?"

"Sounds like you've got a bad line," said Stan.

"Shouldn't you say here rather than there?" Marge said.

"I'll try that," I said. "Is anyone here? Anybody here?"

I was still waiting for Stan to play me for a stooge again when Bob's hand began to tremble convulsively on the glass. "You're just playing the fool," Joan said, but I was no more certain than she really was, because from what I could distinguish of Bob's indistinct face I could see he was staring fixedly ahead, though not at me. "What is it? What's the matter?" I said, afraid both that he sensed something and that he was about to reveal the whole situation as an elaborate joke.

Then the glass began to move.

I'd seen it happen at séances before, but never quite like this. The glass was making aimless darting starts in all directions, like an animal that had suddenly found itself caged. It seemed frantic and bewildered, and in a strange way its blind struggling beneath our fingers reminded me of the almost mindless fluttering of hands near to death. "Stop playing the fool," Joan said to Bob, but I was becoming certain that he wasn't, all the more so when he didn't answer.

Then the glass made a rush for the edge of the table, so fast that my fingers would have been left behind if our fingertips hadn't been pressed so closely together that they carried each other along. The light swooped on the letter I and held it for what felt like minutes. It returned to the centre of the table, drawing our luminous orange fingertips with it, then swept back to the I. And again. I. I. I.

"Aye aye, Cap'n," Stan said.

"He doesn't know who he is," Marge whispered.

"Who are you?" I said. "Can you tell us your name?"

The glass inched toward the centre. Then, as if terrified to find itself out in the darkness, it fled back to the I. Thinking of what Marge had said, I had an image of someone awakening in total darkness, woken by us perhaps, trying to remember anything about himself, even his name. I felt unease: Joan's unease, I told myself. "Can you tell us anything about yourself?" I said.

The glass seemed to be struggling again, almost to be forcing itself into the centre. Once there it sat shifting restlessly. The light reached toward letters, then flinched away. At last it began to edge out. I felt isolated with the groping light, cut off even from Joan beside me, as if the light were drawing on me for strength. I didn't know if anyone else felt this, nor whether they also had an oppressive sense of terrible effort. The light began to nudge letters, fumbling before it came to rest on each. MUD, it spelled.

"His name's mud!" Stan said delightedly.

But the glass hadn't finished. R, it added.

"Hello Mudr, hello Fadr," Stan said.

"Murder," Marge said. "He could be trying to say murder."

"If he's dead he should be old enough to spell."

I had an impression of bursting frustration, of a suffocated swelling fury. I felt a little like that myself, because Stan was annoying me. I'd ceased to feel Joan's unease; I was engrossed. "Do you mean murder?" I said. "Who's been murdered?"

Again came the frustration, like the leaden shell of a storm. Incongruously, I remembered my own thwarted fury when I was trying to learn to type. The light began to wobble and glide, and the oppression seemed to clench until I had to soothe my forehead as best I could with my free hand. "Oh my head," Marge said.

"Shall we stop?" said Joan.

"Not yet," Marge said, because the light seemed to have gained confidence and was swinging from one letter to another. POISN, it spelled.

"Six out of ten," Stan said. "Could do better."

"Shut up, Stan," Marge said.

"I beg your pardon? You're not taking this nonsense seriously? Because if that's what we're doing, deal me out."

The glass was shuddering now and clutching letters rapidly with its beam. "Please, Stan," Marge said. "Say it's a game, then. If you sit out now you won't be able to discuss it afterwards."

DSLOLY, the glass had been shouting. "Poisoned slowly," Stan translated. "Very clever, Bob. You can stop it now."

"I don't think it is Bob," I said.

"What is it then, a ghost? Don't be absurd. Come on then, ghost. If you're here let's see you."

I heard Marge stop herself saying "Don't!" I felt Joan grow tense, felt the oppression crushed into a last straining effort. Then I heard a click from the apartment door.

Suddenly the darkness felt more crowded. I began to peer into the apartment beyond the light, slowly in an attempt not to betray to Joan what I was doing, but I was blinded by the glass. I caught sight of Stan and knew by the tilt of his head that he'd realised he might be upsetting Louise. "Sorry, Louise," he called and lifted his face ceilingward as he realised that could only make the situation worse.

Then the glass seemed to gather itself and began to dart among the letters. We all knew that it was answering Stan's challenge. We held ourselves still, only our exhausted hands swinging about the table like parts of a machine. When the glass halted at last we'd all separated out the words of the answer. WHEN LIGHT COMS ON, it said.

"I want to stop now," Joan said.

"All right," I said. "I'll light the candles."

But she'd gripped my hand. "I'll do it," Stan said. "I've got some matches." And he'd left the table, and we were listening to the rhythm he was picking out with his shaken matches as he groped into the enormous surrounding darkness, when the lights came on.

We'd all heard the sound of the door but hadn't admitted

it, and we all blinked first in that direction. The door was closed. It took a few seconds for us to realise there was no sign of Louise. I think I was the first to look at Bob, sitting grinning opposite me behind his empty bottle of Pernod. My mind must have been thinking faster than consciously, because I knew before I pulled it out that there was only one ticket in his pocket, perhaps folded to look like two by Louise as she laid out his suit. Bob just grinned at me and gazed, until Stan closed his eyes.

—WRATH JAMES WHITE

Wrath James White is a former World Class Heavyweight Kickboxer, a professional Kickboxing and Mixed Martial Arts trainer, bodybuilder, distance runner, performance artist, and former street brawler, who is now known for creating some of the most disturbing works of fiction in print.

Wrath is the author of *The Resurrectionist*, *Succulent Prey*, *Yaccub's Curse*, *His Pain*, *The Book of A Thousand Sins*, *Population Zero*, *Sloppy Seconds*, *Everyone Dies Famous In A Small Town*, *Sacrifice*, *Pure Hate*, *Like Porno For Psychos*, *The Reaper*, and *SKINZZ*. He is the co-author of *Teratologist* with Edward Lee, *Orgy of Souls* with Maurice Broaddus, *Hero* with J.F. Gonalez, and *Poisoning Eros* with Monica J. O'Rourke.

—THE MONSTER IN THE DRAWER

By Wrath James White

Elizabeth's house was an old colonial row home that was over two centuries old and not carrying its age well at all. It was bowed and stooped, ready to cave in upon itself. The house was in need of a total remodeling or, at the very least, a paint job. It still had flecks of white lead paint clinging to the crumbling red brick from its last paint job, sometime during World War I. Five generations had fought, struggled, suffered, and died behind those walls. The home had known few smiles in the two centuries it had stood on this block and even fewer celebrations. This was a house that had grown accustomed to sorrow.

The house's dour, dilapidated visage reflected the history, misery, and depression of its inhabitants. It was the architectural equivalent of the picture of Dorian Gray. Its own decay mirroring the gradual necrosis of those who resided within.

It took only a glance at the collapsing roof, shuttered and boarded up windows, cracked and crumbling concrete porch, and faded, deteriorating brick facade to know that this was not a place of good fortune. Happiness did not grow in the shadows of haunted buildings. It was far too dark to nurture flowers.

This was the house where widows sat in windows waiting in vain for soldiers to come back from war. It was the house where women died during childbirth. It was the house where children played with broken toys and tried to keep their minds off the hunger in their bellies and the sounds of spousal abuse coming from the next room. The house where prayers went unanswered and parents cried themselves to sleep. To Elizabeth, even decorated in Christmas ornaments, her house looked funereal, like a corpse in a party dress.

Everyone knew that ghosts and monsters lived there. *Haunted* was a word Elizabeth had often heard used to describe both her house and its inhabitants. Even the bravest kids refused to pass in front of it during the day or night, stepping off the sidewalk and into the street rather than risk something reaching out from one of the dark, shuttered windows to snatch them inside.

Elizabeth knew why they were afraid. It was because of the monster. The monster that lived with them in the house, the one that had always lived there.

She could hear the young kids passing below her window, daring one another to go up and ring the doorbell. No one would take the dare. The most they would do is come back in the dead of night to throw eggs at the door. No one ever came to visit Elizabeth except to mourn some tragedy or another. She and her family lived in the morbid old house in relative isolation. Just her family and the monster.

Today, Elizabeth was in mourning—kind of. Her baby brother had stopped breathing while lying in his crib the previous night. Family, friends, and relatives braved the frigid temperature outside, trudging through the snow in their heavy winter coats and boots to pay their condolences. They sulked around the drafty old house with shocked, grief-stricken faces, consoling her widowed mother over the loss of her son and ignoring Elizabeth as they always had. Dressed in black, with their sad, pale faces and stunned, hollow eyes, many of the mourners looked as if they were on their way to a masquerade ball. Like they had dressed as vampires and ghouls and were detoured on their way to the party and had simply worn their costumes here, using only a slight alteration in makeup to change their appearances from horrific to tragic. Elizabeth wanted to believe that her relatives took this death as casually as she did, but she knew that wasn't the case. Billy had been greatly loved. The anguished expressions on her relatives were genuine. Store-bought make-up would not have been so convincing.

They called it SIDS, Sudden Infant Death Syndrome.

Though, at three years old, her brother Billy was not quite an infant. No one could make sense of how a healthy toddler could simply stop breathing suddenly. But Elizabeth knew. The monster had gotten him.

She'd heard the creature's mad gibbering coming from her brother's room just as the last episode of the Twilight Zone-a-thon had gone off the air. She'd heard its overgrown toenails scrape the floor and seen its twisted shadow slither across the wall as it made its way down the hall toward Billy's room. She had just dozed off and it had awakened her as she lay in bed with her door locked and the TV flickering blue phantoms across the walls.

Elizabeth had never heard the creature laugh before. She'd never heard it make any sound at all until recently. Still, as soon as she'd heard the high-pitched tittering echoing through the house, she'd known it was the monster. The sound of its ghastly mirth made her skin feel too loose on her as if a draft had slipped beneath it.

She didn't know how it had gotten out. It usually required her to help it out of the drawer. She hated touching it, but its loneliness called to her. Elizabeth understood what it was like to be alone. She knew what it was like to be ugly and unloved. So she often took it out to play with it. She liked to see the hideous little thing smile up at her as she sang to it. When it was happy, that twinkle in its eye almost made it look beautiful. At least to Elizabeth it did. She liked that it needed her. Elizabeth had never felt wanted before, let alone needed. But without her, the monster was almost helpless, or so she'd thought, until her Daddy died.

During the day it shunned the sunlight and hid in her vanity drawer. She'd never really seen the thing leave on its own, but she knew it had. Sometimes she'd be half-asleep in the middle of the night and would hear it scurrying about. Mostly she would see the aftermath of its nightly jaunts when she awoke in the morning to find things smashed or misplaced. She'd often wondered how it could seem so passive and docile during the day, yet at night, when she slept, it would burst free from her vanity and wreak havoc all about the house, throwing and breaking things, leaving a mess for her to clean up. Sometimes, she would hear it out in the hall just beyond her door, throwing a tantrum. It sounded so angry, so violent. Elizabeth would hide under the covers until it stopped. She wouldn't move until the thing had crawled back into her drawer and gone to sleep. Then she'd wake up and stare in awe at the holes in the drywall where it had punched or kicked straight through the plaster, the furniture now reduced to kindling.

Her mother and father never believed the monster could be dangerous either. They always blamed the destruction on Elizabeth.

Sometimes, Elizabeth awoke to find her parents tiptoeing around her, casting nervous and fearful glances in her direction. Often they sported bruises and scratches. Elizabeth knew the monster had attacked them in the night. She wanted to prove it to them, but she didn't want them to take it away from her. It was the only thing that listened to her. The only thing that really loved her. So instead, she bore the blame for its violence and vandalism and watched as her parents drifted further away from her behind a wall of fear and mistrust. Daddy had learned all about the monster though.

He'd staggered home drunk one night and began abusing Elizabeth's mother as he did every Friday night after payday. When Elizabeth shrieked at the top of her lungs for him to leave her mommy alone he had come after her.

"Stop hurting my mommy! Go away! Leave us alone!"

Her father was a large man with big, calloused hands hardened by years working as a brick mason. He'd clamped those hands on Elizabeth's throat and pushed her back into her room onto her bed. He'd done more than beat her that night. She had bled for two days afterward. On the third evening, the monster came out. They'd found her father torn to shreds at the foot of the stairs.

A terrific pool of blood filled the foyer with a thick strawberry pulp containing chunks of torn and masticated flesh. Shattered bone stuck out from the numerous lacerations and avulsions gleaming white against the savaged red meat. His face was the only part of him left unmarred, the expression contorted into a gruesome rictus of purest agony and terror suggesting that he'd been alive through much of the ordeal. By the time the police came, the rats had already gone to work on him. They'd been having a serious pest problem that winter. The police detectives investigating the murder said that some of the local drug fiends had probably broken in and attacked him and that he'd more than likely died trying to protect Elizabeth and her mother. Elizabeth knew better. It had been the monster and it had only come for Daddy, to punish him for hurting her.

The police found her covered in blood at the foot of the stairs, cradling her father's head while the rats splashed around in his blood, retrieving choice bits of his internal organs from the tacky red effluence.

"Daddy? Wake up, Daddy. Wake up. I'll make breakfast. I'll...I'll make eggs and bacon and...and—wake up, Daddy! Wake up!"

No one believed her about the monster. She heard her mother whisper to the police officer that Elizabeth was functionally autistic. She had difficulty staying in the present, distinguishing things in her mind from things in the real world. Most of the time, she appeared normal, but then she'd lapse into a fugue from which it was nearly impossible to rouse her. She'd often found that days would go by without her remembering a thing she'd done or said. They took her father's head from her and sent her upstairs to her room to wash up.

No one bothered to check Elizabeth's drawer. They all laughed at the monster. But Elizabeth knew it was in there and it was getting stronger. It no longer needed her help to get out of the drawer.

Elizabeth knew the monster was getting jealous. It had whispered to her constantly in the weeks prior to her brother's death. It told her it was going to kill the little brat. Elizabeth could hear its voice in her head. Well, not exactly its voice, but its intentions; the violent fury of emotion boiling off it. It didn't like the fact that so much attention was being lavished on little

Billy while everyone seemed to have forgotten that Elizabeth even existed. The monster loved Elizabeth. The monster loved her because she understood it. It was as lonely as she was and needed her company as desperately as she did. It wanted to protect her; to make her happy. So she locked her bedroom door every night to make sure it wouldn't get out like it had the night Daddy died. Still, somehow it had gotten out. Now Billy was dead.

Everything died in this house. Elizabeth stared up at the water stains spreading across the ceiling from year after year of roof leaks and wondered how long they had before the trusses finally rotted away and the entire structure collapsed and crushed them all to death or entombed them alive. She knew it was only a matter of time. Elizabeth looked over at the drawer and it began to rattle and shake as if the thing could sense her staring at it. She had no doubt that the monster would survive when the house finally swallowed them all. This was the perfect house for monsters.

The monster in the drawer was the only friend Elizabeth had left. She often talked to it when she was lonely. And she was always lonely. It talked back to her telepathically or rather she interpreted its body language. She wasn't sure which, but somehow she understood the mute and hideous thing. It mouthed words silently in imitation of her speech but no sound ever issued from its lips, except for that horrible laughter, at night, when it was angry. Still, she'd known of its plans for her baby brother and she'd done nothing to stop it, told no one, and now Billy was dead and a part of her was happy. Even though she was still ignored as Billy's memory took on a presence more vast than he could have ever achieved in life. The thing had martyred him.

Elizabeth watched her mother wail in exaggerated grief as friends and family rushed to console her. Elizabeth knew that her mother's guilt was a selfish one. Now that Billy, with his beautiful blond curly hair, big, blue, puppy-dog eyes, and flawless, tanned, and healthy skin, was dead, there was no longer any proof of her mother's lost beauty. Billy had been the only evidence that remained of her long-faded good looks besides the yellowing photographs on the mantle. Looking at the withered and wrinkled shell, with the hard, bitter, hollow eyes of a prisoner of war, no one would've ever connected her mother with the lovely, vibrant, young bride smiling in those ancient photos, and looking at Elizabeth would've been no help in the matter. Rocking back and forth, staring at herself in the mirror and drooling for hours, lost in her own mind. Elizabeth knew she was no beauty queen.

Her hair was a tangled and knotted nest that stuck out on all sides like a wooly afro and her skin was covered in pimples, which she'd picked until they bled, became infected, and eventually scabbed over. Her eyes were nervous and agitated and flew about in her head when she wasn't zoning out and staring off into the distance, focused intently on nothing. She was a poor reflection of her mother's former comeliness; a distorted mockery, like a funhouse mirror.

Elizabeth had yet to shed a tear over her dead brother and everyone seemed to be waiting for her sorrow to erupt in a hysterical torrent. They kept casting glances her way, trying to catch the exact moment when the outburst would come. The longer they continued to peek at her in expectation without reward, the more their anticipation turned to stern judgment. *"Didn't she care at all?"* they seemed to be asking. *"Didn't she love her brother? Won't she miss him? Maybe she doesn't understand? She's retarded, isn't she? The poor thing."*

"No, I won't miss him! I hated him!" Elizabeth wanted to scream. Instead she turned and walked back into her bedroom, slamming the door with a loud bang. She opened the top drawer of her vanity and stared in at the hideous creature lurking within.

"They all hate me," she said and the thing mouthed her words back at her in uncomprehending silence. She didn't care whether or not the thing understood her. At least it listened.

As she stared, the monster began to cry. It was crying for Billy. She didn't understand. Billy had done nothing to earn its love. Billy was an annoying pest...had been. Billy had stolen all the love Elizabeth should have received from her mother, her aunts, and uncles. Billy had deserved to die. A torrent of tears streamed down the monster's face.

"Stop it! Stop crying! Stop it!" She screamed and shook the helpless little monster, trying to stifle its tears.

"You killed him! You killed Billy! You shook him until he turned blue! I saw you! I saw you do it! Why the hell are you crying for him? Stop crying," she screamed as she continued to shake the silent, grief-stricken thing.

She could still hear the laughter of kids out playing in the street below; building snowmen, forts, and tunnels, having snowball fights, oblivious to the death and madness festering just beyond their sight. None of them knew about monsters that fed on hatred and turned against abusive fathers and innocent boys in the dead of night. They avoided the shadow of her doorstep so that they would never know about such things. So they'd never have to see a monster cry over its dead brother.

Elizabeth's bedroom door banged open and her mother entered followed by her uncles, aunts, and cousins. They covered their faces in horror and pity as Elizabeth continued to cry, and scream, and shake the little mirror.

—TRACIE MCBRIDE

Tracie McBride is a New Zealander who lives in Melbourne, Australia with her husband and three children. Her work has appeared or is forthcoming in over 70 print and electronic publications, including Horror *Library*, *Volumes 4* and *5*, *Dead Red Heart* and *Phobophobia*. Her debut collection *Ghosts Can Bleed* contains much of the work that earned her a Sir Julius Vogel Award in 2008. She helps to wrangle slush for *Dark Moon Digest* and is the vice president of Dark Continents Publishing. She welcomes visitors to her blog at www.traciemcbridewriter.wordpress.com

—BAPTISM

By Tracie McBride

Brother Tomas drew his habit tightly around himself, a futile gesture against the biting sea wind. He eyed the tiny island in the middle of the bay that would be his new home. He had been in Koreka for less than half a day, and already he was homesick for the Secoduna Desert. His superiors had decreed that he be sent here, and they took their instruction directly from God, but sometimes he wondered if they might not occasionally be mistaken in their interpretation. *Have faith, Brother,* he silently chastised himself. Surely, this was no mistake; if anyone could succeed where others had failed, it would be him.

"You're the fourth friar I've rowed out there in as many months," said Mellie, the rawboned young woman who had been assigned as his escort. She gripped the oars with two wind chapped, meaty hands and leaned back, sending the little boat surging against the wavelets. "But I didn't row any of them back, not alive, leastways. What makes you think you'll do better?"

"Greater experience, true devotion to, and faith in, Our Lord, and a plentiful supply of chasteberry tea." Tomas smiled and patted his rucksack. His smile faded as he sniffed the air. "What's that smell?"

Mellie looked over her shoulder. A large log bobbed in the water several feet away. Mellie grinned humourlessly and rowed harder until they grew level with the object. A ripe, overwhelming stench rose from it. The "log" had a face.

The corpse floated on its back, its eye sockets empty and its mouth open to the sky. It still wore its shirt, cravat and jacket, but was naked from the waist down. Its groin was a ragged mess of tattered, bloodless flesh. Tomas retched and covered his mouth and nose with his sleeve.

"What's the matter, Brother?" said Mellie. "Haven't you ever seen a dead man before?"

"I've dealt with many bodies, but they were all..."

"Less chewed?"

"I was going to say *drier.*"

"You'd better get used to it. Most of them wash up on your island." Mellie picked up a pike, hooked it through the dead man's shirt and dragged it to the side of the boat. With a grunt, she hauled it over the side and dropped it at Tomas's feet, sending up a fresh miasma of decay.

"They all think they can withstand the lure of the mermaids' song. We try to warn them, but..." She shook her head.

"...but if you tried too hard, it might be bad for business," Tomas finished. With all the able-bodied menfolk of the town either dead or moved away, their traditional livelihood of fishing was defunct, their nets left to rot on the shore. Perversely, the town thrived, their boats converted from functional fishing vessels to pleasure craft as men flocked from all parts of the country. Most came seeking to satisfy their prurient curiosity, some came to challenge themselves, but save for a few wretched suicides, they all expected to live to tell the tale.

But Tomas was not here for those misguided men. He was here to save the mermaids' immortal souls.

As if in response to his thoughts, a dozen sleek heads broke the surface of the water within arm's length of the boat. Mellie hissed and smacked at the mermaids with her oar. They hissed back and retreated to a safer distance.

"They like to hang around and gloat when we bring in a body, the filthy bitches." She spat into the sea. Her spittle rested for an instant on the surface before dissipating. "Pardon my language, Brother."

Tomas barely heard her. He crossed himself as the mermaids encircled the boat, his eyes never leaving them. He had been told that there were no mermen, and that in the absence of available human partners, mermaids coupled with other sea creatures. Indeed, he could see evidence of this in their features; one had a fat round face that bristled with spikes, suggesting she had been sired by a puffer fish. Another, with her tiny little black eyes set wide on either side of an elongated face, was undoubtedly the offspring of a shark. The impression intensified as she opened her mouth and gave a gurgling approximation of a human laugh, displaying three rows of razor sharp teeth.

He had also been told that, even when they were not singing, the mermaids exuded a malignant glamour, and that to be in close proximity with one was to experience temptation on an almost unbearable scale. His manhood stiffened and pressed against his breechclout, and he shuffled painfully in his seat, anxious to conceal it from Mellie. He had resisted the advances of many a bejewelled Secoduna beauty, yet one look at these creatures and he had to grip the sides of the boat to stop from flinging himself into the water.

"A new man of God!" the shark-like one said. Her voice bubbled like slow-boiling porridge, and Tomas's stomach roiled. "I do hope you will be as...entertaining as the last ones." Her tail undulated, propelling her torso above the water's surface, and she flung back her long black hair to thrust her breasts at him.

Nobody had told him about the gills.

A line of red-tinged slits ran down each flank, pulsating gently in time to the rise and fall of the mermaid's chest. He clutched his rosary beads, closed his eyes and muttered a fervent prayer.

"You're wasting your time," said Mellie. "Praying isn't going to save you—ask any widow in Koreka. The mermaids aren't children of God, they're the spawn of the Devil. And the sooner the Church realises that, the sooner you can stop trying to save their souls and start exterminating them like the vermin they are." She scowled and bent again to her rowing.

"I'd better get you to your island. It's nearly sundown, and I've still got a corpse to bury."

* * *

Tomas's island sloped sharply upwards to a peak in its centre, too steep for him to climb unaided. It was covered in drab, low-lying fruitless scrub, and took less than an hour for him to circumnavigate on foot. Based on the reports from his predecessors, Tomas expected the mermaids to immediately commence a campaign to seduce him, but for several days he was left alone. The only evidence of their presence was a daily offering of freshly caught fish left on the end of the small jetty near his hut. It was while he was collecting this gift one morning that the mermaids resurfaced, by which time he was almost glad to see them.

"Good morning, ladies," he said, inclining his head, and taking care to stand out of reach of their taloned hands. "My name is Brother Tomas Santoyo. Might I inquire as to your names?" The arousal he had felt when he first encountered them washed over him anew. He swayed slightly, dizzy and weak-kneed with lust.

The shark-faced one, evidently their leader, swam forward. She held a hunk of flesh in one hand, and from time to time took delicate bites from it. Tomas could not tell what kind of meat it was.

"My name is Sh'Teth," she said. She named the others in rapid-fire, sibilant mertongue.

"And who is that?" Tomas indicated a small fair-haired mermaid a short distance away at the back of the pod.

"Her? Oh, she is nobody—just a slave we captured."

The mermaid in question swam forward. Unlike most of the others, she looked strikingly like a human female. Whipped by the wind, her fine hair was already almost dry, revealing itself to be a fetching golden blonde. Her father must have been a handsome man, *God rest his soul*, thought Tomas. The mermaid looked up at him with wide blue eyes. As she bobbed in the water, Tomas noticed that her belly was swollen, evidently in the later stages of pregnancy.

"Basha," she said. "My name is Basha."

Sh'Teth snarled, spun on Basha, and struck a vicious open-handed blow across her face. She growled something in mertongue that made the smaller mermaid cringe and retreat, clutching a bleeding bottom lip.

"Pay no attention to her," said Sh'Teth, waving her gory repast at Tomas. "She is lucky we let her live."

"What are you eating?" he asked.

"Baby," she replied. She held the meat outstretched to him on her two upturned palms. "Would you like some?"

At first, he thought that he had misheard her. Then he saw a small white bone protruding from one end of the offering, three tiny fingers on the other, and two pink oozing stumps where the missing digits should be. The blood drained from his face. He stumbled backward in horror and dropped to his hands and knees on the deck. He dug his fingers into the boards and retched.

"Please tell me that child was already dead when you found it," he gasped.

"Of course it wasn't," said Sh'Teth, looking offended. "We are hunters, not scavengers. We took it from another pod last night."

"Then it's not...not human?"

"Oh, Brother Tomas, we would never eat a human baby. That would be a sin."

For a moment Tomas felt a glimmer of hope. If the mermaids had some concept of sin, even a grotesquely distorted concept such as this, then perhaps his predecessors' work had not been entirely in vain.

The mermaids burst into laughter. They were making sport of their heinous crime, and what was worse, they were mocking him. He raised his head and watched, his eyes filled with tears, as they slapped the water with their tails and swam away. Only Basha did not laugh. She trailed behind the others and looked back at him, her face incandescent with sorrow.

* * *

Tomas sat on the end of the jetty and swung his legs like a child. He closed his eyes and turned his face up to the sun. It was moments like these, quiet and pure and simple, when he could almost feel the presence of God.

Almost.

A familiar flood of lust washed over him, and he opened his eyes to see just a gleaming head. No, two heads, he thought with a smile—Basha held a tiny merbaby in her arms. The child was golden-haired, like her mother. Her chubby little hands flailed against Basha's breast as she suckled noisily. Basha swam in tight circles just out of reach of the end of the jetty and made a nervous humming noise in the back of her throat.

"What is it, Basha?"

"I'm not supposed to be here," she said. "If Sh'teth knew..."

"Well, then, we won't tell her." He smiled to reassure her. "Congratulations on the birth of your baby. She is beautiful. What have you named her?"

"That is why I've come to you. The last Brother said that if we were to baptise our babies, then they would go to Heaven." She lowered her head to gaze lovingly at her child. "I like the sound of Heaven," she said, her voice barely louder than a whisper. "It sounds so much better than here."

"I would be honoured to do so," said Tomas. "But she will need a good Christian name. I think I shall call her Constance."

Basha swam closer and held the baby up to Tomas. She was so close to him now, close enough to touch, and he only had to shift his weight forward a little more to join her in the water...

She all but threw her baby into his arms and hastily swam away, as if she feared his touch would burn. Tomas let out a breath, grateful for the minor respite from Basha's glamour. He scooped up handfuls of sea water to sprinkle over the baby's head.

"Constance, I baptize you in the Name of the Father, and of the Son, and of the Holy Spirit."

He felt a little like a fisherman releasing an undersized

catch as he lowered the wriggling infant into the sea and sent her swimming back to her mother.

* * *

Tomas had been on the island for five months, a new record for Koreka missionaries, and he had received a letter from the bishop congratulating him for his piety and fortitude. But Tomas was not celebrating; the mermaids were singing tonight. A string of lights bobbed in the bay as a small flotilla of boats set sail from the mainland to meet them. Most of the men aboard would be bound to a post to prevent them from jumping overboard, but there were always a few wanting to pit their will against the mermaids'. No doubt Tomas would be towing their mangled corpses up the beach in a few days' time.

Sighing, he turned back to his scriptures. He could not sleep while the mermaids sang. He drank chasteberry tea until his tongue was stained blue, stuffed his ears with wads of cotton against their high-pitched wordless wail, and prayed until his knees were bruised, yet still he shook with the effort of keeping his feet on the sand. When they finally fell silent, he knew his dreams would be plagued with visions of their inviting arms, their high, pale breasts, their throbbing, incarnadine gills...

He shook himself like a dog shedding water. The words in front of him ran together into nonsense. He pushed the book aside. It hit the floor, sending up a small cloud of dust. He left it where it lay and took up a pen and parchment.

Dear Bishop Lucian

Thank you for your recent letter. Your words of faith and encouragement were most welcome to me. However, I have come to the conclusion that our mission here at Koreka is one of greatest folly.

Despite the mermaids' superficial resemblance to human women, and their facility with the English language, my work has led me to believe that they are more of the order of beasts of the field and the jungle than of fully sentient creatures capable of receiving the full Grace of God.

Some of the mermaids show evidence of intelligence, comparable even to their feminine two-legged counterparts, and I have been able to engage in some rudimentary theological discussions with them. Perhaps, in time, I might even be able to dissuade them from some of their more abhorrent practices, such as their aggression towards other mermaid pods and their cannibalistic tendencies. Regrettably, it is their means of reproduction that provides the greatest barrier to salvation. Their base nature compels them to seek profane unions with human men, and occasionally lesser sea creatures. They have rejected all attempts to persuade them to live in holy matrimony, and with good reason; removed from the sea, they fail to thrive, and pine away to death in a matter of months. And of course, it is impossible for a human man to live in their environment. They are no more capable of choosing a life of chastity and fidelity than the wolf is capable of choosing not to eat the lamb.

I therefore request that the Koreka mission be closed down, and that I be assigned to a new post where I might be more usefully employed in the service of our Lord.

Your humble servant,

Brother Tomas Santoyo

Tomas read over his letter. He had held high hopes for converting Basha, but since the baptism, she had kept her distance from him, as if she were afraid that he might betray her to the rest of the pod. Surely, he thought, this was the most sensible course of action, for himself, for the Church, for the mermaids...yet he hesitated before putting his seal upon the letter.

Perhaps the mermaids *did* need him. Perhaps he was all that stood in the way of their certain extermination. For if his superiors were to believe his account and were to reconsider the mermaids' status, they surely would not suffer them to live. As much as he despised the mermaids' way of life, he was not prepared to sign their death warrant.

A loud female voice, clearly audible even through his ear plugs, shook him from his reverie.

"Tomas! Please, Tomas, help me!"

Tomas tore the cotton from his ears, snatched up a lamp,

and ran outside. He clattered down the jetty and skidded to a halt. Basha clung to the boards. Deep scratches striped her face and body, her blood glistening almost black in the flickering lamp light.

"We were attacked by another pod...the others escaped, but I was too slow...Tomas, they killed Constance!"

"Oh, Basha..."

Her pain and despair was palpable. Without thinking, Tomas prostrated himself on the jetty and wrapped an arm around her shoulders, drawing her into an awkward embrace. He sought only to comfort her, but the touch of his skin on hers intensified the mermaid's allure beyond his ability to resist. He turned his head and pressed his open mouth to hers. His heart seemed to stop in his chest as she returned his kiss.

Then she grabbed him by the shoulders and pulled. She was strong, freakishly strong, and he offered no resistance as he slid into the water. He clasped Basha to him, and their combined weight dragged them slowly down. Basha wriggled away from him, and he had a moment to consider how lovely her hair looked as it swirled about her in the gentle current, another moment to wonder how it was that he could see her, underwater and in the dark, and then he was shooting skyward.

He drew a deep, shuddering breath as he broke the surface. His lamp had tipped over and set the jetty alight. The heat from the mermaid's kiss flowed outward from his lips to infuse his entire body, mirroring the fire. The flames cast a ruddy glow over the water as they licked at the spilt oil and raced along the boards.

It was as if he were seeing fire for the first time. The flames bowed and pirouetted, seguing from the palest yellow to vivid orange to arterial red; their own hushed roar the song to which they danced. The sea lapped gently at his shoulders, caressing him through his sodden robes as he treaded water. He inhaled again, savouring the scented air. Salt, seaweed, sagebrush, burning pitch, he could distinguish each aroma, yet it all combined into an exquisite perfume. Now he understood why so many men risked death to embrace the mermaids; in one instant Basha had *changed* him. She had brought him anew into the world, immersed him in sensation, she had...

She had brought him closer to God.

He wept. Basha came to him to drink his tears, catching each drop on the tip of her tongue. The sea rippled around him in a dozen different places as Sh'teth and her pod rose to take their turns embracing him. In the dimmest regions of his lust-fogged mind, he wondered if they had used Basha as bait to lure him into the water. Once this would have enraged him, but now it no longer seemed to matter.

He wept as the mermaids' caresses became more insistent. They tugged and tore at his robe and undergarments until he floated naked, and they adorned him with their own bare flesh. He wept as they took their pleasure of him, holding him submerged until he reached the brink of unconsciousness, then allowing him the briefest of respites before dragging him under again. He wept as his own climaxes ripped him apart and reassembled him in strange new ways. Even as the mermaids took him down for the final time, he wept, although whether it was from the agony or the ecstasy, he could not tell.

* * *

The boat sat low in the water under Brother Alton's weight. With every lurch of the oars, water splashed over the sides, soaking the hem of his habit.

"Don't know why you're bothering," said his escort. "You can't convert the mermaids, and there are four gravestones on that island to prove it. I hear Brother Tomas even wrote a letter to the bishop telling him so—right before he died."

"If such a letter exists, then it is the property of the church, and no business of yours," he said. "In any case, Brother Tomas was weak, just like the others." He jabbed at his chest with a podgy forefinger. "Whereas I will prevail."

She raised one eyebrow, and went to speak, when there was a disturbance in the water off the prow of the boat. Alton half-stood to see what it was, sending the boat rocking.

"Welcome to Koreka, Brother," said the thing in the water.

Alton sat slack-jawed and speechless. Nothing he had read or heard about the mermaids could have prepared him for this. She was beautiful, she was terrible, she was completely, unmercifully compelling. As she lifted her body above the waves, he could already feel himself drowning.

—BOYD E. HARRIS

Boyd E. Harris is the publisher for Cutting Block Press, a small press company in Austin, Texas. His books +Horror Library+ Volumes 3 and 4 were nominated for Bram Stoker Awards for best anthology, and his anthology Tattered Souls 2 is nominated for a 2011 Bram Stoker Award.

He is a two-time Black Quill Award winning editor, one for Dark Recesses Press magazine, and one for +Horror Library+ Vol. 4.

As a writer, Boyd has seen dozens of short stories and novellas published in magazines and anthologies, and he fantasizes of a day when some avant-garde travel magazine will pay him to combine his two favorite past times—writing about horrific things and exploring exotic places—into a hair-raising series of travel adventures he'll call "Boyd's White Knuckle Tours".

—ATLANTIS PURGING

By Boyd E. Harris

They hauled it up in the shrimp nets sometime between three and four pm. The medical examiner determined that it had been submerged for six to eight months, decomposing slowly in the chilly waters of the Atlantic. Heavy currents on the Ocean's floor had shoved the torso along, until it rolled its way into East Chesapeake Bay where it was discovered. Both legs, one arm, and the head were missing. When I arrived, they were just beginning to disentangle a protruding bone of the upper arm from the shrimp net to free the remains.

But whose was it? Fingerprint and DNA tests matched it to nothing in any missing person files, and this was with the most advanced network systems in place. Investigators had direct access to the records from every city, state, and federal database in the country.

Just about the time I decided it was a dead story, the second cadaver rolled up on Buckroe Beach; but it wasn't exactly a body. It looked more like the leg quarter of a raw, cutup chicken. The hip section and most of the lower abdomen were still attached. The skin and flesh were blanched, shredded and flapping, with everything under the abdominal wall hollowed out except for eight vertebrae. The spinal column had snagged the steel support sticking out from an old concrete pier post and it swayed with the rips of the water.

I moved in close enough for a few snapshots, but nothing where I had any real good angles. Standing beyond the taped-off area, I wasn't close enough to see, but I was told later that a shark's tooth had been found lodged between two vertebrae.

Then things got interesting. Within a week, three dozen more surfaced, most of them rolling up on Buckroe beach, but a few finding their way through into Chesapeake Bay. None were whole bodies. Most were missing limbs or heads and a few had sizeable chunks gone from their legs or torsos. There were also a few individual heads, hands and feet. The heads were missing eyes, or what was left of them didn't resemble anything of the like. The noses and ears were usually scraped away from rolling along the rough Atlantic floor.

For me, it became a daily ritual to scour the three miles of Buckroe Beach just before sunup, where high tide left a line of seaweed every morning. I looked for bodies as though they were sand dollars or starfish in the prime of the combing season, hoping to happen upon the first body that would be identified. Hoping to get my ugly mug on "Good Morning America." Anything to change a lifelong string of bad luck.

This was my second attempt as a newspaper journalist. The first one had been a disappointment. I'd been a sports columnist and had pretty much pissed off all the local professional athletes. When the star players thumb their noses at you, it's time to move on to something else.

Then I took a short stint into network marketing. You know, the pyramid thing. I failed dismally at that. I figured only annoying people do these things, so I'd probably be pretty good at it, but then I realized that you have to at least have friends to make it work, and that was an area I was sorely lacking in. So I returned to the Times Herald, giving it another go, this time as a big story reporter.

At 5:40 am on July 10th, almost three weeks after the discovery of the first torso, human remains #33 was discovered by yours truly. Unfortunately, like every other discovery in this bizarre series of wash-ups, it would never be identified.

This one was just an arm with part of the shoulder section. It had washed up on the beach not two hundred yards from my condo. It was tangled in seaweed and a dozen or so sand crabs had their pinchers out, picking at it, circling it, trying to decide if there was a meal worth having.

Blanched free of the foul smell you normally get from rotting corpses and so far removed from anything that looked human, it was almost easier to think of it as a washed-up sea creature. These parts just seemed like pieces of raw chicken or pork or whatever you could conjure up in the brain to keep the actuality from seeping through.

Cable news personalities were describing people like me, what I was doing, and commenting on the callousness of it. The exposure was making the front page daily and the competition for the next big break was brutal. Newport News had become a haven for reporters, scientists, and theory specialists. Tourism gave way to freaks and wackos, and there were plenty of those to take up the slack.

One afternoon I got some close-ups of a very disturbing partial corpse. I sold my best photo of it under the table to a shock journalist from *Way Out* magazine. I knew my newspaper wouldn't use it, so I figured it was only fair for me to make a buck.

These were shocking photos indeed. The corpse was missing half its head and all of its arms and legs. It wasn't clear how the chunk had been taken from the head, but it was covered with a layer of skin, almost as if it had tried to heal itself after sustaining the bite or injury. Over the skin, there was a white, fuzzy film covering not only the head, but also pretty much the entire remains. The edges of the injury were smooth, and it looked like the skin covering it was holding in whatever brains had been left behind. There were lumps under the skin, which at least meant something meaty was trapped in there. The remaining eye, plenty deteriorated, was barely visible as it was covered with the same filmy skin.

The media hounded police and FBI investigators for a week, trying to get someone to explain what it was. Finally, authorities from the coroner's office told us it was marine fungus. Fine with me; I had something to report.

On the following day, *The Daily Herald* chief editor, Mike Shields, who also happened to be my uncle, allowed me to print one of my nastiest pictures of the marine fungus-covered remains, so I got twice the mileage on it.

I think everyone around Newport News was becoming desensitized, not just me. I heard that a photographer from the *Newport News Weekly* was caught placing a corpse in different poses for his little photo shoot. Even I probably wouldn't have gone that far given the chance.

Then things went berserk along the shorelines. One morning, eight different parts were reported from eight different bodies along Buckroe beach and smaller neighboring beaches. They washed in at just about the same time. Never whole bodies, always sections and extremities. Multitudes of sand dollar pieces washed up in different times during the year, and only a few whole ones appeared when they were in season. I wondered if there was a human season coming.

On that day, I realized that none of the victims had been found clothed. This meant whoever was dumping them had a purpose other than just dumping them. But then again, to date, only sections of bodies had washed up. Clothes aren't going to cling to a leg and hip, or a head and shoulder section very long. There were a lot of things to consider, but something was happening that was beyond what you'd expect from a mafia hit-and-dump or a drug smuggling operation gone wrong.

Then something caused federal and local authorities to begin smothering the beaches, ready to pounce on every wash-up. They concluded that the curious world had seen enough. Almost every morning a couple of separate body parts were discovered on Buckroe beach, but the authorities were there way too quick for most of us to get to them. They also taped off more and more space between the bodies and us. Something was up—and whatever it was, they were keeping it secret.

And this was about the time the freak show on land cranked into overdrive. There were marine biologists teaming with oceanographers to analyze and form theories on the washed-in human debris. Ocean currents in most parts of the world were said to vary slightly, allowing fair speculation on origination point, but not along the Southeastern coastline of the U.S., and especially outside Chesapeake Bay. Here they were almost impossible to estimate.

Nor could you predict the time of deposit very well. The varying water temperatures of the currents moving through the Atlantic are as unstable as the current directions themselves. This made it difficult to estimate time of death and disposal based on the level of decomposition.

One oceanographer had all her ducks in a row, claiming to have documented the 800 miles of water currents for two years, but her records were discounted as flawed, because most of the bodies and pieces had been bitten by sharks. None of her current stream studies were shown passing through shark-infested waters.

While all this went on, I continued my search for the big break. One morning, while approaching the beach from the back door of my condo, I nearly tripped on a man sleeping on a broken-down cardboard box. From stumbling backwards, I spilt half of my instant coffee and dropped my Pop Tart into the sand. Choking back a scream, I realized this guy was just a bum trying to rest.

He sat up to face me, his silhouette shaking in front of the glowing dawn, and muttered, "Easy does it!"

I stumbled away from him, half embarrassed, but still churning from the scare. After distancing myself a hundred feet or so, resentment set in.

Who was this bum, to choose valuable beach property as a camp? To impose himself on my highly taxed neighborhood community? There were new laws written to remove most of this scum from our way of life. In fact, how had he escaped the *Homeless Relocation Program* of last spring? The city had scooped up, found scrap jobs, homes and mental institutions for these vermin in a record-setting tax dollar usage campaign. This was the first I'd seen of a homeless person since then.

When I returned, the bum was gone and I decided not to report it. With a busy day planned, I didn't need to wait for the cops to come out and do their dog and pony show.

The pieces washing in were growing in numbers, and

yet we still had not found a complete body. Over 250 separate human remains, apparently masticated by sea creatures, notably sharks, and none had been identified.

Because I was classified as an investigative reporter, I decided to do some investigating. I researched drug cartels and mafia activity, cautiously, of course; didn't feel like a Columbian necktie would suit me. I looked into the whereabouts of all Eastern seaboard charter boats and checked for reports on Cuban refugee activity. After exhausting every possibility I could think of, the mystery was no closer to being solved. This type of work wasn't meant for me, but then again, what work was? The self-defeating attitude wasn't helping either.

But I couldn't give up, especially with all there was to gain. There were dozens of out-of-town reporters here to pounce on the next breaking news, but since I was so close to all this, I had to be the one. I was tired of living off my parent's money and going without a girlfriend. Something had to give, even though I had no idea where to look.

Then around noon on September 4th, Manny Bruenstein called. He was my only good contact in Newport News homicide. He had been tight-lipped about this whole thing since early on, but now he wanted to have lunch.

I cabbed it to Hampton marina, getting off at the end of the boardwalk, near the Watertrails Sports fishing dock. I bought a pack of Marlboro's at Deep Eddie's Bait Shop and lit one for the stroll down to the restaurant.

I had grown addicted to spending as much time as possible walking along the water's edge. You never knew what might wash up next, and like anything you get obsessed with, your habits form around the obsession.

Flicking my ashes away from the inward wind of the bay, my eyes caught the bum I'd stumbled over on the beach a few mornings earlier. He was sitting between two wood-sided buildings, also smoking a cigarette, watching me. He was a kid, and though I had not seen his face in the earlier encounter, I knew it was him.

As I turned off the boardwalk toward Blackbeard's entrance,

I shot him a cold stare. My hard facial features, thanks to an overactive acne problem in my adolescence, deep eye sockets, and large cheek and jawbones quickly intimidated most, but this kid kept watching me.

As I sat down, the waitress put a 22 ounce pilsner glass in front of me, frothing over with a crisp local microbrew.

I sipped my beer and spoke of the Braves and their chances at winning a Pennant. Manny enjoyed sports talk, which was a good thing for me. We became friends during my sports column days and I think that helped him see past all my flaws.

He sipped his beer and laughed with me about mundane baseball stats, but I could see something was eating at him.

Manny was a young veteran of the NNPD. He'd joined at 21 as a blue shirt and then worked his way into the violent crimes division. At 35, he was well on his way to running the homicide department. He was a very sharp guy, but a little sloppy with his appearance and sloppier with the company he kept.

He gave me a troubled look, which was my cue.

"What's up, Manny?"

There was trust in his eyes. "One of the bodies has turned up with a positive ID." He chugged a good portion of his beer and wiped the back of his hand across his face. "The Commissioner is having a press conference tomorrow morning. The fed in charge will be with him."

After 392 different body parts turning up and none being identified to date, this was breaking news, but something was wrong.

"Where?" This question needed nothing more. These body parts were washing in from somewhere in the deep blue, but we all wanted to know where they lived before tragedy put them there. Perhaps the answer to what had happened could be answered by learning where they were from.

Bruenstein shook his head. "It ain't where, it's who."

The waitress set my lobster roll and chips in front of me and his sandwich in front of him. She started, "Can I get you anything..."

"Can't you see we're deep in conversation?" I snapped.

Quickly pulling her hands away she said, "Oh, sorry," and scuttled off. I took enjoyment in her humility. I hate wait people who assume they can just interrupt a conversation mid-sentence on the pretext that they are busy.

I looked out over the railing, past the marina to admire the happy blue water of Chesapeake Bay. I reset my focus. "Okay, who?"

"Jerry Collins."

I turned back to Manny. "Wow." That answered the where as well. Collins had been a famous Newport News Banker, who'd allegedly been mixed up in some shady dealings and then suddenly disappeared. We did update after update on his disappearance, but the story had died on the vine and his body was never found.

Manny nodded. "Wow is right."

I leaned back and sipped my beer. "Where'd they find him?"

"Here in the bay. Divers pulled him up."

All this was so awkward. "So how much of him came up?"

"Pretty much his whole body." Manny was uncharacteristically nervous.

"That's odd," I said.

"What do you mean?"

"The first whole body and it turns out to be someone who is identified?" I studied Manny's eyes. He was hiding something.

Things were silent for a moment.

Then something broke our strange stare-off. It was an older woman on the other side of the restaurant deck leaning over the railing and pointing animatedly down into the water.

"No look, can't you see it? There it is, right next to that boat." She was motioning toward a small boat, pulled up on the shore next to several rows of docks.

We turned her way, as everyone did on the crowded deck. I instantly knew what it was and I wasn't impressed. Worn out by it, in fact.

The old man sitting with her said, "I see it too. Is it the lower section of a body?" The excitement in his voice reminded me of myself during my first whale watching expedition as a kid. They were tourists, no doubt. Probably here to enjoy the freak show and maybe be the next to discover a wash-up.

If it was the lower section, then photos wouldn't do much for me. The world had seen plenty of those and was no longer tuning in. Since there was really nothing in it for me, I shouted at the old bag and her husband, "Hey you, people are trying to have lunch here. Have some respect." I shook my head and turned to Manny.

The couple settled down, revealing complete intimidation.

I asked Manny, "Can I print it tomorrow?"

"Of course. That's why we're here."

"All right." Suspiciously, I asked, "What else do you know?"

He bobbed his head a little, indicating there was more. "The body was partly clothed. It was wearing jeans."

I refused to drop my stare. "Hmmm. The first clothed body too."

By now, several patrons and a couple of the wait staff were at the railing, staring at the decomposed section of the washed-up remains.

Someone yelled out toward the water's edge, "Don't touch it. That's police evidence."

Manny stood up. "Guess I need to get back to work."

"Saved by the bell," I said.

We shook hands and I agreed to pay the tab.

Watching Manny walk out, I lit a cigarette and picked up my beer.

A double-take later the bum from the other day was standing on the outside of the deck rail, and he started at me, "Hey dude..."

Keeping indifferent, I said, "Got nothin' for you," avoiding eye contact. I turned back to my food, which was waiting untouched.

"Hey man, I know who you are. You're that reporter guy. You did a story on my dad and me."

I looked back, this time at him. "Yeah?"

"That over there is from Cuckoo Island." He pointed in the direction of the small boat, where Manny was now standing above the visible human remains.

I chuckled and turned to my beer.

"Fine, don't believe me." He threw his hands up, disgusted with my lack of interest.

I turned back and studied him. He was a boy of maybe 22 or 23. His matted hair clung to a dirty, greasy face. His jeans were sliding off his buttocks, his t-shirt looking paper thin, human grease stains making it almost clear.

He mumbled as he walked away, "I saw it from the sky and it ain't a pretty sight." Shaking his head, the kid added, "He promised I wouldn't have to go back there again."

As he walked away, I tried to remember how I knew him, yet he was so out of place here, I couldn't get that off my mind.

Our city had once again become a great place to live. The streets were clean, the boardwalk, not counting the regular wash-ups of human debris, was a pleasant spot for locals and tourists, and the economy was booming. There was no fear of strolling through Hampton Park, no brown bag-covered bottles in the gutters and no stink of piss in our alleyways. Our elected and appointed officials had cleaned up Newport News and I was proud of my city more than ever. Our celebrated mayor was the talk of the nation.

We had removed them all, hadn't we? Incarcerated them, institutionalized them or bused them away to smaller towns, with an enticing amount of cash and booze to make them happy for the move.

Then I remembered who this kid was. He was a bit older now, but yes, I had done a story on him and it was surprising to see him alive. I threw a fifty on the table and jumped over the rail because my story was walking away.

* * *

I recognized Manny Bruenstein's number on Caller ID, but I wasn't playing his games anymore. He'd taken advantage of our friendship and I was disillusioned. From my office on the 3rd floor, I let my cell phone ring four different times before I heard street pebbles clicking against the window. I answered on his fifth call. "What?"

"You have to trust me, Jack. Let me in."

The temptation of having him squirm at the sight of my incriminating evidence was too much to pass up.

I called the security desk and told them to let him in.

It was well after midnight and across many empty desks, a couple of *Sports Day* people lingered.

He joined me at my desk and I stood, folding my arms. This lasted a long moment, before he finally broke the silence. "You can't run the story."

I gave him my best intimidating stare.

"Listen Jack, it's like this. If you run the story..."

"How do you know I even have a story? You've been keeping tabs on me?"

Manny shook his head. "Let me finish. The Commissioner is coming out tomorrow, either way. He's planning to discuss Collin's body. If you run the story, he'll switch his approach."

"Then what are you guys hiding?"

I'd never seen Manny so bent out of shape. He sat on my desk. "Your story is wrong. You have to trust me. I can't go into why."

"Pirelli sent you," I accused. "You guys haven't been following me; you've been following the kid. I'm shocked you all even risked letting him out in the streets."

"The kid's got mental disorders, Jack."

"Ahhh, but he's enough of a threat that you follow him." I smirked. "Now what would you suppose this is." I held up a page that was going into the story, with a photocopy of fingerprints on it. "We can't argue who the kid is. So are you gonna deny Cuckoo Island?"

"The kid drones on and on about this Cuckoo Island. The evil place where we dumped all his street friends. He's clinically schizophrenic, Jack! Come on!"

Then I held up a picture of the inner belly of a 747, crammed wall to wall with unhealthy-looking people dressed in ragged street clothes. "Not exactly on their way to Club Med, eh good buddy?"

He squinted, giving his best confused look. "What's this?"

I pushed it, penetrating him with my stare. "Nice try, Manny."

He forced himself to meet my stare. There was a long, silent, struggling moment for him. His eyes fought back, but mine were stronger. For once, I was winning at something.

Manny broke the silence. "You're so desperate for the big story, that you'll risk your career."

"What career?" I didn't take my eyes off his. "If it weren't for my uncle being chief editor, I would've been fired ages ago. This is it for me. It's my big chance."

Manny shook his head. "You know, this obsession is gonna kill you. You're going off the deep end, Jack."

With my forefinger, I slid one more photo from a manila folder. "Well, looky here?" It was a picture of the kid being pulled from the belly and into the cockpit of the crowded 747. Mayor Pirelli was waiting in the doorway at the top of the ladder, with his arms out. I chuckled. "Father and son reunited after three long years."

Manny stood up and stormed the elevator. Pushing the button, he looked back. "If Cuckoo Island were real, do you think they'd send me over here to talk sense into you? Think about it, Jack. Would you even be alive right now?" The elevator opened. "You run it and they'll make you look like a fool."

The Cuckoo Island story was the most shocking claim of a government crime since Watergate, and yet on some plane, it was a lot worse. My story claimed that Cuckoo Island was created to deal with the overspill of homeless people in our community.

It stated the fact that a city can't just arrest homeless people for wearing inappropriate clothes, pissing in parks or sleeping in alleys and not have a place to put them. There are not enough asylums, jail cells and half-way houses to shelter the crazies. And you can't just bus them to small towns. Not 50,000 of them, anyway. The towns will bus them back just as quickly.

It argued that the answer was a place called Cuckoo Island, though it lies amidst hundreds, maybe thousands of man-eating sharks, and none of it sits above water. It was a damn good article and I had finally achieved something worthwhile.

That was, until 10:30 AM, when Commissioner Andrews and FBI Special Agent-In-Charge Blakely opened their press conference.

I didn't show my face. I'd made my case. I watched, along with my fellow *Daily Herald* associates, on TV monitors from our own press room.

The 408 separate sets of remains that had been autopsied were all found to have several things in common. They were free of clothing, jewelry, tattoos and distinguishing marks for one, and the other—they were all male. This was news, and strange news at that.

But then came the knockout blow that left a sinking feeling in the pit of my stomach. The remains were all found to have the same DNA! Not similar, but identical genetic codes! I was so floored by this that I almost missed the next disclosure. The bone density and muscular mass was identical to that of Atlantic salt water. This meant the remains could float at any depth, not sinking nor rising to the surface. This was evidence that the bodies of these human remains had been birthed underwater. It was impossible, but here they were, announcing it.

Within seconds, I found myself in the men's room examining my breakfast sandwich and coffee floating in the toilet.

Later in the day, a Reuter's release stated that the pictures with the mayor and his son in the 747 had been false. My quality work of superimposing the father and son together over the other photo had been discovered, destroying the validity of the rest of my story.

Manny had been looking out for me after all. I had broken faith, not him.

Worst of all, I would now be the joke of the town.

All eyes were on me as I walked out of the building. I never returned to gather my things. I grabbed some clothes and other crap from my condo and drove home to Nebraska to complete my nervous breakdown.

Within days of the press conference that destroyed me,

President Palmer announced an underwater mission, Operation Atlantis Purging, to search for the source of the mysterious anomaly. There were all kinds of new specialists running around Newport News, spouting all kinds of theories and rumors on what had caused it. I remember a popular one about an illegal stem cell research group who had dumped their failed work in the Atlantic when federal authorities had closed in on them.

Scientists believed the humanoid sea creatures were part of a collective, like corral on a reef, feeding off plankton in deeper waters. Once breaking free of the collective, the parts would die and decompose, taking on gases, causing them to slowly float upward.

The situation worsened and spread. Within a year, these creatures were washing up all along the Eastern Coast of the U.S. After another year, the problem grew and spread to a point where the government became less interested in understanding the anomaly and more in stopping it. By the third year, these things were washing up on beaches all over the world.

I enjoy my new life. Sipping from a cup of Tres Generaciones coffee, I walk out of Howler Monkey Lodge onto Punta Gorda, what used to be the most beautiful Caribbean beach in Costa Rica, and I step into the edge of the receding tide to begin my morning ritual of combing. The tourists no longer visit this area and most of the hotels have closed. Now the most prevalent business here is taxidermy.

At 5:30 am there are only a handful of people walking along, poking through the millions of piled up body parts. This is one of the only places in the world where whole bodies wash up at all, and there is no explanation for it.

The first time out here, I was surprised to find that it smelled the same as any beach. It was odd seeing something much more massive than the carnage of D-Day at Normandy, and yet being able to smell the salty sea breeze.

Though littered with piles of flesh and bone, Punta Gorda's anthropoid season is all but over. Only occasionally will someone happen upon a whole body hidden amongst the shredded fragments. I found one last week, and after the cost of preserving it and shipping; I cleared $2,500. Not bad for a week's work in a third world country.

It's amazing what a little money will do for you here. My new girlfriend, Alicia, is a peach. She's a beautiful "Tica" and she adores me. Probably next week, I'll call it a season and we'll go on vacation somewhere...inland of course.

Life is good. Who knows what next season will bring, but at least for now, I'm successful at something.

—JACK KETCHUM

Jack Ketchum's first novel, *Off Season*, prompted the *Village Voice* to publicly scold its publisher in print for publishing violent pornography. He personally disagrees but is perfectly happy to let you decide for yourself. His short story "The Box" won a 1994 Bram Stoker Award from the HWA, his story "Gone" won again in 2000—and in 2003 he won Stokers for both best collection for Peaceable Kingdom and best long fiction for "Closing Time". He has written twelve novels, arguably thirteen, five of which have been filmed–*The Girl Next Door, Red, The Lost, Offspring* and *The Woman*, written with Lucky McKee. His stories are collected in *The Exit at Toledo Blade Boulevard, Peaceable Kingdom, Closing Time and Other Stories*, and *Sleep Disorder*, with Edward Lee. His horror-western novella *The Crossings* was cited by Stephen King in his speech at the 2003 National Book Awards. He was elected Grand Master for the 2011 World Horror Convention.

—RETURNS

By Jack Ketchum

"I'm here."

"You're what?"

"I said I'm here."

"Aw, don't start with me. Don't get started."

Jill's lying on the stained expensive sofa with the TV on in front of her tuned to some game show, a bottle of Jim Beam on the floor and a glass in her hand. She doesn't see me but Zoey does. Zoey's curled up on the opposite side of the couch waiting for her morning feeding and the sun's been up four hours now, it's ten o'clock and she's used to her Friskies at eight.

I always had a feeling cats saw things that people didn't. Now I know.

She's looking at me with a kind of imploring interest. Eyes wide, black nose twitching. I know she expects something of me. I'm trying to give it to her.

"You're supposed to feed her for godsakes. The litter box needs changing."

"What? Who?"

"The cat. Zoey. Food. Water. The litter box. Remember?"

She fills the glass again. Jill's been doing this all night and all morning, with occasional short naps. It was bad while I was alive but since the cab cut me down four days ago on 72nd and Broadway it's gotten immeasurably worse. Maybe in her way she misses me. I only just returned last night from god knows where knowing there was something I had to do or try to do and maybe this is it. Snap her out of it.

"Jesus! Lemme the hell *alone*. You're in my goddamn head. *Get outa my goddamn head!*"

She shouts this loud enough for the neighbors to hear. The neighbors are at work. She isn't. So nobody pounds the walls. Zoey just looks at her, then back at me. I'm standing at the entrance to the kitchen. I know that's where I am but I can't see myself at all. I gesture with my hands but no hands appear in front of me. I look in the hall mirror and there's nobody there. It seems that only my seven-year-old cat can see me.

When I arrived she was in the bedroom asleep on the bed. She jumped off and trotted over with her black-and-white tail raised, the white tip curled at the end. You can always tell a cat's happy by the tail-language. She was purring. She tried to nuzzle me with the side of her jaw where the scent-glands are, trying to mark me as her own, to confirm me in the way cats do, the way she's done thousands of times before but something wasn't right. She looked up at me puzzled. I leaned down to scratch her ears but of course I couldn't and that seemed to puzzle her more. She tried marking me with her haunches. No go.

"I'm sorry," I said. And I was. My chest felt full of lead.

"Come on, Jill. Get up! You need to feed her. Shower. Make a pot of coffee. Whatever it takes."

"This is fuckin' crazy," she says.

She gets up though. Looks at the clock on the mantle. Stalks off on wobbly legs toward the bathroom. And then I can hear the water running for the shower. I don't want to go in there. I don't want to watch her. I don't want to see her naked anymore and haven't for a long while. She was an actress once. Summer stock and the occasional commercial. Nothing major. But god, she was beautiful. Then we married and soon social drinking turned to solo drinking and then drinking all day long and her body slid fast into too much weight here, too little there. Pockets of self-abuse. I don't know why I stayed. I'd lost my first wife to cancer. Maybe I just couldn't bear to lose another.

Maybe I'm just loyal.

I don't know.

I hear the water turn off and a while later she walks back

into the living room in her white terry robe, her hair wrapped in a pink towel. She glances at the clock. Reaches down to the table for a cigarette. Lights it and pulls on it furiously. She's still wobbly but less so. She's scowling. Zoey's watching her carefully. When she gets like this, half-drunk and half-straight, she's dangerous. I know.

"You still here?"

"Yes."

She laughs. It's not a nice laugh.

"Sure you are."

"I am."

"Bullshit. You fuckin' drove me crazy while you were alive. Fuckin' driving me crazy now you're dead."

"I'm here to help you, Jill. You and Zoey."

She looks around the room like finally she believes that maybe, maybe I really *am* here and not some voice in her head. Like she's trying to locate me, pin down the source of me. All she has to do, really, is to look at Zoey, who's staring straight at me.

But she's squinting in a way I've seen before. A way I don't like.

"Well, you don't have to worry about Zoey," she says.

I'm about to ask her what she means by that when the doorbell rings. She stubs out the cigarette, walks over to the door and opens it. There's a man in the hall I've never seen before. A small man, shy and sensitive looking, mid-thirties and balding, in a dark blue windbreaker. His posture says he's uncomfortable.

"Mrs. Hunt?"

"Uh-huh. Come on in," she says. "She's right over there."

The man stoops and picks up something off the floor and I see what it is.

A cat-carrier. Plastic with a grated metal front. Just like ours. The man steps inside.

"Jill, *what are you doing?* What the hell are you *doing*, Jill?"

Her hands flutter to her ears as though she's trying to bat away a fly or a mosquito and she blinks rapidly but the man doesn't see that at all. The man is focused on my cat who *remains focused on me*, when she should be watching the man, *when she should be seeing the cat-carrier, she knows damn well what they mean for godsakes, she's going somewhere, somewhere she won't like.*

"Zoey! Go! Get out of here! *Run!*"

I clap my hands. They make no sound. But she hears the alarm in my voice and sees the expression I must be wearing and at the last instant turns toward the man just as he reaches for her, reaches down to the couch and snatches her up and shoves her head-first inside the carrier. Closes it. Engages the double-latches.

He's fast. He's efficient.

My cat is trapped inside.

The man smiles. He doesn't quite pull it off.

"That wasn't too bad," he says.

"No. You're lucky. She bites. She'll put up a hell of a fight sometimes."

"*You lying bitch,*" I tell her.

I've moved up directly behind her by now. I'm saying this into her ear. I can *feel* her heart pumping with adrenalin and I don't know if it's me who's scaring her or what she's just done or allowed to happen that's scaring her but she's all actress now, she won't acknowledge me at all. I've never felt so angry or useless in my life.

"You sure you want to do this, ma'am?" he says. "We could put her up for adoption for a while. We don't *have* to euthanize her. 'Course, she's not a kitten anymore. But you never know. Some family..."

"I *told* you," my wife of six years says. "*She bites.*"

And now she's calm and cold as ice.

Zoey has begun meowing. My heart's begun to break. Dying was easy compared to this.

Our eyes meet. There's a saying that the soul of a cat is seen through its eyes and I believe it. I reach inside the carrier. My hand passes *through* the carrier. I can't see my hand but she can. She moves her head up to nuzzle it. And the puzzled expression isn't there anymore. It's as though this time she can actually *feel* me, feel my hand and my touch. I wish I could feel her too. I petted her just this way when she was only a kitten, a street-waif, scared of every horn and siren. And I was all alone. She begins to purr. I find something out. Ghosts can cry.

The man leaves with my cat and I'm here with my wife.

I can't follow. Somehow I know that.

You can't begin to understand how that makes me feel. I'd give anything in the world to follow.

My wife continues to drink and for the next three hours or so I do nothing but scream at her, tear at her. Oh, she can hear me, all right. I'm putting her through every torment as I can muster, reminding her of every evil she's ever done to me or anybody, reminding her over and over of what she's done *today* and I think, so this is my purpose, this is why I'm back, the reason I'm here is to get this bitch to end herself, end her miserable fucking life and I think of my cat and how Jill never really cared for her, cared for her wine-stained furniture more than my cat and I urge her toward the scissors, I urge her toward the window and the seven-story drop, toward the knives in the kitchen and she's crying, she's screaming, too bad the neighbors are all at work, they'd at least have her arrested. And she's hardly able to walk or even stand and I think, *heart attack maybe, maybe stroke* and I stalk my wife and urge her to die, *die* until it's almost one o'clock and something begins to happen.

She's calmer.

Like she's not hearing me as clearly.

I'm losing something.

Some power drifting slowly away like a battery running down.

I begin to panic. I don't understand. *I'm not done yet.*

Then I feel it. I feel it reach out to me from blocks and blocks away far across the city. I feel the breathing slow. I feel the heart stopping. I feel the quiet end of her. I feel it more clearly than I felt my own end.

I feel it grab my own heart and *squeeze.*

I look at my wife, pacing, drinking. And I realize something. And suddenly it's not so bad anymore. It still hurts, but in a different way.

I haven't come back to torment Jill. Not to tear her apart or to shame her for what she's done. She's tearing herself apart. She doesn't need me for that. She'd have done this terrible thing anyway, with or without my being here. She'd planned it. It was in motion. My being here didn't stop her. My being here afterwards didn't change things. Zoey was mine. And given who and what Jill was what she'd done was inevitable.

And I think, *to hell with Jill. Jill doesn't matter a bit. Not one bit. Jill is zero.*

It was Zoey I was here for. Zoey all along. That awful moment.

I was here for my cat.

That last touch of comfort inside the cage. The nuzzle and purr. Reminding us both of all those nights she'd comforted me and I her. The fragile brush of souls.

That was what it was about.

That was what we needed.

The last and the best of me's gone now.

And I begin to fade.

—Brad C. Hodson

A Knoxville native, writer Brad C. Hodson currently resides in Los Angeles. His work includes numerous pieces of short fiction, his upcoming novel *Darling*, the play and upcoming film about Lord Byron, *A Year Without A Summer*, and the award-winning cult comedy *George: A Zombie Intervention*. When not reading or writing, he's usually found dragging heavy weights and throwing sandbags in the park or practicing his Italian while bemoaning the fact that he's still a few decades off from retiring on a farm in Lazio. For articles, reviews, or more info on where to find his work, please visit www.brad-hodson.com

—THE OTHER PATRICK

By Brad C. Hodson

"Can we go?"

His wife ignored him. Anna was too intent on finding the graves of old Hollywood stars. They had only been in Los Angeles for a month, David's public relations firm deciding that now would be the perfect time to diversify and dabble in show business. He hated Hollywood, hated the celebrity culture, and especially hated trudging through cemeteries.

Anna, however, loved every minute of it. "I couldn't care less about the current crop of drama queens," she had said as they entered the cemetery, "but 'The Golden Age' is such a thrill." Even though she knew David would hate it, she insisted on visiting the final resting places of stars like Rudolph Valentino and Faye Wray.

David had made the mistake of being critical of Douglas Fairbanks Junior's massive Roman tomb, complete with a very Caesar-like bust of himself and a reflecting pool, and thought he'd never hear the end of it.

"He was a legend," Anna had said.

"He was a narcissist. He didn't do anything to change the world for better or worse."

"He entertained people. Sometimes that's all we need."

David sighed. This was what he got for marrying someone with her head in the clouds. He saw her interest in acting as a hobby and she knew that. Every time they argued about ridiculous things like this, they both knew it was just a front for the real tension: she didn't feel her husband respected her.

He respected her. He just didn't see why something as self-serving as acting was considered a lofty goal. Not that he had some higher purpose he served, but at least he didn't pretend he did, either.

They rounded a corner in the path and Anna ran down the hill. David wondered what ridiculous grave she had found.

"David. Come look at this."

He shook his head and walked toward her, expecting to find some golden statue of Larry, Moe, and Curly in togas. When he saw the spectacle that had captivated his wife, ice trickled down his spine.

A long wall of hedges ran the boundary of the cemetery. Small tombstones pressed against their length and long, brown vines scrambled up them. What chilled David and obviously fascinated his wife, who snapped picture after picture, were the toys. Thousands of toys were tangled in the vines, offerings to the graves beneath. The empty glass eyes of molded dolls peeked out from behind green leaves while dirty action figures scaled a wall they would never reach the top of. The faded plastic almost looked like a flower arrangement from a distance. He kneeled in front of one. The boy had only been six when he died. The toys surrounding it were old and discolored. A small porcelain doll, a wooden train, and two GI Joes. Someone had burned the soldiers' faces off.

Other graves were similarly decorated. Faded pink dollhouses and fire trucks rusted brown, soggy stuffed animals and plastic tea sets stained the color of soot. Superheroes fought with ivy that threatened to swallow them and plastic circus animals sunk into the dirt at their feet. The entire memorial ran the length of a small city block.

"Morbid," he said.

"I think it's beautiful." Anna snapped away with her digital camera. The sun reflected from a tear rolling down her cheek and David turned away.

"I think one of the Ramones is buried over here." He walked away from the wall. He didn't want her to bring *it* up, was afraid of the topic since she mentioned visiting the cemetery. He didn't turn around to see if she was following. He knew she would wait long enough to compose herself and then catch up with him.

"Oh my God," she said and his heart sank. But then she yelled again. "David. Oh my God, look at this." He turned and walked back toward the wall.

She knelt, face streaked with tears, breath heavy.

He placed a hand on her shoulder. "What is it?"

"The name..."

He stared at the engraving. The letters didn't make sense. He shook his head and looked again. His mind couldn't process what was carved into the stone. He could see the letters, but no syllables formed.

Finally he willed himself to read it: *Patrick Neil Cunningham, Dec 1st, 2001 — July 18th, 2005.*

"Jesus."

"I know." She gripped his hand and squeezed it, squeezed it so hard his fingers lost all sensation. "What does it mean?"

"Nothing, nothing at all. It's just a bizarre coincidence." It had to be a coincidence. It was too strange.

"But the name—"

"Cunningham's a pretty common name," he said.

"But all three names?"

"It happens. I went to high school with another David Neil Cunningham. I even had a college professor named Neil David Cunningham."

"Yeah." She didn't seem convinced. She sniffed and rubbed her eyes with the back of her free hand. "Yeah, you're right. The dates were just so close—"

"But still off by a year and some change on both ends."

They sat in silence for a moment, staring at the grave. David surveyed the toys strung around it. There was a small stuffed dog with a plastic tear in his eye and his arm in a sling. The sling said "Boo-Boo." Above that and to the right was a collection of firemen, soldiers, and police officers that looked like they were part of a Lego set. A big, yellow Tonka dump truck sat on a rock underneath them.

He nearly gasped when he saw the doll.

It was brown, sewn together from a burlap sack. It had black buttons for eyes and its mouth was a straight line of black thread across its face. It wore faded blue overalls that looked like they were cut from an old pair of jeans.

David stood and grabbed Anna's shoulder. "Let's go check out the graves over here." He hoped she hadn't seen the doll.

"Huh? Oh, sure. Yeah." She stood and dusted off her knees. Her hand wrapped around his again, not quite so tight this time, and they walked away. Thank God she didn't see it.

"I'm sorry I was snippy with you earlier," she said.

"I'm sorry I'm such an asshole."

"It's okay. I knew you were an asshole when I married you." She smiled. "It's part of your charm."

He laughed, glad that her mood had changed.

On the drive home they talked about work, Anna's latest audition, and traffic. Anything but Patrick. It was pained and awkward, both of them aware that his name was sitting on the tips of their tongues. He might as well be in the car, David thought. But Anna's laughter, even though it was forced, meant that she was dealing with it.

When they got home, Anna drew a hot bath for herself and David returned a call to an old client back in D.C. They ordered Chinese for dinner, watched a movie, and made love. It was slow and sweet, but not passionate. It was more comforting than anything, like a warm fire on a cold day.

When he was sure she was asleep, he crept into the living room. He sifted through the boxes in the closet until he found the one labeled "Patrick" and pulled it down. To keep Anna from discovering him, he took the box into the bathroom.

He shut the door behind him, careful not to make too much noise. The faucet was dripping and he made a mental note to call the landlord for the third time about repairing it. He lowered himself onto the toilet seat and rested the box on his lap.

He shivered when he opened it. He didn't know if it was because of the cold porcelain pressing against his thighs or the sight of Patrick's clothes folded so neatly inside. He had tried to donate them to Goodwill before they moved, but couldn't.

He had even gone so far as packing them in a garbage bag and leaving them on his porch, but had snatched the bag back inside at the last moment. He grabbed the shirt on top and removed it, tenderly, as though it might crumble to dust. It unfolded in his hands. Big Bird's bright blue eyes stared at him. Patrick loved Big Bird. David pulled the shirt to his face, felt the soft cotton against his cheek. He closed his eyes and inhaled. The shirt smelled like grass and orange juice. It smelled like Patrick.

Tears welled up in his eyes. There in the bathroom, alone and shielded from the world, he let himself cry.

When he was done, he placed the shirt on the floor with the same care that he had taking it out of the box. He turned back and pulled out the rest of Patrick's clothes.

He removed a blanket and this time he did gasp.

There was the doll.

It was almost identical to the one at the cemetery. The only difference was the denim dress it wore, a remnant from before Patrick was born. After his birth, David's mother corrected her mistake by making him a boy version. That was the doll he was buried with. Looking at its sister, David was positive it was exactly like the one in the cemetery.

It was just a coincidence, he reminded himself. The one at the graveyard was probably made by that poor kid's grandmother, too. It had to be a popular thing for women from that generation.

He studied the doll for a few moments, traced his fingers along the stitching that held its cotton ball stuffing in place. Then he wiped his eyes, sealed it back in its box, and returned it to the closet.

He didn't sleep well that night. The dark often brought loneliness and the loneliness brought dreams of his son. Patrick in his playpen with the doll. Patrick's fourth birthday party at the park. Patrick throwing his ball into the neighbor's yard. The dog barking. Patrick wandering over and the dog breaking free of its leash and Anna screaming and—

The alarm clock's buzzing yanked him from the dream. He rolled over, hit snooze, and closed his eyes. He needed another half an hour. But when his eyes shut again, Patrick was there.

The boy's blond hair fell into his eyes as he smiled. He held the doll.

David rolled out of bed and showered.

Anna climbed into the shower with him. "Morning," she said.

"Morning." He lathered up his hair.

"Did you call the landlord about that faucet?"

He shook his head. "Can you do it?"

"Sure." She yawned. "How did you sleep?" She maneuvered past him for the shampoo.

"Not very well."

"Bad dreams?"

"Yeah."

"Me too."

That was the closest they came to discussing their son.

His day ground on between paperwork and mind-numbing conference calls. On his lunch break he found himself driving past the cemetery. He thought about the doll, the name on the grave. It was all just a coincidence. Maybe the name was spelled differently, or the doll wasn't quite constructed the same, or—

Screw it.

He parked at a Subway across the street, bought himself a sandwich, and walked to the cemetery.

As he approached the wall, the same chill shot through him as before approached Patrick's grave. No, the *other* Patrick. He crouched until he was face to face with the doll. It had the same type of construction, the same stitching, and the same eyes and mouth as the one in his closet.

It was too strange. He reached for it, brushed its burlap cheek. His fingers wrapped around it and tugged. A part of his mind screamed at him, *what the hell do you think you're doing?* But his hand worked for itself and pulled the doll away.

He knew he was going to get caught. Someone would bust him. Could they charge him with grave robbing for this? He didn't know.

He tucked the doll in his jacket and went back to work.

The rest of the day, the doll stayed in his jacket pocket.

Periodically, he would reach his fingers in to feel the coarse burlap or trace the line of its mouth. He fought the urge to pull it out and stare at it. He didn't want to explain to everyone in his office why he was playing with a doll.

A doll stolen from a child's grave.

Why did he do that?

Every time he touched it, he imagined his son's doll tucked between his arm and chest in his coffin. His son's fingers curled around its body, hugging it tight against the navy blue suit he was buried in, the holes in his son's flesh sewn together and painted over with make-up.

When he arrived home, he went to the closet and hung his jacket up. Anna walked in as he closed the door.

She grinned. "Putting up your own things, huh?"

"Yeah."

"About time," she joked.

"Don't start with that," he said. He instantly regretted it as he watched her smile fade. He didn't know why he snapped at her, especially when she had been in such a good mood.

She nodded, her face stone, and went into the kitchen. David sighed and sat on the couch. He felt the faint stirrings of a headache coming. He closed his eyes, massaged his temples, and wondered why he wasn't a better husband.

Anna cooked spaghetti and they went for a long walk. They didn't speak much. David was focused on the doll. He couldn't wait for Anna to go to sleep.

When she went to bed, he took the doll from his jacket and collapsed onto the couch. He held it above him and examined it, running his fingers along every curve.

He should return it. What if the other Patrick's parents came by and notice it missing? How would they feel? Tomorrow. He'd take it back on his lunch break. David fell asleep on the couch with the doll in his arms. He wasn't out long when something jolted him awake. He bolted upright, the doll falling from his lap into the floor.

"Anna, I..."

He was alone. The door to the bedroom was still closed.

His hand went to his cheek. What was it that woke him? He thought he had felt Anna's hand on his face.

He must have been dreaming. He leaned over and reached for the doll.

It wasn't there.

It had fallen right beside the couch. He was sure of it. He rolled onto the floor and crawled around patting under the furniture. A sick feeling started to form in the pit of his stomach, a sure sign to David that he would miss the doll.

And Anna would find it.

He sat on his knees and ran a hand through his hair.

It sat on the couch, facing him.

He blinked. Shook his head. He must have grabbed it when it fell and, half asleep, put it back on the couch without realizing it. It was a wonder he didn't carry it to bed with him.

He picked up the doll and placed it back in his jacket. He shut the closet door and leaned his head against it. Eyes closed, he pressed his head harder against the door, feeling the grain of the wood against his skin. He pressed harder, until little white lights sparked behind his lids, and imagined he pressed his head against the lid of a coffin.

After brushing his teeth and washing his face, he stared at himself in the mirror. Why was this hitting him so hard now, three years later? He grieved when his son was gone, as any father would. But his thoughts were never so macabre.

Maybe he'd been hiding it for too long? Maybe avoiding it had only let it build up pressure and now it was going off like a tea kettle.

Or maybe it was the doll. Why did he take that thing anyway? He vowed again to return it tomorrow.

He crept into the bedroom, careful not to disturb his wife. She lay on her side with her back to him, the covers kicked off and tangled around her feet. Her hair spilled over her pillow, down her back, and onto his half of the bed. He kicked off his clothes and slid in next to her, carefully gathering her hair and placing it on her side. The bed swallowed him as he leaned onto his pillow.

He was almost asleep again when the door creaked. He must not have closed it all the way.

There was a faint shuffling, the sound of feet moving through carpet.

Heart racing, throat constricting, he tried to open his eyes but his lids refused.

The shuffling grew closer. David tried to say Anna's name, but could barely breathe.

"Shhhh..."

He forced his eyes open at the sound. A small figure stood beside his bed. Tears formed in David's eyes.

"Patrick?"

"Yes."

He wiped his face and leaned forward. The figure was little more than shadow, but was the right size for a boy. He could make out the hair, though. The boy's brown hair hung down into his face, helping to hide his features.

His brown hair.

"You're not my son."

It placed a dry, withered finger to David's lips. The finger tasted like mold. "I never said I was," he whispered. His voice was high pitched and playful. It was also hollow, like a recording played through blown speakers.

"You're the other Patrick." David sat up. His heartbeat slowed as he realized he must be dreaming.

The boy nodded.

David assumed he was there for the doll. "I was going to bring it back to you," he said.

Little fingers curled around his hand and tugged. David stood and followed the boy through the door.

He was in the cemetery. It was still night, the only light a sliver of moon that hung above their heads. David turned and looked behind him. They had stepped from a large, granite mausoleum. The iron door was open and he could see his bedroom through it. Anna tossed and turned on their bed.

The fingers tugged again and David followed.

As they neared the wall of hedges, he saw movement.

Shadows flickered around the graves. David squinted, trying to see what happened.

They were playing.

Children gathered around their tombstones, pushing cars around in the dirt. Two boys placed army men on a small hill while a group of girls held a tea party around a rotting doll house. As David approached, they stopped. Countless pairs of dead eyes fell on him.

"You took my doll," the other Patrick said.

Out here in the cemetery, under the moonlight, David could see the boy's pale skin and black eyes. Tiny threads of stitching hung from his eyelids and lips. A red t-shirt sat loose underneath a pair of overalls. He reminded David of the doll.

"I'm sorry."

"It's okay. I don't mind sharing. We all share our toys here."

The others turned back to their toys and continued playing.

"I just thought," the boy continued, "that you might want to play with us."

"What?"

"You and the lady seemed so sad. Why?"

"My son..." David choked on the words.

"He has a doll like mine, huh? Was his name Patrick, too?"

David nodded.

"It's good to have toys when you come here," the other Patrick said. "Will you stay?"

A sinking feeling formed in David's stomach and he started to sweat. He shook his head. The boy smiled.

"It's okay. We're not lonely here. I just thought you might be. Do you want to play awhile?"

"Okay."

One of the girls brought over a soggy and faded "Chutes and Ladders" game. "Hi. I'm Alessa." She opened the box and pulled the board out. Her long hair hung down over a faded blue dress. David guessed her hair was once blonde, but had faded to the color of grub worms.

"This is David," the other Patrick said.

"It's nice to meet you. We don't get a lot of grown-ups

playing with us anymore. What piece do you want?"

David pointed to one of the pieces at random. Alessa handed it to him and frowned.

"It's a lot yuckier than it used to be," she said, embarrassed.

"My toys have gotten pretty yucky, too," Patrick said.

"It's okay," David said. "I don't mind."

They played the game for hours, until the rising sun shot streaks of purple through the sky.

"I should take you back," Patrick said.

Alessa smiled and gathered the game pieces up. "It was nice playing with you, David. You're a sweet man." She took her box and rushed back over to the wall of graves.

Patrick's tiny fingers wrapped around David's and tugged him back toward the mausoleum. "Will you play with us again tomorrow?"

"Sure. Yeah, I will." David smiled and stepped through the door.

* * *

He showered and left before Anna woke leaving a note that he had an early meeting. He hoped she wouldn't call him at work and discover he had cancelled his meetings and called in sick.

He drove to the cemetery and parked out front. He waited an hour for the gates to open and then rushed to the wall.

His eyes scanned up and down, running over each of the rotting toys. Finally he saw it: the "Chutes and Ladders" game. Underneath was an overgrown grave. He ripped the vines and weeds away. He fell to his knees when he saw the name.

Alessa Orinkov.

It was real. It happened. He spent the night playing here with these children. He shook his head in disbelief. Blinked. Read the name again.

He stood and stumbled over to Patrick's grave. He took the doll from his jacket and tied it back in place. He scanned up and down the wall again, noting which toys were in the worst condition. Then he left.

* * *

"Thank you for the toys," Patrick said as the children pulled their presents from the vines. Laughter echoed through the empty cemetery and filled David with warmth. It was like watching his son on Christmas morning.

"I brought your doll," David said.

"I know. But I want you to keep it," Patrick said and handed it back.

"Okay."

Patrick smiled and tugged on David's hand. "I'm glad you come to see us so much. My Dad stopped coming. He only visited during the day, with the other grownups. But he doesn't even do that now."

"I'm sorry."

"It made him too sad."

David understood how that felt. He ruffled the boy's hair. "I'm sure he'll be back."

"At least I've got you to play with me now."

Alessa ran up to David, hugging her brand new "Chutes and Ladders" to her chest. "Thank you. Oh, thank you–thank you–thank you."

"You're welcome," David said and smiled.

He played with all of the children that night, showing each of them how to use their new toys. It made him feel good inside, like he was human again. Like he was a father again.

* * *

"Why have you been lying to me?" Anna was angry, angrier than David had seen her in a long while. But he knew she was hurt, too, and so he kept his voice calm.

"I didn't mean to lie to you."

"Why haven't you been to work in a week?"

"I haven't been sleeping well." He shuffled his feet and looked at the floor, unsure what to tell her.

"Then where have you been going in the morning when you leave here? Why have you withdrawn six hundred dollars from our checking account?" Her face was fire, and spittle flew from her mouth.

"You wouldn't understand."

"Is it another woman?" Her body shook as she asked and David's insides hollowed from what he was putting her through.

"No. God no."

"Then what is it?"

"Patrick." He blurted it without thinking. It hung in the air between them and there was no turning back.

She sat on the bed next to him. They were both quiet.

She touched her hand to his knee and asked, "What do you mean?"

"Can I show you something?"

She nodded. David went to the closet and brought back Patrick's box. Anna started to cry as he removed their son's clothes. Her hand went to them, and then recoiled as if she had burnt herself. Finally he pulled out the doll.

He held it toward her. "Do you remember this?"

She nodded, refusing to touch it.

"Do you remember the one that we buried him with?"

"David, why are you doing this to me?"

He pulled the other Patrick's doll from his jacket. She stifled a yell upon seeing it and her hands went to her mouth. She shook her head back and forth.

"I found this one at the cemetery," he said.

"What?"

"It was at Patrick's grave. The other Patrick. The grave that you and I saw that day."

"Why would you take it?"

"I don't know. I just wanted to...I don't know." He shook his head.

"Oh, David. You have to take it back."

"I tried. He told me to keep it."

"Who?"

He swallowed. "The other Patrick. The one at the cemetery."

She paced over to the window and stared out. "We need to see a counselor. You've never dealt with his death."

"And you have?"

"Yes. No. I don't know. But this isn't normal, David. It's not sane."

He could agree with that. After all, was there anything sane about buying toys for dead children? Or playing with them?

But it was real. He knew it was.

"I'm sorry I wasn't there for you like I should have been," he said. "After he died, I shouldn't have poured myself into my work."

He waited for her to say something, but she stared out the window. He continued.

"I'm sorry I never supported your acting. It's not just a hobby. I know that now. It's a compulsion. Something that you have to do."

She nodded.

David went into the kitchen and poured them both a glass of water. He placed hers on her nightstand with two sleeping pills. He gulped down two himself and curled up on his side of the bed. The doll was clutched to his chest.

Later, as he drifted off to sleep, he thought he felt her hand reach around him and take the doll.

When he heard Anna gasp, he opened his eyes and rolled over to find her sitting up, the doll in her hands. She trembled and whispered something. David put his hand on her knee, but she couldn't take her eyes from the boy that entered the room.

"It's okay," David said. He stood and took Patrick's hand. He looked back at his wife. "Come with us," he said and reached for her.

She stared at his hand for a long while before taking it and crawling from the bed.

When they were in the cemetery, Patrick ran to the children already playing with their new toys at the wall.

Anna was sobbing. "Oh my God, oh my God."

David held her. "Shhhh. It's okay. They just want to play." He led his wife to the wall. "This is what I've been spending money on, not another woman."

"The toys..."

"Yeah. Their old toys were in pretty bad shape. No child should have old toys."

Alessa ran up to them, smiling. She threw her arms around David's waist. Anna took a step back.

"Hi, David. Is this your wife?"

David smiled. "Yes. Alessa, this is Anna."

"Pleased to meet you," she said and held out her hand. Anna stared at it.

David laughed. "Don't be rude."

Anna looked to her husband and he nodded. She grabbed the girl's hand and shook it.

"You'll have to forgive my wife. She's not used to being around kids." He winked at Anna.

"That's okay. You guys wanna play a game?"

He looked to his wife. She stared at a group of children playing hide and seek.

"Yeah. You go set the board up and we'll be there in a minute."

"Okay." She skipped off.

"They're...they're so young," Anna said.

"Yeah."

"They look like children."

"They are," he said. "All they want to do is play."

"How...?"

"I don't know. Maybe it's this place. The toys on the wall. I really don't know."

"Do you think other graveyards...I mean..."

David shook his head. "No. I don't know why, but I'm sure this place is unique."

He guided his wife to where Alessa and a group of children had set up their game. They sat on the ground next to the board and Anna handed out the pieces. Patrick came over and squeezed in between David and Anna. David looked to his wife and saw a smile on her face. She hugged the boy.

"Patrick," she said.

Alessa tugged on Anna's nightshirt. "Can you guys stay here with us?"

Patrick buried his head into Anna's side. "Our parents don't come anymore."

"Little kids should have parents," Alessa said.

David took Anna's hand in his. Pale moonlight caught the tears streaking her face. But she smiled.

* * *

The following week, back in their bedroom, David passed a glass of water across the bed to his wife. They kissed and he turned the light off, the dark rushing in, no longer feeling lonely. Instead, he realized as he slid under the blanket and next to Anna, it felt warm and comforting. It felt right.

When their bodies were finally found, he knew it would be ruled a double-suicide. The bottles of pills on the bedside table would give it away if an autopsy report didn't.

Police would never be able to explain the thousands of dollars they had charged at toy stores around Los Angeles or where the toys had gone. The possibility of foul play would be ruled out when security footage revealed the couple paying for the toys, hand in hand and smiling. As he took his wife's hand under the blanket, he was positive anyone watching that footage would see a happy couple and that this would confuse the police even more.

There would be no note found, only a small doll stitched together from a burlap sack, tucked in bed between them.

—Shaun Hutson

Shaun Hutson has had more than 60 books and a number of short stories published since 1981 (32 of these books under his own name and the rest under six different pseudonyms). He has also written for radio and TV and has appeared in a couple of low budget horror films just to illustrate that as an actor he's a very good writer! He also lectured to the Oxford Students Union back in the early 90's. Needless to say he's never been asked back. He lives in Buckinghamshire.

—A QUESTION OF MORALITY

By Shaun Hutson

I am not a paedophile.

I despise those people and what they do as much as I detest being labelled with that same derisory and derogatory name. Any man or woman who sexually abuses a child should be destroyed in the same way a sick animal would be destroyed. Put down. Executed. Use whichever term you wish, but no one who sexually abuses children should be allowed to live.

This is not a reactionary statement. It is one that comes about when any modicum of sense and morality is applied to the whole subject of sex with children. It is never forgivable and it should never be accepted by the law or by anyone with any shred of decency. People who indulge in this kind of monstrous act are scum. There is no other word for them.

I am not a paedophile.

People have accused me of this and I will defend myself and refute these foul accusations until the day I die. It is too easy these days to brand people unfairly. To tar them with the same brush. That is what happened to me. I lived alone. I had no choice. My wife had died, we never had children. My parents were gone. I was alone because I simply had no one. I didn't want to be alone. Just as I didn't want to be targeted by the fools and the idiots who peered at me from behind their twitching curtains and who were pleasant to my face and yet malicious behind my back. I can imagine the things they said about me. How I was always in the house and hardly ever went out. As if living a solitary life was a crime. I never bothered them because I didn't want to impose. People pretend to be friendly and they say they are there to help, but they don't really want to be bothered. I knew I was the same. I liked my privacy. I enjoyed not being responsible to anyone or for anyone.

I loved my wife more than words can say but caring for her through her illness for two years was painful and trying, and although I was heartbroken when she finally died, there was a part of me that breathed a sigh of relief. And don't think I haven't felt guilty about that these past few years. I would give anything to have her back with me.

If she had been here now, perhaps I would not be in this position.

With her I had a purpose in life, without her I began to wonder what the point was to even my own existence. There was no one to share a joke with. No one to comment to about the rubbish on television in the evenings. I still miss her now. And when I left our home because I couldn't bear to stay there accompanied by so many memories, I moved into another area and wished I hadn't. The people there were much younger than I. All seemed to have small children and they all seemed wary of me from the first day I moved in.

I could sense them looking at me as if I was an outsider. They spoke to me out of enforced politeness. They didn't welcome me into their community.

And when I spoke to one of their children, they glared at me with accusing eyes, and I could imagine what they were thinking and saying about me behind my back. I could almost hear what they were calling me. But they were wrong.

I am not a paedophile.

What is so wrong about merely speaking to small children? I was never furtive in my approaches to them. I saw them in the street, children I knew lived around me and, out of nothing more than friendliness, I spoke to them. Laughed and joked with them. What is so terrible about that? My wife and I always spoke to children when we were out shopping. No one thought anything of it when we were together. No one viewed our approaches as sinister or potentially dangerous, but because I continued my friendliness as a single man, I was viewed with mistrust and eventually hatred. And yet no one had any evidence against me except what they invented in their own twisted minds. They were the ones who were sick, not, as they intimated, myself. What kind of mentality could accuse a man of some of the things they accused me of? What kind of warped and abnormal thought processes could come up with some of the offences they said I was guilty of?

When the police were called, I couldn't believe it. More to the point, I couldn't believe that these men and women who were supposed to represent the law were so hostile towards me.

They had arrived at my house to interview me about the disappearance of four local children and their presence had been prompted by nothing more than hearsay. The malicious and poisonous gossip of those who lived around me and who viewed me with such mistrust and fear. I was confused and angry that my neighbours had done this to me. I was furious that their small-mindedness had caused them to react in such a way. They condemned me without knowing any facts. Simply because I was not one of them, I was singled out for persecution. I told the police that, but they seemed unimpressed. They were on the side of the accusers rather than on mine. There was no benefit of the doubt given. They had, it seemed, condemned me as surely as those who had clamoured for my arrest.

When the police arrested me, many of my neighbours stood at their front doors and shouted abuse at me as I was being taken to the police car. Some even spat in my direction and they yelled names like *paedophile*.

I am not a paedophile.

I have never sexually abused a child in my life. I never would. Those that I kept in my cellar were treated well. Right up until the time I ate them.

—JONATHAN TEMPLAR

Jonathan Templar has had stories published by, among others, Open Casket, Wicked East Press and Smart Rhino Publications. He has contributed to the forthcoming shared-world anthology *World's Collider* and his novella *The Angel of Shadwell* is due in spring 2012.

Jonathan can be found hiding from the sunlight at www.jonathantemplar.com

—THE MEAT MAN

By Jonathan Templar

Charlie worked with rats.

Well, not literally, although sometimes he'd beg to differ. No, he dealt with the vermin, brought violent closure to their flea-ridden lives. He was an exterminator, although that was a word no longer in fashion. Respectable people recoiled when you used the word *extermination*, as if they imagined that rats would be taken to a new life somewhere on a carpet of cheese, pleasuring themselves all the way, rather than dying in agony as poison took a hold of their tiny little systems. People, ordinary people, had gotten so soft that they even romanticised rodents.

They were fucking idiots, the lot of them.

Charlie had seen what rats could do, seen them gnawing down on the body of some old dear who had died on her own and had nobody to clean her up, who'd just been left there to be fed on. He had witnessed firsthand the mewling abhorrence of a pack of blind newborns sucking the teats of some vast mother rat lying bloated in a hole under the ground, and once you saw that kind of thing, you would never think of them as anything other than unholy, filthy beasts.

Charlie's trouble was that he looked a bit like a rat, and he smelt like one as well. To every other human he might as well be vermin himself. This had coloured his relationship with most people he'd met. He didn't have friends and he had never had so much of a sniff of the prospect of a wife and children. Charlie was wandering aimlessly into his 50's with the growing knowledge that the stuff he was coughing up in the mornings suggested things inside his body were starting to decay, that the cigarettes he constantly held between his thin lips were indeed killing him as his mother always said they would.

Dying didn't frighten him, not really. His life had been grim enough, there was little that he would fight to hang on to, and anything he did enjoy slowly killed him. But he had his job, and he enjoyed it, enjoyed the solitude it allowed, enjoyed that it gave him the power of life and death over things that were smaller and stupider than he was.

Charlie worked the underground. They say you're only ever ten feet away from a rat in a city. In the underground, the little buggers might as well be sitting on your shoulder. They were everywhere, scampering through the dark tunnels and the drains and culverts that made a maze beneath London, happy in their domain but stupid enough to poke their heads out into the light from time to time and become what the sanitised folk who lived above ground termed *a nuisance*.

Charlie had some sympathy for their situation. They lived under the ground where the light didn't shine and kept mostly to themselves. If people chose to come down and dig tunnels it wasn't the rat's fault if they couldn't always get out of the way. This was their turf after all.

But they did pop up, and so Charlie had been sent to see them off.

It had been a couple of years since his supervisor, Dale, sent Charlie down here. Dale was a halfwit 20 years younger than Charlie fresh from some management training course. The sort of man who wore a tie under his red work clothes as if the vermin might be somehow more impressed by him. Dale always talked to him while breathing only through his mouth, and Charlie knew this was because he thought Charlie stunk, that he was unhygienic and that his lack of attention to his own personal health constituted a disciplinary offence on the grounds that it was anti-social. Charlie knew this because he'd snuck a look at his own personnel file. He had read in the many, many dispatches sent from their office that Dale had taken to his post of supervisor with a zeal and a professionalism that the company in general would never bother to appreciate. His request for disciplinary hearings and time management reports would simply be scoffed at by the brass. They had had been doing this for years and were well aware that pest control hardly attracted the cream of the employment market.

There had been no disciplinary for Charlie, but when the chance had arisen to bury him in the underground, a permanent posting that came with a one room base camp and no daily supervision, Charlie didn't even get the chance to put his name forward, he was down the tunnels, never to be seen again.

Charlie *loved it.*

He was left alone, he kept his own hours and he had a comfy little room all to himself with a nice chair and a radio, a kettle to make frequent cups of tea and it was next to a heating exchange, so it was toasty warm all year round.

About a year ago, Charlie had stopped going home in the evening. He only had a one room apartment near King's Cross which stunk from its proximity to the communal toilet and got broken into by drug-addled scum at least once a month. He only had enough belongings to fill a shoulder bag so he packed them all up and brought them down here. A few times a week he'd pop up to the surface, take out some cash from the bank, from an account that filled up quicker than he could possibly spend it with no outgoings. He'd do a tiny bit of shopping, he had simple needs; some tinned sardines, packs of instant noodles, some custard creams and a box of teabags. He didn't drink, but he'd stock up on his smokes from a Ukrainian who came round once a week selling knock offs, flogging his dirty wares across the network.

It was a shit life, but then it always had been, at least he didn't have anything to worry about down here.

And he still did his job; he did it properly and with a degree of pride. Charlie would place traps wherever he found spore, he'd put poison down in the places where people would never go, the dark corners and the places between, if any of the stations had an infestation he'd make his way across the network (they even gave him a free ticket!) and he'd deal with it quickly and efficiently. And if the people he met doing his job tended to recoil from him, then what did he care anymore? He was long past worrying what other people might think of him.

He first met the Meat Man deep down in the tunnels where few others ever ventured. The Meat Man was from Africa, or somewhere dark and distant anyway, he wasn't English and Charlie rarely had much time for anyone who wasn't English. But he took to the Meat Man.

The Meat Man had a number of tasks; he was officially termed a *Sanitation Officer*, a nice title that hid the truth of what he did. He was paid to sanitise. To wipe things down, to keep things clean. But nowhere on his job description did it mention just what it was he was usually wiping up.

"I clean up the guts," he said, after a long, long draw on the unfiltered cigarette Charlie had passed him. It was a sackable offence to smoke down here. It was illegal, even. It didn't matter; there was never anyone else down here in the dark to notice.

"What guts?" Charlie asked him, innocently.

The Meat Man whistled through brown, stained teeth. "Anyone what gets themselves in front of one of them trains. Anyone or anything."

"People you mean?"

"Mostly. Happens more often than you think, they decide it's time to end it all, throw themselves in front of a bloody train. Ruin everybody else's day along the way. Make them all late for work. Ha!"

"Blimey."

"There's the tramps, of course, they get squished as well. Down here trying to find somewhere warm to kip, find themselves on the wrong track at the wrong time. Silly buggers. Most times the driver doesn't even know he's hit them, it's not like he's driving a car and the bastards have flown over his bonnet. No, he just carries on driving with what's left of a man dragging along underneath him. By the time he gets back to the depot, he's left quite a mess behind him."

"And you have to clear it all up?"

The Meat Man took another drag and smiled again. He

smiled a lot. "That is my job. To go up and down these tunnels and mop up what's left of dead folk."

"You must have quite a stomach,"

The Meat Man shrugged. "Don't matter to me. It's all just meat, isn't it? I ain't never killed nobody. I like to think I show them the proper respect when I scoop "em up."

"I suppose so."

"It's not like you, Charlie. You're the Bringer of Death, my friend. The bodies you end up with in your bucket, you have their blood on your hands in a whole different way."

"They're just rats though," Charlie said as he lit another cigarette "Not the same is it?"

"Be the same if you're a rat, eh? I wonder if Our Lord Jesus judges us like that, what price is a rat's life compared to that of a man's?"

Charlie pondered this. "Rat hasn't got a brain like a man, does it? Doesn't have, what they call it, consciousness?"

The Meat Man nodded.

"Doesn't have *consciousness*," Charlie continued. "They're sly little bastards, I'll give them that, but that's all they are. They don't think like a man thinks, they just scamper about in the filth, hunt and eat and fuck."

The Meat Man patted him on the shoulder. "That sounds a pretty accurate definition of a man to me, my friend. I would have thought with all your experience down here, you'd have seen enough strangeness to know that there are more things on heaven and earth than you are ever likely to see on bloody television."

"I've seen plenty of strange things, but a rat is still a rat."

The Meat Man stubbed out his cigarette, collected his bucket and headed back to his duty. "You just keep telling yourself that, Charlie."

Things got stranger after that. Charlie remained uncertain if the Meat Man's words had been a warning, a prophecy or just bullshit coloured by coincidence. But whatever the reason, the behaviour of the rats became decidedly odd.

For a start, they kept themselves deeper, out of sight. Charlie was used to at least a couple dozen sightings being reported a week, and knew that was the tip of the iceberg as most people would just ignore the things when they saw them. It was mainly station staff who contacted him to tell him that there were vermin out and about, but for a couple of weeks now his phone had been deathly quiet.

Charlie hadn't seen many of them either, and the ones he did had been quick to scuttle away as soon as they were spotted, none of the bolshie bravado they often exhibited, the confidence that they may be small but they were still in their element, in their domain with its network of passages and short cuts that only they could squeeze their way through. They seemed to be actively avoiding human contact far more than usual, and despite the plethora of traps that Charlie had set across his patch, he hadn't found a single rat corpse for over a week.

He met the Meat Man again later in the week. He was dressed in his blue protective outfit, gloves and a facemask as he gathered pieces of a person from tracks they had been smeared over while humming a cheerful melody. He waved at Charlie with a blood-stained glove and mimed the action of smoking. Charlie nodded his agreement, stepped over pools of gore and joined his strange friend.

"The rats are being a bit peculiar," Charlie said.

"I thought that the rats were just rats, Charlie? Sly but stupid, wasn't that it?"

"I'm not saying otherwise. All I am saying is that they're acting odd. Furtive, like. Barely seen one of the bastards all week."

"So you've had a quiet week. Well good for you, my friend, good for you," the Meat Man pointed with his cigarette at the discarded gloves he had placed on the ground. "At least you have no blood on your hands."

Charlie was largely illiterate when it came to interpreting the intent of other people, was less than a master when it came to reading between the lines. He tended to take most of what was said to him literally. He did so now.

"They don't tend to bleed much," he said bluntly. "The poison gets them, makes them stiff as a board but they don't bleed."

The Meat Man just smoked with a smile. "There are many different ways to bleed," he eventually said softly.

"What do you do with all the mess?" Charlie asked him.

"The mess?"

"The bits. All the meat you collect. The rats get burnt up; someone from the council comes and collects them every week. What do you do with the people?"

"Oh much the same thing Charlie, much the same thing."

"Yeah?"

"Of course. What other use could there possibly be for a bucket full of flesh?"

And Charlie couldn't think of an answer. But even he, uncultivated in the ways of others, could see that the Meat Man was not being honest with him.

The next time Charlie saw a rat, it was in the most unexpected place. It was on his chair, his *special* chair with the high back and the red cushion, the chair that he spent long hours sitting upon in his office, the chair which only his backside was allowed to grace, the only piece of furniture that he cherished. Hell, the only possession of any kind he cherished.

He had returned from a tour of the traps. Once again he had found them all empty, not a poisoned rodent in any of them. Charlie hadn't received a call from any of the stations in six days either, not a single report of activity anywhere on his patch.

For the first time, his slight concern had escalated into a worry. What if this went on? Had he done his job *too* well? Had he driven them all away, out of the tunnels and the dank holes and into another refuge that was someone else's responsibility to patrol? What if the council came this week and there were no bodies for them to take away for burning? Would they be pleased? Once or twice perhaps, Charlie might get a pat on the back and recognition for his talents. But if it carried on, would they decide that he wasn't needed down here anymore, that he might be better assigned to a new post somewhere else, away from the precious office that he now called home? This made his stomach revolt. Charlie loved his life down here, he couldn't return to the surface, couldn't go back to working with other people every day, living among them, *talking* to them.

He was thinking all this with a furrowed brow when he opened the door to his kingdom and saw the rat on his chair, raised up on its hind legs, its vermin face looking right at Charlie, whiskers twitching and black eyes staring. It didn't scamper when he burst in, didn't become the fast moving blur that rats usually transformed into as soon as they were in the company of humankind.

It simply stared.

It was so bold that Charlie hesitated. He had his mouth open to shout at the little bastard, but then he clamped it shut. It looked at him, Charlie looked back. They shared something for a moment, a brief conjunction between them. Then it slowly climbed down, weaved its way across the floor on tiny claws and passed Charlie, heading away to the dark of the tunnels. Charlie just stood in the doorway, unsure of what had happened.

His relationship with the rats had changed. He wasn't sure yet if he understood what it had changed into.

He didn't have to ponder for long.

Charlie spent a restless night full of fitful dreams. In those dreams *he* was the rat and the hole he was scurrying down was a long mouth lined with teeth which keep slicing into him, diminishing him one bite-sized chunk at a time. He woke up yelping twice, and on each occasion he was certain there had been the sound of sharp claws scratching at his door as he awoke.

The following day, tired and feverish, he set off on his tour of duty. At the first junction, the first place where his traps were laid and baited, he found a row of perhaps a dozen rats in a line waiting for him.

His heart leapt. Initially, he was overjoyed to see them, to know that they were back and that he could catch them, that he could keep his job down here, that he was still *needed*. But they didn't run as he approached, they stayed in their line and patiently watched, as if they had been expecting him.

He stood before them, they stared up, and again they shared a moment of union, as if something was passing between them that lay beyond the limitations of language, a communication that Charlie couldn't understand as such, but comprehended on a level deeper than he would have recognised in himself.

He didn't like it. It made him feel sick.

Charlie raised the case he was carrying, the device for taking dead rats back to base, that he had brought with him today more in hope than any expectation that he might fill it. He hurled it at the party of rats and finally they moved, darting back into the gloom, to the dark places where he wouldn't follow.

All of them but one. The same one that Charlie had found on his chair the day before. He didn't know why he was so certain it was the same one. It was a rat; all rats looked the same, the same stupid vermin faces and senseless black eyes. But he *knew* it was the same one. It stared at him again, looked inside him.

"Just fuck off," he shouted at it. But it didn't. It twitched its head to the side, an almost human gesture.

This way, it was saying. *Follow me.*

And it trotted away, slowly, keeping a pace that Charlie could easily follow.

And so he did.

The rat led him along darkened tracks, and then to the side, through a maintenance tunnel. Charlie had to use his torch to follow the rat's movements, these tunnels weren't lit, didn't need to be on a regular basis.

The rat stopped occasionally, looked behind to make sure that Charlie was following then continued on its journey.

Eventually, after they had passed through tunnels so low that Charlie had to hunch to get through, old tunnels from forgotten sewer networks and walled-up inlets from the River Fleet, they came to a door. The rat squeezed its way underneath. Weak yellow light peaked out from the frame of the doorway. Charlie turned off his torch, turned the handle and went inside.

He'd seen lots of rats in his time, more than he could

probably count. But he'd never seen this many all at once. There were hundreds of them, thousands probably. They lined the floor, covered it like a carpet of wiry flesh and dirty fur, all those sly black eyes looking at him as he stepped inside, not a sound from any of them. They just sat and watched him. They'd been waiting patiently.

The room was an old, old chamber with an arched ceiling made of crumbling stone, a green hue from the moss that had risen over it. It was damp; water ran down the walls in torrents in a number of places.

At the far end of the chamber was a raised alcove, thick metal bars at its furthest edge leading to a dark recess beyond that led to who knew where. It looked like a stage, and standing upon it was the Meat Man, next to something large and bleeding covered in a tarpaulin.

The Meat Man waved fondly. "Hello, my friend! I'm glad you could join us, they insisted that you would come sooner or later."

Charlie didn't understand any of this and the presence of this rodent army made his skin crawl. "What are you talking about?" He wanted to use the Meat Man's name but realised he didn't know it.

The Meat Man gave his familiar smile. "They've been working for such a long time on this Charlie, I wasn't sure they'd persuade you to come but they have."

"Have you gone mad? What is going on here?"

"Oh Charlie, my friend, don't you see? You've spent so much time down here in the dark that your eyes have begun to fail you. You've been out there every day killing these creatures, poisoning them by the hundreds, and all along they have seen in you the thing they have always been looking for, the wisdom they have always sought. You are their *god*, Charlie. They have come to worship you, to pay homage to your image. They are yours to command! They are your army, your children, yours for ever more."

Charlie wanted to leave, wanted to get out of this room and put the madness behind him, to run through the tunnels and back to the surface, to get away from this. But the rats were looking at him, all of them, and he considered for the first time that what he took to be the vacant look in their eyes, the emptiness he had always seen could indeed be something else.

Were they looking at him with sheer, mindless devotion? They loved him. They *did* worship him. Why had he never seen it before?

"They came to me in the tunnels, Charlie, they told me all this, that you were a cruel god, that they could not venerate you in the way they desire for fear that you would strike them down. So they asked me to help them, to build a monument to you so that you might understand them, understand the love they have for you."

He pulled the tarpaulin away. Charlie felt his face freeze in a twisted mix of awe and horror.

It was *him*. They had built a statue of Charlie, a sculpture formed not from stone or marble but from the raw material that the Meat Man had brought them. It was an eight foot high Charlie moulded from the remains of a hundred corpses, slapped together from the gore that had been shovelled up from the tracks and scraped from the front of trains.

It was a literal Meat Man.

"This is their love for you," the other Meat Man said, and cackled with the insanity he could no longer hold in.

The army of rats bowed their vermin heads as one, and gave honour to their god.

And Charlie felt their love overwhelm him.

—LEE THOMAS

Lee Thomas is the Bram Stoker Award and Lambda Literary Award-winning author of *Stained*, *Parish Damned*, *The Dust of Wonderland*, and *In the Closet, Under the Bed*. Recent releases include the critically acclaimed novel, *The German*, and the novella, *Torn*.

—A Man in Shape Alone

By Lee Thomas

From a distance you look like a man of above average size, though you have known only a few days of life. Your features are poorly defined with a flat nose that looks as if someone has attached a spare thumb between the uneven rectangles of your eyes, and your mouth is little more than a hole Deborah gouged in the gob of clay she fashioned for your head. She called you, *Golem*.

You look at Deborah lying on the floor and experience a collection of sensations you don't understand. Memories of her smile make you think of sunlight, warm and nourishing. You always felt safe with her eyes upon you. Conversely, seeing those eyes cold and blank like bubbles on the surface of a lake, as they are now, crash and cut as if deep within you a shelf holding an array of precious bottles has collapsed, peppering you with brightly-colored shards. This is the only pain you've ever felt, and you want it to end. You stare down at Deborah, the red hole above her ear and those empty bubbles that once looked upon you with wonder, and you know the pain will continue as long as you look at her.

So you turn away, and leave the apartment and your murdered parent behind.

It is night and the streets whisper with mostly unfamiliar noises. There is laughter, which you have heard, and shouting, which you know so well, but amid these recognizable human sounds are hums and buzzes and clangs and grindings. Some draw you and others repel. You wander with no destination, equipped with a past too short and too sheltered to use for reference or direction. You don't know where to go because Deborah can no longer tell you.

After many hours of wandering, you are still in the city. Dawn breaks, filling the sky with blue and casting wedges of gold on the heads of the buildings towering above. You still walk in shadow, but already the day's warmth works into your material. The streets begin to fill with men and women. A little girl, not like Deborah in the least but reminding you of her all the same, skips in circles on the sidewalk ahead. She notices you and cocks her head to the side as if trying to decide if she's familiar with your face. You turn into an alley to avoid her gaze.

You find the towering walls comforting, protective. The sun cannot reach you here, cannot emphasize the imperfections of your face, and you lie amid the filth and trash, where you are determined to remain until night returns. A chocolate-stained candy wrapper affixes to the surface of your back. A chicken bone jabs at your hip until your weight settles and the bone is enveloped in clay, now permanently a part of your composition. The same can be said for the shard of compact disc at your shoulder and the toy car molded of cheap metal now lodged in the back of your head. Other bits of waste ornament you, but even if your vanity demanded their absence, you would be incapable of freeing them. Your hands are flat slabs designed to bludgeon, not fabricated with the detail required for delicate acts of grooming.

As you lie there, looking upward through a tunnel of dirty, chipped bricks and iron ladders at a sky of splendid light, a cat creeps from beneath the dumpster at the alley's end and cautiously approaches. Finding you neither a threat nor a delicacy, the animal pushes into the cradle between your head and shoulder; its tail, soft yet slick with motor oil, lies across your cheek. It is not Deborah's touch but reminiscent of that touch and it comforts you, even when the restless cat paws at your collar, taking bits of you beneath its claws before it settles into sleep.

Though you do not sleep, you dream. Deborah's image moves through you like a possessing spirit, only comforting and welcome—her face the first sight of your life, her voice the first sound.

On the night of your creation, she recounted the murder of her husband at the hands of local villains—men who behaved like cruel lords of the city streets. She called them *gangsters*. Upon finishing her story, she placed her hand on your cheek. That same hand and its twin had worked hatred and sorrow and the profoundest of love into your material. Its touch awakened these feelings in you, just as the scroll perched in the cave of your mouth first awakened your thoughts. She had sculpted with the intent of revenge, but that simple word encompassed myriad complexities like a greenhouse that sheltered and nurtured a hundred different species of flora.

The following night you left Deborah and walked the streets, drawn to the brutal men she had named. You found them in an apartment, not very unlike the one in which you had recently left. They appeared surprised when you entered the room, splinters of the smashed door jutting from your arms. The two men shouted and fired guns. The bullets passed through you like stones through water. You brought your hand down on the head of the first man. Neck bones snapped as the impact drove his skull low until his jaw shattered against collarbones. His head opened. Blood and bits of gray, not unlike the clay of you, bathed your arm. Teeth poured over his chest amid a wash of crimson. One tooth stuck to the lapel of his coat, and you looked at it, fascinated by its contours and its fine details. Your regard lasted only a moment, and then the brutal man swayed and crashed to the floor. You turned to the other and swung your arm like a club. This second man lifted his arms in defense but they snapped away, bone tearing through muscle and skin and cloth, as you wedged him against the wall with your arm. His mouth was open as it had been during his shouted protests, though blood now spilled in place of words. You pulled your arm from the trench it had made in his chest, and he too collapsed on the floor.

You wanted to remain there for a time so that you could examine the intricacies of the men's anatomies—what skilled hands must have been at work to form such tiny pieces and parts. You speculated on this mystery because you could conceive of no craftsman equal to the task. Your own parent had only managed flat slabs where hands should be and thick blocks of clay for feet. You then reminded yourself that you were a man in shape only, like a shadow cast against a grim wall. Your origin was not their origin.

Returning to Deborah, you saw so many people walking the streets, and you were curious to know more about them. Again, you wished to pause to observe and absorb their behaviors, but Deborah had made her wishes clear, and you obeyed because that is your nature.

On your second night of life, Deborah cried as she picked the bits of wood from your arm and mended the bullet holes, filling the tunnels in your torso with fresh clay before smoothing your chest and belly with her warm palm. She wiped away the men's blood and tissue with a dampened cloth and your body shimmered in the dimly lighted apartment until the fresh moisture evaporated.

All night she spoke to you, her finely wrought hand resting on the blunt arch of your knee. Laughter and tears punctuated her conversation, as she continued to reminisce about the dead man she had loved.

On the third night, Deborah explained that you needed to go away, telling you that your work was done, and though you didn't understand her meaning, you were introduced to an intimate fear. Your time with Deborah was coming to an end, and what might follow was beyond your imagination.

Was there anything before Deborah's face? Could there be anything after?

No answers would be given to those questions on this night. Her *thank yous* and apologies were interrupted by a knock on the door. She asked you to stay still. Then Deborah left for another part of the apartment, and you remained motionless, even when the sound of thunder rolled through the room.

Several minutes later, you took a step forward and the motion surprised you. Despite Deborah's command for stillness you were able to walk and you did so, feeling excitement and trepidation with each step.

You found Deborah lying by the front door with a red hole above her ear. You thought about thunder and remembered the gunshots that had sounded just before bullets passed through you in that other apartment, and you thought that Deborah, too, had been damaged.

You knelt down and ran your thick hand over the wound, trying to smooth it as Deborah had done for you the night before. But the maladroit and fingerless wedge of your hand only tangled her hair and smeared the blood, making her less beautiful, so you stopped. Looking at your palm, you saw the red of her painting the gray of you. Strands of hair ran like capillaries through the clay.

That was when you stood and gazed down upon her just before you left.

Lying in the alley with the cat pressed against your neck while you watch cottony clouds pass beyond the tunnel of weathered brick and iron, the few memories you have play forward and backward, moving with a disarming rhythm like a tree beside a window bent into view by gusting winds.

When night falls, the cat is gone. You lift yourself from the garbage and walk into the streets. You try to avoid people but it seems impossible in this place. All around you are apartment buildings like immense rectangular hives. Abrasive noises play in never-ending loops. For you, this is the world. You know nothing else, but you sense there might be more, so you walk to the west.

And you keep walking for days and weeks. The city falls behind you, giving way to smaller structures and diminished populations. By day you remain hidden and still, replaying your accumulated memories, wondering at the things you've witnessed: a man sitting in his car by the side of a road, sobbing; two boys fighting over a toy airplane; a woman humming a sad melody to herself as she pecks at her computer's keyboard; a man and a woman embracing in a room as you stand beyond the window to observe their union. All along your route, you've encountered men and women joined, whether in conversation or in physical embrace, and you think of Deborah, speaking with such profound love for the husband she lost. Even the people you see walking alone in yards and on sidewalks and down long roads, even these people you imagine are merely fractured elements, temporarily separated from their companions. And you wonder if you too are fractured. Deborah was not of your kind. Her gentleness and care were more the actions of a parent than a mate, which makes you wonder if any such complement to your being exists. Are you unique? Or merely misplaced and left to search for your own tribe?

One evening, you walk through a playground, now deserted. Glass from a shattered bottle slides into the sole of your foot. A condom filled with dried semen affixes to your heal to join the refuse accumulating in your clay, and you wonder on the purpose of each new ornament, though you understand they are meaningless to you. These are items cast away by man, and you are not a man. You only wear one's shape. You've seen men and women eat and drink and sleep and breed just like all of the other species you've encountered on your journey: all except you. You require none of these things, and though you recognize your difference, only now does the extent of that difference work into you like another jagged piece of broken glass.

Drops of rain begin to fall. The first lands on your shoulder and you feel an insignificant part of yourself wash away with the water. A vivid fear emerges. You imagine that each drop of rain will take a little more of you until nothing is left, and this possibility terrifies you, so you seek shelter.

Beneath a child's fort constructed of thick redwood beams, you lean against a tree and make a decision. Though you are not a man, you will live like one. Perhaps your kind has different customs, different norms, but you have found no other like you to provide example or tutelage, so you use the patterns to which you have become familiar. And with the decision made, you feel less vulnerable to the rain, though you still do not dare to continue your journey until it stops.

One day you are wandering through a field and find a shack.

It is hardly taller than you and constructed of weathered boards, uneven at the seams. Like you, the wood is gray. A window of filthy glass looks out on a mountain range in the distance. Tall grasses surround the building, running over sweeping hills to the forest at your back. The shack is infested with mice and insects; several of them join the accumulation on the soles of your feet as you absently stomp around the shelter's dirt floor, testing the way you fit in the space.

Satisfied that you have found a home, you sit in a corner and begin the process of memory. Months of experience play back to you. Some of these memories are more pleasant than others, and these are the ones you want to recall, want to see with the most frequency, but foul recollections are given equal if not greater weight than the agreeable ones.

Days go by while you sit motionless in the shack, engulfed in reminiscence. Rain and sunshine and night and day pass hardly noticed. Finally you are satisfied with the memories, certain you remember each moment of your brief existence. Only then do you leave the shack to explore the peaceful environment you have discovered.

At a riverbank you watch the current race from north to south. You wonder what lies beyond the river, but you fear straying too far from your shelter. Each afternoon has brought rain, and there is no reason to believe this one would be different. Instead of pursuing an expedition you sit on the bank and scrape lines in the mud, a substance not unlike your own material. Deborah fills your thoughts, and you wish she were with you to share your home.

But Deborah is gone. You have found no other like her. No other like yourself.

Rising to a crouch, you push your hand into the mud. It tingles as if infused with energy. And you begin to dig.

You scrape the mud together, leaving long troughs on either side of an oblong mound, which is as long as the distance between your feet and shoulders. The form's edges are ragged and you look at your hands, understanding their inadequacy for the finer work ahead. From the field, you take a twig and force it through the flat edge of your hand. With the wood you score the oblong, starting at the middle and drawing a line to one of the tapered ends. At the other end, you round the boxy mass and create divots to designate the contours of a delicate neck. You want this form to resemble Deborah, but it never will. The level of artistry necessary to achieve that miracle is far beyond your meager skills. As you stab the twig into the rounded lump of mud crafting the first eye, you tell yourself that creating the general form will suffice, so you gouge two holes. With the eyes complete, you move on to the mouth. Gently, you dig a narrow hollow and the mud pushes back and away, forming a rough ridge of lips. An hour passes as you draw and pause, trepidation often stilling your hand as you trace a strand of hair or separate toes with the edge of wood. What you began in desperation, its completion so utterly imperative, now fills you with uncertainty.

You drop the stick and walk into the field, determined not to look back, resolute in your decision to abort this ridiculous activity. But ahead of you is the shack, hardly a crate in the distance, and the emptiness of your days strikes your chest like stones.

When you return to the shape in the mud, you look down at the face and find it beautiful. Already you've forgotten your recent hesitation. Unable to resist, you kneel and press your lips to hers.

Gravity takes hold of the scroll in your mouth, and it falls, rolling over your lips to rest against the mud at the back of your creation's throat. You die in that moment, the life-giving document no longer touching the clay of your form.

But she lives and returns the kiss, rising to you. Her material and yours meld and in this moment you are resurrected, the power of the document passing through mud and clay. Consciousness surges, and you experience a frisson of joy, fueled by the sensation of touch.

You think of her as Deborah, and for a time, you are happy— the scroll passing from you to her in the moments of embrace. Sometimes the world goes away and you live no longer until she returns to again pass the document from her mouth to yours. You share this intimacy and a single life. You and this new Deborah have no language. When you are alive she is not, but some days you wake to find scratches in the dirt. You interpret a wavy line with an arrow as the river and understand that Deborah visited its banks that day. A jumble of lines erupting in wings suggests your companion has come across a nest of birds, and Deborah has drawn a clumsy map so that you might find it too. You adopt the practice, leaving symbols in the dirt for her. These are oblique communications but they are the only means you have to interact beyond the physical.

Initially this is satisfying, but as the months pass you wonder if you've added to your existence or diminished it. And there is always the transient death.

You begin to dread those moments of darkness, imagining that one day Deborah might wander from the shack and never return—gone like the first Deborah—leaving you to erode in the wind gusting through the cracked boards or to suffer at the hands of some passing strangers, incapable of defending yourself because you are nothing but an unconscious shape.

When the fear becomes too great you stay to your side of the shack, forsaking the intimacy that could pass the life between you. No touch. No kiss. No comfort. Only the certainty of continued existence, and that is enough.

One day, you leave the shack with the sculpted mud that once served as your companion propped against a wall and you walk through the field and to the riverbank, and instead of turning back you follow the river to a bridge, then cross, heading toward a horizon serrated by mountain peaks.

This time you travel during the day, allowing the sun to warm you, and at night you recount the sights and the sensations. You encounter no men, only simpler creatures—the rodents, the birds, the insects, the scavenging coyotes—concerned with the fundamental needs of existence. You envy the ease of their thoughtless pursuits: gathering food and finding shelter and rutting. They exist by instinct. Regret is impossible for such beasts.

Days pass before you reach the base of the mountain ridge.

You imagine that if you climb this incline you might see the entirety of the earth spread out before you, but you resist the urge to scale this peak, and you look back at the way you have come.

Instead of beginning up the mountain, you sit on a rock. You think of Deborah, but not Deborah the woman. Instead, the name recalls the figure of dirt with which you shared the scroll. You think about the pictures she scratched in the ground to greet you when both the document and life were returned. You want to go back to her and draw the mountain ridge before waking her and holding her tightly to you so that your kiss provides enough life for you both.

But there will be darkness. There will be death.

The day ends as you sit on the rock. Through the night, memory eludes you. In its place are silence and a mental twilight against which no images play.

Before the dawn, you rise from the rock and begin the trek home. The earth is too large and there will always be something new to see, something new to experience, but if such discovery requires casting off equal measures of acquisition, then what is gained? It is merely a trade, for which novelty is the only means of differentiation. And novelty is little more than moisture, glistening and smooth but soon evaporated and forgotten.

As you approach the shack, you are startled to see a man there, standing in the open doorway. He is old and bent at the middle. You pause in the field with the green grasses waving against your legs, watching intently as the old man scratches his head. Finally, he shrugs and closes the door and walks away. In moments the blades of grass obscure him completely.

You run forward, imagining the terrible things this man might have done to Deborah. The guilt for having left her crashes down with palpable weight, causing you to stumble. When you reach the door your awkward hand has trouble opening it, but you manage to work it free and throw it wide.

With relief you see Deborah propped against the wall as you'd left her all of those days ago. In your eagerness to touch her, you don't even bother drawing the mountain ridge on the ground for her. Instead, you kneel down and lower your mouth to hers, your hands simultaneously reaching out to hold her close.

Before your lips can touch hers, she crumbles. Her seemingly solid constitution comes apart into a multitude of specks, at first a cloud, then merely soil on top of soil, indiscernible from the earthen floor of the shack.

Her loss confuses you, and you grow angry. You imagine the old man did this, performed some murdering rite on your companion, and your primary urge is to find this man, to shatter his skull and crush his chest, reducing him to dirt the way Deborah has been reduced, but already you understand the blame cannot be reassigned. You took too long to return, and Deborah died because of your neglect.

Running your hand through the precious dirt, mixing it with the common earth, your anger continues to blossom, growing hard and sharp-edged in your chest. You stand and punch the rickety wall. The entire shack cants and creaks with the impact. With another blow, you punch through the dried gray boards, and you continue this destruction until the shack is reduced to ragged slats and shards of broken window.

And still Deborah is gone, and still your guilt enrages you. You stomp away from the shack and into the field toward the river. The banks there are deep with mud. You'll make another companion—another Deborah. You'll make a hundred of them so that when one crumbles others will remain to assuage your grief.

On the river's edge you watch the current rush. Above you, the afternoon rain clouds have gathered. They are black and cover the sky like tumors. You dare the rain to come now. It can't hurt you, could never truly hurt you so long as the document rested in your mouth. To prove this you wade into the river to let the coursing water caress and tug at you, and as you suspected, you are unharmed. When you walk out, your legs and feet glisten but they have not been weakened.

Yet in those few moments, wetted by the river, your resolve to fashion new companions waned. You look at the rich mud on the bank and think it is only mud. There is no Deborah to be found in that substance, just dirt and minerals and moisture, not unlike yourself.

It returns to you then, this lost realization: though you dreamed of life as a man, you are not a man. You are merely a collection of silica and ore with aspirations of humanity, given consciousness and mobility by a scrap of rolled paper. You can't know what a man thinks or what he feels or how to walk the paths he's carved. You can merely observe and mimic his behaviors in an awkward pantomime of life.

The first drops of rain fall, but you hardly notice them. They will come and go forever as long as there is moisture and a sky, and your thoughts are too thick to be bothered by such a mundane occurrence.

Strangely, you have found the knowledge of your dissimilarity amusing, even comforting. If man is one thing and you are another, why should you measure yourself against this dissonant calibration?

As the rain beats down, you sit in the wet field and wave your arms like blunt scythes bending the damp grasses. You entertain memories of the first Deborah, who gave you life, and the second, who gave you her touch and sketches in the dirt. Between them are a hundred memories of sights and sounds, none yet lost, none traded for fresh experience and evanescent novelty. Your clay shimmers and the rubbish clinging to its surface washes away, though so much remains embedded in the material of you—strands of Deborah's hair, a few bones, and the toy, metal car secure at the back of your head.

—BENJAMIN KANE ETHRIDGE

Benjamin Kane Ethridge is the Bram Stoker Award-winning author of the novel *Black & Orange* (Bad Moon Books 2010). He has several new novels slated for 2012 and beyond. Benjamin lives in Southern California with his wife and two creatures who possess stunning resemblances to human children. When he isn't writing, reading, videogaming, Benjamin's defending California's waterways and sewers from pollution.

—SOLUTION

By Benjamin Kane Ethridge

A tremor passed through the ship and glass beakers jiggled in their holding racks. Some solutions had been deep red once (Py remembered) and now were dull pink. Other solutions had been vital and blue once—Py remembered—and now were spotted gray lesions on the glass. All solutions had dried up, but discolored memories still remained.

Py didn't like the lab, yet he felt he belonged there. It was a confusing little room, both enlightening and deterring. The lab was a womb; the lab was a tomb. He couldn't change that.

He uncrossed his legs and got on his knees. The freezing floor eventually chilled him. Something in that cold streak through his nervous system brought his senses back. He understood few things and only in simple terms, but connections were suddenly easier to make again.

Something on this ship was broken and he was the only one to fix it.

He tossed through the starchy pages of the ship's blueprints, passing plumbing sheets and sewage disposal schematics, passing air and water conveyance, and passing a guidance manual for the pressure line control system, which had somehow been mixed in with the rest.

Py set down the manual carefully and shook his head. He was about to run his fingers through his hair when a stabbing instinct caught him. It was a black road-sign stuck at the side of his subconscious highway: *No touching the body.* He wouldn't think about why he obeyed either. Asking that particular question was dangerous for some reason and he had enough problems. Didn't he?

His thoughts eventually bobbed away; attention deficit disorder kept the terror from stacking too great. He breathed deep into his lungs but felt only a snakelike twinge in his chest. *Am I a ghost?*

He stood up—surely ghosts had no need for legs or feet. His eyes tilted down and sprung back up quickly. Py wouldn't look. He'd seen himself once in a mirror in the lavatory. What had been in the reflection? He couldn't remember. But he knew that looking once had been too much.

Where were the other passengers? They had gone into their Displacement Chambers during the prep for light speed. He had seen them go in from his own D-Chamber. He'd seen a couple smiling faces and a few complacent stares behind the transparent shields. Then their bodies had turned over, went out, slipped away, vanished to vapor, just as the airlock to Py's chamber had hissed opened and spilled him out.

He stole a glance out the lab window. No stars, only black-black nothingness, no reference to elucidate whether they'd made light speed. Py wagered the bridge display would be able to answer that easily enough. But if light speed had been reached, wouldn't the artificial gravity have powered down? And how could his body withstand the force? Maybe he wasn't withstanding anything; maybe he was a ghost after all. He didn't want to sit in the lab forever and think negatively like that though. After all, he might be able to help the others stuck in limbo. Could a ghost do such a thing?

He had to find the bridge on foot. The blueprints hadn't given any ideas. They were too disorienting. Finding himself in the main hallway, Py glanced east and west. The light panels in the ceiling dripped down and the shadows from dead rooms etched the spreading maze of dusty aluminum floor tiles.

Where was he going again?

Since light speed initiation, thoughts had become more

slippery to hold, even for Py. Right before his D-Chamber popped open, he had felt some displacement occur, as though he'd begun to fall into limbo with the others, only to return from that temporary death.

The others—did he remember them? There had been only one woman, a geobiologist, and the rest had been men: two navigators, a network specialist, and a medical doctor. Py remembered occupations, not names. He remembered his own occupation as well and wondered whether his male shipmates would appreciate a lowly operations mechanic rescuing them. Py had no expectations of being branded a hero though. Perhaps it wouldn't matter. The others could have loved him or ridiculed him or ignored him, but he did not know. Thinking back to anything, even to five minutes ago, was like looking through layers of gauze; there were shapes and colors, but definition had taken leave.

He needed to get to the bridge for some reason. Probably when he got there everything would make itself known. He went west and touched the wall plate. His fingers glided through. He felt this but did not look; he wouldn't look at any part of his body, no matter how small, ever again. His fingers met the plate a moment later, as though the real plate lived inside the wall, a mixture one part reality and one part concept.

After a pause, the door slid open. The command center was a hollow landscape of catwalks and windowed computer rooms. Nothing operated. High above on the vaulted ceiling, light globes looked like distant suns, readying for collapse. Something far away pulsed. He ignored it and went up the center catwalk.

Room after room, he checked for supplies in cupboards and in trunks. Plenty of food rations and water were left. This was good. He did have the urge to eat and drink sometimes. But had he eaten recently? Did ghosts eat?

"I'm not a ghost." His words tumbled backward and forward like a collision and counter-collision. He hurried into the hall, disgusted with his lot and searching his mind for an answer. Why had he gone up to the second floor? What was he after?

The bridge. He nearly slapped his forehead but stopped. He needed to go down to the ramp. He disregarded the countless footprints tracked in the dust, for they were too long and pointed to be his. His footfalls landed heavily, plaintive hammers in a labyrinth forge.

Up the ramp, he noticed the bridge airlock had sealed and an alarm-light slapped around like an orange and white cyclone in the hall. He walked past the obnoxious blaring light into darkness and sidled up to a display that fried away the gloom: *Error in atmospheric configuration; airlock disrupt, program change, or failure. D1ZNNi00-s(0iE)subnet.12: HW-9 Partition pneumatic plug disengaged. User command 12/567 during atmospheric system diagnostic.*

Concepts climbed the treacherous ascent to his brain. The HW-9 partition ran on the port side of the ship and its pressure lines serviced all airlocks therein. Someone, maybe even him, had fouled up during system-check and flattened the plug indefinitely. That meant the ship had never made light speed. The contingency programming overrode auto-navigation when any life support system failed. Had he once known this?

The assemblage of logic was born too quickly for Py to question its origin. His eyes stretched to their limit, which felt like ten oblique expansions. His D-Chamber must have had a natural seal long enough before displacement began, but when the ship's pressure changed, his hatch opened. His lone chamber was connected to the HW-9 partition, unlike the other chambers on the starboard side. It seemed possible that if he found the pressure line control guidance manual, he could seal the partition. With the right protocol he could do this inside the D-Chamber and displace with the others. The ship would resume its intended itinerary and all of this would be over.

He had to search for the guidance manual. And fast. With the other plugs engaged, the pressure would intermittently throw all the release valves at once. That wasn't good for the ship's structural integrity. Repeated pressure release could weaken other systems and rupture the lines. Probably give the ship one hell of a quake too.

The fuzzy sound of clinking beakers returned to his ear. The guidance manual had to be in the lab somewhere. He ran. Py's heart tripled as his feet dropped faster on the powdery floor beneath. Freedom became a desperate taste on the tongue as his last move came nearer.

Something waved in the corner of his vision and he jerked to a halt. Across from the lab was a black room. Had he just seen someone in there? There had been movement, he was sure. Long footprints on the dusty floor went inside. His eyes strained, bleary and ineffectual, until they discovered the truth. There *was* someone inside the room, grinning at him from the dark.

"Hello?" he attempted. His own words corrupted his ears, sounding hoarse and randomly arranged. *Lello-He.*

The watching man did not reply. Py wanted to continue on, to get the guidance manual, to go back into the D-Chamber and finish this, but he wanted to see this man more. He needed to see someone. There had been too much loneliness, past and present, to forgo an opportunity at another face.

He reached for the light dial on the wall. Breathlessly, carefully, his fingers wiggled out and spun it. The dial met his touch a second later and the room brightened.

In the lavatory mirror, he saw himself. He saw Py.

Strings of muscle, both long and spiraling, drifted every direction like a cosmic explosion prior to disconnection. Two eyeballs curled in and out of shape, white spheres that unraveled to silver waste. Py shouted and his neck muscles bunched together and stripped away in strands. It took a minute to realize he was screaming and that his heart filled, pumped and drained into ether. When it beat faster the heart sucked in and turned inside-out, over and over in reptilian dances.

Thoughts forced consciousness down. His brain floated through the atmosphere, so much a meaningless sea plant in a cruel current. Memories were crushed by dread. Py knew this moment would not disappear in his mind, though. It would latch on forever—it was the foundation of his life beyond certainty. He would remember not to remember what the mirror had showed him.

He threw his conceptual hands to his hypothetical face and roared. Everything twisted inside, his limbs pretzeling and bones breaking and reassembling. Pain and peace seesawed. He saw the rollercoasters of vermillion and thatches of slimy, colorful organs colliding in the mirror's reflection. With little sense remaining, he spun the wall dial down, so that this barbarism would not light in his eyes for a second longer.

Something sloshed into the hallway.

What was its name this time? What was the name this ghost represented? A mongrel shape tumbled into the lab. Its helix-arm slashed the walls for support. In the dim illumination, horror bridged confusion. The thing fell to the floor. Its soul was still entwined in antimatter. It felt its arms slip apart and some awareness returned. While it attempted to uncross the legs, it threw painful glances around the room. A wall calendar above the caustic storage showed a cartoon strip of a walking pi symbol. How did one spell that? Pye? Pai? Perhaps Py?

The curdled thing tried its legs again. Thing?

That is...Py, yes: Py knew that if he unfolded his legs, if he stopped this perversion, something good was bound to happen. That was his mind's sole passenger, only the primitive resolve: *no touch is good.*

His legs uncrossed finally and he got to his knees. Everything dropped fathoms inside him and struggle was lost like a fleeting itch behind a barrier of numbness. *Had he been looking for something?* Yes, something needed fixing on the ship. He was the mechanic. He had to fix all broken things.

The ship's blueprints lay scattered on the floor. He must have been looking these over. He browsed carefully and considered. The pages fell, one after the other, past engineering specs, plumbing, water and air, and a guidance manual for the pressure line control system. How had it gotten mixed in with the blueprints? He slipped the thin manual under the stack to get it out of the way.

Py remained there for a time, trudging through musty reasoning. Answers were on the ship somewhere, even if he hadn't found the right questions yet. Perhaps the bridge would tell him. He would go and see, and avoid any mirrors. But what had been in the mirror? Something bad? He could not remember.

The silence was murderous. *Am I a ghost?*

A cold moment later, the spacecraft shuttered and the empty beakers shook.

—RICHARD SALTER

Richard Salter is a British writer and editor living near Toronto, Canada with his wife and two young sons. He edited the short story collection *Short Trips: Transmissions* for Big Finish Productions and is now working on *World's Collider*, an apocalyptic anthology. He has sold over twenty short stories including tales in *Solaris Rising*, *Gotrek & Felix: The Anthology*, *Phobophobia*, *Bigfoot Tales* and *Machine of Death 2*. Visit him online at www.richardsalter.com

—TO AND FRO

By Richard Salter

Tuesday April 10th

Major breakthrough today. Marie had an astonishing leap of pure guesswork and managed to freeze a coffee bean. It doesn't sound very impressive, I know, but really it's a big deal. We injected the bean with a radioactive isotope with a rapid half-life. Then we switched on the field for 20 seconds. When the field was switched off, we tested the bean and discovered that the radioactivity had decayed as if only two seconds had passed, not 20.

So what does that mean? Quite simply, we practically froze the bean in time. It aged 10 times less than everything else. I would never say something like this on any of my official recordings for the project, but hot damn! Yeah, this is my private journal so I can say whatever I want. When you've been working on something for two years of your life, it feels amazing to make a breakthrough.

Tomorrow we're going to try 30 seconds and we'll keep expanding it from there. Once we've frozen the bean for an hour, it's time to move on to the next phase of the experiment. That's when things get really cool.

One day we will announce our results to the world. One day when we have achieved true success. Who knows if the final tests will work? Today's accomplishment is one step on the journey, but a significant one.

* * *

Wednesday April 11th

Today Mr. Franklin stopped by to see the first results of his investment. Mr. Franklin is an internet billionaire. He's about 40—though he looks better than most men 10 years his junior. He's gorgeous and toned, with a roguish grin and a sharp dress sense. He's divorced, apparently. When he made his fortune, the rumor is that his wife dumped him and took half of it. Poor guy. At least he still has all his hair. And, er, half of all that money. Anyway, whenever he visits I make sure I'm wearing my sluttiest skirt and high heels, and the lab coat that best shows off my figure. Marie says I'm being obvious, but I tell her men don't get subtle. She should be encouraging me. If Mr. Franklin and I get married, I'll get half his fortune and Marie's research has guaranteed funding for as long as I live!

Mr. Franklin was looking especially dishy today. He was wearing one of those tailored suits and a swanky tie. He stared at the coffee bean like we were insane. He nodded and smiled when I explained to him that the bean had been frozen in time. It was, to all intents and purposes, one hour younger than everything else in the world. I don't know if he fully understood, but he graciously congratulated us on our breakthrough and promised us another lump sum deposited in the research account. Marie estimates we'll have the results he is looking for in about a year. At this rate, I reckon it's going to be much sooner than that, but she's wise not to oversell it. We've had setbacks before.

He stayed for longer than I thought he would. He took us both out for a really posh lunch, which was beautiful—the best food I've eaten in a while. Then he told us to keep up the great work. Well, after a glass or two of champagne the afternoon was pretty much a write-off. I swear when he said goodbye his hand lingered on mine for just a touch longer than is appropriate. Marie thinks I'm imagining things but if anything I'm a realist.

I know he has his pick of every hot young thing that passes his way. A girl can dream, though.

* * *

Thursday May 3rd

Another breakthrough today. This one is beyond exciting. I got to call Mr. Franklin and tell him personally. He's in Milan right now, but he said as soon as he returns to Chicago, he will stop by and take a look. I can't wait to see him again.

Oh, right, the breakthrough. Today we were able to do more than just freeze a coffee bean, or the orange we froze for an hour last week. This week, we took our humble coffee bean and sent it back in time. This is what we've been trying to achieve all these months! The theory has become a reality. It works! Sure, the coffee bean only went back one second into the past, but for a moment—just for a moment—two beans occupied the same space. I've never seen anything like it. Marie joked that they might explode but no, they co-existed. It was the strangest thing. The coffee bean seemed hyper-real for a moment, like it was *more* real than anything else in the room, or indeed the universe. Then its double disappeared as it was sent back in time, and we were left with just one coffee bean 1.24 seconds older than the rest of reality.

Let me just repeat that, because I'm having trouble believing it myself. Instead of "freezing" the bean for an hour so that it didn't age, and ended up younger, we actually sent the bean back in time one second, so it in effect lived the same second twice. That now makes it *older* than everything else.

It's so exciting. Tomorrow we will try to send it back two seconds into the past. Eventually, if we get good enough at this, we can send it back far enough that it will actually start to appear on the "launch pad" before we even place it there. How weird will that be?!?

* * *

Wednesday June 6th

After weeks of not really getting anywhere, today we made a giant leap. We've been increasing the amount of time we send the bean back in time, but only by increments of .01 of a second. Hardly noticeable and certainly not impressive to the eyes of a billionaire internet mogul with amazing dress sense and a chin cut by diamonds. Sorry, got distracted.

So today, just in time for Mr. Franklin's visit, we managed to extend the field to send the bean back a whole five seconds. It doesn't sound like a lot, but now we are actually witnessing the impossible. This time, Mr. Franklin was seriously impressed. I felt like I was 15 again, back in high school, when my favorite teacher, the dreamy Mr. Hockley, was assessing my science project. I had built a miniature power station that actually powered a dolls house, right down to the desk lamps and the mini fridge! He was so impressed he gave me a gold star and shook my hand—lingering just a little longer than appropriate...

But I digress. So, right in front of Mr. Franklin's eyes, I held a coffee bean in my hand just inches from the launching pad. To his astonishment, an exact replica of the bean appeared on the pad. Three seconds later, I placed my bean into exactly the same space, where it had that hyper-real quality again. Two seconds after that, it returned to normal. That bit wasn't impressive, but the bean appearing out of thin air *before* I placed it on the launch pad—now that was impressive.

Mr. Franklin told us that this achievement alone would make us the most famous scientists on the planet. He urged us to continue. *We would make history*, he said. He sounded excited. He hugged us both in delight. His hug with Marie was a little awkward, but I didn't care because then he embraced me like he meant it. I can't decide which one was the highlight of my day, the successful time jump or the hug. Both were pretty awesome. He told us he'd dreamed of travelling in time since he was a little boy, and had always vowed that one day he would be rich enough to fund the finest minds in the country to unlock the secrets. He knew he was not good at science, but if he could enable others, that would feel just as good.

He truly is a wonderful man. And he smells so good too! I hope he isn't gay.

After he left, Marie said something to me that gave me chills of anticipation. Okay, she complained that Mr. Franklin hugged me for far too long. But as well as that, she said that any day now, something could arrive on the launch pad out of thin air, sent back by our future selves to this point in time. It can happen at any time, now that this breakthrough has been made. When that day comes and something arrives on the launch pad, we will know for certain that our research *will* uncover the secret of time travel. It must, or else we could not have sent ourselves anything. *The future has been unlocked*, she said. I find that so exciting! I wonder what we will send ourselves! I hope it's more exciting than a coffee bean.

* * *

Thursday June 7th

I have a date! A week Saturday. And guess who asked me out? OMG, it's Mr. Dishy himself. He sent me an e-mail today, saying he enjoys spending time with me and would I like to go to a very swishy and expensive restaurant. Okay, so he didn't actually call it a very swishy and expensive restaurant. That was me paraphrasing, but who cares? I'm so excited! Saturday can't come soon enough!

Marie just tutted. She seems kind of sullen about it. I think she has a little secret something for him too. Frankly, who the hell wouldn't? She is more his age, but that's never stopped me before. A little competition between co-workers? Bring it on!

* * *

Saturday June 16th

I'm home! He kissed me goodnight but was the perfect gentleman. I never give out on a first date! So we said goodnight and he kissed me and I stopped worrying about my shoes and whether they were posh enough for the restaurant, and oh my God I might be in love. Too soon to say that I suppose, at least not to his face! It'll be our little secret, you and me, dear journal. Harriet, you'll say, I won't tell a soul.

* * *

Tuesday June 26th

Everything is a mess. The whole thing is in ruins. I don't know how we will ever get over it. I'm not talking about me and Mr. Franklin—sorry, Craig—that's going just swimmingly. In fact, we went out three times last week and again on the weekend.

It's the experiment that's kaput. Maybe I should explain.

Today we tried to send a pineapple one day back in time— or at least we will tomorrow. How do I know that? Well we planned to. But also, the pineapple arrived this morning. There was a metal pin on it with tomorrow's date so we know where it came from.

Problem was, the pineapple itself was bad. Rotten. Not just gone off, but different. We sliced it open and it was rancid all the way through. No maggots or anything, but not a bit of it was a golden yellow color. It was like ashes.

It was a bust.

Marie was devastated. She asked me not to tell Craig for the time being, at least until we've run some more tests. I'm seeing him later tonight—it'll be tough to hide my disappointment. Maybe there was something wrong with the pineapple?

* * *

Thursday July 5th

It wasn't the pineapple. Everything we sent back a day or more was the same, even the coffee bean. Everything organic, that is. The metal pins we attached with the date on them looked a bit burnt, but stayed intact. Whatever we pinned them to came back ruined.

Marie has become increasingly sullen over the past couple of weeks, but today she was worse than ever. She's banned me from her office, told me off for being late today—I slept in with Craig—and even threatened to fire me. She looked beaten. She couldn't even bring herself to look at me. She is usually so well put together, yet today her hair was a mess and there was a stain on her lab coat. God only knows what was up with her, but she cheered a bit when I made a suggestion.

So, we set the date into the future this time, and sent our brave (fresh) pineapple into tomorrow. It disappeared and didn't come back for the rest of the day. Fingers crossed.

* * *

Friday July 6th

It arrived! The pineapple arrived! And...wait for it...it wasn't rotten. It was as fresh as if it had been bought that day. I was over the moon about this. Marie merely smiled. She did perk up a bit. She even offered a theory. *Yesterday is already written*, she said. There are no alternatives to established history, so it's harder to insert an object from today into the fixed past. Like trying to crush another CD into a box full of them—some are going to get their cases cracked.

But tomorrow, well that's a different story. Anything could happen tomorrow. There's much more room to wiggle in a little pineapple goodness.

So today we sent three pineapples forward, five minutes

apart. Tomorrow, if they arrive okay, we'll send something two days forward, and then we upgrade from pineapples to Misty. She's not a stripper, she's a mouse. If that works, we go shopping for a new cat.

* * *

Wednesday July 18th

Misty made it just fine! Craig was here to see her arrive, healthy and happy on the launch pad, exactly one day after we sent her. We took a blood sample and tested it, and yes, she is a day younger than anything else on the planet.

Craig was seriously impressed. Then I told him I love him. Not in the lab, later, at dinner. All these dinners are playing hell with my waistline, but Craig seems to be into me for more than just my figure. He asks me about my hopes and my dreams, and seems to be taking note of what I say. Maybe I will get to go to Hawaii and swim with dolphins! Can't wait! He bought me the most beautiful necklace. It has my name on it; in fact it calls me his *love*! It's covered in diamonds. It's beautiful. It took my breath away. It still does, every time I hold it up and watch it sparkle.

Marie is still sullen, despite our successes. She seemed to be talking to someone in her office today, but with the blinds down I couldn't be sure. She might have been on the phone, but I saw someone stumble against the blinds at one point. She came out looking even more upset and wouldn't tell me what was wrong. I didn't see anyone come out of her office before I left for the day.

I told Craig how worried I am about Marie. He told me she's always been given to mood swings. Some weeks she'll be upbeat and happy, then suddenly she'll be withdrawn and unhappy— for no reason. He's known her longer than me, but I've never seen her so pissed off before.

* * *

Monday August 6th

Tomorrow is the big day. Craig's here and he hates the idea, but this is why I joined the project in the first place. Marie can't go in case something goes wrong. Craig's way too important to lose in the time vortex. But me, I've always wanted to time travel. I'd be the first human on the planet to do it. The Doctor (that's the cat—I named him, my little joke) travelled a whole week forward in time with no ill effects. So now it's my turn.

Today I became the first human in history to travel in time. It was only a minute, and I felt nothing but a weird tingle all over, but here I am, one minute younger than everything else on Earth. Except the cat.

Craig hugged and kissed me when I materialized—so already I know I'm going to love the future.

Even Marie seemed a little happier. This is a major fucking breakthrough—pardon my French—after all.

I actually travelled in time! And you know what, I feel younger too!

Tomorrow I'll go for an hour. On Wednesday I'll go a whole day. We've planned to have me go forward an entire week on August 15th! I cannot wait. How amazing will that be? Better make sure my DVR is set to record my shows while I'm away!

* * *

Tuesday August 14th

11.49pm: I can hardly type. I'm in shock. Will write more later.

* * *

Wednesday August 15th

1.00am: I have to write this down. If I don't, I'll forget the details and they're important. Tonight, Craig and I sneaked back into the lab after Marie had gone home. It was my idea. I said I wanted to have sex there. We did, it was great, but that wasn't the real reason for the visit. When we were leaving, I said I had to go back and get my purse.

Once I was alone, I went straight to Marie's office. I had to know what was going on in there.

She locked the door of course. I had to spring the lock with a screwdriver. It was dark inside, and the light switch didn't work.

There was a shape in the corner of the room. I fought the urge to flee and stepped inside. There was a desk lamp and I headed towards it, but froze when I heard the noise.

It was a wheezing sound, like an asthmatic struggling to breathe. The shape in the corner was stirring. I reached out with a trembling hand, my eyes never leaving the dark mass huddled behind the desk. My fingers fumbled with the lamp, searching for the switch. When I found it, I hardly dared turn it on. My hair stood on end, my heartbeat hammered in my ears and every rational thought in my head told me to run the fuck away...

I had to know.

The light wasn't strong, but it was enough to illuminate the pitiful creature in the corner. It struggled to lift its head. Its eyes spoke of pain and desperation. It was human-shaped, more or less. Its skin was grey and crumbled like ashes. One arm was half missing, broken off at the elbow. Its head was misshapen and its body warped. The facial features were so damaged, its identity was a mystery. It struggled for every breath. As it raised its eyes towards me, it seemed to have trouble focusing. When it did manage to make out my face, a pitiful wail escaped its crumbling lips, a cry for help.

I don't think I moved for well over a minute. My hand was

still on the lamp. I tried to speak but no words came out. I stared into those eyes and a terrible realization gripped me.

This poor wretch had travelled back in time. So that's what Marie had been hiding! Without my knowledge, she had sent some unsuspecting victim back to last week, or perhaps even further. Why? We all knew what happened to the pineapples. Why would Marie risk sending a person back? Why would this poor husk ever consent to such a journey?

I tore my eyes from the pitiful horror on the floor, to something that had caught my eye on the desk. It was a metal pin, like the ones we attached to everything we put through the time machine. I picked it up, feeling sick at the blackened state of it. Clearly it had been put through the machine and sent back in time. I could still read the date on it though.

Wednesday, August 15th

This creature would step into the machine tomorrow—now today!—and be sent back in time. Why would anyone choose to do that? Perhaps they were tricked. Perhaps they thought they would be travelling into the future...

Underneath the pin was a photograph. It was in color but clearly a couple of decades old. A wedding photo. The bride was Marie. The groom? I could hardly believe it. Craig.

Shit. I knew they were old friends. I didn't know they were once married! My imagination seized this revelation and ran with it. Did this explain Marie's coldness towards me? Had Greg left her and she wanted him back? Did she hate me enough to...?

Slowly, with mounting dread, I turned to find the creature had locked its bloodshot eyes on me. It probably hadn't looked away since I turned on the lamp. That crimson gaze bored into my soul with such startling familiarity, it left me struggling to breathe.

Only one way to be sure.

I took a step nearer. The thing on the floor tried to back away but was too weak to move more than a few inches. The effort caused its right foot to disintegrate. It whimpered in distress. I crouched down to its eye-level. Still I drew closer.

I reached out, hesitating before I touched its delicate skin. Its eyes implored me. Its moaning rose to a desperate high-pitched whine as it tried to recoil. I saw it then, a slight glint of metal beneath its withered chin. My fingers made contact. It was like touching broken eggshells. The surface crumbled at the slightest movement of my hand. I hooked a finger around the metal chain.

I jumped back as the creature's neck imploded, the weight of its head too much for its shoulders to support. The head crashed through the creature's collarbone and kept falling, opening a dreadful gorge through the chest cavity and into its abdomen. Its pelvis shattered and its legs crumbled. The skull hit the floor and exploded into tiny pieces. Chunks of grey flesh skittered across the floor and broke apart.

I was left holding the gold chain in my trembling fingers, crouching over a mess of shattered bones and dust. The diamond-encrusted pendant looked as though it had been in a fire, but I could still read the inscription on the back. As I read it, my free hand went to its twin fastened around my own neck.

To Harriet, my love.

—F. PAUL WILSON

F. Paul Wilson is the award-winning, bestselling author of forty-plus books and nearly one hundred short stories spanning science fiction, horror, adventure, medical thrillers, and virtually everything between. His novels regularly appear on the *New York Times* Bestsellers List. *The Tomb* received the Porgie Award from *The West Coast Review of Books; Wheels Within Wheels* won the first Prometheus Award. His novella *Aftershock* won a Stoker Award. He was voted Grand Master by the World Horror Convention and received the Lifetime Achievement Award from the Horror Writers of America. He also received the prestigious San Diego ComiCon Inkpot Award and is listed in the 50th anniversary edition of *Who's Who in America.*

In 1983, Paramount rendered his novel *The Keep* into a visually striking but otherwise incomprehensible movie with screenplay and direction by Michael Mann.

The Tomb has spent 17 years in development hell at Beacon Films (*Air Force One, Thirteen Days,* etc.) as Repairman Jack. The plan is to make Repairman Jack a franchise character. Godot might arrive sooner.

Over nine million copies of his books are in print in the US and his work has been translated into twenty-four languages. He also has written for the stage, screen, and interactive media. His latest thrillers, *The Dark at the End* and *Nightworld* star his urban mercenary, Repairman Jack. *Jack: Secret Vengeance* is the last of his YA trilogy about Repairman Jack as a teen. Paul resides at the Jersey Shore and can be found on the Web at www.repairmanjack.com

—PLEASE DON'T HURT ME

By F. Paul Wilson

"Real nice place you've got here."

"It's a dump. You can say it—it's okay. Sure you don't want a beer or something?"

"Honey, all I want is you. C'mon and sit next to me. Right over here on the couch."

"Okay. But you won't hurt me, will you?"

"Now, honey—Tammy's your name, isn't it?"

"Tammy Johnson. I told you that at least three times in the bar."

"That's right. Tammy. I don't remember things too good after I've had a few."

"I've had a few too and I remember your name. Bob. Right?"

"Right, right. Bob. But now why would someone want to hurt a sweet young thing like you, Tammy? I told you back there in the bar you look just like that actress with the funny name. The one in *Ghost*."

"Whoopi Goldberg."

"Oh, I swear, you're a funny one. Funny and beautiful. No, the other one."

"Demi Moore."

"Yeah. Demi Moore. Why would I want to hurt someone who looks like Demi Moore? Especially after you were nice enough to invite me back to your place."

"I don't know why. I never know why. But it just seems that men always wind up hurting me."

"Not me, Tammy. No way. That's not my style at all. I'm a

lover not a fighter."

"How come you're a sailor, then? Didn't you tell me you were in that Gulf War?"

"That's just the way things worked out. But don't let the uniform scare you. I'm really a lover at heart."

"Do you love me?"

"If you'll let me."

"My father used to say he loved me."

"Oh, I don't think I'm talking about that kinda love."

"Good. Because I didn't like that. He'd say he loved me and then he'd hurt me."

"Sometimes a kid needs a whack once in a while. I know my pop loved me, but every once in a while I'd get too far out of line, like a nail that starts working itself loose from a fence post, and then he'd have to come along every so often and whack me back into place. I don't think I'm any the worse for it."

"Ain't talking about getting 'whacked,' sailor man. If I'd wanted to talk about getting 'whacked' I woulda said so. I'm talking 'bout getting *hurt*. My daddy hurt me lotsa times. And he did it for a long, long time."

"Yeah? Like what he do to hurt you?"

"Things. And he was all the time making me do things."

"What sort of things?"

"Just...things. Doin' things to him. Things to make him feel good. Then he'd do things to me that he said would make me feel good but they never did. They made me feel crummy and rotten and dirty."

"Oh. Well, uh, didn't you tell your mom?"

"Sure I did. Plenty of times. But she never believed me. She always told me to stop talking dirty and then *she'd* whack me and wash my mouth out with soap."

"That's terrible. You poor thing. Here. Snuggle up against me now. How's that?"

"Fine, I guess, but what was worse, my momma'd tell Daddy and then he'd get mad and *really* hurt me. Sometimes it got so bad I thought about killing myself. But I didn't."

"I can see that. And I'm sure glad you didn't. What a waste

that would've been."

"Anyway, I don't want to talk about Daddy. He's gone and I don't hardly think about him anymore."

"Ran off?"

"No. He's dead. And good riddance. He had an accident on our farm, oh, some seven years ago. Back when I was twelve or so."

"That's too bad...I think."

"People said it was the strangest thing. This big old tractor tire he had stored up in the barn for years just rolled out of the loft and landed right on his head. Broke his neck in three places."

"Imagine that. Talk about being in the wrong place at the wrong time."

"Yeah. My momma thought somebody musta pushed it, but I remember hearing the insurance man saying how there's so many accidents on farms. Bad accidents. Anyway, Daddy lived for a few weeks in the hospital, then he died."

"How about that. But about you and me. Why don't we—?"

"Nobody could explain it. The machine that was breathing for him somehow got shut off. The plug just worked its way out of the wall all by itself. I saw him when he was just fresh dead— first one in the room, in fact."

"That sounds pretty scary."

"It was. Here, let me unzip this. Yeah, his face was purple-blue and his eyes were all red and bulgy from trying to suck wind. My momma was sad for awhile, but she got over it. Do you like it when I do you like this?"

"Oh, honey, that feels good."

"That's what Daddy used to say. Ooh, look how big and hard you got. My momma's Joe used to get big and hard like this."

"Joe?"

"Yeah. Pretty soon after Daddy died my momma made friends with this man named Joe and after a time they started living together. Like I said, I was twelve or so at the time and Joe used to make me do this to him. And then he'd hurt me with it."

"I'm sorry to hear that. Don't stop."

"I won't. Yours is a pretty one. Not like Joe's. His was

crooked. Maybe that's why his hurt me even more than Daddy's."

"How'd you finally get away from him?"

"Oh, I didn't. He got hurt."

"Really? Another farm accident?"

"Nah. We weren't even on the farm no more. We was livin' in this dumpy old house up Lottery Canyon way. My momma still worked but all Joe did was fiddle on this big old Cadillac of his—you know, the kind with the fins?"

"Yeah. A fifty-nine."

"Whatever. He was always fiddlin' with it. And he always made me help him—you know, stand around and watch what he was doin' and hand him tools and stuff when he asked for them. He taught me a lot about cars, but if I didn't do everything just right, he'd hurt me."

"And I'll bet you hardly ever did everything 'just right.'"

"Nope. Never. Not even once. How on earth did you know?"

"Lucky guess. What finally happened to him?"

"Those old brakes on that old Caddy just up and failed on him one night when he was making one of his trips down the canyon road to the liquor store. Went off the edge and dropped about a hundred feet."

"Killed?"

"Yeah, but not right away. He got tossed from the car and then the car rolled over on him. Broke his legs in about thirty places. Took awhile before anybody even realized he was missin' and took almost an hour for the rescue squad to get to him. And they say he was screamin' like a stuck pig the whole time."

"Oh."

"Something wrong?"

"Uh, no. Not really. I guess he deserved it."

"Damn right, he did. Never made it to the hospital though. Went into shock when they rolled the car off him and he saw what was left of his legs. Died in the ambulance. But here...let me do this to you. *Hmmmmmmm.* You like that?"

"Oh, God."

"Does that mean yes?"

"You'd better believe that means yes!"

"My boyfriend used to love this."

"Boyfriend? Hey, now wait a minute—"

"Don't get all uptight now. You just lie back there and relax. My *ex*-boyfriend. *Very* ex."

"He'd better be. I'm not falling for any kind of scam here."

"Scam? What do you mean?"

"You know—you and me get started here and your boyfriend busts in and rips me off."

"Tommy Lee? Bust in here? Oh, hey, I don't mean to laugh, but Tommy Lee Hampton will not be bustin' in here or anywheres else."

"Don't tell me he's dead too."

"No-no. Tommy Lee's still alive. Still lives right here in town, as a matter of fact. But I betcha he wishes he didn't. And I betcha he wishes he'd been nicer to me."

"I'll be nice to you."

"I hope so. Tommy and Tammy—seemed like we was made for each other, don't it? Sometimes Tommy Lee was real nice to me. A *lot* of times he was real nice to me. But only when I was doin' what he wanted me to do. Like this...like what I'm doin' to you now. He taught me this and he wanted me to do it to him all the time."

"I can see why."

"Yeah, but he'd want me to do him in public. Or do other things. Like when we'd be driving along in the car he'd want me to—here, I'll show you..."

"Oh...my...*God!*"

"That's what he'd always say. But he'd want me to do it while we were drivin' beside one of those big trucks so the driver could see us. Or alongside a Greyhound bus. Or at a stop light. Or in an elevator—I mean, who knew when it was going to stop and who'd be standing there when the doors open? I'm a real lovable girl, y'know? But I'm not *that* kind of a girl. Not ay-tall."

"He sounds like a sicko."

"I think he was. Because if I wouldn't do it when he wanted me to, he'd get mad and then he'd get drunk, and then he'd hurt me."

"Not another one."

"Yeah. Can you believe it? I swear I got the absolute worst luck. He was into drugs too. Always snorting something or popping one pill or another, always trying to get me to do drugs with him. I mean, I drink some, as you know—"

"Yeah, you sure can put those margaritas away."

"I like the salt, but drugs is just something I'm not into. And he'd get mad at me for sayin' no—called me Nancy Reagan, can you believe it?—and hurt me something terrible."

"Well, at least you dumped him."

"Actually, he sort of dumped himself."

"Found himself someone else, huh?"

"Not exactly. He took some ludes and got real drunk one night and fell asleep in bed with a cigarette. He was so drunk and downered he got burned over most of his body before he finally woke up."

"Jesus!"

"Jesus didn't have nothin' to do with it—except maybe with him survivin'. Third degree burns over ninety percent of Tommy Lee's body, the doctors at the burn center said. They say it's a miracle he's still alive. If you can call what he's doing livin'."

"But what—?"

"Oh, there ain't much left to him. He's like a livin' lump of scar tissue. Looks like he melted. Can't walk no more. Can barely talk. Can't move but two or three fingers on his left hand, and them just a teensie-weensie bit. Some folks that knew him say it serves him right. And that's just what I say. In fact I do say it—right to his face—a couple of times a week when I visit him at the nursing home."

"You...visit him?"

"Sure. He can't feed himself and the nurses there are glad for any help they can get. So I come every so often and spoon feed him. Oh, does he hate it!"

"I'll bet he does, especially after the way he treated you."

"Oh, that's not it. I make *sure* he hates it. You see, I put things in his food and make him eat it. Just yesterday I stuck a live cockroach into a big spoonful of his mashed potatoes.

Forced it into his mouth and made him chew. Crunch-crunch, wiggle-wiggle, crunch-crunch. You should have seen the tears— just like a big baby. And then I—

"Hey. What's happened to you here? You've gone all soft on me. What's the matter with—?

"Hey, where're you goin'? We were just starting to have some fun...Hey, don't leave...Hey, Bob, what'd I do wrong?...What'd I say?...*Bob!* Come back and—

"I swear...I just don't understand men."

—JOHN F.D. TAFF

John F.D. Taff's career as a horror and dark speculative fiction author spans 25 years, with more than 60 stories in print in magazines (*Cemetery Dance, Eldritch Tales, Deathrealm, Aberrations, Morpheus Tales*) and anthologies (*Hot Blood: Seeds of Fear, Hot Blood: Fear the Fever, Shock Rock II, Best New Vampire Tales, Vol. 1* and *Best New Werewolf Tales, Vol. 1*). Four of his stories have been chosen as honorable mentions by Datlow and Windling in their *Year's Best Fantasy & Horror* anthologies. His short fiction will appear this year in *Big Pulp, Evil Jester Digest Vol. 1, Horror Library 5,* and *Call of Lovecraft.*

Little Deaths, his first collection of short fiction, will be published by Books of the Dead Press this April. Visit him at www.johnfdtaff.com and follow him on Twitter @johnfdtaff

—THE DEPRAVITY OF INANIMATE THINGS

By John F.D. Taff

The movies.

That's where they started, you know?

The voices.

I watch a *shitload* of movies...pretty much *every* movie that's released. From the box office smashes to the stuff that's so bad you can tell the actors are wondering how they managed to land in such a piece of shit. All of 'em—cartoons, weepies, chick flicks, period dramas, sci-fi, horror.

And I watch them all, from opening to end credits.

Nick, that's my name.

Everyone knows it.

Every *thing* knows it.

I work for a living, naturally. You could say I distribute movies. Yeah, that's good. *Movie distributor.* I make sure that some of the less fortunate among us get to see shit like *Iron Man II* and *Harry Potter*, either in a theater or in the comfort of their own homes.

Being a movie distributor lets me dress like I want and live like I want. So what if I'm not wearing fuckin' Armani suits and driving a Ferrari? I still have money for a house, a sweet whip (one of those new Chevy Camaros, black, tinted windows, leather seats, deluxe audio package, nav system), nice clothes, kicks, a little bling...and, yeah, plenty of money for the ladies.

No, dickhead, not *those* kind of ladies. Nice ones. Well, nice looking, anyways. Got enough money to get them presents every once in a while, take them to dinner, to the movies.

Yeah...the movies.

Anyway, it was one of those superhero movies. I can't remember which one, they all look the same to me. Some fruity guy in a cape flouncing around or some punkass kid in spandex pajamas CGIing all over the screen. Whatever, not my cup of tea, you know? I like horror movies, axes and blood and shit. Yeah, give me a good splatter movie where a guy gets his shit chopped off and fed into an industrial meat grinder any day over a fucking super hero movie.

I was getting ten clicks for this one, after just racking up 15 clicks for that last *Harry Potter* flick. It was shaping up to be a good summer for me.

There I was, in my seat, planted, ready to sit perfectly still for two hours.

Don't understand, do ya? Well, let me instruct you in the ways of movie distribution.

You see, our friends in Asia account for more than half of the population of the planet, probably more like three-quarters or something. But they also account for only about 2% of its wealth. Yeah, I'm making this shit up. What do I look like, Google?

But these people want the same stuff we all do—the Chevy in the driveway, the nice house, the high-def TV, the G.I. Joe with the kung-fu grip. They want to see *The Hangover Part II* and *Twilight* just like everybody here in the good old US of A. Trouble is, they don't have money like we do.

So, my employers pay me to go into a theater, a nice one here in the Midwest where most of the operators aren't on the lookout for guys like me. I buy the overpriced, watered-down sodas and the stale popcorn in the giant tubs.

I take a seat, adjust the ball cap I'm wearing. Under the hat is a small, high-def camera with a very sophisticated mini microphone and an even more sophisticated wireless device. I tether this to my *very* smartphone, for which I have a pricey, unlimited data plan. I check the phone's touchscreen to make sure the movie screen is centered and nicely framed and in focus. I make sure the microphone is picking up.

Then, I sit perfectly still, perfectly quiet and watch a movie for two hours. I don't eat, I don't drink, I don't fucking move or blow my nose.

As I watch, it streams over wifi in real time to some servers in Chicago, and from there it goes...well, who the hell knows? It goes to a lot of places I ain't never been and ain't never gonna go, depending on who's paying me.

When they get the feed, it's downloaded, cleaned up, and burned to DVDs. In a couple of days, literally, what I just watched in an air-conditioned theater in a cushy suburb of Boston winds up on the streets of Islamabad and Manila and Macau, in Phnom Penh, in Hyderabad, in fucking Moscow.

Huh?

Yeah, I think I'm doing the world a service. Fuck those guys in Hollywood with their fucking Interpol warnings and shit. They've got enough money as it is. And they could care less about my customers.

Yeah, I provide a service that helps people. So what if I make a few bucks doing it? Who am I hurting? Arnold Schwarzenegger? George Clooney? Stephen Fucking Spielberg?

OK, so there I was sitting in that fruity superhero movie, not paying much attention, when the worst thing for someone like me happens.

Kids.

I try to avoid 'em, choose midweek matinees and shit when I know they'll be in school. But there they were, right in the row in front of me.

They start whining about something or other. Probably had to take a piss, what do I care? Except they were cluttering my audio, and I'd have to stay and watch the fucking movie again.

Again, with the capes and shit.

So I, trying not to be too loud, to move too much, shushed them.

That got me a dirty look from the mother or the babysitter or whoever she was.

Worse, though, she turned around to deliver it, turned around and rose in her seat, her head in frame, completely ruining the shot.

And that's when it happened.

Hit her with me. I'm hard. If you turned me on edge, I think I could knock her out, maybe even draw blood. And if you hit her with me a couple of times, well...

Clear as day, like it was coming from someone sitting in the seat next to me.

My phone's screen, lying on my thigh, was on, lit.

Confused, I lifted it to my ear.

"Hello?" I whispered, but there was no one there.

The bitch in front of me took this opportunity to sharply remind me that cell phones were a no-no in the theater.

"I know that," I said, rising in my seat and digging my hands into my pockets for the car keys.

You could stab me through her eye, deep, deep into her brain.

You could kill her with me.

I heard this voice as clearly as I hear yours now.

I stared down at the keys in my hand.

"What did you say?" I asked, looking at the keys.

"Sit down!" someone hissed from behind me.

So, yeah, I left. Fucking left. I knew I'd have to come back again, but not this time. This shot was ruined, and I was freaking out.

When I went outside, I took my hat off, turned off the camera, the mic, the wifi. I tossed it onto the passenger seat of the car. My eyes were still dark-blind from the theatre. I stood there rubbing them, the car door open, black heat rolling out in waves.

Then, some fucker honked at me, wanting to get into the space next to mine.

My car talked to me.

Hop in, it said. *Hop in, back out, and we'll run him down while he's walking through the parking lot.*

If that weren't enough, I heard four little voices after that, all talking together.

Yeah, yeah, let's run him down, grind him into the asphalt. Let our treads drink his blood.

I stood there for a few more minutes, like a fucking retard, until the guy just pulled in around me. He got out, slammed his door, flipped me the bird, walked away.

That shook me, and I got into the car quickly, fired it up and pulled out.

Because, just for a moment, I thought about listening to those voices.

So, I went home, to crash and drink. I figured maybe a few beers would calm me down. I had a couple tallboys, followed that with an entire bottle of Cristal I had in the fridge from the other night.

Anyways, there I was lounging on the couch, getting my drink on, scratching my dog Max's head, when I get a call from my current girlfriend.

I'm talking to her, and she's pissed about something or another. They're always pissed about something, aren't they? It's like God didn't hang the sun right from the beginning, as far as they're concerned. Right?

So, there I was pretending to listen, and then she notices. Because they notice sometimes, if you slip up and really aren't listening. If the "yeahs" and the "okays" and the "uh-huhs" you're throwing out don't exactly line up with what they're saying, they get all pissy.

She knew I wasn't listening and called me out.

Before I could answer, though, I heard the voice.

Nick, it says. And now it knows my fucking name, is using my name like we're best friends or some shit.

Nick, it says, and I know it's the champagne bottle, don't ask me how. I just know.

Nick, it says, *why don't we just go round and you can bash me upside her head, break me against her stupid skull. Once she's unconscious, use one of my sharp edges to slit her throat.*

I gotta tell ya, my blood iced up. I dropped the bottle, and was a little surprised that it didn't make a noise when it hit the floor.

That it didn't say anything...anything *else*.

"Nicky!" she shrieked in my ear, rattling the little speaker in the cell phone.

"You're not fucking listening to me now, are you?"

"What did you say?"

But I wasn't talking to her, get it?

I was talking to *it*.

The motherfucking champagne bottle on the floor, empty.

I shut the phone off, more to stop her chirping in my ear than anything else, tossed it onto the coffee table.

It rang and rang and rang, but I didn't pay any attention.

I gotta tell ya, I stared at that champagne bottle for a long, long time before I fell asleep on the couch.

When I woke, I felt like I'd been skullfucked, probably from the Cristal. Max was curled up on the opposite end of the couch, on top of my feet.

I sat there with my head in my hands, and the phone rang, making me jump like I'd been goosed, sending a jolt through my head.

I fumbled around the coffee table for it, answered it.

Yeah, it was her again. I held the phone away from my head as she yelled at me. I caught words, mostly names she was calling me. Max even sat up and stared at the phone.

I tried to put the phone back to my ear, but she was shouting now, and crying I think...yeah, I think so. Makes me feel miserable now, but then it made me mad. I mean, Christ, I didn't do anything, leastways not to her.

Leastways not then.

But as she went on yapping, I heard other voices over hers, nearer, all around me.

I looked at the glass bong I kept on the shelf next to the plasma TV. Yeah, a bong. So, arrest me. Hah!

Break me against the wall and slice me across her stomach and watch her guts spill onto the floor, Nick.

I looked at one of the throw pillows on the couch.

Put me over her face, Nick, and hold down hard, until she stops kicking, until she stops breathing.

At the books on the shelf, mostly King and Koontz and Straub.

Hit her head with my spine, Nick. Hit her head hard, over and over, until her brains spatter everywhere.

At the rug under the coffee table.

Nick, use me to roll up her dead body and take it to the dump.

At the empty beer bottles...the wine opener, the lamp, the fan, the fucking TV...

All talking.

Use me.

Cut her. Hit her. Hurt her.

Kill her.

I couldn't take it. I jumped up and yelled, "Stop it! Shut the fuck up!"

Scared the shit of out Max, that was about it.

The voices faded, but didn't stop.

I saw my car keys on the table, the same keys that had wanted me to kill that woman in the theater just the day before. I grabbed them, clenched them tight in my fist like that could stop them from talking.

I took the car back to the theater, found the movie that those fucking kids had ruined yesterday. It started in 20 minutes, so I grabbed my hat rig and hot-shoed it inside, bought my ticket, my bushel of popcorn, my gallon of Coke, took my seat.

Then I realized that I didn't bring my phone. Without the phone, all the high-tech stuff was worthless. I couldn't check the framing, couldn't connect the wifi, couldn't download the movie.

Fuck yeah, I was pissed. But, I thought, what the hell, ya know? Maybe sitting here alone, in the dark, watching this stupid movie would take my mind off things, quiet the voices.

It didn't.

About a third of the way into the movie, the big guy who plays the hero in the fruity cape, you know, the blond guy, what's his name? Anyway, he's macking on the lead actress chick, getting ready to super-score or something, and suddenly he's talking.

Nick, buddy, listen, the best thing you can do right now to get some relief is head over to her house and smack her around a little. Or a lot, if you know what I mean.

"Huh?" I asked, and a few kernels of popcorn fell out of my mouth.

Ever strangle someone with a phone cord?

"A phone cord?"

Oh yeah, cordless phones. Well, how about a bath towel? A big one, rolled up, then looped around her neck. Pull it tight from behind her, and bingo!

"A bath towel?"

Someone in front of me turned around, shushed me loudly, but the two on the screen were still talking.

Bath towels and phone cords? said the female lead, the one with the dark brown hair and the big, dopey eyes. *Ugh. Leave it to a guy to screw that up. Just be direct. Push her out of a window. Or toss a toaster in the bathtub.*

Well, that's fucking stupid, he said. *Ever heard of ground-fault interrupters? That won't work.*

Your ideas are any better? Bath towels? I mean, Christ, what's he gonna do, dry her to death?

You know, you're a bitch...and the entire crew knows you're screwing the producer.

Yeah, well your breath is awful. And I read in the rags that you're gay.

Suddenly, I was on my feet. The giant soda sloshed to the floor, spilling down the slanted concrete. The popcorn flew in the air.

The guy in front of me, a lover of superhero films if there ever was one—you know the type, middle-aged, fat, pasty faced—turned and shushed me again.

I ignored him, lurched out of the row and stumbled down the darkened aisle to the exit.

As I left, I could hear the two stars still advising me.

That asshole who's shushing you? Just a short, sharp jab upwards with the heel of your palm against the bridge of his nose. Drive the shards of his nose into his brain.

I went home and drank about a six-pack. Thankfully, they didn't talk to me, so I went to bed. The voices didn't start in until right as I was drifting to sleep, so I didn't pay any attention to them. Just jammed my head under the pillows and let the beer carry me off to sleep.

About three in the morning, I woke up about to piss my diddies. Forgetting everything else, I danced over to the bathroom and drained the lizard right before it ended up going down my leg.

As I stood there in the bathroom, though, they came back.

Jam me into her mouth and just keep pushing until you hear bone, said the toothbrush.

What am I here for, anyway? Slit her throat, said my razor.

Hold her down and force her to eat every fucking pill. Don't induce vomiting and don't call poison control, said the open, super-size bottle of ibuprofen.

Roll me into a ribbon and strangle her with..., began the towel hanging near the shower, as if it had been to the same fucking movie I saw earlier.

"SHUT! THE! FUCK! UP!" I screamed, and it was loud enough that I actually hurt my throat.

Well, from there it was about a solid week of mostly sleeping, taking stuff I had around the house, Darvocet, Percocet, Oxycotin, anything, anything I had to take the edge off, to numb me, to let me sleep in silence.

Because every time I got out of bed, to take a leak or a shit, to eat something, to scratch my nuts, I heard them. All of them. It was like every fucking thing in the house had suddenly found its voice and wanted to talk to me nonstop.

I couldn't figure out why, still don't know.

And I don't know why they were all so fucking *angry*, so filled with hate.

So filled with murder.

I'd get the mail, and the umbrella stand near the door wanted me to run out with an umbrella and *shish kabob* the mailman.

I'd get a phone call, and 15 things within earshot were all offering themselves as a way to off the poor bastard who called.

I'd spot a neighbor when I looked out the window to see what time of day or night it was, and the curtains wanted me to strangle him with them. Or the window wanted me to shatter it and slice the guy up. Or the cord to the blinds wanted me to...

Get the idea?

By about day three of this, I was pretty loopy.

By day seven, I was fucking crazy.

She came over on day 10.

Yeah, Stacey. The girlfriend of the moment.

Yeah, the one on the phone.

I was still asleep, nice and peaceful, when I heard Max suddenly go ape shit.

Someone was at the door, knocking.

Why did I ever give her a key?

That key, that motherfucking key ruined everything.

And it never had to say a word.

Max came bounding into the room just ahead of her, circling and yipping, tail going a mile a minute.

He was excited.

She, definitely, was not.

"Nick!" she yelled at the top of her lungs at the foot of my bed. "What the hell's going on? I've been calling and calling and you don't answer. You don't listen to your messages? You don't return calls?"

I was awake by then, who wouldn't be with that going off right in your bedroom, but I lay there with my head under the pillow.

Lay there *waiting*.

She smacked the pillow covering my head hard, and I heard her bracelets jangle, her nails claw the pillow case.

"Nick! Nick? You awake or dead?"

You know how a southern accent, like from Georgia or Alabama, sounds so hot on a girl, so smooth and silky? Yeah, well, let me tell you that a South Boston accent is just the opposite. It's like fingers on a chalkboard. Especially when they're pissed.

I took my head from under the pillow.

"Hey, Stacey..."

"Don't you 'Hey, Stacey' me, motherfucker," she said. Sweet, ain't she?

I opened my mouth to reply, but they started.

All of them.

Everything in the entire house, all at once.

Cut her, Nick.

Bash her, Nick.

Smotherherstabherdrownherslashherpushherhither.

I couldn't stand it anymore, you know? It was too much, too much.

I was tired, freaked, strung out.

Afraid.

So, I jumped out of bed and grabbed her.

To shut them up, you know? Just to shut them up.

She was too surprised to do anything.

I wrapped my blankets around her like a cocoon, knocked her to the ground.

I could hear her screams, muffled, distant, drowned by the other voices.

I grabbed the...clock radio, I think...and bashed the covered lump of her head until its plastic casing cracked. Tossing it aside, I saw my golf driver leaning next to the closet door.

A few tee-offs with that, and I dropped it, bent and useless.

The voices were louder now, insistent, gleeful, manic.

A book, a lamp, a knife from the kitchen, a baseball bat, an electrical cord.

I was sweating, panting when it was over.

Max was sitting in the corner of the room, watching it all with his dark, dog eyes, confused, wary.

The voices were dull now, as tired as I felt.

But still there, like whispers from the row behind you in a dark theater.

The lump, *her* lump lay on the floor before me, still wrapped like a mummy in my sheets, in my comforter. There were a lot of tears in the fabric...Jesus...blood, blood soaking through it all.

She didn't move, no noises.

I remember swallowing, and it tasted like my tongue took a shit in my mouth.

I remember hearing a single voice above the others, and I tripped through the house looking for it.

It was my cigarette lighter.

It told me what to do.

And I did it.

To shut them up.

That's when it happened, the fucking thing that drove me over the edge, that pushed me right over.

Yeah, wise ass, I wasn't *already* over the edge.

As I stood there, watching my house burn down in front of me, feeling the heat of all of the things inside it press against my face, I felt something rub against my naked ankle.

I looked, and there was my dog, Max. Good old Max.

I reached down to absently scratch the top of his head, and as I did, he looked up at me.

About time, he said to me, tilting his head toward the burning house. He spoke as matter-of-factly as if we talked every day. *She was just like all the rest of that shit in there. They just couldn't shut the fuck up, none of them. It got so bad, I couldn't hear myself think.*

Yeah, that's it...that's what did it.

Having a little chat there in the yard with my dog, with the house burning.

That's when I fainted.

I didn't want to hurt her, do you get me? I didn't want to hurt *anyone*.

But they wouldn't leave me alone, not for a minute.

They wouldn't shut up about it, not even after I did it...what they said.

Eventually even that didn't shut them up, so I burned the fucking house down.

I just hope to Christ that worked.

Can we take a stretch now? Can I get a Coke or something? I'm getting a little thirsty from all this talking.

I haven't talked all that much lately, if you know what I mean. Kind of like the silence.

Sure, I can sit here by myself for a minute, no problem.

No, you don't have to worry about me. Go ahead.

Jesus Jumped-Up Christ!
Finally, you're back.
Your goddamn pencil.
You left it here, on the table when you went out.
I guess you figured I was handcuffed, what could I do?
And you were right.
But you wouldn't believe the shit it said.

For my friend, T. J. Lewis

—G.R. Yeates

G.R. Yeates was born in Rochford, Essex in the UK. He studied Literature & Media at the Colchester Institute and he has lived in China where he taught English as a foreign language. In 2011, he began to self-publish a series of vampire novels set during World War One entitled *The Vetala Cycle*. He is currently working on three novellas that were originally considered 'too sick and disturbing' for publication. You can find out more about him and what he is up to at www.gryeates.co.uk

—THE LIFT

By G.R. Yeates

No one used the lift these days, not after the accident, not after the rumours, not after all the blood that was found. That's what they said anyway.

The office building was a dirty grey lump of forsaken masonry erupting out of the city's concrete and mortar. A carbuncle with cracked glazing for eyes and a narrow aperture overhung by worm-eaten wood for a mouth, or entrance, however you wish to perceive it. Everything about the place was broken and gracelessly ageing. The light bulbs within, depending as eyes might do from the frayed cords of their electrified optical nerves, flickered beige and sepia shadows across the walls. Their low-wattage lives were short and sour, quickly fused by the ancient wiring threading the ceilings like black-rot veins. The computers occupying the splintered desks were white, battered boxes with dust-heavy screens scrolling steady streams of green text over pitch-black backgrounds. Not as ancient as the wiring but, in popular terms, these computers were antiques. Their constant static humming set teeth on edge and made eardrums ache. The heat emanating from these over-worked, out-of-date machines in this cloistered environment created a precipitative atmosphere and the workers of the building blamed this for the stench permeating every single floor. Every face was a sunken, loose mask of slightly yellowed flesh, shoulders were slumped in a permanently defeated attitude and nostrils always twitched, cloggily sniffing. The stench was an all-pervading misery they dutifully endured, but it was not the thing they feared most in the building.

"No one uses the lift these days. You're best to use the stairs if you want to get up and down to anywhere."

The speaker was a young woman; strikingly slim, cobalt blue hair and as untouched by the building's oppressive blight as her colleagues were its sure and certain victims. Her eyes were crystal clear and glacial whereas theirs were foggy, threaded with shifting veins of some milky foreign substance. Her skin was as unblemished as theirs was stained and sallow, hanging from their porous bones. Her fingers and toes were finely-sculpted whereas doubtless theirs were stunted, callused clumps of mallow. Her name was Raya and she was showing the new boy the ropes. His name was Stuart and he was as clear-eyed and untainted as she, for now.

Stuart followed Raya dutifully; the docile beta to her domineering alpha. He wondered at how she had managed to keep herself clean and pure in this diseased environment. Every so often, as she took him from desk to desk, from team to team, explaining the tedious and repetitive work cycles they all observed in the same way as nature observes its seasons; he felt the urge to ask her why she was so different. But, each time, he thought better of it. Nothing had been said, yet there was an air of the inviolate about her—Raya was not to be questioned. She was to be accepted as surely as Athena, Aphrodite, and Freya once were.

The comparison to goddess might seem excessive, but Stuart could see it in the eyes of the people they passed as they awkwardly shuffled to their feet to shake his hand with their clammy paws. Their well-worn faces seemed to be long past the point of exhibiting feeling, even incapable of showing the stronger emotions for fear of what it might do to the atrophied muscles beneath the skin.

And that was it.

Fear.

A sparkle of it, a mote, a light in the dull, bovine darkness of their eyes. It was there whenever Raya came close, whenever she was near enough to touch. These people were tentative enough after their years of drudgery but, in her presence, they became positively meek in their submissiveness.

Stuart was sure there was the faintest hint of a smile, thin with calculated meanness, pulling at the corners of her mouth whenever Raya witnessed this occurring.

* * *

It was later and the tour of the offices was done.

Not that there was much to see in terms of variety, there was just a lot of the same-old same-old, stacked up high, floor upon floor. The thrumming office cubicles of disintegrating wood and over-heated plastic were much of a muchness. All leading into and out of one another, creating a colossal labyrinth of mouldy, muttering faces, rustling stacks of poor-quality printouts and the ever-flickering off-colour light bulbs that, unshaded, swung as elderly eyeballs from overhead. The stench, he could taste it, overripe, on his tongue, feel it burrowing into the moist cells clustering at the back of his throat. He felt sure he could take a bite out of it if he had a mind to.

"Doesn't the air conditioning work in here?" he asked.

"No, the Directors wouldn't let us install a system. They said it would spoil the building's character."

"The character's pretty well spoilt already if you ask me."

She did not laugh.

"We have other candidates for this role, Mr Williams. You don't have to be here."

"I was only joking."

She looked him up and down, curtly dismissive, wrinkling her pert nose as if she had finally caught a whiff of the stench that seemed to touch and sicken everybody else except for her.

"Look, I'm sorry, I really need this job. I apologise, it was a stupid joke."

She snapped a smile at him, "Yes, it was."

They walked on through the maze of shuffling paperwork, teetering file-mountains and peering puckered visages for some time. The only sounds passing between them being the *klakt-*

klakt of her stilettos on the grubby tiles of the floor and the duller *snap-snap* of his laceless patent leather shoes. They came to the lift, passing it not for the first time, but this time it arrested Stuart's attention, "You said no one uses the lift these days."

"That's right."

"Why not? Is it broken?"

"No, we just don't use it anymore."

"But that makes no sense. All these stairs, all these floors in the building, surely using the lift would make life a lot easier."

She stopped walking, turned sharply to face him, "We *don't* use the lift. The Directors decided it was to be considered closed after the accident."

"What accident?"

This time her smile was not a snap but a long, slow development across her lips tapering out to just below her incisive cheekbones, "There was a boy, a new starter, just like you. He asked too many questions, was too curious, too ambitious, too *keen*."

"What happened to him?"

"Like I said, there was an *accident*. So don't use the lift, don't make jokes and don't ask questions, always say yes, never say no and you'll be *fine*, just like everybody else here."

She spread her arm out, encompassing the nearest ninety degrees of nullity, ambulatory depression and washed-out, wheezing despair. Stuart nodded dutifully. There was a recession on, the world was crumbling financially, he had no choice when it came to answering her inevitable question. The job would pay well, he couldn't complain.

"When can you start?"

* * *

Stuart was finishing late.

Over the days, weeks and months that he had been here, he tried to keep to his contracted schedule. Work in the morning, break for lunch, work in the afternoon, leave by early evening. Though it was the season for the nights to be drawing in, he still should have been leaving when there was some light in the sky, a trace of amethyst, the slightest turquoise smear. No, he was still here, working later and later and his lunch breaks were gradually growing shorter and shorter with no end to the accumulating piles of printouts strewn across his desk.

What on earth was the purpose of it all?

The interview process had made the job out to be administrative support at a senior level with considerable training built in and advancement options, horizontal and vertical. But, as far as Stuart could see, all he did was printing, photocopying, filing, stamping, hole-punching and clipping papers into place. It all swam before his eyes, becoming no clearer, making no sense other than a very disturbingly empty nonsense. The few colleagues he spoke to could tell him nothing, which told him everything. There were no prospects, there was no training programme, only people shuffling reams of paper and the ceaseless drone of dying machinery.

But it paid well, so he couldn't complain.

Or could he?

* * *

As the days went by, after he made his complaint, Stuart thinned and found that he was growing a little yellow like the other workers in the building. His hair began to come out, first lone strands, then as clotted lumps going grey and brittle at the roots, virtually snapping off like strings of glass. His skin absorbed moisturiser and heavy smears of foundation make-up as a desert drinks away water, leaving his flesh starting to sag away from its bones, just like the other workers. And his little flat, whenever he sat in it alone for a while, was beginning to bear the tell-tale odour of the stench.

And he dreamed.

He dreamed that he was passing through dense layers of obscurity, with no colour to them that he could name, all heaving and shifting laboriously around him. He could see people moving about in it, their shapes but not their faces. He could hear the sounds but not the words they were speaking, if indeed they were words. In his hand was the letter of complaint, crumpled tightly into his fingers. He was going to give it to the Directors in person, that would show them.

The things, the people here, became clearer.

Some were sitting. Some standing and gesturing.

They were Human Resources and they served the Directors. Well-made latex skins were drawn tightly over what was nameless, mottled and passed for their flesh. Their voices were titters and flirting giggles coiling through the ripe air. He could smell their sutures. He could hear the splitting of stitched scabs unpeeling as they scratched at themselves. Not a patch of the skin on them was healthy. Glistening insects peered out from the drooling ulcerous recesses of their congested eye-holes. Their perfume was a caustic fusion of formaldehyde and bleach catching at the sensitive membranes of his throat's tissue. What horrors were crawling around inside them, he wondered, laying dewy eggs, fucking and bleeding, then coming out to lie down in empty corners and die, alone and unseen. They cooed and called out to him, such enticing necrophiliac forms.

He crushed the letter in his hands, drawing some strength and resolve from the anger laced into it.

He moved through the pressing bodies towards the office doors resolving out of the smog before him. Plain pine surfaces broken up by squares of frosted glass. Looking in, he could see nothing for sure but the space within was a pregnant roiling opacity, a rancid fog of amniotic waves. The Directors were in there, somewhere, waiting, indistinct and tremulous. The stench, the sour, uncirculated, substantial *stuff* that ran throughout the building must be their doing, he thought. They *need* it. He rested his hand on the door handle, meaning to twist it hard, turn it harder, stride in with purpose, make himself heard.

Then it came!

Rushing from out of the depths of the office, seething and amorphous. Violently pink and scar-tissue raw. Enraged sloth. A mouth, *many* mouths, perished rectums oozing fluid, hanging wide open, hungry and gnawing. Limbs were outstretched, stumpily twitching as it struck against the other side of the door. Glass squeaked, shrill and high, a great weight went dragging down over it, fumbling at the door handle, making it turn, turn, and turn.

Opening the door!

It was then that Stuart woke up, in the dark, breathing heavily and all he could taste in the air was the stench. Overhead, he saw his bedroom ceiling as loam composed of compacted cemetery earth, teeming with charnel orgies of grave-lice, their moist and corrupt forms as moon-silvered as silk worms. A steady rain of stinking black soil and bone-nuggets was spilling down onto him. And in the outer gloom, the Directors lurked, hissing fumes out from their flatulent bodies. They spoke to him, a damp choir of synthesised gastric bowel harmonies.

He saw her standing there, their PA, their pale puppet, this was why she never became tainted or aged like the rest of them. Wood lasts, flesh rots. Raya smiled at him and it was a smile born of red, wet, awful dreams as she translated the foul speech of the Directors.

"When can you finish?"

And this time he was awake, rushing to the bathroom, emptying himself of what little food and water he could bear to consume these days.

* * *

Breathing hard and heavy, Stuart approached the entrance to the lift, drawing glances from beady, sticky eyes tired of staring at computer screens and endless mounds of printout paper.

Arbeit macht frei.

Work sets us free.

He heaved the metal doors apart. He was not sure if he was here for real or here in a dream. He listened, as he admired the dangling outcrops of blackly-greased machinery, to the echoes travelling up and down, up and down, unable to escape out into the light and the air of the external world. No, for them, forever, was this vertical tunnel of unlit interior horror where their last moments were smudged and scraped into the crumbling brickwork. He chanced a glance up into the blackness above, feeling woozy, so sick on his feet.

Falling, falling, smashing, crashing, bones breaking through bleeding pulp, fractured ribs stirring as stiff fingers through him, splitting open his insides and spilling his blood and fluid as unappetising spatters of steaming raw soup all over the place.

The lift-shaft was an open black throat waiting to swallow him.

He was leaning over, looking down into the pit. He saw them, all of them down there at the bottom of the shaft. Lumps of leprous blubber in mildewed suits and skirts, splitting at the seams. Pasty faces made hoggish and bloated by time, by decay, smeared with crusty traces of blood and sputum. The source of the stench, what was rotten about this place, the bodies of those who said no.

Arbeit macht frei.

Work sets us free.

And he heard movement behind him, lots of pairs of little shuffling feet, towers of paper printouts slumping and falling as they were disturbed by the passage of squared shoulders and bulbous hang-dog heads. The masses of the workforce, his dull and dead-eyed colleagues, were there, encroaching, and he was retreating before them, nowhere else to go. They were herding him, guiding the sacrifice to its final resting place. They had their work to do. The lift-shaft exulted, issuing an ecstatic groan that was dreadful and dimensionless, emanating from a deep, dark place that few of the living can knowingly perceive.

And Raya was there, at the rear of the herd, smiling, her cobalt blue hair shining. She ran the corpse-white slug of her tongue across her lips and gave him a lingering wink. He was sure he heard the *klakt-klakt* of wood on wood.

"We don't use the lift. Something else does."

Stuart stepped backwards one last time and, when he cried out, there was an echo, ascending and descending. The doors shut without a sound. The floor was no longer there. There was no more light. And Stuart went tumbling, crashing and smashing on down, as he had been doing his whole life, as we all do, falling from one uncertain point to another, not knowing what waits but knowing it is there, out of sight but always there, waiting to claim us as its own.

Waiting to set us free.

—RENA MASON

Rena Mason is a SUNY nursing graduate whose minor studies were in Language Arts. She currently lives in Las Vegas, Nevada, is a member of the Pacific Northwest Writers Association, a supporting member of the Horror Writers Association, and has been a member of the New Orleans Saints & Sinners Literary Festival where she was a guest reader and panelist on YA fiction. She is preparing her suburban sci-fi/ horror novel, *The Evolutionist*, for submission. This short story is her first published work.

—The Eyes Have It

By Rena Mason

It's true what they say—the eyes are the windows to the soul. I discovered this lying on the rooftop of my workplace. I was dying from a stab wound to my lung. The last breath I took bubbled through the knife slit between my ribs, then my pupils dilated. From the inside, I saw a soft glow at the end of a long, gloomy tunnel. I reached up, but the flickering incandescence disappeared before I could ascend. I sensed that instead of *me* departing, something else entirely—something not of this world—came in.

* * *

When I was ten years old, I prayed to see angels. Shadow people came instead. They visited on the darkest nights, after I'd had long days and my eyelids felt their heaviest. Sheer black figures huddled in the corner of my room, hidden by the darkness. They whispered unintelligible white noise. I lay awake those nights with the covers pulled up to my eyes. Light from outside shone through a slit in the window beside my bed, and somehow I knew they could not cross it. They were waiting for the time when they could. I stopped praying to see angels, and when I became a teenager I never saw them again.

* * *

Ray Briar was head of the accounting department where I

worked. I was in sales. He was in his mid-thirties, tall, brown hair with premature gray salting the sides, and deep mocha eyes—handsome in a mature, authoritative way. Everyone knew about his wife and kids, he kept framed family portraits on top of his desk. Those pictures; however, a display of his loyalty, did not seem to deter him from flirting with me. For months he came over to my cubicle and told me how beautiful I was. In return I walked over and told him he looked good in some particular color tie. When we were at the water cooler together, he always handed me a full cup with a big smile. He told me on more than one occasion he liked the way my skirt flounced against the back of my legs. I always felt his eyes on me when I walked away. It was harmless, but something in his stare and the tone of his voice often unsettled me.

Ray was my only on-the-job friend. No one else would talk to me for more than five minutes unless it had to do with work. I often wondered why, and eventually chalked it up to jealousy in order to protect my pride. I was the youngest sales supervisor in the history of the company, and a woman. Then I learned from Gina, the office gossip, that Ray told everyone he and I had been having a secret affair. Everything came to light for me then. It explained the last few months of unprovoked scowls, sneers, and hushed whispers behind my back. I was furious, helpless, and desperate. Ray made me the office pariah, and I wanted to know why. I wanted the truth.

* * *

My moment came a few days later when Ray and I were alone at the water cooler. "How's it going?" he asked. He gazed into my eyes, smiled big and innocent, then drank some water.

"Just great, because apparently you and I are having an affair."

Water spewed from his mouth. He quickly put his hand up and coughed into it. He was still catching his breath when he asked me who I had heard that from.

"Do you deny saying it?" I asked. "Telling *everybody* a lie?"

He would not answer. Ray lowered his head then leaned his face in front of mine. I thought he might kiss me, and as angry as I was, my heart still fluttered with lovesick desire. He glowered down at me for a moment then looked away.

I refused to yield. "I don't think you should play games like this, Mr. Briar," I said.

He stepped back and forced an automatic smile. "Me either. Let me get back to you on this." He slowly relaxed his stance then casually walked away.

After lunch break he came over to my cubicle with some phony paperwork. On top of the papers, there was a handwritten note. *I can't stand this anymore. Please stay late and meet me on the roof. I promise, I'll explain everything. Shred this when you're done reading it.* I looked up at him and smiled. I turned around and dropped the paper into the shredder.

"I'm counting the minutes."

He grinned, then went back to his desk.

I had never been up to the roof before. It's where all the office smokers hang out. I was nervously excited to hear what Ray was going to tell me. My mind raced with a multitude of scenarios.

After work there were still several people hanging around. I pretended to wait in front of the elevators until it was clear. I carefully opened the door to the stairwell, stepped in, and let it shut gently behind me. I snuck up the steps and opened the door out to the roof. A strong wind gust whipped hair around my head, blinding me. I stumbled onto the rooftop and the door slammed shut behind me with a clang.

I supposed it looked like any other rooftop. A bevy of tube shapes, squares, and rectangles, probably air vents and electric boxes, were painted taupe and jutted up from the drab gravelly surface. Cigarette butts lined the edges of pipes and vents shielded from the wind. I wanted the vantage point to spot Ray as soon as he came out, so I walked several feet toward one of the vents, and sat down. It was a nice view all around. Indigo domed the uppermost sky and melted into brilliant citrine. It would soon be dark.

Then Ray came through the doorway. He saw me look at him, smiled, then waved me over. He stepped onto the roof, but held the handle and closed the door quietly. He had an intense look in his eyes. As soon as I reached him, he wrapped his arms around me and held me tight. "I love you," he said. "I've always loved you." He spun us around then pushed me up against the brick wall next to the door. I was shocked, had lost my breath and train of thought. He put his hand up my skirt then forced his way between my legs. He buried his face into the side of my neck. He was kissing, licking, biting—mumbling. I was confused. I struggled, but it felt both good and wrong. His murmurs grew louder, but none of it made any sense. Finally, I was able to get one of my hands free. I grabbed hold of his hair and yanked his head back. "What the hell are you saying?" I asked.

He looked deep into my eyes. "I love you," he said, "but I love her more." And that was when I felt it—an icy, quick sting in my side. His hand clenched into a fist against my blouse. The handle of something extended from his grasp. It dawned on me what he had done.

He stabbed me.

I opened my mouth to scream, but he slid his fingers from between my legs and shoved them down my throat. I bit down on his hand. He thrust the knife deeper, lifting me off the ground. I writhed and kicked, but I couldn't catch my breath, and my strength drained away. Both of my shoes came loose and I heard them clunk against the rooftop. I was helpless, unable to scream or fight back. I just stared at him, trying to make sense of what was happening. The sound of rain pitter-pattered against my shoes, but when I looked up at the endless onyx sky, no moisture fell upon my face.

He pulled his hands back and I slumped to the ground. Slick crimson dripped from the blade—it was *my* blood. My shoes were sprawled out next to me in a pool of urine. What I'd thought was the sound of rain was me wetting myself. My mind screamed out in silence, but I felt nothing, aside from the gut-wrenching anguish that radiated through me.

A crackling, gurgle sound filled my ears each time I tried to breathe. Ray knelt next to me and I waited for him to say something. Tell me why, or tell me he was sorry. "You're not the first *other* woman I've ever loved, and you won't be the last," he said. He wiped the knife handle off on the bottom of my skirt and that was it. He stood up, and looked down at me one last time. He walked toward a vent with spinning fan blades inside, slid the knife between the slats, and dropped it in. In a casual stride, he went back over to the door, opened it, and left.

Left me to die.

* * *

Death is darkest of all places, and in that desperate, final moment before it became my lasting abode, I prayed again to see angels. Creatures of cold and darkness came through my dying eyes—hissing shadows of death with no sympathy or conscience. They whispered white noise I could now comprehend. I knew they came to garner my soul.

The dim light at the end of the dark tunnel appeared again. Everything human about me dried up that instant and became sheer, black ash. The shadow people led the way, and we floated upward to hover just above my lifeless body lying dead on the rooftop. We formed a circle like friends around a campfire. The shadowy figures still resembled those of humans, but they were composed of fine particles. Any motions they made caused the grains to spread apart then immediately coalesce again. They were fluid, black static mannequins and I had become one of them.

"What am I to do?" I asked. My own voice unfamiliar to me.

"You will know," they replied. "Follow what you feel. We will return when it is done."

"When what..."

And they were gone—vanishing up into the air the way ashes rise from a fire then disappear.

Well, now what? I really didn't know. A car engine thrummed below. I moved in a flash toward the edge of the rooftop—amazed I could flee instantaneously.

It was Ray in his Lexus, about to pull away. I moved back to the rooftop door and grabbed the handle. My shadow hand exploded into a trillion flakes of black ash then came back together when I moved it away. I tried again and again, but the same thing kept happening. He was leaving the parking lot. I knew I had to go with him. He did this to me—*him!* Once more I moved in a flash and dove from the rooftop. Suddenly I found myself in the passenger seat next to him. Not quite sitting, something more like hovering. I reached out to feel the dashboard and my shadow hand disappeared into it. *That could not be right.* If letting me have my revenge was what the shadow people wanted, it would be impossible without physical touch. In a fit of rage, my black ash fingers became talons, and I lashed them out across Ray's face.

"Ouch!" he yelped, swerving his car into oncoming traffic. Horns blared, lights flashed. He pulled back into his lane, vigorously rubbing his cheek. He moved his hand away and glanced at himself in the rearview mirror. There was an angry red gash in the side of his face. So—it seemed my touch affected him after all.

I wanted to kill him, but the timing felt off, and the others said I would know when. As hard as I tried to muster the will to strangle him, it wasn't there.

He drove with a smug smile through quiet suburban neighborhoods. Every street lamp we passed under buzzed exceedingly loud. Faint, ambient sounds of the neighborhood were amplified and echoed. At last, he pulled up a driveway with short white picket fences on either side. The house was a nice brick Tudor style. Exactly the kind I imagined he lived in. Bicycles and kids' toys appeared hurriedly abandoned out front. The garage door opened and he pulled his car in. Before going inside, he looked himself over. He touched the gash on his cheek. His hand jerked back and he swore in pain. He looked down at his fingers and they were clean. Apparently satisfied with the rest of his appearance, he entered the house.

I rose through the roof of his car and followed him in like a mist of fine ash—a disembodied shadow. The garage entrance led straight into the kitchen. He emptied his pockets, and tossed his keys on the counter. He walked down a long narrow hall. Near the end, he went left through an open doorway and turned on a light. I came in behind him and hovered in the darkest corner.

It was a bathroom. He turned the water on and let it run while he leaned closer to the mirror hanging above the sink. He examined his wound carefully. "Damn," he said. "This better not scar."

An orange Tabby cat slinked up next to the doorframe. It stretched its neck out and rubbed against the jamb. It looked up at me, arched its back, and hissed. Ray spun around and kicked the cat down the hall. "Boris! You stupid fucking cat." It took off with a yowl. Ray turned and faced the sink again. He pumped a couple squirts of soap into his palm then washed his face and hands. When he was done he pulled a small towel from a wall hook and gently patted his cheek dry. The slash was split apart like a fissure. Yellow glossy ooze filled it, and inflammation surrounded its edges.

"Thanks Boris," he said to his reflection. "We *really* can't have psychotic scratching cats running amok with the girls around, now can we?"

He left the bathroom, went back down the hall, then headed up a flight of stairs. To the right of the landing there was a door decorated with butterflies and flowers. He held his hand on the doorknob for a second, appearing to ponder a deep thought. He turned it slow, careful not to make a sound. I wondered what his intentions were. He was obviously capable of murder, but maybe he could do worse things too—horrible things. My thoughts filled with gruesome images of his victims. He did say there would be more. Maybe I was supposed to stop him in the act, and yet, I still did not feel the urge to kill him.

The door opened and he stepped inside with me at his heels. A child's night light was on. It was one of those kinds that spin around and projects moons and stars on the walls.

Eerie rainbow lights and shadows danced around the room in a carousel nightmare. Two little beds were also in the room. One was against the far wall and the other closest to the door. They were separated by stacked bins filled with toys. A small table stood in the middle with two small chairs pushed in on either side. A miniature tea setting was laid out on top. Above one of the headboards, in big bubble letters read the name *Caitlin*. The other one spelled *Candice*.

Something inside me began to stir, but it was not scorn or rage. Strangely enough, it felt more like hunger, which made no sense considering I was dead. I waived it off and continued stalking Ray's every move. He walked over to the bed by the door then leaned down.

A little girl lay sound asleep. She had rosy lips and cherub cheeks—an angel. Some of her curly blonde locks matted around her temples with sweat. I hovered directly above the both of them in case I had to stop him from attacking her. He moved closer to the child and I drifted down a little lower. I waited for the impulse to strike, but it did not come. All I felt was starved. He puckered his lips, kissed the child softly on the forehead, and pulled the covers up. He walked over to the other bed, and did the same thing with the other little girl.

I waited, stunned at the nothing-but-hunger I felt. I held my place, not knowing quite what to do, but knew I couldn't leave just yet. Ray did though, and shut the door behind him. I tried to go after him, but was unable to move. Instead, I drifted down even more and hovered only a few inches above the little girl, Caitlin. That was when I smelled it—an irresistible aroma that called to me. It was somewhere on the child, and I had to find it. I moved in closer and sniffed her hair, her forehead. I even smelled her breath. As I was about to move away and dismiss it as nonsense, she opened her eyes. The overpowering scent seemed to be emanating from there. I came in a little closer and sniffed her eyes. Yes, that was it! What was in there making me want it so badly? The aroma was indescribable. It's a mouthwatering smell that binds your insides into knots. I could think of nothing else, and would not be satiated until I had it.

Her eyes widened into big blue saucers, she took in a deep breath, and I could tell she was about to scream. I blanketed her with my shadow ash body, and she could not move. I forced my thumbs into her mouth to keep her quiet. She bucked and writhed underneath the weight of the monster I had become. I thought I might be crushing her, but I could not let go. Still driven by the maddening aroma and unnatural curiosity, I moved my index fingers close to her eyes and quickly poked one just a little. A clear fluid rose through the surface of her cornea and I lapped at it with a forked tongue of dark mist. It only accentuated the delectable smell, and I could no longer hold back my uncontrollable urge. She squeezed her eyes shut, and thrashed her head from side to side. Crazed, I thrust my thumbs deeper into her throat, pinning her head down while she gagged and choked. I pried her eyelids open with my middle and index fingers. She twitched a few times then finally stopped. Her little body went still underneath me. Simultaneously, I prodded both of my fingers straight down into each one of her eyeballs. I slowly pulled my finger out of her right eye and put it in my mouth. Good god, nothing was ever so right and wrong! I put my lips over the puncture wound and suckled out the substance. When I couldn't get any more, I moved my tongue inside and scooped up the last little bit.

Ah...the soul...a gelatinous ocean behind the eyes, right down to the salty organic taste it left in my mouth. Powerless to stop, I pulled my finger from the left eye then repeated the grisly act. Overwrought with violent hunger, I crossed the room to the bed with the bubble letters *Candice* above the headboard, and devoured her the same way. She hardly put up a struggle compared to her twin, and my technique had become swifter and more concise.

When I was through savagely dining on their vitreous jelly souls, I looked up and gasped at the gore I had left strewn across their angelic faces. Four, small, flesh sockets appeared to gaze blankly at the ceiling. It struck me all at once—I had just killed two little girls! This should not have happened. Killing

Ray—should have happened. I felt deceived. Infuriated, I left the girls' room in search of the master bedroom.

I moved down the hall and shifted through a door, where I saw two figures lying motionless under a king-sized comforter. A single, smaller form clung to the edge of one side, while Ray was miles away on the opposite side. He killed me so he could come home and sleep so far from the woman that he *loved more?* It didn't look at all like love to me.

I floated over to his wife and hovered a foot above her. She was on her side with a pillow scrunched between her hands. Her hair was long and dark, like mine. I waited to feel the hunger, but it didn't come. I simply felt the urge to kill her. I spread a black ash hand over her mouth and nose then lowered my body onto hers. I clung to her like layers of heavy plastic wrap. She struggled and squirmed, which only fortified my hold. I speared her side with two fingers from my other hand. Her eyes opened wide, and I looked straight down into them. She could not see me. Her children did though. They had the horror of me in their eyes.

His wife's fight for life was as futile as mine. The thought made me drive my fingers in deeper, and then deeper still. I jabbed my fingers into her the same way he did to me with his knife. I stabbed and twisted them into her organs. When her death throes ceased, I moved my hand from her face, put my head down close, and listened to the last breath rush from her mouth.

"*He loves you more,*" I whispered.

It was done. I removed my fingers then floated over to Ray. They will blame *him* for this.

Outside on the curb, the shadow people waited for me. I felt a fleeting remorse for what I had done. "When I was alive, I was a good person," I told them. "I was supposed to go to Heaven when I died, and I prayed to see angels."

"And you have," they replied. "We are angels of death, creatures of the darkness. If you had only taken the souls of the children, you would have gone to Heaven. Now you must suffer our fate."

"Shadow people," I whispered to myself, recalling my childhood memory of them. Even though they had left, I always knew they were still waiting—waiting for me in the dark.

—GARY MCMAHON

Gary McMahon's short fiction has been reprinted in both *The Mammoth Book Of Best New Horror* and *The Year's Best Fantasy & Horror*. He is the British-Fantasy-Award-nominated author of the novels *Hungry Hearts* from Abaddon Books, *Pretty Little Dead Things* and *Dead Bad Things* from Angry Robot/Osprey and *The Concrete Grove* trilogy from Solaris. You can find more at www. garymcmahon.com

—ROAD FLOWERS

By Gary McMahon

"Wow!" Tom's voice rose from the front seat of the Freelander, hanging uncertainly in the muggy air before floating out of the open side window. "That's a bit special."

Marge sat up and turned her head, staring out at the display that adorned the roadside. At first her eyes failed to take it all in, but slowly the finer details began to emerge and engaged her senses. It was indeed a bit special—there was no denying that fact. But it was also rather eerie.

A curved metal crash barrier wound along the blind curve of the road, and decorating this fiercely functional structure were literally hundreds of fresh flowers. Daisies. Lilies. Tulips. Fat-headed roses. It was an arresting sight, and the sheer sentimentality of the impromptu arrangement took Marge's breath away...until she realised what it was the floral tributes represented.

"Oh," she said, simply, bluntly.

"What's that, love? Something wrong?" Tom was nothing if he wasn't sensitive to her needs, especially these days. In the past, empathy had not been one of his stronger virtues, but now he paid more attention to her emotional state.

"It's just...well, you know. Those things—those flowers— have been put there to remember an accident. They're a tribute to someone who was killed on this stretch of road."

Silence. Darkness. Lights blinking in the distance: the peering eyes of twin headlamps as they emerged from the blackness ahead, watching from another vehicle somewhere up the road.

"I know. Sad, isn't it?"

Marge nodded, knowing that he could not see her. She repositioned herself on the wide back seat, feeling a dull ache driving into the base of her neck, right between the shoulder blades. She'd slept for at least a couple of hours; the last lingering scraps of daylight had still hung in the sky when she'd lain down to rest her eyes.

"You know what's funny?" asked Tom, glancing into the rearview mirror. He waited for her to prompt him, and when she failed to do so, he carried on anyway, in love with the sound of his own voice, the weight of his argument. "You never actually see anyone placing the posies at the kerb. They just seem to appear there, laced to road signs, leaning against barriers, scattered along the verge like lost children. And when they die, they're put out again."

The headlights far ahead of them had vanished; they must have been on the back of another vehicle, and the car or lorry had sped away from Marge and Tom, leaving them behind. Leaving them in the dark.

Marge twisted in her seat and looked out of the tinted rear window. The diminishing view of the flowers seemed to glow for a moment with phantom light, like the gases above a swamp; and then the light died, swallowed by all that darkness swarming down from the hills like a pack of hungry wolves. Marge thought she saw someone—remarkably thin, unusually flexible—bending down towards the flowers, perhaps adding to the arrangement. But the view did not last; it, too, was soon eaten up by the night.

She glanced over at two-year-old Heather, who was sleeping fitfully in the baby seat. The girl's eyes were still half-open, as if she were peeking at the world, but her head was tilted, her small pointed chin resting on one shoulder. Heather's mouth was agape; drool spilled in a thick swathe from between her slack lips.

Marge took a tissue from her blouse pocket and gently

wiped her daughter's face. Then she kissed the sleeping toddler on the bridge of her freckled nose.

"I hope we find this place soon." She leaned forward, her hands going up and wrapping around Tom's thick neck. His flesh was warm to the touch, it stirred beneath her fingers; she could feel his pulse as it beat out a secret rhythm of life deep inside the sanctity of his muscular body.

"I'm sure it's just up ahead. We should see a sign pretty soon."

Summoned by Tom's words, a sign jerked up from the ground as if on springs: ROSEGRAVE 3 MILES.

Tom chuckled, his chest hitching; Marge felt strangely afraid, as if someone was playing games from which she'd been excluded for a reason she did not understand.

* * *

The streets were empty as they drove into the outskirts of the village. The green spaces held dark corners; all the houses and shops were doused in black. It felt to Marge that a heavy lethargy had enveloped the entire town, sending even the buildings into a deep and dreamless slumber. Her skull seemed to writhe and expand, as if filling with a soft and doughy matter, and an intense drowsiness slowed her thoughts and movements.

"The hotel's up here. I can see a sign." Tom guided the big vehicle through the narrow entrance and parked it close to the main doors—the better to carry little Heather inside without disturbing her.

White light pressed against the glass doors, trapped inside the foyer; thin stalks of people moved in lazy patterns beyond, like fat bluebottles held in a jar. Marge shook her head, felt cobwebs drift from her brow. Clarity remained just out of reach, but she managed to focus on the warm bed that waited for them indoors.

Tom carried their bags to the reception desk and registered while Marge struggled to release Heather from her seat; she cradled the youngster's head against her breastbone, acutely aware of the sharpness of bone beneath her moist skin. Heather murmured in her sleep: nothing but meaningless babble; somnambulistic babytalk.

"Thank you, we'll be fine." Tom was just finishing up at reception, and he dangled a key from his thumb and pointed towards the lift doors situated beneath a huge framed watercolour of familiar hills and a long straight stretch of road bereft of crash barriers.

Marge smiled and pressed the button to summon the lift. Hidden machinery hummed. The pretty receptionist whispered something that sounded like "Always, more of them come" and somebody laughed just before her heels clattered loudly and threateningly in the large open space of the lobby.

Marge looked sidelong at Tom, but he was concentrating intently on the lights of the control box, counting off the floors as the lift descended to meet them. He looked tired; it had been a long drive from London and despite having been born in Yorkshire, he was lost in the countryside in more ways than could be accounted for by mere geography. The hushed whisper of leaves and the shrill tone of birdsong were alien to his ears, like lyrics sung in a foreign tongue.

The lift arrived; the doors opened and inhaled them inside.

* * *

At first she thought she was truly waking, but then the certainty that she was still inside the confines of a dream coated her like a thin residue, a tacky nectar from a secluded grove situated somewhere outside her usual realm of experience.

When she opened her eyes, the room was filled with flowers. A sea of colour filled her vision. The smell of them invaded her nostrils, suddenly drowning out all other senses. It was dizzying in its intensity.

Flowers lined the walls, the ceiling, were lain waist-deep on the floor; they spilled onto the bed and gathered between her bare feet. The surface of this floral ocean soon began to writhe and undulate, and she became afraid of what might emerge from beneath the buds and blossoms and stems and petals. She did not want to see what was under there, concealed for now by the temporary beauty; the corruption that dwelled under the attractive façade...

The scrawny shapes of wasted bodies twisted and turned beneath their sheet of flora; faces formed of stamens, pollen sacs, and the dusty flesh of pulpy petals threatened to break through. Just before the figures sat up, announcing their presence, the flowers falling away like discarded suits of clothing, she opened her eyes again—

* * *

The next morning the sky was leaden; streaks and striations of grey decorated this sullen expanse and feathery clouds broke apart in wispy streamers, like bands of smoke from a chemical fire. They'd planned to go for a long walk, perhaps even follow a local nature trail, but the weather prohibited such activities, so they decided instead to explore the village centre.

As Tom picked up a few brochures from a stall in the lobby, Heather chuntering away like a scratched CD at his side, Marge approached the front desk. There were no other guests in evidence, and the receptionist looked bored. It was a different member of staff from the one on duty last night; she was shorter, quite plain, and held an aura of sullenness.

"Can I help you?" The girl's voice was deep and intimidating in timbre, but once she smiled that surly manner evaporated and she looked keen to please.

"Yes. I was wondering about all those flowers on the main road into the village. Beside that crash barrier. Did someone lose their life there, in a road accident?"

The girl seemed unsure of how to answer: her brow furrowed, her eyes went dull, losing interest. "No, madam, Not that I know of."

Marge persisted: "But all those floral tributes, like a mat of flowers on the verge. Quite beautiful...and so very sad."

"I'm sorry, madam, but I really have no idea what you're

talking about. There hasn't been a serious incident out here for ages. People tend to drive safely on the roads around the village. This is a small, quiet community; we look after each other." These last words were weighted with an intractable element of threat; they could easily have been meant as a warning.

Marge smiled, but the expression was nothing more than a weak mask. Was this girl deliberately deceiving her, or had she simply not been informed of the accident?

"I can check, if you'd like. It's easily done." The girl's mouth was hard, set in stone; her cheeks were rigid, the muscles there visible beneath the taut skin.

Nodding her head, Marge turned away. She was suddenly desperate to hold her daughter, to feel the warmth of her cheek and the heaviness of her body. The *solidity* of her presence.

* * *

The morning was a wash-out. The museum was little more than a small front room filled with badly painted portraits and sketches of local dignitaries, past and present. The Roman fort was a couple of old stones and a crooked plaque. The teashop was closed for refurbishment.

"What now?" Marge asked Tom, holding tightly to the polyester reins that kept Heather within touching distance. She was trying to get away on her sturdy little legs, but the harness kept her in check, despite the occasional whining complaint.

"Well, there's a war memorial next to the Village Green. We could take a look, and maybe get a photo of you and Heather standing next to it."

Marge grinned. "Oh, don't we have such exciting and decadent holidays?"

Tom shook his head, resigned to her wry comments. "I know, I know. My fault. Next time, I promise to do more research. But remember, tomorrow we're heading for Brontë Country—that should be much more interesting!"

She slipped her free hand into one of his, squeezing his fingers. "Don't worry, hon. I know this place doesn't exactly live up to its promise. But it *did* look lovely in that film—by the way, can you even remember what it was called?"

Tom stared at her, his eyes wide, lips slightly parted; they both giggled.

"Shit," he said. "You know, all I remember is that it was filmed here, and yes, it did look wonderful. The film itself was rubbish."

They walked on in a comfortable silence, both watching Heather's back as she struggled against her bonds, drawing smiles and appreciative glances from the few other pedestrians they passed.

The film that acted as such a good advertisement for Rosegrave was on television a year ago. Both she and Tom were so enamoured with the location (if not the film itself, a cheesy and instantly forgettable love story) that when they'd decided to come to Yorkshire, a detour here had immediately sprung to mind. Unfortunately, they didn't expected the village to be so *sedate*.

The war memorial consisted of a squat stone slab standing upright behind a low wooden bench on a few square feet of neat turf. Several people milled aimlessly on the grass, some of them reading the list of names etched into the side of the monument.

As they drew level with it on the opposite side of the road, Marge sensed rather than saw two slender figures stand up and quickly move away from the site, their outlines shimmering like sunbeams caught in an updraft of warm air. A small boy raced across the grass, chasing a football into the road; a man on a moped swerved to avoid the child, honking his horn and shaking his fist as he hiccupped by.

Flowers were laid across the footpath and around the fat legs of the bench, a carpet of them leading up to the modest stone monument. Posies. Bouquets. Bundles. Wreaths left in memory of a traffic accident.

Marge tensed; she tightened her grip on Tom's hand. Heather instinctively fell back alongside her parents, and Tom picked her up and carried her the rest of the way, looking both ways as they crossed the road.

"There seem to be a lot of road accidents in Rosegrave."

Marge did not respond; she couldn't find the words. She was too afraid to even look for them. But afraid of what?

Slowly, she moved around the war memorial, studying the flowers attached to the grainy stone, tied to the bench, scattered on the trimmed turf. Hidden amid the blooms were sympathy cards and hand-written notes bearing messages of grief—"Miss you", "Rest in peace, mummy", "To my beloved", "We love you with all our hearts".

When she saw the photograph, Marge could barely move; just a hand raised slowly to her mouth, a slight tilting of the head, a tiny stumble as she almost lost her balance. The world seemed to slow down in its revolutions around the sun, gravity turned to sludge. Time came to a halt around her, and even the grass stopped growing as she bent down to pick up the weathered Polaroid.

It would be incorrect to state that the woman in the picture only resembled Marge. It *was* Marge, right down to the slight cast in her left eye, the tiny scar on her chin she'd picked up from falling down two concrete steps when she was just four years old, the way her hair sat on her scalp in a manner that Tom often jokingly referred to as looking like a wig.

"What's wrong?" Tom's hand fell onto her shoulder like a rock. His voice grated in her ears, sounding like it didn't even belong to him.

"This photo," she managed to say, her voice breaking along with her heart.

Tom took the Polaroid from her shaking hands, held it up to his face, and peered at it with great deliberation. "That poor, poor girl," he said, no recognition on his face, in his eyes. Nothing. "And she was *so* pretty."

When Marge tried to speak she found that the words had stuck in her throat. So she picked up her daughter and held her, held her as tightly as she dared without causing pain.

* * *

Tom was bathing Heather before putting her to bed, so Marge took the opportunity to slip downstairs unnoticed. The dumpy receptionist was still on duty; she recognised Marge, and her tight smile was guarded.

"Did you check?"

"I'm sorry, madam?" The girl's smile faltered, breaking like expensive crystal.

"The flowers. The *accident.*"

"Oh, yes. Actually, I asked my boyfriend—he's a police constable. Traffic police. He said that there have been no serious road accidents in the area for years, since even before he was on the job. We're actually quite famous for our road safety record. The government has funded studies." Her eyes glittered, but it was a false glamour, like the joyless lustre of fool's gold or costume jewellery.

"What about the war memorial? We went there today, and there are flowers everywhere. Wreaths and messages and photos...of a *young woman.*"

"I'm sorry, madam, but you're mistaken. There are some lovely award-winning planting beds near our memorial, but there hasn't been any road accident. No wreaths. No sympathy cards."

Marge was powerless in the face of such unwavering denial; there was no way of getting through to this girl, of reaching the truth, whatever it was.

She spun away from the desk and headed for the cramped hotel bar, ordered a small brandy from a sad-eyed barman who looked, at most, a year or two out of his teens. The liquor burned a track along her throat but it did not erase the dread that nestled within her chest. She paid for the drink and went upstairs, determined to get out of there.

* * *

Tom was sitting on their bed in his thick terrycloth robe when she entered the room. His eyes were locked onto the screen of the portable television perched on the dressing table, watching a sports show. His team had played earlier that day, and he'd been keen to catch the result of the game.

"I want to leave." The words sounded foolish, but they needed to be said. They hung in the air, refusing to budge until he acknowledged them, hovering over his head like predatory birds.

"Yeah, tomorrow." Tom's attention was still caught up in the show; football results scrolled down the screen, a surfeit of information he needed to plough through for what he required.

"No, Tom. We need to leave *now.*"

At last she had his attention; he muted the TV and slowly turned to face her, his eyes flashing weirdly in the peculiar flat light from the screen. "What are you on about, love? What's the problem?"

Heather was sleeping soundly on the sofa bed under the big window. The top pane was propped open, letting in a gentle breeze. Intermittent skirmishes of rain spattered the glass.

"There's something happening here, Tom. Something's not right. I don't pretend to understand what it is, but we need to go. Now."

He sighed; it was all she needed to hear.

"You don't believe me, do you?" She urged him to contradict her, to get up, get dressed, and help pack their cases.

"It's not that, Marge. It's just...well, is this like the time you thought our neighbours had it in for you? Or when you were convinced your mother was poisoning Heather's milk?"

Marge winced; he'd hit a nerve—*every* exposed nerve she had. "No. That was the postnatal depression." She felt like she was speaking to a child. "This is different. This is *real.*"

When he stood and approached her she slapped away his hands, disgusted that his faith in her was so fragile. "Don't patronise me, Tom." She did not raise her voice; she needed to sound rational.

Tom backed away, hands held palms-outwards. They stood there in silence, facing each other across the miles of cheap carpet, both afraid of saying anything more in case they said too much. The moment seemed to last forever, and was broken only when Heather mumbled something in her sleep.

* * *

She knew he was awake by the sound of his breathing, and when she slid her hand onto his thigh, he slowly moved his fingers across her knuckles, covering her hand with his own.

"Remember last night, when we saw those flowers by the roadside?"

"*Mmm...*" Was he falling asleep, or just faking it?

"When you said that it's strange how we never see anyone putting them there; that the flowers just seem to appear overnight?"

"*Mmm...*"

"What if that's true? What if...what if whoever sees the people who put out the flowers becomes the next victim?"

"*Mmm...*"

She took her hand away from his leg. There was no resistance as his arm fell away from his side and onto the plastic mattress. When Tom began to snore, she almost screamed.

* * *

She kept her speed under 40; she was unfamiliar with the controls of the four-wheel-drive and there was certainly no need to tempt fate. Safety was the byword.

She'd left a note for Tom requesting that he meet her in the hotel near Otley they'd booked over a month ago. The holiday could continue as planned; the only difference being that she was travelling on ahead and he'd have to rent a car to catch up. It served him right. He should have listened to her.

The hills rolled past as if on castors; darkness stained the landscape like spilled ink; shapes that might have been narrow, bedraggled figures twitched away from the headlights whenever she rounded a bend. The village was three miles behind; soon she would reach the spot where they'd first seen the flowers, where the warning had been ignored.

She saw the crash barrier first, and when she slowed the car it became apparent that the flowers had been cleared up and taken away. Stopping an adjacent lay-by, she switched off the engine and wound down the window. She stared at the metal barrier, looking for a clue to the mystery that Tom thought only existed in her mind.

The shapes that bobbed in the darkness drew closer to the car, and only when she saw the flowers clutched in their withered hands did she realise they were upright figures. Swaying to some unheard rhythm of the road, they stepped up to the barrier and began to arrange their many tributes. The torn rags of clothing hung from their damaged frames; hands that resembled clusters of dried-out stems relinquished posies and wreaths and placed them on the ground at the foot of the barrier.

As Marge started the engine, biting down the panic that was welling in her torso, she caught sight of snapshot images in the narrow beams of the headlights—dried, skinned parodies of faces, the dented helmets of skulls, shoulders shorn of so much more than off-the-peg shirts and jackets.

The rear wheels skidded on loose gravel as she pulled away, refusing to look back, denying the magnetic pull of the sights that beckoned from the mirrors. The road ahead seemed to close in like a throat in the act of swallowing, restricting her route towards salvation, and when Heather stirred on the back seat, Marge sent out a silent prayer to the gods of the road that her daughter would not wake.

She stepped on the brake, more shocked than afraid, until the fear became solid, tangible, a living thing contained within the feeble coat of her skin. Figures lined the carriageway. They stood in ragged lines and unruly groups, hundreds of victims clutching their own floral tributes—the wilted flowers they needed to bequeath to whoever came next.

Marge reversed the car and spun it around in the middle of the road, a ferocious manoeuvre designed to warn off her passive assailants. She headed back the way she'd come, planning to reach town and wake Tom, show him the reality of what was happening here. And as she approached that same spot in the road—the glinting serpentine crash barrier—a sudden and undeniable urge overtook her mind and body.

She watched as the last of the flower-bearers placed their burdens on the ground, near the road; and as she watched she knew exactly what was expected of her. Marge had finally witnessed the grieving, needing, remorseful figures, and now she must join their ranks.

Without thought, without delay, and wary of any sudden movement that might wake Heather, she calmly and deliberately turned the wheel and swerved her vehicle towards the barrier.

—Norman L. Rubenstein

Upon graduation from Northwestern U. (B.A. in Philosophy & Political Science) and Loyola U. of Chicago Law School (J.D.), Norm spent 20+ years as a litigation atty., then was appointed as an Administrative Law Judge for the City of Chicago, presiding in thousands of trials and hearings.

He currently resides in Surprise, AZ, with his Retrievers, Sunny & Coco. He's an Active Member of both the Horror Writer's Association (HWA), and of the International Thriller Writer's, Inc (ITW).

He's a prolific Horror & Thriller Genre book and film reviewer and magazine columnist and has extensive experience as a freelance Editor for numerous Specialty Presses.

His most recent published works are in the nonfiction reference, *Thrillers: 100 Must Reads* and as co-author with Carol Weekes of "The Closet," in the fiction anthology, *Fear Of The Dark*. Norm's busy writing screenplays and stories.

—Steven W. Booth

Steven W. Booth decided in early 2010 to finally use his MBA (much to his mother's delight) to start a company that helps authors self-publish. After a few years of learning the how to build books for other authors, he decided to become a publisher and build books for himself. Steven's first novel as both publisher and an author, *The Hungry* (co-written with Harry Shannon), was released in 2011, and has helped pay the rent. The sequel, *The Wrath of God*, will be released in mid-2012. Genius Publishing, his imprint, has upcoming books from Gene O'Neill, Brian Knight, Carol Weekes, Tim Marquitz, Christopher Conlon, and Karl Alexander.

Steven lives in Encino, CA with his wife and far too many cats.

—THE WIDOWS LAVEAU
By *Steven W. Booth & Norman L. Rubenstein*

That Honore Laveau's crypt was in a common mausoleum surprised many in the community, given how he was known to be extremely wealthy, as well as very powerful. Some felt his untimely demise left his widow little time to have a proper, private mausoleum built. Others, however, speculated that Honore's widow, Desirée, was perfectly happy to let Honore rot in a crypt barely suitable for a coachman or baker, if only to save Honore's vast fortune for herself.

It was widely speculated that Honore was related to the famous (or infamous, depending upon one's view) "Voodoo Queen of New Orleans," Marie Laveau, a widow in her own right, and they'd been seen frequently together in public enjoying each other's company. While Honore officially claimed to be a cousin of the formidable lady, rumors from respectable sources identified him as one of the many bastard sons of Marie's—and by all appearances, one of her favorites. Honore's reputation as a ruthless businessman earned him respect, and the whispers that Honore was Marie's disciple, and a powerful Houngan, a Voodoo priest, meant that he was almost universally feared.

His young wife—now widow—Desirée was the only daughter of a powerful tobacco and cotton tycoon from Mississippi, who knew nothing of voodoo and even less of New Orleans. But in the five years of their marriage, she had blossomed into a socialite of great reputation for generously supporting orphans and the poor. Desirée dedicated as much energy and effort in giving away—some said squandering—

Honore's fortune as he invested in creating it.

Consumption had overtaken Honore in the course of a few days. The doctors shook their heads and wrung their hands, but there was nothing they could do for Honore, and he was dead within a week. Some said it was just deserts for an evil man practicing the black arts. Others went on with their lives. One, however, did not accept his untimely demise with the same casual attitude as the rest of New Orleans society.

Though the Funeral Mass had been a roll call of New Orleans elite, the interment was, by design, sparsely attended. Only the priest, Desirée, Honore's servant François, and two cemetery workmen were present. Much gossip spread through the city as to why the Widow Laveau refused to have even the pallbearers stay for the committal. The reality, however, unknown to almost all, was that Desirée wanted nothing more than to deprive Honore of the respect he had earned, rightly or wrongly, throughout his otherwise charmed life.

The priest executed the Rite of Committal as rapidly as his vows would allow, as the widow and her newly inherited servant were anxious to be as far away as possible, and as soon as dignity would permit them to leave.

When the priest had finished, he nodded to the workmen, who caused the casket to be lifted from the ground and inserted into the crypt that would be Honore's last resting place. Desirée and François were already gathering their things as the workmen began sealing the crypt. They did not bother to read the inscription.

HONORE ANTON LAVEAU
JANUARY 19, 1809 – OCTOBER 7, 1849
REST IN PEACE

As widow and servant made their way to the waiting carriage, Marie approached from the shadows. She pointed a finger at Desirée and scowled, causing François to step in front of his mistress, shielding her from whatever spell Marie might cast. Marie cackled at this futile display.

"The dead know all secrets," she said softly, "and I know the dead. For he wrongly taken, know you my curse—he shall return and do unto you, worse. For she who robs a mother of her son, let the agonies she suffers never be done!"

Marie made a quick, furtive motion of her hands and walking stick toward the younger woman, then abruptly turned her back to them. She smiled at the two startled cemetery workers standing awkwardly nearby and handed each a gold coin. She said, "Ferrymen, see that he gets safe passage," and walked away, soon to be lost from sight amongst the trees.

* * *

"No respect," said Jacques, the lead workman, as he tightened the clamps that would hold Honore's crypt closed tight. He showed none of his usual calm, distant acceptance of the actions of the grieving mourners. Another day, he would have said nothing about the odd behavior of the younger Widow Laveau, nor of being personally singled out by Marie Laveau herself. Today, however, he seemed agitated, anxious even. "No respect at all. A man like him deserves a burial fit for a king," he said.

Guillaume sought to calm Jacques down. "'Tis nothing, my friend. Come the rapture, we will all be judged the same, king and pauper, and the manner of our burial will come to naught."

Jacques hopped lightly off the short ladder that allowed his diminutive stature the reach he needed to finish the job. Guillaume looked down at the much smaller man, who came up no higher than his shoulders, as Jacques scowled.

"Some will be judged more harshly than others, Guillaume! Betrayal, adultery, and murder never escape the Lord's sight." He spat on the ground, precisely where Widow Laveau and her servant had stood during the committal.

Guillaume gaped at the violence in his friend's eyes. "Perhaps you sympathize too much with Monsieur Laveau's passing. Come, it is late. I will buy you a good wine, and we will forget all about this."

Jacques scowled, then his expression softened. He looked up at Guillaume and replied, "Forgive me, old friend. I've been feeling rather oddly ever since today's interment. Perhaps a nice glass of wine will help both my headache and my disposition."

They gathered their tools and set them on the small handcart. Guillaume lifted the handles, and began pushing the heavy cart toward the outbuilding where they spent much of their time between burials. Jacques lagged behind, and Guillaume could hear snippets of the conversation Jacques held with himself, which consisted of small guttural sounds that resembled the barking of a rabid dog. Guillaume said nothing as he put away the tools in their rightful places. He took up a lantern and lit it. He locked up the outbuilding, and with lantern in hand, put his arm around Jacques's shoulder and led him toward the entrance to the cemetery.

Jacques followed distractedly, but when they were just outside the church grounds, he halted as if his feet had become rooted to the earth.

"We cannot let them get away with their crime," insisted Jacques.

"Who? What crime?"

"Who else, you fool? Desirée and that horse's ass, François. You saw them, their guilt dripping from their pores in the same way that their tears did not. Honore Laveau's ghost cries out for vengeance, and we must answer the call."

Guillaume stood before his friend, and with kindness in his heart, said, "The only call we must answer is the one that leads us to the local ale house, and then to bed. Besides, Laveau was no saint, as you well know."

Jacques's eyes snapped up to bore into Guillaume's. "Just what is meant by that?"

"Nothing, friend. Nothing." Guillaume put his hands on Jacques's shoulders and said, "What is wrong tonight? What possesses you to speak so?"

"I..." began Jacques, but he paused. Again, something of his old kindness came into his eyes, and he said, "It is nothing. I let the moment get the better of me. Here, let me buy you a glass of wine. Come, I know a place nearby."

He began walking, not toward their usual tavern, but in the opposite direction. Guillaume, in order to avoid bringing on another argument, followed a step behind.

They walked a long time in silence. Guillaume presumed that Jacques held his tongue to prevent himself from lashing out at whatever demons tormented him tonight. But when his feet, already sore from the day's work, began to protest the long walk, he ventured a comment.

"Jacques?" he said. "Might there not be a closer place for us to have a drink?"

The words had barely left Guillaume's lips when Jacques whirled around to face him, his face red, and thrusting his chin up aggressively toward Guillaume, said through gritted teeth, "We're almost there."

Yet after walking another quarter hour, with only homes in sight, Guillaume began to wonder about Jacques's powers of navigation.

Just as Guillaume had worked up his courage to question his friend again, Jacques announced, "We are here."

Guillaume looked to and fro, searching for Jacques's proposed tavern, yet none appeared. The light was failing, and home was another hour in the opposite direction. Though it was a warm night, a shiver ran up Guillaume's spine.

"Where might 'here' be?" said Guillaume.

"The place where it happened," replied Jacques.

"The place where *what* happened?"

Jacques looked Guillaume directly in the eye. "Laveau's murder." Guillaume could think of nothing to say, and Jacques hardly gave him a chance. "We must not let this crime go unpunished," he said.

"Jacques—" ventured Guillaume.

"Tonight," continued Jacques, "we are agents of the Holy Spirit. We are avenging angels. It is our mission to make the sinners pay for their heinous acts."

"Jacques, if I hadn't been with you this hour and more, I would swear you were drunk. We know nothing of a murder—"

"We do!" Just as quickly Jacques then lowered his voice. "The evidence of their guilt was written on their faces. Even the great lady Marie Laveau could see it." He glanced up and down the street, as if seeking those who might oppose him. "It is up to us, don't you see? We are the only ones who can affect this revenge. And we will be amply rewarded." Jacques paused. "You know as well as anyone in New Orleans that Laveau was rich. You have no idea how rich, my friend. And I promise you, Laveau's wealth is ours if we carry this out. It is our due. You heard the nearly—sainted Marie Laveau herself all but accuse them, and you saw that she gave us each a piece of gold already." He held his coin up to the light of the lantern, though surely it seemed to glow with its own light. "How can you doubt that Madame Laveau wants us to do this thing? It is so clear! So clear..."

"I don't know," said Guillaume. "I don't think this is a very good—"

Jacques snatched the glowing lantern out of Guillaume's hand, and quickly extinguished it. "The entrance is this way," said Jacques, turning toward the house, leaving Guillaume feeling there could be no room for argument. He led Guillaume down a narrow alleyway on the north side of Laveau's manse. Without hesitation, Jacques entered a small gate set into the barrier wall. He impatiently held the gate for Guillaume, who hesitated just outside. "Come on, we haven't much time," insisted Jacques.

"What about the servants?" asked Guillaume.

Jacques grunted. "Mireille is ancient, and Gaspar is usually off carousing at this time of night. I rather expect François is here, though," he sneered. "Do not concern yourself with them. Now, come!"

Guillaume took a step through the gate, and Jacques closed it behind him. "How do you know so much about the comings and goings of the servants?" Guillaume whispered.

"I told you, I am guided by Marie Laveau and the spirit of Monsieur Laveau himself. Their intent is as clear to me as the moon in the sky. Now, shh!" admonished Jacques in a whisper. He led them through the thick foliage to the back of the house.

There he headed unerringly to a particular plant and thrust his hands down, rummaging around at its base. He soon produced a small, burnished brass key. He proceeded to open the servant's entrance with it, and stepped quickly inside.

This is not a good idea, thought Guillaume. Nevertheless, he followed.

The house was dark, and smelled of cooked meat and sweet spices. Jacques moved with the quiet self-assurance of a denizen of the house. Guillaume did his best not to bump into furniture and generally make himself known to the occupants. If his heart could be heard as well by the household as it could in his own ears, the alarm would have already been raised.

"Are you sure they're home?" whispered Guillaume.

"Silence!" hissed Jacques. As if on cue, footsteps sounded from the floor above. A woman's laugh. The creak of a bed. Then the rhythmic, unmistakable sound of lovers copulating.

The sounds only seemed to make Jacques even more upset. He headed confidently for the stairs, and Guillaume strove to follow without knocking over the statuary that occupied the niches along the stairwell.

Jacques stopped at the landing at the top of the stairs, and was nearly trampled by Guillaume in the darkness. Jacques turned to his companion and whispered almost silently, "Do as you're told, and we shall be home before you know it." He clapped Guillaume on the shoulder, and ventured a smile. But it was an evil smile, a smile bent on murder, and it made Guillaume shudder.

The young widow Laveau moaned with lust and pleasure, and Jacques tightened his grip on Guillaume's shoulder. "It is time," said Jacques. He turned and went to the door, placing his hand on the knob. He gestured for Guillaume to come close. Then he threw the door open and charged in.

The room was lit by only a few candles, giving it a soft, intimate glow. The fireplace was dark, as it was a warm evening. Desirée Laveau faced the headboard on her hands and knees, her long, luxurious blonde hair covering her face in a cascade, and François, Laveau's trusted manservant, took her from behind with great energy and enthusiasm. Both turned to the sound of the door opening, and François shouted in anger.

"Who are you?" he bellowed as he disengaged himself from Desirée. He was a large man, though not as large as Guillaume, and appeared very intimidating despite his utter nakedness. "What are you doing here?" He raised his fists.

"Guillaume," said Jacques, "shut him up."

Guillaume brought his fist around, slamming it into the side of François's head, casting him across the room. He crashed into a large bureau and crumpled to the floor. He did not move.

Desirée ventured a scream. It was a piercing sound, and Guillaume was sure that someone would hear her.

Instead of ordering Guillaume to quiet her as well, Jacques crossed the room and gave her a stinging slap to the face, knocking her down onto the bed.

"Slut!" he shouted. "Your husband is hardly cold in his grave, and you defile his bed with that over-muscled jackass, François!"

"What do you want?" she whimpered. "Don't hurt me."

"You shall get what you deserve, and nothing less." He turned to Guillaume. "Come here," he ordered. Guillaume approached, still unsure of what he had gotten himself into. "Hold her," Jacques said.

Guillaume reached for Desirée's wrists. She pulled them away, covering her breasts, and cried, "No!" She kicked out at him, but Guillaume seized her by her ankle, and drew her to him. She struggled, but she was no match for the much larger man. He took her wrist, and twisted her arm painfully. She squealed and fought, but Guillaume managed to turn her over, wrenched her arms behind her and held her face down on the bed. He looked up at Jacques for instructions.

"Keep her there. I need to fetch some things." Jacques turned to go out the door, but paused to kick the unconscious François in the head on the way out.

"Please," said Desirée softly. "Please don't rape me. I have money. You could be a very rich man."

"Shut up," said Guillaume. He wondered how he found himself in Laveau's home, holding the man's terrified, naked wife captive, as his good friend went to gather Lord only knew what. Guillaume prayed that Jacques was only seeking out the money he'd mentioned, but he knew there was really no hope of that.

François began to stir. Guillaume fought off panic as he wondered how he would maintain control over both Desirée and François without Jacques's help. François groaned and tried to find his feet, but to no avail. He fell back down to the floor, and lay there, gasping.

Guillaume was about to call out to Jacques to hurry when he appeared at the doorway. Jacques held a length of rope, a knife, and a hammer. He locked the door behind him, and deposited the key in his shirt pocket. With Desirée face down on the bed, she could not see what Jacques had brought, but Guillaume could see well enough, and his blood ran cold.

"Stand her up," said Jacques. "I want her to see this."

Guillaume pulled Desirée off the bed, and turned her around. Tears ran down her face, and she struggled a little, but her exertions proved futile against Guillaume's grasp.

Jacques measured a length of rope, and cut it with the knife. He quickly and efficiently bound François's hands behind his back. He then took much of the rope, and tied it into an elaborate knot. Finally, Jacques took up a nearby chair, and dragged it over to where François lay. Guillaume could see he was struggling to regain a clear head. Jacques encouraged him by drawing the knife along the length of his thigh. Blood dribbled out where the blade touched him, and he squirmed as his eyes fluttered open.

"Stand up, betrayer!" ordered Jacques. At knifepoint, François struggled to right himself, and eventually found his feet. Jacques made him sit in the hard, wooden chair. Then Jacques threw the rope over an exposed beam near the ceiling, and put the knotted loop around François's neck.

"No!" screamed Desirée. It was a useless gesture, as Jacques pulled the free end tight, making the still groggy François stretch to preserve his breath.

"Stand on the chair, François, or I promise you, I will drive this knife through your heart."

François stood, crying and choking, and Jacques took up the slack, and ultimately tied the rope off on the leg of the bed.

"What are you going to do to me?" asked François with as much courage as he could muster. "Am I to be hanged?"

"That is up to you," sneered Jacques. "If you move, you will surely hang yourself." Jacques went to where he had placed the hammer, retrieved it, and went back to François. "This need last only as long as you choose," he said. And with that, he brought the hammer down on François's foot. Guillaume could hear the bones crush beneath the blow. François bellowed in pain, but he kept his balance.

"What do you want?" cried François.

Jacques raised the hammer, and held it poised to fall again. "Vengeance," he growled.

Without hesitating, Jacques brought the hammer down again on the same foot. Jacques tried to move it out of the way, but only succeeded in placing his toes under the path of the hammer. Blood spurted from the crushed toe, splattering Jacques.

"Mercy," begged François, his voice clogged with tears and pain.

"Mercy?" asked Jacques. "Is that what you showed your master when you poisoned him?" Jacques gestured with the hammer again, and François jumped back, almost tipping over the chair. Jacques laughed a laugh so evil that Guillaume felt the devil himself possessed Jacques's very soul.

"I know nothing of poison," offered François.

Jacques only laughed again. He brought the hammer up a third time, and held it, ready to strike. He gazed into François's eyes.

"I can take no more," cried François. "It was her! She seduced me. She promised to share everything with me and to marry me if I helped her." He was crying in earnest now, deep rasping sobs, his nose running freely down his face and onto his chest.

Desirée screamed out at her lover, "Liar!" She turned to Jacques and spat venomously, "Don't believe him. He seduced *me*. He convinced me that Honore was possessed by the devil and meant to steal my immortal soul." She struggled against

Guillaume's grasp. "François showed me his altar to Satan, and I watched as he took part in sacrificial rites with that old witch, Marie Laveau. He told me that Honore and Marie were lovers, and convinced me that the only way to protect myself was to follow his evil plan to kill Honore."

Jacques became as wild as a wounded alligator. "Marie is no witch! She is the high voodoo priestess, and you owe her and her son veneration, not plots and murder!"

Jacques next put the hammer aside, and picked up the knife.

"What...what are you going to do with that?" asked Desirée.

Jacques turned to her and grinned. "I want to give you a gift, my dear." He turned the knife over in his hand. "It is clear that you chose François's manhood over your husband's life. It seems only fitting that you should have the object of your desire. But I am going to leave it up to François as to whether you will receive this gift." Jacques looked up at the bleeding, naked man, and said, "The choice is yours."

"What...?" began François, his eyes wide.

Jacques approached him with the knife. He took a hold of François's flaccid penis and testicles and placed the knife next to them. "The choice is yours, François. Give your mistress this gift and live, or keep them for yourself in death. For only by kicking the chair out from under you will you keep these intact."

Jacques touched François's skin with the knife. François squealed like a young girl, then looked again at his tormenter, and his eyes grew wide. "It's you, isn't it, Honore," he whispered hoarsely, an accusation.

Guillaume couldn't believe his ears. "What's that?"

Jacques must have responded by tightening his grip on François's genitals, for the naked man shrieked in pain. Jacques repositioned the knife, ready to sever man from manhood. François made his decision. He shifted and knocked the chair out from under himself. He dangled a few inches from the floor, his face turning blue and his tongue protruding from his lips. His eyes became bloodshot just before the light went out of them. Then François's bowels loosened, and he defecated on the floor. He twitched once, twice, then moved no more.

"A shame," said Jacques simply. Then he turned to Desirée. "I suppose we know which was more important to him now."

"You sick bastard!" she shouted.

"You have no idea," replied Jacques. He approached her with the knife.

Desirée stared at the small man confronting her. "I recognize you now," she whimpered. "You're the two cemetery workers at Honore's funeral. How do you know so much about my husband? Did Marie tell you to come here? Tell you what to do and say?" She struggled against Guillaume's sweaty grip, but he held her fast. "What do you want with me? It was François! The coward admitted his guilt and took his own life. Look at him! He's the one who did evil to Honore, who poisoned him. Go to Marie and tell her that you have extracted vengeance for Honore. I had nothing to do with it, I tell you. Nothing!"

Jacques shook his head sadly. He opened his mouth, and began talking in a voice that startled Guillaume, who'd never heard his friend use such a tone in all their years together. It was far deeper and more mellifluous, more refined and colorful than Jacques had ever sounded. Indeed, his voice was that of an entirely different person altogether.

"You, my dear, shall pay the price for your faithlessness," he said.

Desirée suddenly grew wild and fought like a tigress, trying to break free from the frightened and puzzled Guillaume. Jacques, again speaking in the new, strange, deep voice, said, "Guillaume, hold her down on the bed."

Guillaume was nauseated from all he'd just witnessed. "Haven't you done enough, Jacques? Let's just take the money and go."

"No!" shouted Jacques. "I shall show the same sympathy for my murderers as they did for me!"

"Your murderers?" asked Guillaume. "What are you talking about?"

"Desirée knows, don't you, my dear?" asked Jacques, his voice deep and resonant.

Desirée's eyes grew wide with recognition. "Honore?" she

gasped. "It can't be!"

"Oh, but it is, my dear. You didn't think you could get away with it, did you?"

"Honore, forgive me," she exclaimed. "Had I known..."

"Had you known that I would return from death, you wouldn't have killed me, is that it? Well, it is too late for your regrets, Desirée. Your husband is dead. Your lover is dead. Soon you will join both of us. Guillaume," he said, never taking his eyes off Desirée, "hold her down."

Guillaume hesitated.

"Guillaume," warned Jacques-who-was-Honore.

Guillaume released Desirée's wrists, and pushed her to the far corner of the bedroom.

He shook his head. "No, Jacques, or whoever you are. I won't let you do it."

Jacques's eyes became cold, almost dead. "You cannot stop me," he said.

"I can try," said Guillaume. He moved quickly, more quickly than Jacques could counter, and he knocked the knife out of Jacques's hand. Guillaume put his fingers around Jacques's throat, and squeezed as hard as he could.

Jacques struggled against Guillaume, a strange smile spread across his face. Guillaume felt something cold rush through him, as a river might rush into a sea. Behind his eyes, he could see the face of Marie Laveau. He knew why she was there, and what he must do, and a sense of depraved glee came over him. Guillaume continued to squeeze, and after a long moment, the light went out of Jacques's eyes permanently. Guillaume held him that way for a while longer. Finally, Guillaume released him, and Jacques crumpled to the floor.

He turned to Desirée. She had covered herself and stood in the corner of the room, the look of terror draining from her face. "Thank you," she said. "Thank you for saving me."

"It was nothing," he said. He reached into the dead man's pocket and pulled forth a small key, along with a gold coin. He walked to the bedroom door, Desiree following close behind him, anxious to see him gone, and proceeded to unlock and slowly open the door.

There, waiting just outside was Marie Laveau, who walked inside the bedroom staring all the while at Guillaume, while Desiree, seeing her, instinctively shrank back farther into the room to avoid her, uttering a small cry.

"Is it done?" Marie asked as she approached the large man.

Guillaume responded with a smile. In the same deep, resplendent voice that had earlier issued from the mouth of Jacques, Guillaume said, "Yes, mother, it all happened just as we'd planned. Thank you for this gift."

Marie leaned up and kissed Guillaume on his cheek as she said, "Please, my son, what mother would not protect her beloved child?" She turned her gaze upon her deceitful daughter-in-law, who'd now sunk down upon her knees, and was shaking in fear as her eyes kept flitting back and forth between the room's two other occupants. "Now, what to do with her?"

Guillaume-who-was-Honore replied as he approached Desiree, "Oh, she's inspired me. I've thought of a number of interesting ideas. Would you care to join me, Mother?"

As they each took hold of her arms, Desiree began to scream.

It was a start.

—JOHN MANTOOTH

John Mantooth is an award-winning author whose short stories have been recognized in numerous years' best anthologies. His short fiction has been published in *Fantasy Magazine*, *Crime Factory*, *Thuglit*, and the Stoker winning anthology, *Haunted Legends* (Tor, 2010), among others. His first collection of stories, *Shoebox Train Wreck*, will be released by Chizine Publications in March of 2012.

—THIS THING THAT CLAWED ITSELF INTO ME

By John Mantooth

Back before drugs came to Jefferson City and back when people lived to die of old age and not festering gunshot wounds or drug overdoses or cancer brought on by the gasses from the landfill, back when you could walk along a moonlit path at night and not see broken glass and old syringes nor fear for your life, back in that time there was the bus that rode only at midnight. Its driver was a shadowy man whose face was like a terrible mirror and looking into it would suck your soul right out of your chest and into his.

I saw the bus many times. It was yellow, nearly faded to white, and it glowed like one of those stars I had stuck to my ceiling, except this glow never faded in the dark. Instead, it pulsed and burned, and hurt your eyes if you stared too long.

I only saw the driver once.

The night it came for my grandfather, I stood at the window, watching as Pa Paw stumbled, zombie-like toward the bus. That night, I'd struggled to see the driver through the window, but the glass was fogged, and he was nothing more than a shape, a hunched and darkened blot on the other side of smoke.

When the door opened, folding in on itself, I shut my eyes tight as I had been taught to do. When I opened them, the bus and Pa Paw were gone.

The next morning I was surprised when his body still lay in the hallway outside my mother's room. My grandmother stood over him, touching his face, praying.

"Granny?"

"Shush."

I waited. There were certain times my grandmother would not be interrupted. One was while reading the Word. The other was when she was in prayer.

When she finished her prayers and goodbyes, she turned her face to me. Granny had been kicked by a horse when she was seven and it made her jaw grow wrong, and one of her eyes never stopped moving. You've seen the little dolls with the silly eyes that move when you shake them? This was not unlike my grandmother's eye.

"I saw the bus come last night, Granny. I saw it take him."

She nodded. "I saw it too, Mary Louise."

"Then why is he still here?"

Granny smiled at me then. I think that's why grandpa married her. She was ugly with her crooked jaw and wiggly eye, but when she smiled, you could see her true beauty, what lay underneath the crookedness.

"He's not here, Mary Louise. He's on that bus."

"But—"

"But nothing. This is just where he lived. An empty house that will rot and decay because there's nobody left to take care of it anymore." She held out her hand for me to help her up. Granny was so old she'd stopped counting birthdays. Her bones creaked, and I thought about the old swing I used to sit in on her front porch, how when the wind blew, the chains groaned and it sounded like it meant something.

Once on her feet, she put her hand on my shoulder. "You didn't try to look at the driver did you?"

"No ma'am."

She nodded, her eye bobbing crazily. "Promise me when I go, you won't look either."

"I promise."

"It'll be hard then because me and you have the thickest blood in the family, Mary Louise. Your mama is crazy, your daddy is dead, and now grandpa is too. Your brothers think I'm an old, superstitious fool. That leaves you and me. Our blood is thick. It'll hurt when I go and there'll be a part of you that wants to go with me, but don't dare look in them doors when he flings them open. Don't dare."

"I promise I won't, Granny."

* * *

A year later, almost to the date, my granny lay deep in her bed of death. It fell to me to take care of her because my mother had locked herself away in the attic by then, the smell of her waste seeping out of the ceiling, me and Granny wondering what she was eating, how long she'd last.

The bus was coming for Granny soon, she knew it, and I knew it. I sat by her bed, wiping her face with a wet rag. It was late September, and still hot, but Granny's sweat came from her fever. Something burned inside her and I knew it was her soul looking for a way out, and when she found it, the bus would come clanging up that hill, and I'd have to close my eyes or have my own soul sucked out of my body too.

Still, I had to wonder if it would be that bad. Mama might not come down again until the bus came for her. My brothers were mean and violent and did not believe in anything except fists, guns, and hard drink. At least I would go with Granny instead of being left behind here.

One of my brothers, Leroy Jake, came in hollering about being hungry and why wouldn't I cook him some supper.

I kissed Granny and met him out in the kitchen. "Why should I cook for you, LJ? Cook for yourself."

He made like he was going to slap me but stopped. The last time he'd tried that, I'd snuck into his room when he was asleep and bitten his ear so hard there were still teeth marks.

"You're a girl. Girls cook."

I was about to ask him where he'd found that written down when Granny cried out.

"That bus will be coming soon," I told him. "You best hit the woods."

"I don't believe in no phantom school buses."

I ignored this last and went back to Granny. I held her hand as she began to squirm and kick, and I knew it was her soul trying to find a way out.

An hour later, I heard it.

First it was just on the wind, a distant sound like the cry of a coyote from up in the hills, but gradually it came closer, the straining engine, the clanking, grinding gears, the crunch crunch of tires on the gravel road.

I went to the window and pulled back the curtains. I switched off the lamp and sat in the darkness, holding Granny's hand, watching the space right below the live oak in our front yard. It's just where it parked when it took Grandpa, and probably where it'll park when it takes me.

Unless I go tonight.

As if she read my mind, Granny sat up suddenly and pulled me to her. I hugged what felt like a dry sack of bones and something else, something barely alive, beating miserably inside.

"Don't look," she said or maybe she didn't say a word. Maybe it's only what I thought I heard. Doesn't matter. It's what she wanted me to know.

Then the bus was outside. The low hanging branches of the live oak scraped the roof as it pulled to a stop

I felt her hand loosen on mine and then I saw her stand up, but not all of her. Just her soul. She left the house behind, laying broken in the bed and walked silently across the hardwoods, her feet not even a whisper against the dusty floor, and out through the window, never pausing, only walking through it like it was a wall of thin smoke.

I watched, leaning forward, intent on seeing her all the way, and maybe further. I confess, I did not yet know what I would do when the door folded in and revealed the driver. I felt a powerful urge to see him, to test Granny's words, I also wanted him to take me just like she said, to suck my soul out of my chest and leave my body here with Granny's.

That's when I heard LJ screaming. Like my other brothers, he never believed the stories of the bus. He'd been asleep when Grandpa went, but now he was awake, and I knew he was looking out the kitchen window, watching a woman who had not been able to stand for the last three months, walk with a startling kind of grace toward a glowing school bus.

The door began its slow fold inward and I leaned forward, dropping Granny's hand, my breath forming a mist on the window.

What I saw is still frozen in my memory today. I might try to shake it, I might try to forget it, but it still comes back in my dreams.

His body was slight, thin like a sapling grown in the shade. His neck long and crooked, but his face was handsome and young, and smiling. It was the smile—a death grin—that held me. I felt struck, slayed as Granny used to say, in the spirit. My soul was half out of my chest and I felt the other things trying to come in, wedging their way beneath my fingernails and seeping inside my ears, the very pores of my skin prickling with their probing fingers.

I fought it as hard as I could, my fists clenched so tight, the next morning, I found the marks of my nails fresh and deep in the fat of my palms. Even though I fought, I still felt a part of me open up, and things slipped out of me, even as others clawed their way in. They were dying things, sad things, the things that no man could fully understand, much less any young girl.

And all the while it was happening, I couldn't stop looking at the driver, and he did not stop smiling at me.

At last the door unfolded itself like a bat's wing and filled the cavernous doorway of the bus, blotting out the night and sending my soul flying back into my chest.

Have you ever been punched hard in the gut, punched so hard, the wind was knocked out of you and you knew your lungs were stuck, sealed up tight forever until they weren't, and you were breathing again, thankful for air you'd always taken for granted?

This was what it felt like when my soul was returned to me. It landed with a slap that rattled my ribcage. I was slammed back against the wall, and I lay there for a long time wondering if I would ever breathe again.

And when I did, I lay there even longer, wondering why.

* * *

LJ wasn't so lucky. To this day, I don't know if I fought harder than him or if those dying things just wanted him more, but he wasn't ever the same after that night. We found him the next morning, still standing over the sink, his face slammed hard against the kitchen window, mouth open slack. The other brothers proclaimed him dead, but I went up and put my arms around him and walked him to his bedroom where he slept with his eyes open for days.

When he came out of his room, we pretended things were normal for awhile, but there's only so much pretending that a person can do when their brother doesn't remember his name, or how to run a trot line, or skin a deer.

He wasn't evil, and I suppose that was a true blessing because of the things I felt clawing to get inside of me, at least half of them were downright wicked. LJ was just off, almost empty, but I've come to believe that certain kinds of emptiness are worse than evil. It's true that LJ's strength did grow, and some of my other brothers were amazed by this. He lifted a dead deer carcass by himself and swung it up into the bed of Henry's truck. He swung an axe with such force it became permanently wedged inside a birch tree, and once, he single-handedly pushed Daddy's old truck out of the mud.

I changed too. I often wonder if one of those evil spirits clawed its way inside me after all. I still felt the same about most things, but I didn't feel any of them as deeply as before. I felt like I was a pond without rain and gradually, I grew more shallow, more callous and dry in the sun.

It was an emptiness too.

I was thankful that I had my soul, that it hadn't gone on that bus with Granny, but I hated the new space inside me, and wished I could kick it out of me and feel the old things again, and oftentimes my brothers found me bent over in the grass, coughing and hacking, trying to send it back out.

—STEPHEN BACON

Stephen Bacon lives in the UK, with his wife and two sons. His short stories have been published in magazines like *Black Static*, *Shadows & Tall Trees* and *The Willows*, and in the anthologies *Murmurations: An Anthology of Uncanny Stories About Birds*, *The Horror Library Volume 2*, *Where the Heart Is*, several editions of *The Black Books of Horror*, *Dark Horizons*, *The Journal of the British Fantasy Society*, and the final three editions of *Nemonymous*. His debut collection, *Peel Back the Sky*, was published by Gray Friar Press in 2012. You can visit him at www.stephenbacon.co.uk

—SOMEWHERE ON SEBASTIAN STREET

By Stephen Bacon

Somewhere on Sebastian Street lies a place that isn't governed by the usual laws of nature; a place where the walls of reality are at their thinnest, and darkness occasionally bleeds through from beyond, tainting the people and objects it touches. Somewhere on Sebastian Street exists a portal between worlds.

The residents of Sebastian Street once dreamed of life and distance and time, bearing witness to sights that no one should ever see. Unspeakable acts. Their presence has long since faded from within the walls. But houses dream, too, and sometimes those dreams become nightmares.

* * *

I'm nearly finishing my second pint by the time I spot Gary enter the pub, threading his way between lunchtime workers and the ubiquitous assortment of regulars. He winks as he draws close to my table. He hasn't changed a bit in the five years since I last saw him; the sparkle in his eyes is still present, the brush of red hair lending his face a good-humoured appearance.

We shake hands and he asks what I'm drinking, then ventures to the bar. I watch his flirting fail to impress the barmaid. He returns a minute later with my pint and a Coke for him. I make some comment about how his drinking habits have *definitely* changed, and he laughs enthusiastically, pointing out that he's working. We deal with the pleasantries.

"So what're you doing back here? You said on the phone you

needed help with access to a site?"

I nod. "The old Swinston estate."

He frowns. "There's nothing there now, mate. The last row of houses was knocked down last year."

"I know. I read about it on the internet. How come it took so long?"

Gary shrugs. "Some fuck-up between the council and the property developers. The demolition started back in the nineties when it was just used by rent-boys and junkies. The last row was delayed 'cause of some administrative cock-up—that's Leeds-fucking-Council for you. Anyway, finally the courts decided they could knock the lot down."

"Right. Well, I just need half an hour. Only to take some photos, soak up the atmosphere." I take a puff on my inhaler, feeling like my nerves are betraying me.

"There's nothing there no more—just rubble."

"That's okay. Just for old-times' sake. A final goodbye."

Gary eyes me strangely, as if he's just realised I've lost my mind. He's probably thinking about the woman that was killed there in the early 80s; those stories about how her body was mutilated and defiled.

"Please, Gaz. I won't cause a problem." I try to compose my best *trustworthy, old school-friend* face. I think I succeed.

He takes a drink of his Coke. I can hear the ice clinking against the glass. He wipes his mouth with the back of his sleeve. "I can give you twenty minutes."

* * *

His council van smells of stale sweat, hamburgers, and engine oil. The dashboard is littered with old newspapers and Post-it notes with addresses scrawled on them. As he drives, I can hear his toolboxes rattling in the back. He asks me what I'm doing back in town.

I explain about how my parents have just moved out of the family home into a smaller bungalow in Beeston, and how I've been helping them with the process. I mention how I've been sorting through some storage boxes from my old bedroom in an effort to thin out their belongings. I tell him it stirred up old memories from my childhood. This is all true. Needless to say, I don't tell him the entire truth.

I finger the plastic walkie-talkie in my pocket. Its rubber aerial pokes against my chest like a knife.

Soon we enter the industrial estate. Business offices and flimsy-looking warehouses stand conspicuously in the centre of deserted car-parks. All the company logos affixed to the buildings' walls look identical. Ahead, the road is barricaded by a framework of red and white plastic cordons. Behind it, a solid eight-foot wooden fence encircles the perimeter of the building site.

Gary pulls over and yanks on the handbrake. "Right." He unclips a Yale-key from the fob dangling from his ignition and passes it to me. "The entrance is over there. This is for the padlock." He looks at me strangely again. "I'll have to get back once I've had my dinner. That give you long enough?"

I nod and smile, climbing out of the car. The walkie-talkie in my pocket seems suddenly fragile and I cup it as I hurry over to the door that's cut into the roughly-erected fence. The metal of the padlock feels icy-cold and I'm relieved once it gives and I gain entry. I step through the door and close it behind me, pushing the swollen wood together with some effort.

It's difficult at first for me to reconcile what I'm seeing. The flat expanse of ground is broken up by piles of rubble—mainly heaped house-bricks, but also twisted metal struts, faded UPVC window frames and smashed paving slabs. Jewels of broken glass glisten in the afternoon sunlight. It resembles nothing of the place it was the last time I was here.

* * *

There was something about the empty houses that made them look sinister. It may have been the way their doors and windows had been barricaded up; as if the authorities were trying to prevent some obscene force from escaping. Perhaps local legends added to the sense of despair that attached itself to the deserted streets. Swinston estate had been left to rot many years ago; Leeds city council, it seemed, had thrown in the towel.

The boys were well aware of the stories. Everybody was. The depravity that once went on in Sebastian Street was discussed in hushed tones, but still the kids heard about it. Lurid schoolyard stories kept the tale alive, passing it through generations as if it was part of the community, a fabric of local colour.

In 1982 a woman's mutilated corpse had been discovered inside one of the rows of terraced houses. Six different types of semen were found within her battered and abused body, as well as a length of bubble-wrap. Someone had slashed arcane symbols into her flesh. There was even a rumour that one sample of the semen had been equine.

The three boys stood on Sebastian Street and regarded the final row of terraced houses with something approaching reverence. Metal security shutters enclosed the doors; wooden boards were nailed across the windows. It symbolised all that was forbidden. Years before, heroin-addicts had frequented the houses. Ironically the only street to survive the estate's demolition had been the one with such notoriety.

"Why didn't they knock *these* ones down?" murmured Sam. Absently he fished out his asthma inhaler and took a blast.

Mal shrugged. "Which one was where it happened?"

Cameron poked the ground with a wooden stick. He glanced up and studied the row.

Sam tried to detect fear in the boy's expressionless face, but saw nothing. He glanced at the row himself. The security covers made the houses look like impassive faces staring back at them. Almost challenging.

"Not sure which one." Cameron's voice was indifferent. "They all look the same."

Several tiles were missing off the roof, which extended the length of the terrace. Only the individual chimney pots gave any indication of which house was which.

Sam took out the Spider Man walkie-talkies, handing one to Cameron. He accepted it silently.

"My brother told me that men sometimes bum other men inside there." Cameron blinked. "For money."

Mal grimaced, but said nothing. He knelt on the kerb. "You still up for this?"

Cameron nodded. "No problem."

Despite the younger kid's bravado, Sam noticed the damp patches under his arms. He considered again whether they were being fair—Cameron Glover was the school's misfit, seemingly friends with no one, a withdrawn introvert who took the butt of most of the pranks. Mal and Sam had offered him the opportunity to join their small circle of friends...at a price; first he'd need to prove his worthiness.

The sense of desolation that permeated the Swinston estate seemed a stern enough challenge. Its abandoned streets and silent, debris-stricken plots appeared to harbour darkness. Shadows gathered on the corners. Discarded rubbish thrived amongst the ruins, and overgrown weeds sprouted from the cracked tarmac. Parents warned their children not to venture onto the estate in the daylight, let alone during the hours of darkness. The place was synonymous with death and depravity.

Cameron studied the row of terraced houses and swallowed. He gripped the wooden stick tightly, almost brandishing it. Somewhere nearby, a plastic bag, half-buried by soil and bricks, flapped in the breeze like a frantic bird.

"How does this thing work?" The younger kid licked his lips and peered at the walkie-talkie.

"Just press the button and speak into the top. We'll hear you."

Cameron nodded slowly. Sam watched the younger boy walk towards the row of houses, clambering over the remnants of a fallen wall. Overgrown grass reached through the rubble like spindly fingers. Sam's eyes followed Cameron's progress until he disappeared round the back. He crouched on the kerb next to Mal. For a moment they listened.

Sam finally spoke into the walkie-talkie. "Can you see the hole in the board?"

There was a pause and then a short burst of static. "I'm in

the kitchen already."

Mal pursed his lips and nodded approvingly.

"What can you see?" asked Sam.

"It's just a kitchen. It's dark, though. God, it stinks."

Sam smiled, detecting the faintest trace of fear in the younger lad's voice. "Go on."

"Nothing much. It's dusty. All the worktops are filthy."

"Go into some of the rooms."

There was silence for a few minutes. Then, "Right. I'm at the bottom of the stairs."

"What's it like?"

A tinny laugh. "Just stairs."

"I mean, is it dark?" Sam stared at the entranced Mal. "And scary?"

"No." But Cameron's voice sounded slender and taut.

"See what's upstairs."

"Okay."

For a few minutes there was just silence. Mal scratched his head. He said to Sam in a low voice, "Don't you think he's a weirdo? I'm not sure if we want him hanging around with us, anyway."

"What do you mean?"

"Seen his arms? He's got cuts all over them. He always wears that long-sleeved vest for PE but I saw it when he was washing his hands. I think he's into that *cutting-yourself* shit."

Sam searched for the word. "Self-harming?"

Mal nodded. "That's it."

Sam shrugged and stared at the row of houses. He didn't speak. His eyes tried to picture the kid inside, wandering around in the darkness.

A plaintive caw broke the silence. Sam watched a huge black crow land on the roof. It unfurled its wings slowly as if to catch the sun, making it look like it was wearing a cloak. Mal stood and threw a stone. It missed by a mile, striking the sagged guttering with a crack that echoed across the estate like a gunshot. The crow flapped into the air and flew languidly away.

There was a burst of static and the walkie-talkie crackled

into life. "There's nothing up here. Just empty rooms."

Mal grabbed the handset from Sam. "Watch out for the ghost of the dead woman." He laughed exaggeratedly, maniacally.

Cameron's next words halted the laughter. "Hey—there's a hole in the wall. I can see something moving."

Sam stared at Mal's stunned face, listening intently. He reclaimed the walkie-talkie.

There was the sound of movement in the speaker. Bricks falling.

"Are you okay?" Sam cleared his throat and pressed the walkie-talkie.

"Just opening up a bigger gap."

Sam could hear him scrabbling around. When Cameron's voice returned, it was made gruff by his panting breath. "I can see into the bedroom. Looks like the house next door. There's something on the floor."

"What is it?"

"Hang on." Sounds of effort, a succession of knocks.

"Eugh. There's black stains on the floorboards. It looks like...dried blood."

"Shit, that must be where—"

"Hang on, what's that?"

The silence was unbearable. Mal stared at Sam expectantly, open-mouthed.

"What is it?" Mal prompted eventually. His breath was shallow.

"Stone steps. Going down."

Mal frowned.

Silence again for several moments. Then Cameron's voice returned: "God, they go on forever. I'm walking down them." He sounded breathless. "I'm on some kind of landing."

Sam continued to listen. He was aware that Mal was also holding his breath. "Is it still dark?"

No reply. When Cameron spoke again, his words chilled Sam to the bone: "I'm at the bottom. I can see something. It looks like...a lake."

Sam turned sharply, frowning at his companion. "I thought

he said *lake*."

Mal's eyes were huge. "He did."

"Wow, it's lovely. There's...there's trees and a cornfield and... some massive dragonflies." He sounded awestruck.

Sam spoke slowly. "Cameron, are you okay? You sound a bit funny." He took a puff of his inhaler.

"Ah, they're not dragonflies. They're...what're they called?—hummingbirds?" His voice had taken on a dreamlike quality.

Sam yelled at him to stop being stupid, pleading with him to return. Mal's face was aghast. Pale. He stared dumbstruck as Sam shouted into the walkie-talkie, urging the younger boy to come back out. Cameron ignored him, instead continuing to describe impossible sights.

Sam stood with his head pressed against Mal's, listening to the younger boy speak. He was becoming detached from reality, carried away by Cameron's warped madness, the narration fuelling his fear and transporting his imagination. Sanity was being abandoned. Certainty was unravelling.

Eventually the walkie-talkie fell silent and Sam stared miserably at the row of houses, numb and broken. Nearby, Mal shivered, his hands laced together as if in silent prayer.

Sam's chest felt constricted and wheezy. Fear deterred any notion of rescue; Cameron's words were lodged like barbs in his mind.

They turned to go, stunned and terrified. Their abandoned bikes seemed like they'd lain there for years, the frames coated with dust and grit. It was impossible to ride them because they had Cameron's spare bike to accommodate now. They hurried as best they could. Mal lived on the far side of town, so they separated at the boundary of the park, exchanging hushed farewells. Sam resisted the urge to ditch the bikes, instead negotiating the journey by clumsily pushing one on either side. By the time he arrived home and alerted his parents, he was aching and shivering.

Sam knew they'd never see Cameron again.

* * *

Much later—several weeks after the police had scoured the estate with forensic teams and assistance from a nearby force, weeks after Cameron's brother—whose arms also sported similar cuts and cigarette burns—was taken into care by social services, ages after Cameron's dad was arrested and the local press had reported the sickening catalogue of abuse—Sam returned to Sebastian Street and stared at the row of houses with eyes that had lost their innocence.

He'd learned things about the world that could never be unlearnt; ugly truths that soured his trust and crumbled the foundations of his belief system. It had only been three weeks since Cameron's disappearance, yet it felt as if the world had changed; things had advanced.

It was early evening and the sun was descending beyond the rubble-strewn site, creating a black silhouette of the houses, rendering them flat and unreal. Sam had no idea why he'd brought the walkie-talkie. Maybe it felt like the single remaining link to Cameron; a fragile thread of contact. Perhaps it symbolised the final vestige of his own childhood.

He clicked on the button of the walkie-talkie and pressed it to his ear.

* * *

I take the walkie-talkie out with trembling hands and hold it for a moment, staring at the mountain of rubble that now approximates Sebastian Street. The silence is eerie. A breeze sweeps the site, combing through the overgrown weeds and sending dust rattling across the debris. Clouds race overhead. The sky presses me to the ground. I close my eyes.

I can remember how it felt to lie in bed at night, listening to the static's howl as I held the walkie-talkie to my ear. At first Cameron sounded frightened, his voice high-pitched and frantic, distorted by the swirls of interference. Sometimes I tried to answer him, but there was never any sign that he could hear, just the tortured warbles of sound. Eventually the noises faded and there was nothing but static; cold, black static. The batteries ran down and I never replaced them.

I examine the gaudy red and black plastic now, testing the weight in my hand. The new batteries seem to make it heavier than it once felt, even though I know that's impossible. I hold it up and carefully press the receive button.

It feels like I stand there forever holding my breath, listening to the crackling, whooshing white-noise. My imagination conjures swirls of vocals in the static but I dismiss that as lost hope. A cloud passes in front of the sun and it suddenly grows cold. Somewhere in the distance, a dog begins to bark. And then at once I hear a faint snatch of Cameron's voice—not words as such, just the murmur of his conversation. He's still a little boy, his pitch high and unbroken, but this time not by fear. He sounds excited and...*settled*. Comfortable. There is a squeal of interference and it all goes silent, but not before I make out a final, brief snatch of dialogue. *I'm okay.*

Satisfied, I return the walkie-talkie to my pocket and shuffle back to the door, sensing countless eyes watching my progress. I throw a final glance back to the rubble-strewn site before I step through the fence and padlock it behind me.

Gary looks relieved as he sees my approach. Across the city, I hear the low squeal of a police siren. Nothing much changes.

* * *

Somewhere on Sebastian Street lies a portal between two worlds; a place where salvation exists for those that seek it, an escape from the stark brutalities of life. Somewhere on Sebastian Street lurks a darkness that seems forbidding and threatening to some, yet welcoming and hospitable to others. This lost district provides refuge to those individuals whose despair is sufficient to enable passage into this realm of solitude. Somewhere on Sebastian Street, a boy chooses to remain young forever, electing to spend eternity alone rather than endure a tortured mortality. He inhabits the darkness alone...but he's never lonely.

Somewhere on Sebastian Street, that boy dreams of a life less real. Once his dreams were filled with love and hope and goodwill, but he always knew in his heart that these things would be denied him.

Somewhere on Sebastian Street lies a sanctuary for the forlorn, a haven for those beyond hope, and whatever dwells within its imaginary walls will never dwell alone.

For Gary McMahon

—DANICA GREEN

Danica Green is a UK-based writer whose work has been featured in over 50 literary journals and anthologies, including flash fiction, articles and short stories in *Smokelong Quarterly, Eclectic Flash, Neon Magazine, PANK,* and *The Stone Hobo,* as well as anthologies by Cinnamon Press, Rainstorm Press, Silver Bow Publishing and others. She is currently working on her first novel and you can read more about her work on her Facebook author page: https://www.facebook.com/Danica.Green.Author

—JUNE DECAY

By Danica Green

Lola flicked through a magazine, trying to ignore the smashed glass and decay that surrounded her, trying to draw her mind away from the rhythmic thumping that was resonating through the door behind her. Her eyes wandered to the broken window as a shadow walked past on the street, a red sash across its body and a flashlight shining into every home on the way. Lola went still. As the shadow left her sight, she breathed a sigh of relief and turned to look at the door from which the noise was emanating. She always feared the Watchers would hear, see the worry on her face, bust their way in and descend with their pistols to the basement, but as of yet she had managed to avoid suspicion. She stood, walking to the kitchen and taking the thawed raw chicken that she had left defrosting on the side. She had fifteen minutes until another Watcher would walk past and she liked to be there, sitting in the family room, making a show of normality and getting on with her life. She tucked the chicken under her arm and pulled a key from a chain around her neck, unlocking the door and going down into the darkness. The thumping stopped, the sound replaced with a low snarl coming from the back of the room, and Lola flicked on the light switch. The basement was small and gnawed bones surrounded her in piles, the occasional blood splash and piles of excrement in various places on the floor.

"June," she whispered softly. "June, are you hungry?" A bundle of rags in the back corner shuddered, then suddenly jumped and ran towards Lola, stopping sharply two feet away.

The eyes of the child were milky white, the hair thin, her teeth chipped, gnashing, and a grasping arm with curled fingernails reached desperately for Lola's face. The chicken was thrown into the middle of the room and Lola walked back to the steps and sat on the bottom, teary-eyed and wistful. She knew the child would not eat the chicken until she had gone, only as a last resort when there was no living food available. The child still strained against the tight handcuffs that held her to a water pipe, not caring whether it was the pipe, the cuffs, or her arm that broke, just desperate to get to Lola and fill her gnawing stomach. After ten minutes, she stood and began to walk back to the family room.

"I love you, June," she said sadly, having to speak louder over the pained wails of the little girl behind her.

She locked the door and sat down on the couch, staring at her magazine as another Watcher walked by the window like clockwork. Lola sighed and dragged the toe of a shoe through some broken glass in front of the coffee table, pushing together little patterns as she did. Both ends had come quickly, the end of the world, then the end of the threat, but it had been enough time for thousands upon thousands to succumb and suffer the same animated death as little June. She remembered the screaming as her husband's shoddy fortifications had failed the instant they arrived, the planks across the windows snapping under the multitude of pushing, throbbing bodies that sought their beating hearts and flowing blood. She looked through to the kitchen and thought about the instant she went from wife to widow as a dozen living corpses feasted upon his screaming form. She remembered taking June by the hand and running out the back door, leaping fences with a wailing child clinging to her back, dodging the rending fingernails of her neighbours and ignoring any shouts for help she heard. The freshly animated were hard to distinguish and you only knew they had turned when you caught a glimpse of those milky eyes, or when their first reaction was to try and snap your neck. Her reverie was broken by a beam of light that blinded her and she shielded her face, blinking furiously.

"Hey Lola, you okay?" What a stupid goddamn question she thought, taking care not to voice it aloud. Instead she looked through the window to the cool night and gave a slow nod.

"As well as can be expected, Mary-Ann."

"Aye. We have all suffered great pain." Lola seethed a little, knowing that Mary-Ann and the rest of her family had been away during the tragedy and she had lost no one and nothing. Even her house had sustained little damage, as being empty it had attracted no attention from the changed ones. "I hear you're going with the Seekers tomorrow. Are you sure that's a good idea?"

"We must all do our part," Lola said curtly, picking up her magazine and staring hard at blurred words until Mary-Ann moved off into the dark.

Lola was the only woman to have signed up for the Seekers, most women naturally assigning themselves to the cleaning crews and those who were housing orphans and invalids whose carers had died. Some even joined the Watchers, though there hadn't been a single incident in the two weeks since the town had come back to some semblance of normality. The streets here were surely tempting, with plentiful meat as many of the townsfolk returned, but the abandoned sections of town where the stragglers still wandered were full of corpses to satiate them and given a choice, they often chose to feast upon those they knew would not retaliate. It was to these abandoned sections that Lola and the rest of the Seekers would head tomorrow, pistols and axes in hand, to flush out the remnants of the dead so the town could finally be rebuilt.

Lola stood and yawned, whispering a prayer at the basement door before heading up the stairs to her bedroom. She didn't change out of her clothes, the feeling that she might have to leave in a hurry still fresh in her mind, and she lay down with her face buried in the pillows. She had her own reason for joining the Seekers and that was to see the so-called zombies up close. She didn't like that word, though it was what all the newspapers and magazines were flashing about, but when she looked at her broken daughter she didn't see a creature of horror stories and b-movies, just a sick little girl who needed a cure. The long and fearful run from the house on the day her husband died had not given her time to study them as she desired, her eyes were fixed in front of her as she ran, focused solely on keeping moving.

The only time she had seen one of the creatures up close that day had been when it happened. When June slipped off her back and the creature crawled out of the darkness, a broken leg and one eye missing, hissing through the gaps in its teeth. Lola pushed the thought away and replaced it with a plan for the morning. Study, kill, study. She knew they could die, starve, she knew they slept and breathed, but what she needed was a way to prove that their minds could be brought back, the insatiable flesh-rending desires quelled and their memories and personalities renewed. It was the only hope that kept her going.

When the dawn came, Lola changed into a fresh set of clothes and went downstairs to take a ham hock from the fridge. It seemed this processed meat wasn't as nutritious to June as bleeding flesh and many times Lola had planned to find a butcher shop that was up and running again, ask for all their offal and raw junk meat, but she feared it would be too suspicious so she kept her going with joints from the grocery store. As she went down to the basement and sat on the steps, ham lying ignored on the floor while June's unrestrained hand grasped and grabbed, spittle dribbling down greying unhealthy skin, Lola found herself questioning her own logic. Was this thing really still her baby girl? Could the balding head and teeth filled with chunks of rotting meat really return back to the glossy perfection of a beautiful five year old? It didn't seem likely, sitting there in the dimness with the child to whom she had given life trying so desperately to kill her, but even with all her doubts and fears, she couldn't ignore the fact that without living flesh, June would soon die her final death.

Sighing, she left the basement, locked the door, and made herself toast and coffee, brushing her hair in between bites and sips. She was to meet the rest of the Seekers by the town hall in an hour and she went through the checklist she had been given in her mind. Clothing should not be too tight or long enough to interfere with walking or arm movements, sensible shoes, make sure you've eaten because you'll need the energy. She laughed to herself as she recalled giving a similar set of instructions to June the first time she went on a field trip. She'd only just started school so it was a day trip to the park to learn about the wildlife in the river, but she had been so excited, jumping up and down and squealing about newts and ducklings and...

Lola stopped herself. *Getting emotional is going to make this whole thing harder,* she reminded herself. They had tried to talk her out of it, what place does a woman have hunting down dangerous creatures, especially one so recently widowed and childless? She didn't care. Let them think she'd lost the will to live, was running blind into a suicide. If there was a way to help June it was there among those who were like her and joining the Seekers was her only option to examine them.

When Lola arrived at the town hall, fifteen men stood crowded around it brandishing weapons and comparing them with their fellows. Guns had proven ineffective against the zombies; hand held weapons worked best. Many of the men had discussed acquiring cutlasses and samurai swords, but at the end of the day they lacked the finesse to make use out of them, so every hand gripped a common axe, heavy, sharp and needing no specific expertise to wield. An axe, gun, whistle, and a small jar of paint were handed to Lola as she joined the group, most of the men ignoring her, some sneering and a couple even looking at her with sympathy, as though her losses had driven her to madness. The man who had put himself in charge of the Seekers did a quick headcount and then shouted at the throng to gather around him.

"Okay, there's sixteen of us, so I'm putting everyone into fours." The man began to divide everyone up with many of the men shooting glances at Lola, unwilling to have the woman on their team.

"Hi, I'm Paul," said one of the men assigned to work with her. He shook her hand cordially and hefted the axe on his shoulder. Lola smiled and turned to the others.

"Ian," said an older man with still visible muscles despite

his grey hair. "I joined to serve in 'Nam the last few years of the conflict, the day I turned eighteen, so you're in good hands with me." He smacked the flat of the axe blade against his palm and grinned. "I've seen worse than zombies." Lola cringed at the use of that word, picturing June in the basement, chewing frantically on a ham bone. She turned to the last man, who scowled at her and pointedly addressed himself to the other two men instead.

"Conner," he stated, not offering his hand. The Seeker's leader called back to the groups and everyone gathered to hear him.

"We're going to walk to the section of town we're clearing today. When we get there, we split up, but as the zombies are few and far between, it's unlikely you'll come across more than one at a time and it's nothing that a group of four can't handle. We're working Park Street and all the side lanes, up to the intersection for Mill Road. Don't go any further than that! Once a house is clear, put an 'x' on the door with your paint so we don't go checking the same place twice. The most important thing to remember is, don't split up. These damn creatures are ruthless and strong, they don't get incapacitated by pain and injury..." The man continued to talk but it was drowned out by Conner hissing softly at the group.

"Like we don't fucking know this already. Just a few weeks ago, I was pressed against the wall of my kitchen, fending the fuckers off with a carving knife..." The man seemed volatile but Lola was forced to agree. Everyone had fought, many had died, some had been infected by whatever the creatures carried in their blood and passed on to others. There was no one here who hadn't done this before, and now they were a thousand times more prepared than they had been that night, when a hoard of the things came running into town in the darkness, smashing windows and climbing in, hundreds dead before the rest of the town was awoken by the chaos. She pictured her husband screaming, trying to board the windows while Lola woke June and they stood in the kitchen and cried. She, and every other man in the crowd, would take great pleasure in their task today.

"...and last but not least, if you get into trouble, blow your whistle and keep blowing until help comes. If you hear a whistle, leave whatever you are doing *immediately* and go to assist. Is everyone clear?" The man finished and the group was nodding around him, aiming pistols into the distance and testing the edges of their blades with careful thumbs.

They began to walk through the town, people watching them as they passed, awed at their bravery or horrified at their stupidity, Lola couldn't tell which. As the people thinned out, they entered streets closed in with newly built fences, the areas already cleared by the Seekers being prevented from re-infestation until the whole town was safe. The final plan was to build a large stone wall that circled them completely, the construction having begun almost before anything else. The cities were safe again; the military and police forces having dedicated themselves almost exclusively to them, and many of the villages had been permanently abandoned and thus held no interest to the walking dead. It was the towns that were suffering the most, those too small to warrant government attention and the area around Leverton, Lola's town, was surrounded by other similar ones that had been left to deal with the crisis on their own. While the people of Leverton had banded together and begun to rebuild their shattered lives and homes, some had not been so well organised or determined, and stories had floated back and forth about towns that were still in the grip of the chaos, hiding in their homes and watching their loved ones die or worse. It wasn't hard to see how it could spread again and without military assistance their only option was to isolate their town from the world.

When they reached Park Street, they were quietly directed to the side streets, Lola and her group taking the first on the left. As they entered between the rows of houses, the smell hit them, rot and decay, bones picked clean in the streets, adults, children and animals, amid broken glass and scattered possessions that the stupid ones had tried to rescue as they fled, losing their lives in the process. Conner took the lead and headed straight to the first house, smashing his axe into the door even though the windows were broken open.

"Are you trying to draw them here?" Ian hissed, hard-trained muscles tensing. Conner just sneered and shrugged, pushing down the wreckage of the door and entering. Ian followed and Lola stood in the doorway with Paul, watching the street in case any others came.

"I don't think you've gone mad," Paul offered, out of the blue. Lola turned to him, almost tempted to yell at him for his blatant pity, but saw genuine sympathy in his eyes.

"Thank you. I...appreciate it."

"I lost my sister," he continued, kneeling down and sifting through some of the broken possessions on the street.

"I'm sorry to hear that."

"Well...we weren't really close. She was just visiting for a week. It had been a while since I saw her. My house is on the very edge of town and the rest of us were woken by her screams. My wife and I managed to escape while they were..." He stopped, voice choking up and Lola knelt beside him with a hand on his shoulder.

"We have all suffered," she said. "It's not much comfort though, I know. At least she died." Paul glared at her intensely and Lola hastily finished her thought. "No, please, don't misunderstand. I just mean that those who were bitten instead of eaten...well it could have, I mean, she could have suffered a worse fate." Paul's face softened and he nodded.

"There was another Seeker on the team a couple days ago. He joined up to look for his wife. He'd defended her from a group of the things while she ran but he couldn't find her again when he escaped himself. I was on his team and we were doing the houses up by the mini-mart when she appeared, leapt at him, ripping out one of his cheeks and snapping his arm. He shot her right in the face. Then he shot himself. I don't know whether he did it from grief or because he knew that he would have turned into one of them, but it's a memory that will haunt me longer than that of my sister's death."

Conner and Ian returned from inside the house and Ian painted an 'x' on the door with his finger.

"Nothing," he said as he did so.

"Not nothing," said Conner, holding up a fistful of bills and grinning.

"You would steal from the dead?" Paul yelled, making a grab for the money as Conner snatched it away. "Anything of value is meant to help rebuild the town, not line your pockets."

Conner just laughed, pushing through the three of them and heading to the next house. This time Lola and Paul entered while the others waited, climbing through one of the windows into the kitchen. Lola gagged on the smell, the fridge lying open on the floor with its contents rotting inside it. The table was pushed up against the door and they pulled it back with an effort before cautiously opening it and looking round the sitting room. The house was as empty as the first and they worked their way up one side of the street, finally reaching the supermarket.

Conner smashed the glass doors in, grinning while he did so, and the four of them entered. The smell inside was worse than any of the houses, an entire warehouse of rotting food. Lola found some comfort in knowing that since the town had been infested at night, no one would have been here and they were unlikely to come across any dead shelf stackers or cashiers. Ian and Conner walked to either side of the store, looking down aisles as they went, and Paul started to walk towards the back. Lola wandered up and down the supermarket lost in thought, memories of death, running, the horrible gut-squeezing pain of knowing that June would soon die. She was so absorbed that she nearly walked into the hunched figure standing in the aisle ahead of her. The figure turned, and a whimper escaped from Lola's throat as she stood immobile in the aisle. Her hand moved unconsciously to the whistle hanging from her neck as the zombie began to advance on her, slowly, cautiously. It had obviously taken a beating in the mass escape to the town hall that happened the night of their invasion, as its entire lower jaw had been ripped away and it walked with a limp. Lola backed up, hand moving from her whistle to her gun and just as the creature began to run she emptied her cartridge into its brain and turned to get away.

The smell hit her the second she did, coming face to face

with another zombie covered in smears of food from smashed jars, a streak of blood and excrement running down one side of its body. She backed into the shelf, pistol empty, axe dropped too far away when she pulled her gun out, feeling behind for anything that could help her, hope dying as her fingers touched bags of pasta and rice. The first zombie was still up, though wounded enough that it would bleed to death sooner or later, but the second was whole, milky white eyes in the face of a middle-aged man, an illegible tattoo emblazoned on its forearm. It leapt, then shuddered to a halt as it was hit with six pistol shots in its vital areas, eyes, elbows and kneecaps. It crumpled on the ground and Lola looked up to see Ian crouched on top of the shelves, glaring at the jawless zombie shuffling towards them. He hefted his axe and jumped down in front of her, but as he went to swing, Conner came running around the corner of the aisle and buried his own axe into its back, again and again, splitting the creature in two. The blood flew in every direction and splattered across Lola's face.

"I told you she'd be useless," Conner said, pulling his axe from what was now just a corpse. He looked over to the second zombie which was incapacitated but still writhing on the ground. Sensing Conner's bloody intentions, Ian stepped over and cleanly sliced off its head.

"Shit," said Ian. "Where's Paul?"

A long, shrill whistle blast echoed around the store and Lola grabbed her axe as the three of them took off across to the rear doors which moved in and out sporadically, the mechanism broken, and through them they saw Paul in the middle of the parking lot, a ring of zombies thick around him. Ian charged, swinging his axe wildly and Conner knelt in the doorway, firing his pistol into chests, taking down three and missing three others. As he joined Ian, Lola stood, axe hanging limply in her hand, watching Paul's terrified form flashing back and forth in her mind between himself and her dead husband, screaming at her to run. Half the zombies had turned to pay attention to the others, wailing with rage and surrounding them from all sides. The rest still advanced on Paul who was carving a way towards

Lola.

Two of the creatures saw her and ran as fast as they could in her direction, screaming with punctured throats and rotting lungs. She blinked furiously, the tears blurring her view, and swung her axe heavily at the legs of the first one that reached her. They flew from its body, the rest of it thudding to the ground and starting to crawl towards her with its arms and bleeding stumps. The second one came at her. She swung, missing it, and it crashed into the side of the building, dazed. The one at her feet grabbed for her ankles, trying to take a bite and she rammed the heel of her shoe into its face over and over without looking away from the zombie in front of her. She swung her axe again and the zombie ducked, the weapon ricocheting off the wall and flying from her hands, skidding across the gravel. Lola jumped over the one still biting for her feet, its face smashed beyond recognition and she rolled across the ground in one fluid motion, rising with the axe in hand and sliced cleanly through the neck of the creature coming for her. She turned around. Piles of corpses lay scattered across the lot and the men each had three more to deal with. Lola ran for Paul, burying her axe into the skull of the one closest to him as he took the second one in the stomach and the third in the face. Lola couldn't get her axe out from where it was embedded in bone and when she finally wrenched it free, all three men were walking towards her, the rest of the zombies destroyed. She sensed a snarky comment from Conner and cut him off.

"Should we go and find the rest of the groups? We can't deal with this many on our own." Paul nodded hard and Conner shook his head, spitting on the ground. Ian simply stood and looked at the piles of the dead at their feet. His arm went into spasm, then a leg, and he turned around just as the milky whiteness began to creep over brown irises and the blood from where he had been bitten seeped across his shirt hem from the hip.

"No, no, no," he was whispering, though Lola wasn't sure if he even knew they were there anymore. She felt the weight of the axe in her hand, looking to the other two men who were watching Ian with horror. Ian started to convulse, his eyes becoming completely clouded and a string of spittle started to make its way down his chin. Just as the first uncontrollable taste for flesh became clear on his face and a snarl escaped his throat it was cut off, the sharp suddenness of Conner's axe connecting with his skull. Paul covered his face with his hand and Lola started to cry again.

"Shut up you stupid bitch," Conner spat at her. "I'm sick of you. Let's get going."

"We're walking back to the others?" she asked plaintively, failing to project an ounce of confidence into her voice.

"Of course we're fucking not. This place is nothing but corpses anyway, what's one more? They'd only tell us to grow some balls and get back to work." Lola cringed at his anger and noticed Paul nodding his head to the side.

"If it had simply been Ian's death, then yeah, they would have. But there could be hundreds of these things and this is something that a larger group should be handling."

"Whatever, pussies," Conner growled, pushing Lola out of the way and heading back to the supermarket doors. "Go back if you want. I've got zombies to kill." As he left, Lola felt an arm slip around her shoulder and looked into Paul's face.

"I'll leave the decision up to you," he said, obviously trying to sound calm, though a hint of a tremble ran through his words. Lola wiped her eyes and smiled at him, focusing hard on the successful kills she had achieved and trying to get back to that state of terrified adrenaline.

"We can't let him just go off alone. He's a jerk, yes, but he's part of our team. Without our help he'll be dead by the time anyone else can get over here."

"You say that like it's a bad thing," Paul laughed, as they both began to follow Conner onto the street. The road was empty of life as Paul painted an 'x' on the side of the store. They checked the next house along, but that too was empty, of both Conner and the undead.

"Maybe he went back anyway?" Paul offered, looking in the direction of Park Street.

"Not that guy," Lola said bitterly, shaking her head. "Do you still have bullets?"

"A full chamber. The zombies in the parking lot took me by surprise; I bent down to tie my shoe and when I looked up there was a dozen of the bastards closing in on me. Shall we look for Conner or just keep checking houses?"

"Houses, I guess. Conner has his whistle if he needs help, though he's probably too stubborn to use it. We don't know where he is and we could spend the rest of the day looking." She squinted along the street, the houses still continuing far into the distance, and sighed, beckoning for Paul and smashing open the door of the next house. The morning wore away as they worked, finding no other zombies with the exception of a changed cat that leapt for Lola's throat as they entered someone's bedroom. Paul had shot it out of the air before it reached her. When they got to the end of the street, they crossed over and began to search the houses on the other side, starting with a quaint, white-washed little house with roses in the yard and a swing set next to them. Paul soothed her as she looked at them. They had found few corpses during their checks, most of the dead picked clean to bones already, but when you found the skeleton of a child it was still heartbreaking. The door was open, hanging off one hinge and the bottom floor was clear, clean, and neat.

"It's almost like the house wasn't invaded," Lola said, confused.

She left Paul looking for a basement and cautiously climbed the stairs. Then, she vomited. A pile of zombies lay in the hallway, eyes still open, arms still reaching out. They were truly dead, rotting, flies swarming around the pile of them that lay under an attic hatch. Paul ran at the sound of Lola's retching and nearly joined her as he took in the sight. Lola gestured to the hatch and Paul tentatively climbed the mound of death to pull it open. The ladder slid out and they started up. The attic was very large, boxes of miscellaneous items lay stacked atop each other as far as they could see, and the stench of death was coming from somewhere, not just the pile below them. They navigated through books and clothes and broken toys to the back of the attic. Lola looked around the room, her gaze stopping on the blocked off section of the attic with no door. Bricks lay haphazardly cemented from floor to ceiling, the occasional one knocked out and lying jaggedly broken. Paul walked over and wiggled a few more bricks free of the wall in a line, the hasty job making them unstable. He peered through and gasped.

"Lola," he whispered. "Stay over there. You don't want to see this." Lola snorted, walking over and peering into the secret room. The light of the attic shone through the missing bricks and illuminated two adult skeletons and the half-eaten remains of several children. A little boy lay sleeping in the corner amid the carnage. Paul raised his pistol.

"Wait!" Lola yelled, knocking his gun away. Paul looked at her with shock but still lowered it.

"What is it?"

"He's just a child..."

"But he's one of them. He'd tear your eyes out as soon as he's free. What else can we do?"

The child was stirring, woken by the shouts and the second he caught the scent of flowing blood he ran towards the light and stuck both hands out of the gap, reaching and snarling. Paul and Lola backed away and Lola looked into the milky eyes of the growling child, with splinters of his mother's bones implanted in his gums. Her mind flashed back to her husband, the kitchen, the running, through the gardens and down the main street, June slipping softly off her back and the deadly creature crawling towards her. The images flashed wildly, the creature eyeing both of them, not sure which to go for, June crying on the road and, finally, the memory of thrusting out her finger, desperately pointing towards her daughter as she backed away from them both, sealing June's fate, and her own.

"Come back, Mama." A whispered plea with a strained voice as the zombie came eye to eye with her child. The scream, as it pinned her down and tore a chunk out of her leg, and the memory of continuing to back away as June watched. She didn't know the name of the young man who had come running down the road and impaled the creature, then tried to grab Lola away. June was still whimpering for her mother, bleeding, convulsing, the change coming swiftly as her eyes began to cloud over. Last of all she remembered running, running with the young man to the safe house at the town hall, the zombie that had been her daughter running desperately and rage-filled down the road behind them, her tiny legs unable to keep up despite her lust for their blood. She snapped sharply back to reality and Paul had a hand on her shoulder, pity in his eyes as her own filled with tears and spilled over. Lola looked at him, then at the child whose hands were clawing single-mindedly through his brick prison, and finally nodded to Paul before turning around to climb down from the attic. She stood in the hall and sobbed as she heard the gunshots.

When Paul appeared beside her, they didn't speak. It was well known that Lola had lost a child and she could almost feel her own guilt mirrored in Paul, almost palpable in the strained atmosphere of the room. Only Lola knew that she was still yet a mother. When they exited the house, Lola was still weeping and Paul offered to check the next house on his own, leaving her to stand in the street and think about her daughter. The initial cleansing of the zombies hadn't been too hard, the town hall was secure and the creatures crowded around it hungrily, making easy targets for the men and women who deployed bullets, shells, and burning oil from the top windows. After a couple of days when no more of the zombies were directly outside, teams were sent and eventually they secured the section of the town around the hall, which included Lola's house. She remembered returning home, starting to tidy, going to the kitchen to throw away the rotting food and seeing her little girl, still in her nightdress, curled up asleep on the floor.

She had almost gone to wake her before she caught herself, forced to remember the situation as it was. In the end she had fetched a pair of handcuffs and grabbed the girl by the back of the head. She had snarled and twisted as she awoke, but zombie though she was, she was still just a small child and Lola had few problems holding her head immobile, getting her to the basement and handcuffing her to the pipe without injury. When Paul returned from the house, Lola was racked with deep sobs again and couldn't stop herself, though she tried. He put an arm around her.

"This is ridiculous. Let's go back and find the other groups." Lola nodded and the two of them started back down towards Park Street, jogging as they cast their eyes around for trouble.

The only time they stopped was when they found Conner's mutilated corpse in the middle of the road, but it amounted to no more than a quick glance and they ran on. When they exited the side street, the other groups were already waiting, two of them each missing a member, all of them with crimson streaks on their skin. The leader of the Seekers didn't ask questions about their losses, simply took the names of the dead to inform families and the twelve of them that remained headed back to the safe part of town.

The next morning, Lola was cooking breakfast for herself when a knock sounded at the door. She wiped greasy hands on her skirt and went to answer it, smiling a little as she saw Paul standing there with a bunch of lilies.

"A gift. I told my wife bout you so she got you these." Lola took them with a small laugh and gave him a quick hug. It was only after she had invited him in for coffee that her eyes flicked to the basement door and she realised that June could start rattling her handcuffs or thumping the floor any second. She took the lilies to the kitchen and put them in a vase on the table, then eyed up Paul.

"What is it?" he asked. Lola took several deep breaths, fingernails tapping on the table.

"I have something I want to show you." Her heart was quickening as she led him to the basement door and quietly unlocked it. She pointed Paul ahead of her and he walked carefully down into the darkness with Lola behind. She shut the door after them, silently locking it and coming to stand next to Paul at the bottom of the steps.

"What's that sound?" Paul whispered, straining to hear the quiet breathing that came from the corner, the small whines that escaped with the breath. Lola felt for his arm and led him three paces forward into the dark. A chain clanked softly, a small sound of something moving across the stone floor.

"I'll just turn the light on." Lola walked behind Paul, but there she stopped, grabbing him by the shoulders.

She pushed. Paul's screams were immediate and bloodcurdling, and when he managed to break free and run towards the stairs, Lola grabbed him again and threw him back. The sound of cracking bones accompanied his terror, the sounds of gorging, of blood spattering hard onto the wall. As Paul's screams grew fainter, turning into whimpers, Lola placed a hand on the light switch with trembling fingers, then withdrew it and headed back to the stairs. The sounds of feasting continued, though the pained whines had faded away to nothing. As Lola put her foot on the bottom step, she turned around in the darkness.

"Feel better, baby. I love you, June."

—LAIRD BARRON

Laird Barron is the author of several books, including *The Imago Sequence*, *Occultation*, and *The Croning*. His work has appeared in many magazines and anthologies. An expatriate Alaskan, Barron currently resides in Upstate New York.

—SHIVA, OPEN YOUR EYE

By *Laird Barron*

The human condition can be summed up in a drop of blood. Show me a *teaspoon* of blood and I will reveal to thee the ineffable nature of the cosmos, naked and squirming. Squirming. Funny how the truth always seems to do that when you shine a light on it.

A man came to my door one afternoon, back when I lived on a rambling farm in Eastern Washington. He was sniffing around, poking into things best left...unpoked. A man with a flashlight, you might say. Of course, I knew who he was and what he was doing there long before he arrived with his hat in one hand and phony story in the other.

Claimed he was a state property assessor, did the big genial man. Indeed, he was a massive fellow—thick, blunt fingers clutching corroborative documents and lumpy from all the abuse he had subjected them to in the military; he draped an ill-tailored tweed jacket and insufferable slacks over his ponderous frame. This had the effect of making him look like a man that should have been on a beach with a sun visor and a metal detector. The man wore a big smile under his griseous beard. This smile frightened people, which is exactly why he used it most of the time, and also, because it frightened people, he spoke slowly, in a big, heavy voice that sounded as if it emerged from a cast-iron barrel. He smelled of cologne and Three-In-One oil.

I could have whispered to him that the cologne came from a fancy emerald-colored bottle his wife had purchased for him as a birthday present; that he carried the bottle in his travel bag and spritzed himself whenever he was on the road and in too great a hurry, or simply too hungover for a shower. He preferred scotch, did my strapping visitor. I could have mentioned several other notable items in this patent leather travel bag—a roll of electrical tape, brass knuckles, voltmeter, police issue handcuffs, a microrecorder, a pocket camera, disposable latex gloves, lockpicks, a carpet cutter, flashlight, an empty aspirin bottle, toothpaste, a half roll of antacid tablets, hemorrhoid suppositories and a stained road map of Washington state. The bag was far away on the front seat of his rented sedan, which he had carefully parked up the winding dirt driveway under a sprawling locust tree. Wisely, he had decided to reconnoiter the area before knocking on the door. The oil smell emanated from a lubricated and expertly maintained thirty-eight-caliber revolver stowed in his left-hand jacket pocket. The pistol had not been fired in three-and-a-half years. The man did not normally carry a gun on the job, but in my case, he had opted for discretion. It occurred to him that I might be dangerous.

I could have told him all these things and that he was correct in his assumptions, but it did not amuse me to do so. Besides, despite his bulk he looked pretty fast and I was tired. Winter makes me lazy. It makes me torpid.

But—

Rap, rap! Against the peeling frame of the screen door. He did not strike the frame with anything approaching true force; nonetheless, he used a trifle more vigor than the occasion required. This was how he did things—whether conducting a sensitive inquiry, bracing a recalcitrant witness, or ordering the prawns at La Steakhouse. He was a water buffalo floundering into the middle of a situation, seizing command and dominating by virtue of his presence.

I made him wait longer than was necessary—to the same degree as his assault on my door was designed to set the tone and mood—although not *too* long, because sometimes my anticipatory juices outwrestle my subtler nature. I was an old man and thus tended to move in a deliberate mode anyway. This saddened me; I was afraid he might not catch my little joke.

But—

I came to the door, blinking in the strong light as I regarded him through filtering mesh. Of course, I permitted a suitable quaver to surface when I asked after his business. That was when the big man smiled and rumbled a string of lies about being the land assessor and a few sundries that I never paid attention to, lost as I was in watching his mouth, his hands and the curious way his barrel chest lifted and fell under the crumpled suit.

He gave me a name, something unimaginative gleaned from a shoebox, or like so. The identity on his State of Washington Private Investigator's License read Murphy Connell. He had been an investigator for eleven years; self employed, married with two children—a boy who played football at the University of Washington, and a girl that had transferred to Rhode Island to pursue a degree in graphic design—and owner of a Rottweiler named Hellestrae, after his favorite lineman. The identification was in his wallet, which filled an inner pocket of the bad coat, wedged in front of an ancient pack of Pall Malls. The big man had picked up the habit when he was stationed in the Philippines, but seldom smoked anymore. He kept them around because sure as a stud hound lifts its leg to piss, the minute he left home without a pack the craving would pounce on him hammer and tongs. He was not prone to self-analysis, this big man, yet it amused him after a wry sense that he had crushed an addiction only to be haunted by its vengeful ghost.

Yes, I remembered his call from earlier that morning. He was certainly welcome to ramble about the property and have a gander for Uncle Sam. I told him to come in and rest his feet while I fixed a pot of tea—unless he preferred a nip of the ole gin? No, tea would be lovely. *Lovely?* It delighted me in an arcane fashion that such a phrase would uproot from his tongue— sort of like a gravel truck dumping water lilies and butterflies. I boiled tea with these hands gnarled unto dead madrona, and I took my sweet time. Mr. Connell moved quietly, though that really didn't matter, *nothing* is hidden from these ears. I listened while he sifted through a few of the papers on the coffee table— *nothing of consequence there, my large one*—and efficiently riffled the books and *National Geographics* on the sagging shelf that I had meant to fix for a while. His eyes were quick, albeit in a different sense than most people understand the word. They were quick in the sense that a straight line is quick, no waste, no second-guessing, thorough and methodical. Once scrutinized and done. Quick.

I returned in several minutes with the tea steeping in twin mugs. He had tossed the dim living room and was wondering how to distract me for a go at the upstairs—or the cellar. I knew better than to make it blatantly simple; he was the suspicious type, and if his wind got up too soon...well, that would diminish my chance to savor our time together. Christmas, this was Christmas, or rather, the approximation of that holiday, which fills children to the brim with stars and song. But Christmas is not truly the thing, is it now? That sublime void of giddy anticipation of the gaily-colored packages contains the first, and dare I say, righteous spirit of Christmas. Shucking the presents of their skin is a separate pleasure altogether.

But—

Mr. Connell sat in the huge stuffed recliner with springs poking him in the buttocks. It was the only chair in the room that I trusted to keep him off the floor and it cawed when he settled his bulk into its embrace. Let me say that our man was not an actor. Even after I sat him down and placed the mug in his fist, those accipitrine eyes darted and sliced from shadowed corner to mysterious nook, off-put by the cloying feel of the room—and why not? It was a touch creepy, what with the occasional creak of a timber, the low squeak of a settling foundation, the way everything was cast under a counterchange pattern of dark and light. I would have been nervous in his shoes; he was looking into murders most foul, after all. Pardon me, murder is a sensational word; television will be the ruin of my fleeting measure of proportion if the world keeps spinning a few more revolutions. *Disappearances* is what I should have said. Thirty of them. Thirty that good Mr. Connell knew of, at least. There were more, many more, but this is astray from the subject.

We looked at each other for a time. Me, smacking my lips

over toothless gums and blowing on the tea—it was too damned hot, as usual! He, pretending to sip, but not really doing so on the off chance that I *was* the crazed maniac that he sought, and had poisoned it. A good idea, even though I had not done anything like that. Since he was pretending to accept my hospitality, I pretended to look at his forged documents, smacking and fumbling with some glasses that would have driven me blind if I wore them for any span of time, and muttered monosyllabic exclamations to indicate my confusion and ultimate verification of the presumed authenticity of his papers. One quick call to the Bureau of Land Management would have sent him fleeing as the charlatan I knew he was. I ignored the opportunity.

Mr. Connell was definitely not an actor. His small talk was clumsy, as if he couldn't decide the proper way to crack me. I feigned a hearing impairment and that was cruel, though amusing. Inside of ten minutes the mechanism of his logic had all save rejected the possibility of my involvement in those disappearances. No surprise there—he operated on intuition; *peripheral logic,* as his wife often called it. I failed the test of instinct. Half blind, weak, pallid as a starfish grounded. Decrepit would not be completely unkind. I was failing him. Yet the room, the house, the brittle fold of plain beyond the window interrupted by a blot of ramshackle structure that was the barn, invoked his disquiet. It worried him, this trail of missing persons— vague pattern; they were hitchhikers, salesmen, several state troopers, missionaries, prostitutes, you name it. Both sexes, all ages and descriptions, with a single thread to bind them. They disappeared around my humble farm. The Federal Bureau of Investigation dropped by once, three years before the incident with Mr. Connell. I did not play with them. Winter had yet to make me torpid and weak. They left with nothing, suspecting nothing.

However, it was a close thing, that inconvenient visit. It convinced me the hour was nigh...

The tea grew cold. It was late in the year, so dying afternoon sunlight had a tendency to slant; trees were shorn of their glory, crooked branches casting crooked shadows. The breeze nipped and the fields were damp. I mentioned that he was going to ruin his shoes if he went tramping out there; he thanked me and said he'd be careful. I watched him stomp around, doing his terrible acting job, trying to convince me that he was checking the value of my property, or whatever the hell he said when I wasn't listening.

Speaking of shadows...I glanced at mine, spread out across the hood of the requisite '59 Chevrolet squatting between the barn and the house. Ah, a perfectly normal shadow, if a tad disfigured by the warp of light.

A majority of the things I might tell are secrets. Therefore, I shall not reveal them whole and glistening. Also, some things are kept from me, discomfiting as that particular truth may be. The vanished people; I know *what* occurred, but not *why*. To be brutally accurate, in several cases I cannot say that I *saw* what happened, however, my guesswork is as good as anyone's. There was a brief moment, back and back again in some murky prehistory of my refined consciousness, when I possessed the hubris to imagine a measure of self-determination in this progress through existence. The Rough Beast slouching toward Bethlehem of its own accord. If leashed, then by its own device, certainly. Foolish me.

Scientists claim that there is a scheme to the vicious Tree of Life, one thing eats another and excretes the matter another being requires to sustain its spark so that it might be eaten by another which excretes the matter required to sustain the spark—and like so. Lightning does not strike with random intent, oceans do not heave, and toss, axes do not ring in the tulgey wood or bells in church towers by accident. As a famous man once said, there are no accidents 'round here.

Jerk the strings and watch us dance. I could say more on that subject; indeed, I might fill a pocket book with that pearl of wisdom, but later is better.

Mr. Connell slouched in from the field—picking about for graves, by chance?—resembling the rough beast I mentioned earlier. He was flushed; irritation and residual alcohol poisoning in equal parts. I asked him how he was doing, and he grunted a perfunctory comment.

Could he possibly take a closer look at the barn? It would affect the overall property value and like that...I smiled and shrugged and offered to show him the way. Watch your step, I warned him, it wouldn't do for a government man to trip over some piece of equipment and end up suing the dirt from under my feet, ha, ha.

This made him nervous all over again and he sweated. Why? Two years before this visit, I could have said with accuracy. He would have been mine to read forward and back. By now, I was losing my strength. I was stuck in *his* boat, stranded with peripheral logic for sails. Mr. Connell sweated all the time, but this was different. Fear sweat is distinctive, any predator knows that. This pungent musk superseded the powerful cologne and stale odor of whiskey leaching from his pores.

To the barn. Cavernous. Gloom, dust, clathrose awnings of spent silk, scrabbling mice. Heavy textures of mold, of rust, decaying straw. I hobbled with the grace of a lame crow, yet Mr. Connell contrived to lag at my heel. Cold in the barn, thus his left hand delved into a pocket and lingered there. What was he thinking? Partially that I was too old, unless...unless an accomplice lurked in one of the places his methodical gaze was barred from. He thought of the house; upstairs, or the cellar. *Wrong on both counts.* Maybe his research was faulty—what if I actually possessed a living relative? Now would be a hell of a time to discover *that* mistake! Mr. Connell thought as an animal does—a deer hardly requires proof from its stippled ears, its soft eyes, or quivering nose to justify the uneasiness of one often hunted. Animals understand that life is death. This is not a conscious fact, rather a fact imprinted upon every colliding cell. Mr. Connell thought like an animal, unfortunately, he was trapped in the electrochemical web of cognition, wherein curiosity leads into temptation, temptation leads into fear, and fear is considered an impulse to be mastered. He came into the barn against the muffled imprecations of his lizard brain. Curiosity did not kill the cat all by itself.

His relentless eyes adjusted by rapid degrees, fastening upon a mass of sea-green tarpaulin gone velvet in the subterranean murk. This sequestered mass reared above the exposed gulf of loft, nearly brushing the venerable center beam, unexpressive in its obscured context, though immense and bounded by that gravid force to founding dirt. Mr. Connell's heartbeat accelerated, spurred by a trickling dose of primordial dread. Being a laconic and linear man, he asked me what was under that great tarp.

I showed my gums, grasping a corner of that shroud with a knotted hand. One twitch to part the enigmatic curtain and reveal my portrait of divinity. A sculpture of the magnificent shape of God. Oh, admittedly it was a shallow rendering of That Which Cannot be Named; but art is not relative to perfection in any tangible sense. It is our coarse antennae trembling blindly as it traces the form of Origin, tastes the ephemeral glue welding us, yearning after the secret of ineluctable evolution, and wonders what this transformation will mean. In my mind, here was the best kind of art—the kind hoarded by rich and jealous collectors in their locked galleries; hidden from the eyes of the heathen masses, waiting to be shared with the ripe few.

Came the rustle of polyurethane sloughing from the Face of Creation; a metaphor to frame the abrupt molting bloom of my deep insides. There, a shadow twisted on the floor; my shadow, but not me any more than a butterfly is the chrysalis whence it emerges. Yet, I wanted to see the end of this!

Mr. Connell gaped upon the construct born of that yearning for truth slithering at the root of my intellect. He teetered as if swaying on the brink of a chasm. He beheld shuddering lines that a fleshly tongue is witless to describe, except perhaps in spurts of impression—prolongated, splayed at angles, an obliquangular mass of smeared and clotted material, glaucous clay dredged from an old and abiding coomb where earthly veins dangle and fell waters drip as the sculpture dripped, milky-lucent starshine in the cryptic barn, an intumescent hulk rent from the floss of a carnival mirror. To gaze fully on this idol was to feel the grey matter quake inside its case and reject what the moist perceptions thought to feed it.

I cannot explain, nor must an artist defend his work

or elucidate in such a way the reeling audience can fathom, brutes that they are. Besides, I was not feeling quite myself when I molded it from the morass of mindless imperative. Like a nocturnal flower, I *Become*, after that the scope of human perception is reduced and bound in fluids nameless and profane. There are memories, but their clarity is the clarity of a love for the womb, warmth, and lightless drift; fragmented happiness soon absorbed in the shuffle of the churning world and forgotten.

Mr. Connell did not comment directly; speech was impossible. He uttered an inarticulate sound, yarding at the lump of cold metal in his pocket—his crucifix against the looming presence of evil. Note that I refrain from scoffing at the existence of evil. The word is a simple name for a complex idea, an idea far outstripping the feeble equipment of sapient life. It is nothing to laugh at. As for my investigator, I like to remember him that way—frozen in a rictus of anguish at wisdom gained too late. Imagine that instant as the poor insect falls into the pitcher plant. He was an Ice Age hunter trapped in the gelid bosom of a glacier. It was final for him.

I reached out to touch his craggy visage—

My perceptions flickered, shuttering so swiftly that I could not discern precise details of what occurred to big Mr. Connell. Suffice to say what was done to him was...incomprehensible. And horrible, I suppose most people would think. Not that I could agree with their value judgment. I suffered the throes of blossoming. It tends to affect my reasoning. The ordeal exhausted me; yet another sign.

Mr. Connell vanished like the others before him, but he was the last. After that, I left the farm and traveled north. Winter was on the world. Time for summer things to sleep.

* * *

I only mention this anecdote because it's the same thing every time, in one variation or another. Come the villagers with their pitchforks and torches, only to find the castle empty, the nemesis gone back to the shadowlands. Lumbered off to the great cocoon of slumber and regeneration.

In dreams I swim as I did back when the oceans were warm and empty. There I am, floating inside a vast membrane, innocent of coherent thought, guided by impulses to movement, sustenance, and copulation. Those are dim memories; easy to assume them to be the fabrications of loneliness or delusion. Until you recall these are human frailties. Interesting that I always return to the soup of origins, whether in dreams or substance. Every piece of terrestrial life emerged from that steaming gulf. The elder organisms yet dwell in those depths, some hiding in the fields of microbes, mindless as jellyfish; others lumbering and feeding on what hapless forms they capture. Once, according to the dreams, I was one of those latter things. Except, I am uncertain if that was ever my true spawning ground.

In fairness, I do not ponder the circumstance of my being as much as logic would presume. My physiology is to thank, perhaps. There come interludes—a month, a year, centuries, or more—and I simply *am*, untroubled by the questions of purpose. I seek my pleasures, I revel in their comforts. The ocean is just the ocean, a cigar is just a cigar. That is the state of *Becoming.*

Bliss is ephemeral; true for anyone, or anything. The oceans have been depleted several times in the last billion years. Sterile water in a clay bowl. Life returned unbidden on each occasion. The world slumbers, twitches and transforms. From the jelly, lizards crawled around the fetid swamps eating one another and dying, and being replaced by something else. Again, again, again, until you reach the inevitable conclusion of sky-rises, nuclear submarines, orbiting satellites, and *Homo sapiens* formicating the earth. God swipes His Hand across Creation, it changes shape and thrives. A cycle, indeed a cycle, and not a pleasant one if you are cursed with a brain and the wonder of what the cosmic gloaming shall hold for you.

Then there is me. Like the old song, the more things change, the more I stay the same.

When the oceans perished, I slept and later flopped on golden shores, glaring up at strange constellations, but my contemplation was a drowsy process and bore no fruit. When the lizards perished, I went into the sea and slept, and later wore the flesh and fur of warm-blooded creatures. When ice chilled and continents drifted together with dire results, I went into the sea and slept through the cataclysm. Later, I wore the skins of animals and struck flint to make fire and glared up at the stars and named them in a language I don't have the trick of anymore. Men built their idols, and I joined them in their squalid celebrations, lulled by flames and roasting flesh; for I was one with them, even if the thoughts stirring in my mind seemed peculiar, and hearkened to the sediment of dark forms long neglected. I stabbed animals with a spear and mated when the need was pressing. I hated my enemies and loved my friends and wore the values of the tribe without the impetus of subterfuge. I was a man. And for great periods that is all I was. At night I regarded the flickering lights in the sky and when I dreamed, it occurred to me exactly what the truth was. For a while I evaded the consequences of my nature. Time is longer than a person made from blood and tissue could hope to imagine. Ask God; distractions are important.

But—

Memories, memories. Long ago in a cave on the side of a famous mountain in the Old World. Most men lived in huts and cabins or stone fortresses. Only wise men chose to inhabit caves, and I went to visit one of them. A monk revered for his sagacity and especially for his knowledge of the gods in their myriad incarnations. I stayed with the wizened holy man for a cycle of the pocked and pitted moon. We drank bitter tea; we smoked psychedelic plants and read from crumbling tomes scriven with quaint drawings of deities and demons. It was disappointing—I could not be any of these things, yet there was little doubt he and I were different as a fish is from a stone. The monk was the first of them to notice. I did not concern myself. In those days my power was irresistible; let me but wave my hand and so mote it be. If I desired a thought from a passing mind, I plucked it fresh as sweet fruit from a budding branch. If I fancied a soothing rain, the firmament would split and sunder. If I hungered, flesh would prostrate itself before me...unless I fancied a pursuit. Then it would bound and hide, or stand and bare teeth or rippling steel, or suffocate my patience with tears, oaths, pleas. But in the end, I had my flesh. That the monk guessed what I strove to submerge, as much from myself as the world at large, did not alarm me. It was the *questions* that pecked at my waking thoughts, crept into my slumberous phantasms. Annoying questions.

Stark recollection of a time predating the slow glide of aeons in the primeval brine. The images would alight unasked; I would glimpse the red truth of my condition. Purple dust and niveous spiral galaxy, a plain of hyaline rock broken by pyrgoidal clusters ringed in fire, temperatures sliding a groove betwixt boiling and freezing. The sweet huff of methane in my bellowing lungs, sunrise so blinding it would have seared the eyes from any living creature...and there were memories layered behind and beyond, inaccessible to the human perception that I wore as a workman wears boots, gloves, and warding mantle. To see these visions in their nakedness would boggle and baffle, or rive the sanity from my fragile intellect, surely as a hot breath douses a candle. Ah, but there were memories; a phantom chain endless as the coil of chemicals comprising the mortal genome, fused to the limits of calculation—

I try not to think too much. I try not to think too much about the buried things, anyhow. Better to consider the cycle that binds me in its thrall. For my deeds there is a season—spring, summer, autumn and winter. Each time I change it becomes clearer what precisely maintains its pattern. That I am a fragment of something much larger is obvious. The monk was the first to grasp it. There was a story he mentioned—how the priests prayed to their gods, good, and bad, to look upon men and bestow their munificent blessings. They even prayed to terrible Shiva the Destroyer, who slept in his celestial palace. They prayed because to slight Shiva in their supplication was to risk his not inconsiderable fury. Yet, the priests knew if Shiva opened his eye and gazed upon the world, it would be destroyed.

But—

In the spring, I walk with the others of my kindred shell, nagged by fullness unsubstantiated.

In the summer, I see my shadow change, change and then I learn to blossom and suckle the pleasurable nectar from all I survey. Nail me to a cross, burn me in a fire. A legend will rise up from the ashes. Invent stories to frighten your children, sacrifice tender young virgins to placate my concupiscent urges. Revile me in your temples, call upon Almighty God to throw me down. No good, no good. How could He see you if not for me? How could He hear thy lament, or smell thy sadness? Or taste thee?

In the autumn, like a slow, heavy tide, purpose resurges, and I remember what the seasons portend. A wane of the power, a dwindling reserve of strength. Like a malign flower that flourishes in tropical heat, I wither before the advance of frost, and blacken and die, my seeds buried in the muck at the bottom of the ocean to survive the cruel winter.

I know what I am. I understand the purpose.

I left the farm and disappeared. One more name on the ominous list haunting law enforcement offices in seventeen states. I vanished myself to the Bering Coast—a simple feat for anyone who wants to try. An old man alone on a plane; no one cared. They never do.

There is an old native ghost town on a stretch of desolate beach. Quonset huts with windows shattered or boarded. Grains of snow slither in past open doors when the frigid wind gusts along, moaning through the abandoned FAA towers colored navy grey and rust. The federal government transplanted the villagers to new homes thirteen miles up the beach.

I don't see anyone when I leave the shack and climb the cliffs to regard the sea. The sea hangs there, a dark, scaly hide marred by plates of thickening ice. Individual islets today, a solid sheet in a few weeks, extending to the horizon. Or forever. Stars flicker as twilight slips down from the sky, a painless veil pricked with those beads and sparks. Unfriendly stars. Eventually I return to the shack. It takes me a very long time—I am an old, old man. My shuffle and panting breath are not part of the theatre. The shack waits and I light a kerosene lamp and huddle by the Bunsen burner to thaw these antiquitous bones. I do not hunger much this late in the autumn of my cycle, and nobody is misfortunate enough to happen by, so I eschew sustenance another day.

The radio is old, too. Scratchy voice from a station in Nome recites the national news—I pay a lot of attention to this when my time draws nigh, looking for a sign, a symbol of tribulations to come—the United Nations is bombing some impoverished country into submission, war criminals from Bosnia are apprehended in Peru. A satellite orbiting Mars has gone off line, but NASA is quick to reassure the investors that all is routine, in Ethiopia famine is tilling people under by the thousands, an explosion caused a plane to crash into the Atlantic, labor unions are threatening a crippling strike, a bizarre computer virus is hamstringing two major corporations and so on and on. The news is never good, and I am not sure if there is anything I wanted to hear.

I close my rheumy eyes and see a tinsel and sequined probe driving out, out beyond the cold chunk of Pluto. A stone tossed into a bottomless pool, trailing bubbles. I see cabalists hunched over their ciphers, Catholics on their knees before the effigy of Christ, biologists with scalpels and microscopes, astronomers with their mighty lenses pointed at the sky, atheists, and philosophers with fingers pointed at themselves. Military men stroke the cool bulk of their latest killing weapon and feel a touch closer to peace. I see men caressing the crystal, and wire and silicon of the machines that tell them what to believe about the laws of physics, the number to slay chaos in its den. I see housewives scrambling to pick the kids up from soccer practice, a child on the porch gazing up, and up, to regard the same piece of sky glimmering in my window. He wonders what is up there, he wonders if there is a monster under his bed. No monsters there, instead they lurk at school, at church, in his uncle's squamous brain. Everyone is looking for the answer. They do not want to find the answer, trust me. Unfortunately, the answer will find them. Life—it's like one of those unpleasant nature documentaries. To be the cameraman instead of the subjects, eh?

Ah, my skin warns me that it is almost the season. I dreamed for a while, but I do not recall the content. The radio is dead; faint drone from the ancient speaker. The kerosene wick has burned to cinders. A flash from the emerald-colored bottle catches my eye; full of cologne. I seldom indulge in cosmetics; the color attracted me and I brought it here. I am a creature of habit. When my affectations of evolution decay, habit remains steadfast.

Dark outside on the wintry beach. Sunrise is well off and may not come again. The frozen pebbles crackle beneath my heels as I stagger toward the canvas of obsidian water, leaving strange and unsteady tracks on the skeletal shore. There is a sense of urgency building. Mine, or the Other's? I strip my clothes as I go and end up on the cusp of the sea, naked and shriveled. The stars are feral. They shudder—a ripple is spreading across the heavens and the stars are dancing wildly in its pulsating wake. A fulgence that should not *be* begins to seep from the widening fissure. Here is a grand and terrible happening to write of on the wall of a cave...God opening His Eye to behold the world and all its little works.

I have seen this before. Let others marvel in my place, if they dare. My work is done, now to sleep. When I mount from the occluded depths what will I behold? What will be my clay and how shall I be given to mold it? I slip into the welcoming flank of the sea and allow the current to tug my shell out and down into the abyssal night. It isn't really as cold as I feared. Thoughts are fleeting as the bubbles and the light. The shell begins to flake, to peel, to crumble, and soon I will wriggle free of this fragile vessel.

But—

One final kernel of wisdom gained through the abomination of time and service. A pearl to leave gleaming upon this empty shore; safely assured that no one shall come by to retrieve it and puzzle over the contradiction. Men are afraid of the devil, but there is no devil, just me and I do as I am bid. It is God that should turn their bowels to soup. Whatever God is, He, or It, created us for amusement. It's too obvious. Just as He created the prehistoric sharks, the dinosaurs, and the humble mechanism that is a crocodile. And cockroaches, tarantulas and humanity. Just as He created a world where every organism survives by rending a weaker organism. Where procreation is an imperative, a leech's anesthetic against agony and death and disease that accompany the sticky congress of mating. A sticky world, because God dwells in a dark and humid place. A world of appetite, for God is ever hungry.

I know, because I am His Mouth.

20291309R00215

Made in the USA
Lexington, KY
01 February 2013